THE FEDEROV LEGACY

Copyright © 2013 Rosella Leslie
01 02 03 04 05   17 16 15 14 13

All rights reserved. No part of this publication may be reproduced, stored in a retrieval system or transmitted, in any form or by any means, without prior permission of the publisher or, in the case of photocopying or other reprographic copying, a licence from Access Copyright, the Canadian Copyright Licensing Agency, www.accesscopyright.ca, 1-800-893-5777, info@accesscopyright.ca.

Caitlin Press Inc.
8100 Alderwood Road,
Halfmoon Bay, BC V0N 1Y1
www.caitlin-press.com

Text and cover design by Vici Johnstone.
Edit by Rebecca Hendry.
Cover image of Russian woman from alamy.com CPN331.
Cover image of the Kronverk embankment in Saint Petersburg from Istock 000001148926.
Printed in Canada

Caitlin Press Inc. acknowledges financial support from the Government of Canada through the Canada Book Fund and the Canada Council for the Arts, and from the Province of British Columbia through the British Columbia Arts Council and the Book Publisher's Tax Credit.

 Canada Council   Conseil des Arts
for the Arts   du Canada

Library and Archives Canada Cataloguing in Publication

Leslie, Rosella M., 1948-
    The Federov legacy / Rosella Leslie.

ISBN 978-1-927575-06-2

    I. Title.

PS8623.E849F44 2013   C813'.6   C2013-900534-X

The Federov Legacy

ROSELLA LESLIE

CAITLIN PRESS

This book is dedicated to my son, Nathan Alvarez.

Special thanks to the Quintessential Writers Group for their constant support.

Contents

AUTHOR'S NOTE	5
CARIBOO, BC— *Late May 1914*	7
A VILLAGE IN THE CARPATHIAN MOUNTAINS OF GALICIA—*Mid-June 1914*	16
ST. PETERSBURG—*June 26, 1914*	28
ZGARDY—*July 1914*	35
GRANDFATHER GALIPOVA—*June 27, 1914*	41
ZGARDY—*September 1914*	56
ST. PETERSBURG—*September 1914*	65
ZGARDY—*October 2, 1914*	77
FRONT LINES BETWEEN LODZ AND WARSAW—*Christmas 1914*	86
ZGARDY — *May-September 1915*	92
EASTERN FRONT BETWEEN GRODNO AND MINSK—*Early September 1915*	105
ZGARDY—*September 1915*	109
PETROGRAD—*November 1915*	124
ZGARDY—*Summer 1916*	136
PETROGRAD—*September 1916*	145
ZGARDY—*October 1916*	153
PETROGRAD—*January 1917*	173
ZGARDY—*November 1917*	184
PETROGRAD—*June-December 1917*	191
ZGARDY—*Spring 1918*	208
WESTERN RUSSIA—*December 1917-November 1918*	228
ZGARDY—*May-July 1919*	248
KIEV, UKRAINE—*November 1918*	264
ZGARDY—*July 1919*	276
EPILOGUE: IMBYR RIVER, ZGARDY—*September 1919*	287
ACKNOWLEDGEMENTS	288

Author's Note

In 1815 the Congress of Vienna established the Kingdom of Poland, with the Tsar of Russia as its head of state, and incorporated the surrounding territories into the Russian, Prussian and Austro-Hungarian empires. Over the next hundred years these boundaries remained relatively intact—as did the determination of the Lithuanian, Polish and Ukrainian people within those boundaries to regain their autonomy. While repeated insurrections were quelled by brute force, each uprising led to concessions, especially to the Polish landlords and aristocracy, and this led to an increasing rivalry between the better-educated Poles and the more agrarian Ukrainians.

After Austria's defeat in the Austro-Prussian War of 1866, that nation sought to fortify its internal support by granting unofficial autonomy to its northeastern province of Galicia partly in present-day Poland and partly in Ukraine. The official languages were changed from German to Polish and Ukrainian, although, once again political power remained concentrated in the hands of Galicia's Polish population. Meanwhile, the Galician Ukrainians were gradually becoming divided into Russophiles and Populists. The former promoted stronger ties with Russia and a Ukrainian-Russian language, while the Populists believed they could achieve greater reforms by working with the Poles and their Austrian overlords. After the Austrian and Polish authorities branded the Russophile leaders as traitors, the Populists were given more and more cultural and educational concessions. By the turn of the century, although the Poles still maintained their hold on the provincial government, the Ukrainian Populists were becoming serious rivals.

Galicia's southeastern region included a part of the Carpathian Mountains inhabited by three distinct Ukrainian ethnic groups—the Lemkians, the Boikans and the Hutsuls. The Hutsuls were highlanders who spoke a distinctive Ukrainian dialect and had their own unique customs, belief systems and architecture. These are the people who are featured in this story, which takes place just before and during World War I.

CARIBOO, BC
Late May 1914

It was a stand-off, eighteen-year-old Alice Galipova on one side of the table, her father, Sergei, on the other. "No! Absolutely not," she repeated. "I will not be packed off to Russia as Tusya was."

Sergei pushed away from the table. "*Ya tvoy otets! Vy budete delat' kak ya govoryu!*"

Alice drew herself up to her full height, a technique she used with recalcitrant patients. "Yes, you *are* my father," she agreed in English, hoping the formality of her uniform hid her uneasiness at questioning his authority. "But in Canada *I* get to say what I do and where I go, not you!"

He stared at her, but instead of shouting as she expected, his lips thinned and he shook his head. Continuing in Russian, he said, "So this is what you learn at that nursing school, hmmm? To be disrespectful?" He sat down and turned his attention to the silver-embossed letter that had sparked the argument. "The countess has arranged for your passage from Montreal to England in two weeks. You will write at once to Ottawa for your passport and have it delivered to the ship."

"I'm not going, Father."

His grasp on the letter tightened, his cold expression a warning Alice could not ignore. She shifted from one foot to the other and nervously repositioned several strands of blond hair that had escaped from beneath her cap. "Even Tusya said it isn't safe, Father. He said workers are always going on strike and being arrested and sent away ... ."

"And what of it?" Sergei scoffed, waving disparagingly at the stack of newspapers on the table. They came weekly from Victoria, Toronto and Russia to the post office at nearby Willow Bar Creek. "Your brother would find it is the same here. Do you forget last summer when soldiers and police attacked the striking coal miners in Nanaimo? It is the same everywhere."

Of course Alice remembered. After her brother had left to attend university in St. Petersburg, she had inherited the job of reading the Canadian papers to their father. Every time a union leader was arrested or workers were forced back to work without having their demands met, she was forced to endure endless lectures on the merits and perils of socialism, a subject that had not interested her then and did not interest her now. And since it was obviously not helping to further her cause, she tried a different tactic.

"But who will look after the house if I go to Russia?"

His right brow rose in surprise. "Pete Lereux, of course. The same man who did so while you were at that ... that school. He does what needs doing here and," he added emphatically, "he also cleans the bunkhouse without complaining."

When he's not drunk, thought Alice, who had to admit that she complained bitterly whenever she was assigned bunkhouse duties. She walked to the window and gazed out at the ranch yard. Although it was only the middle of May, it had been weeks since it had last rained, and the horses standing in the corral stirred up small dust clouds every time they moved. "I still don't understand why your cousin wants me to come. Surely they have plenty of nurses in St. Petersburg."

"The countess wants a nurse with the new ways. Someone she trusts."

Alice gave an involuntary snort. "Trust? She doesn't even know me, Father!"

"She knows *me*," he said curtly, as if that settled the matter. Then, trying a fresh tack, he added in a more amiable tone, "I owe her my life, Alicia. What she asks, I cannot refuse."

She turned and looked at him suspiciously. Her father rarely discussed his past and hadn't once indicated that his life had ever been in danger. "When was this?"

He shrugged. "It is of no matter. Besides, you saw our last letter from Tusya. He tells us your Grandfather Alexandrei is not well. He needs a nurse, and you are a nurse, so you must go."

Alice had never met her grandfather and knew him only by his infrequent letters that were filled with academic matters about the university where he had been an assistant professor of literature—the same university Tusya was now attending. When her grandmother died shortly after Sergei had left Russia, her grandfather had gone to live in the countess's home. According to Tusya, he now spent most of his time absorbed in his books. She started to ask exactly what ailed her grandfather but stopped when she heard the front door open. Footsteps sounded in the hallway and a moment later the portly frame of William Bearcroft filled the doorway.

"Well, you two certainly look in fine fettle," he said jovially. He advanced toward the table, his hat in one hand and the other outstretched.

Sergei shook the man's hand and asked, "What brings you to Galipova Ranch, *moy drug*?" He waved the doctor toward a chair. "Please sit."

Doctor Bill, as William was known to Alice and Tusya, had been the only doctor in the whole area for years, and when she was younger Alice had accompanied him on his rounds as an unpaid assistant. She had loved working with him and it was he who encouraged her to attend nursing school in Kamloops and spent long hours arguing with her father until he finally gave his permission.

"I can't stay," he said apologetically. "I've just come to borrow your daughter for a few hours. I figure the sight of a pretty nurse will calm old man Carter down while I change that dressing on his leg."

Sergei splayed his hands, palms up, toward Alice. "You say nothing of this?"

"I was going to, Father," she said, smoothing the apron of her uniform, "but you sprang this Russian trip on me before I could get a word out."

The doctor looked from one to the other. "Russia?"

Alice grimaced. "He wants to send me to St. Petersburg. My grandfather is ill and Father thinks Russian nurses aren't capable of looking after him."

"That is not what I say," Sergei retorted. He snatched up the letter and shook it in her direction. "It is for countess!

"But shouldn't you be the one to go, Father?"

Sergei faltered for a brief moment and then said, "I cannot go." There was a finality in his tone that denied questions. "I can never go back."

The doctor cleared his throat. "Personally, I don't think this is the time for anyone to go to Russia," he offered. "There's trouble brewing in the Balkans that could erupt any day."

Sergei snorted and tossed the letter back onto the table. "Always there will be trouble in Balkans!" he said dismissively. "Too much shedding of blood for peace ever. Are we to stop living because of Balkans? *Nyet!*" He scowled at Alice. "You will go to Russia, Alicia ... or you will not be my daughter."

Without giving her a chance to respond, he clamped his hat on his head. "I bid you good-day, William," he said, and with an abrupt nod to the doctor he strode from the room.

As the outside door slammed, Alice moved a chair and sat, her hands clasped in her lap.

The doctor stood uncertainly.

"He didn't mean that, Alice," he said gently. "He'll come around."

She shook her head. "Oh, he meant it, all right. You've seen the way he is. You do what he wants or he cuts you off." Being shunned by their father had always been an unspoken threat hanging over herself and her brother. It had grown worse after their mother died when Alice was ten. Both siblings had often declared they would rather face a beating than the long silences their father inflicted upon them whenever they were disobedient. Even now, although she was strangely tempted to call his bluff, she wanted to rush after him and promise she would do his bidding. She heard the sound of hooves pounding out of the yard and knew he was heading for the range where he would probably spend the night. It was one more way of punishing her, and as always, it left her feeling bereaved and alone.

The doctor cleared his throat and she suddenly remembered the reason for his visit.

"I'm sorry," she said, getting to her feet. "This is not your trouble, Doctor Bill. I'll just get my cape and be right with you."

"It *is* my trouble," he called after her as she left the room. "I'm losing my nurse before I even had a chance to get used to her."

෧෬

On the first Monday in June, Alice found herself in Montreal standing before a gangway that led to the deck of the *Empress of Britain*. Stepping back from the line of passengers steadily making their way up the incline, she surveyed the great black hull half-hidden in the thick fog that had blanketed the port all morning. She could just make out two rows of portholes running along the side, the twin tiers of snowy-white upper decks and above them, two tall funnels that spoke of mighty engines below. *The ship looks very rugged,* she thought, and tried to reassure herself that it was sturdy enough to cross the Atlantic and would not sink as its sister ship, the *Empress of Ireland,* had done just a few weeks earlier. Not that it was the Atlantic she really had to worry about, for the *Ireland*'s sinking had occurred in the protected waters of the St. Lawrence River. More than a thousand passengers had been lost when the ship was gored by a Norwegian collier that had lost its way. *In a fog just like this,* she thought glumly as she finally joined the line of passengers and started up the gangway.

Once on deck she was directed to the cabin she was to share with a roommate she had never met and who had not yet made an appearance. She deposited her valise on one of the two small beds on either side of an even smaller desk and paused a moment to tidy her hair before a mirror near the door. As usual, the chignon she had carefully crafted that morning had collapsed, even though she had used a dozen pins, and as a consequence her wide-brimmed straw hat, instead of tilting cheekily on her head, was clamped over her ears and covered half of her forehead. After hastily redoing the chignon and replacing the hat, she smoothed the fawn-coloured fabric of her raincoat, liking the way it looked and that it reached almost down to her ankles. Although they made her look a little more severe than she would have liked, the coat and the blue serge suit she wore beneath it had been the only ones available at the dress shop she visited in Kamloops. However, having watched other women boarding the ship, she was reassured that the outfit was entirely suitable for her journey.

Opening the door, she hurried off to the purser's office to collect the letter of request, which served as a passport in Canada. The cable she had received from the lieutenant-governor's office just before leaving Willow Bar Creek had said it would be waiting for her on the ship, but she wanted to make sure it had arrived. For almost an hour she stood in line waiting to speak to the short, bespectacled clerk in command of the purser's counter, only to discover when it was finally her turn that no such letter existed—at least, none that was addressed to her.

"But I must have it!" she exclaimed, fighting back panic.

The clerk frowned, his attention already turning to the passenger behind her. "I am sorry, Miss, but there is nothing I can do. It is perhaps at head office, but I have no way of knowing that."

Alice glanced at the clock on the wall of the tiny office. It was almost noon and the departure time was four o'clock. If the head office wasn't too far away, she could still make it there and back before the ship sailed.

"And where is this head office?"

Giving a sigh of exasperation, he pulled a small map from a file and pointed to a square that said Windsor Station. "But you had better hurry," he cautioned, handing her the map. "The ship will not wait."

Biting back her own exasperation as she realized the head office was located in the station from which she had just come, Alice hurried back to the gangway where the purser's warning was repeated to her by the ships' officer on duty. When she asked him to point the way to the streetcar stop, he shook his head.

"They've walked off the job, Miss," he said bleakly. "You'd best take a taxi." He nodded toward a cab just pulling up with more passengers. Alice followed a porter who was hurrying to help them, and a moment later she was in the cab speeding along Peel Street.

Although she reached the station in less than twenty minutes, finding the office where her mail might be held took much longer, and after being redirected to four different clerks she was almost ready to admit defeat. At first she had been polite and when that hadn't worked she had shouted, threatened and begged, but each clerk said the same thing: there was no letter. It did not seem to matter to them that without it she could not enter Russia, and as she walked slowly down the long, third-floor hallway leading to yet another office, she wondered why it suddenly mattered so much to her. She had not wanted to go on this journey in the first place and had consented to it only because she did not dare to find out if her father really would disown her. Why then was she not rejoicing at this perfect excuse that was none of her fault? But she knew the answer before she even asked the question. She did not like to lose. Once she had committed herself to a course of action, she would let nothing stand in her way. "Especially not a few ridiculously incompetent clerks," she muttered, and marched into the office ready to do battle once more.

There were two women behind the counter, one thin, tall and starched who was inserting manila folders into a filing cabinet, the other a medium-sized mouse-like girl seated at a desk. Deciding the tall clerk was the one in charge, Alice said crisply, "My name is Alice Galipova. I was told you have a letter for me that I need at once. Can you please get it for me?"

The woman frowned at her. "I beg your pardon?"

Realizing too late that boldness would not work with this particular clerk, Alice adopted a more conciliatory tone and explained her dilemma. But the damage was already done and without even looking, the woman denied the existence of any such letter.

"Surely you could take a few minutes to check?" Alice wheedled. "Perhaps it has just come in."

"I would know if it just came in," the woman sniffed. "I suggest you come back tomorrow."

"But tomorrow will be too late!" Alice's frantic gaze swept the office and came to rest on the mousy clerk, who was staring at a basket labelled "out-going mail." On the top of the assortment of letters and packages protruding from the basket was one with large black lettering, and although Alice could not make out the full name, it began with GAL. Certain it was her letter, she pointed an accusing finger at the basket. "It's right there! I'm sure of it. See, it has my name."

The woman barely glanced at the basket. "And I'm sure it is not," she retorted and returned to the stack of manila files. "Come back tomorrow."

Alice contemplated leaping over the counter to snatch up the letter, but such an act would probably get her arrested. Instead she said, "You can give me that letter or I shall go to see your supervisor." When the woman still didn't move, Alice turned toward the other clerk, who appeared ready to burst into tears.

"So be it," Alice said and left, slamming the door behind her. In the hallway she stood fighting back tears. She had absolutely no idea where she would find the woman's supervisor, nor was there much hope of getting any satisfaction if she did. Steeling herself for yet another battle, she headed for the elevator, but when footsteps sounded behind her, she stopped and turned. The mousy clerk was skittering down the hallway. She halted in front of Alice, glanced furtively behind her, then pulled from her pocket the envelope with the black writing on it. As Alice had suspected, it was addressed to her.

"Please don't go to the supervisor, Miss," the clerk begged, thrusting the envelope into Alice's hands. "We will both be let go if you do." Without waiting for a response, she turned and skittered back to the office.

"Don't worry," Alice called quietly after her. "I don't have time to complain to anyone."

The streetcar workers had still not settled whatever grievance had caused their impromptu walkout, so when she exited the station, Alice looked about for another cab, only now the sidewalk was crowded with passengers who had just disembarked from an incoming train and there was not a taxi to be had. She glanced up at the golden clock beneath the main archway and realized with a sickening feeling that she now had less than an hour before her ship was to sail.

She peered through the thick mist that all but obscured the street and tried to remember her original route to the quay or the route the taxi had taken later. It seemed logical that by simply keeping to Peel street she would eventually come out at the docks. In any case, since no taxi was available, there was nothing to do but try. Turning up her collar against the damp, she started walking as fast as possible, thankful she was wearing sturdy oxfords.

Two blocks later, she heard the muted beating of a drum. Suddenly out of the mist emerged a noisy parade and before she had time to step aside she was engulfed in a sea of angry-looking men. Many of the marchers were wearing the uniform of streetcar conductors and all were waving banners advocating workers' rights. They chanted in unison, "Workers of the world unite! You have nothing to lose but your chains!" Pulled and pushed along as if she were a stick in a swollen river, Alice clutched her purse and tried to work her way to one side where she might break free. "Excuse me," she cried to ears deafened by enthusiasm. "Excuse me, please. I have to get to the ship!"

By sheer force of will she managed to squeeze almost to the outside of the crowd, but was stuck there for several blocks until suddenly a tall, well-muscled man grabbed her arm and thrust her forward with such force that she stumbled and would have fallen had he not been holding her fast. She tried to yank free then realized that with his help she was actually emerging from the human river and a moment later they were both free.

"Thank you," she gasped, steadying herself with his arm as she caught her breath and her racing pulse gradually stopped pounding against her temples.

"Are you all right?" he asked, letting go of her arm at last. When she nodded, he turned to rejoin the parade that was rapidly disappearing in the fog.

"Wait!" she cried. "I don't know which way to go."

He paused. "Where are you headed?" When she told him, he looked regretfully after the crowd then took her arm once more and guided her up the street to another intersection. "Just keep on this street and you'll end up at the docks." Letting go of her arm, he shoved a pamphlet into her hand then turned and hurried after his companions.

Within a few blocks she could hear shouting and the clanging of chains. Certain the ship was about to embark without her, she began to run. Twice she stumbled over the uneven sidewalk and barely saved herself from falling, and more times than that she wondered if the man had played a cruel joke on her and sent her in the wrong direction. Then at last she saw the ghostly image of the *Empress* looming in the fog. She also saw that the gangway was about to be raised and she began running even faster.

"Wait!" she cried breathlessly. "Please! Stop!"

Her voice was muted by the fog, but for some reason the worker directing the operation looked her way. At once he signalled to the others to stop.

"You almost missed it," he said accusingly, helping her onto the gangway. She gasped her thanks and hurried up to the deck where the ships' officer rebuked her for making them late. Too breathless to respond, Alice joined the other passengers at the rail and only when her breathing had returned to normal did she realize she still held the worker's pamphlet. It was covered with slogans and on the back was the picture of a half-roofless farmhouse beside which, dressed in the tattered clothing of a peasant, stood a human skeleton gazing beseechingly at an equally skeletal horse. It made no sense to Alice and after tucking the brochure into her purse, she turned her attention to the activity on the dock. The gangway had been lifted, the cables fastening ship to shore had been cast off and with a belch of steam and a long, muffled blast of its horn, the *Empress* was underway.

A VILLAGE IN THE CARPATHIAN MOUNTAINS OF GALICIA
Mid-June 1914

Natalya Tcychowski raced across the meadow toward the wooded trail and as soon as she saw her father emerge from the shadows she began to shout, "Papa! Papa!"

Vasyl Tcychowski, leading a black Hutsul stallion hitched to a stout log he'd dragged through the woods, halted at his daughter's approach. Braids askew, her homespun shift wet and clinging to her small frame, she stopped, breathless, in front of him. "Farmer Andronic is killing Oleksi!"

He dropped the reins and grabbed her arm. "What are you talking about?"

"Farmer Andronic stole Oleksi's pig right out of our yard," she cried, gesturing back the way she had come. "Catherine saw him and threw herself onto the pig and he dragged her through the dirt but Oleksi grabbed Farmer Andronic's whip and pulled him off his horse and now they're fighting and ..."

"Where?" Vasyl barked. "Show me!"

With her father close on her heels, she raced back across the meadow. Moments later they reached the rough track where the two men were wrestling in the dirt. Twice as heavy as Natalya's eighteen-year-old brother, Yurri Andronic had Oleksi pinned in a tight headlock and was pounding his fist into the younger man's already bloodied face. He was about to administer another blow when Natalya launched herself at his back and tried to grasp his arm.

"Let him go!" she shrieked. "Let go!"

The farmer flung her aside, and she fell back against her sixteen-year-old sister, who was cringing beside Andronic's white stallion and shouting at the two men to stop. The horse sidestepped nervously and the large boar roped behind it squealed in terror.

"What's the meaning of this, Andronic?" Vasyl demanded, his hand resting on the sheathed axe attached to his belt. It was well known among the villagers that he could throw that axe with deadly accuracy.

Andronic lowered his fist and got to his feet, hauling Oleksi, still confined in the headlock, up with him. "This whelp assaulted me," he rasped, his fleshy cheeks puffed in ruddy indignation.

Vasyl's eyes narrowed. "Well, since he is obviously not assaulting you now, I would suggest you let him go."

The two men glared at each other.

"Now... Andronic!"

Sullenly the farmer released his hold and thrust Oleksi forward, but with such force he fell face first into the dirt. Scrambling to his feet, he lunged for Andronic.

"Enough!" Vasyl roared, grabbing his son from behind.

"I won't let him take my pig!" Oleksi struggled to break away but, although he was almost as big as his father, he was no match for Vasyl's vice-like grip.

"It is *my* pig as everyone in the village knows," Andronic spat.

Natalya said indignantly, "It would have died if Oleksi hadn't—" Catherine's hand muffled the rest of the sentence.

Andronic flicked Natalya a scathing glance. "Your children would do well to learn some manners," he said triumphantly, and she realized that, while her father gave no outwardly sign of it, she had shamed him with her outburst.

"But," Vasyl said coolly, "the girl is right." Letting go of Oleksi, he released his axe from its holder and grasped the long, ornately carved shaft with one hand while slapping the flat side of the razor-sharp blade against his other palm. "My son found that boar in our woods when it was nothing but a half-dead runt that had been left for the wolves. He nurtured and fed it and now it is his right to butcher the animal."

The farmer took a step back. "You may be chief forester, Vasyl Tcychowski, but the law is the law."

"Yes, and according to the law that pig belongs to my son," Vasyl said. Transferring the axe to his left hand, he reached up to the cantle of Andronic's saddle with his right, unfastened the rope and handed it to Natalya. "I'll return the rope to you tomorrow."

Andronic's cheeks bulged and grew so red that Natalya was sure they would explode. Then, carefully avoiding Vasyl's axe, he grabbed the reins of his horse and when he was safely mounted, snarled, "No thieving Russophile is going to get away with stealing what belongs to me!" And angrily spurring his horse, he galloped down the track.

Vasyl replaced his axe in its holder. "Your mother will have our dinner waiting," he said quietly and, swinging about, stalked toward the farm.

Oleksi took the rope from Natalya's hands, and pulling the squealing pig, he followed Catherine, who had already started up the trail after their father. Natalya lingered behind and watched the farmer and his horse turn off the trail that led to the eastern Carpathian city of Yeremeche and disappear down the track to the village. As the dust settled, she raised her eyes to the conical peak of Gora Syvulia. Crowned with the glow of the setting sun, it was surrounded by numerous lower mountains with rounded crests and slopes greened by forests of spruce and pine. Natalya knew there were other Hutsul settlements scattered among those hills, but she had never been to any of them. From where she stood she could see the trickle of the Imbyr River that over the centuries had carved out a wide valley from north to south. At some point in its history, the river had narrowed and looped westward, leaving on the eastern bank a large flood plain that was now checkered with grain fields. The village of Zgardy bordered the loop like the single strand of a necklace, and in the gathering dusk, smoke from the village chimneys mingled with the river mists and wisped over Andronic's barley fields, which took up most of the eastern half of the valley and several of the slopes below her.

As she always did at this time of day, Natalya was engulfed in a mixture of melancholy and peace. Then, drawn from her reverie by the thought of supper, she followed the others to the log house that nested into the steep hillside as naturally as the thick grove of beech trees that surrounded the family farm.

⁂

Vasyl Tcychowski loved to tell his children how he had constructed their two-storey home by himself, devoting exhausting hours after each long day at work to create a building that embodied both function and beauty. Each time he told this tale he would point out the Hutsul patterns he had painstakingly carved into the ceiling beams and on the posts of the front porch that extended the full length of the southern wall. "We have the best house in all of Zgardy," he would brag.

"You anger your neighbours with such boasting," his wife would scold then quote from one of Father Ishchak's sermons, "Pride goes before destruction, Husband, and a haughty spirit before a fall."

Vasyl would laugh heartily at her warning. "Is it my fault, Zhanna Pylypovna Tcychowski, that our neighbours have no ambition?"

Despite her father's lack of concern, the destruction predicted by her mother worried eleven-year-old Natalya, especially after she overheard a conversation while she was hiding from Yuliya and her friends in the shadows of Ivan Shevchenko's barrel-making shop. He and his wife, Galyna, the matchmaker of Zgardy, had just arrived home and had paused before going up to their living quarters above the shop.

"Vasyl Tcychowski is a fool," Galyna had scoffed. "He builds a palace for his bride but doesn't join it to his barn."

"He should have married a Hutsul woman," said the barrel maker.

Galyna spat on the ground she could never keep free of the shavings and sawdust generated by her husband's carpentry. "Her mother was a Lemko. It is no wonder that, except for his first-born, all of his sons die before they take a breath."

Her husband nodded sagely. "Just what one would expect of a fancy woman from Lemberg who thinks she knows more than our molfar."

Vasyl had laughed when Natalya repeated the conversation to him, but there was an edge to his laughter. "Your mother is a nurse," he had said dismissively. "Of course she knows more than a man who relies on spells and potions."

Once, after they had pestered her for details, Zhanna told her daughters how she had been visiting her father at his forge in Lemberg when she met Vasyl.

"Your papa was having a special gate built for Baron Potocki," she told them, her stern face momentarily relaxing into a satisfied smile. "I decided right then that he was the man I was going to marry." Absently pleating her apron, she had added, "Of course, it wasn't easy for me to come to this village. People here don't like strangers."

Vasyl's mother, who had lived with them for the first five years of their marriage, taught Zhanna the Hutsul ways and she became a devout member of the Ukrainian Greek Catholic church that most of the villagers attended. But she had insisted on teaching her children to speak Russian and Polish as well as the Hutsul version of the Ukrainian language.

"She creates a tower of Babel with her children talking in so many tongues," complained Galyna Shevchenko, who only spoke the Hutsul dialect.

"Who would want a wife who can complain in three different languages?" Ivan asked then laughed at his cleverness.

Now, as Natalya passed the house on her way to the pig's

enclosure and smelled the sweet aroma of *borscht*, she forgot about the villagers and her worries. Suddenly all she cared about was getting to her place at the table.

※

After his horse had been unhitched from the log and enclosed in the pasture and the pig was once again secure in his pen, Vasyl and his children cleaned up at the washstand near the well. As they trooped into the house, Zhanna, heavy with yet another pregnancy, was standing beside the stove. Her eyes widened when she saw Oleksi's battered face and Catherine's scraped arms and soiled dress, but she said nothing. Instead, as her husband seated himself at the head of the table, she lifted the heavy pot of soup, carried it across the room and placed it in front of him.

Natalya's two other sisters were already settled on a freestanding bench facing the table and beneath the room's only window. Plump and bossy, fourteen-year-old Yuliya eyed the pot hungrily, clearly more interested in dinner than in her brother's battered face. Leysa, who was a year younger than Yuliya and the most fragile of the Tcychowski siblings, paled as Oleksi and Catherine took their places on the opposite bench. Like her mother, she asked no questions but quietly shifted her position, allowing Natalya to squeeze between her and Yuliya.

Natalya glanced around the table and felt, not for the first time, that in this family she was *stranny chelovek*, a Russian phrase her mother used to describe someone who was different. For while her two eldest siblings were dark and tall like their father, and Yuliya and Leysa were blond and blue-eyed like their mother, Natalya's unruly hair was copper-coloured and her eyes an ever-changing green and brown.

※

When everyone was served, Zhanna sat beside Catherine, where she could easily reach the soup pot, bowed her head and said the evening dinner prayer. Her "Amen" was scarcely out before Yuliya crossed herself and began slurping up her soup, but Natalya was so eager to tell her mother the story of the fight that she barely touched her meal. She watched impatiently as her father emptied first one, and then a second, bowl of hot *borscht*. When he nodded to his wife for a third helping, Natalya was unable to restrain herself.

"Oleksi is going to be arrested!" she exclaimed. She winced as Yuliya's elbow dug sharply into her side, and she moved closer to Leysa. Aware of the disapproving glare her mother had fixed on her, Natalya didn't dare to say more, and it was Catherine who quietly related what had happened. "I held onto the pig," she finished, gripping her spoon, "and even when Farmer Andronic kept going, I didn't let go!"

"But surely you told Yurri Andronic he can have what is his?" Zhanna said to her son as she ladeled more soup into his bowl.

Oleksi shook his head. "That boar is mine, Mama."

"Ai-yi-yi!" Zhanna brandished the ladle at him. "Do you forget that Yurri Andronic is a friend of Bailiff Wojcik?"

"But I have done nothing wrong, Mama!"

"And since when does right or wrong matter?" Her hand trembled as she passed the bowl back to him.

Forgetting herself once again, Natalya said, "Farmer Andronic called Oleksi a thieving Russophile."

Too upset to reprimand her for yet another outburst, Zhanna turned and stared at the far wall. "It is because of that accursed rug."

Even in the dim light of the brass oil lamp that sat in the centre of the table the colours and workmanship of the elegant tapestry was visible. Hanging above a large chest on which a small altar had been fashioned, the rich, woven fabric held the image of the Madonna holding the infant Jesus. Crowning the image was the Romanov double-headed eagle crest in burnished gold.

"No, Mama," said Oleksi, "it is because we speak Russian. Andronic believes anyone who can speak the language of the tsar is an enemy of the Austrian empire. He says if the war comes, he will see to it that we are sent away."

"What kind of foolish reasoning is that?" Zhanna shook her head. "We are not at war, and our emperor himself speaks Russian. As does Baron Potocki."

She jumped when Vasyl's thick fist crashed down on the table, rattling dishes and cutlery.

"Enough!" he thundered. "Can a man not eat his dinner in peace?"

The family fell silent, but while the others busied themselves with eating, Natalya stared boldly at her father's scowling face. Although he often bellowed like the bull in Andronic's field, Vasyl Tcychowski had never once lifted a hand to his wife or children, a peculiarity that provided even more fodder for the village gossips. Still, when Yuliya's elbow once again dug sharply into her ribs, drawing Zhanna's frowning attention, Natalya resisted the urge to elbow her sister back, lowered her eyes and resumed eating. Beside her, Leysa had stopped eating and was rubbing a small wooden cross that hung from her neck. Their father had carved one for each of his children and Leysa's was worn thin from constant worrying.

When Vasyl finally finished his meal, he pushed his bowl aside and leaned back in his chair. "You are wrong, Wife, to suggest a gift from the tsar of Russia might bring harm to our household. Perhaps it is because you have forgotten how your husband acquired such a masterpiece."

While Oleksi and Catherine grimaced, Natalya felt a warmth creep through her. The others might find their father's stories tiresome, but to her they were adventures come to life, and she loved the tale of the tapestry most of all.

Vasyl faced his son. "I shall tell you again, Oleksi, and this time you must listen carefully for it is of concern to you after the affairs of this day."

Oleksi nodded in respectful silence.

"When I was young and only a gamekeeper, I would travel from one end of Baron Potocki's forests to the other tracking down poachers. This is how I came upon a lady who was being robbed by a band of thieves, and since her cowardly escort and servants had run off, I did what any Hutsul man would do. I charged forward with my axe, knocking this one and that one about until they fled into the forest. Then I accompanied the lady to the tavern where her chaperone and servants were telling lies about how they had fought valiantly but were unable to save her."

At this point, as he did every time he told the tale, Vasyl rolled his eyes in contempt of the cowards.

"Several weeks after I returned home, a box arrived containing that tapestry and a letter signed by none other than Countess Catherine Stanislavovna Federov, daughter of the late General Stanislav Stanislavovich Federov of the Grand Duke's Imperial Army. The letter thanked me for saving her life and instructed me to come to their home in St. Petersburg if ever I needed her help."

Vasyl paused. "I keep the tapestry in a place of honour," he said, his voice thick with emotion, "because it reminds me that even the humblest of men can affect the affairs of their nation and the world. Had Catherine Stanislavovna died that day in the woods, it would not only have been the thieves who reaped the fury of the Grand Duke's army, but the Hutsuls, young and old, who would have been blamed and punished—an act of revenge that could well have brought on a war between Austria and Russia. And I, who was nothing but a gamekeeper, prevented that from happening." He nodded solemnly as if affirming his own statement. "And that, Oleksi Tcychowski, is how you must live your life, knowing that, while every act you commit might affect no one but you, it might also change the fate of a whole people."

"I understand, Father," Oleksi said.

"Do you?" Vasyl's voice was calm and quiet. "Because for a long time Bailiff Wojcik has wanted to reduce the chief forester's influence with the Potocki family and to have his own son take my place. He will do anything in his power to bring grief to our home, and when he returns from Warsaw next week, he will address Andronic's accusations with great relish."

Oleksi splayed his hands in frustration. "But how, Father? How can he find fault with me for defending myself and my property?"

"As bailiff, Wojcik can find fault wherever he pleases. And it will please him to send you off to serve in the Imperial Austrian Army."

"But I won't go!"

Vasyl shook his head sadly. "You won't have a choice, my son."

Natalya felt the blood drain from her face. Her brother might be her greatest tormentor, but at the thought of his leaving, she suddenly felt like weeping.

Oleksi's face betrayed his fear. "Vitovskyi's brother was forced to join Austria's army two winters ago. They have received no word of him since."

"Nor will they," his father said flatly. "The Austrian commanders treat their new recruits worse than Andronic treats his swine. Tomorrow we will travel to Yeremeche and from there you will take the train to Russia."

"No, Vasyl!" Zhanna rose and went to stand behind her son, placing her hands on his shoulders. "Sending him to join the tsar's army will surely brand us all as Russophiles." She dug her fingers into Oleksi's shoulders, pushing him down against the bench as if to keep him physically in place.

He squirmed in her grasp, but his mother maintained her hold.

Catherine said quietly, "Last week someone told the bailiff that Father Ishchak was distributing Russian propaganda in the reading room. He wasn't, of course, but now he has removed all of his Russian literature—even the poetry journals."

Zhanna nodded vigorously. "You see? It is better that Oleksi apologizes to Yurri Andronic and gives back his pig! He can offer to work for him for free as payment for making such an error in judgement."

"Hutsul men do not apologize," Vasyl said coldly. "Especially not to a toad like Andronic, who would sell his own mother for a better price on his corn." Getting to his feet, he walked heavily to the chest below the tapestry and, after removing the ornaments and icons that formed the altar, lifted the lid. A moment later he returned with an ornate envelope bearing the Romanov seal. He handed it to Oleksi.

"You will take this to the Countess Stanislavovna Federov in St. Petersburg, and she will find you a position within the army where you will be treated with respect. And if the war comes, you will at least be on the winning side."

Freeing himself from his mother's grasp, Oleksi stood, took the letter and ran his trembling fingers over the seal. "Do you really think the Russians could win the war, Papa? It is said in the village that the German army has more guns and better railroads ... ."

"Bah!" Vasyl snorted. "Germany does not have the heart of the Russian peasant, or the fighting spirit of a Cossack tribesman. I promise you the tsar will make short work of the Kaiser's guns and railroads."

Zhanna sank onto the bench, bowed her head and clutched the metal cross that hung from her neck. Her fingers worrying the inlay of small coloured stones, she began to pray.

Vasyl put a hand on Oleksi's shoulder. "We may be under the thumb of Austria and Hungary, my son, but we are still Hutsul, and we—not our oppressors—shall decide where we will spill our blood."

He turned to Zhanna. "Go now, Wife, and prepare a travelling bag for Oleksi so he can leave tonight and be three days gone before Bailiff Wojcik returns from Warsaw." Retrieving his hat from a peg near the door, he went outside.

Natalya followed her father down the steps and across the yard, but when they reached the track leading to the village, he held up his hand. "Tonight I must go alone, little one," he told her sternly then headed alone down the hill.

Many hours later, Catherine slid from the bed shared by the four sisters and crept silently downstairs. Without disturbing Yuliya and Leysa, who were both snoring softly, Natalya also climbed from the bed. Knowing better than to show herself, she hid in the shadows on the narrow stairwell's top step and peered down into the kitchen where Catherine, Oleksi and her parents were gathered near the stove. Although they were talking in voices so low she could hear little of what they said, Natalya understood that her father had made an arrangement with his chief raftsman, Yevhen Hutopila.

The forest reserve where Vasyl's timber crews were currently felling trees was so rugged and far from a proper road that the logs could not be hauled out by horses but instead were gathered into rafts to be floated down the Imbyr River. Narrower at the front end, these rafts were held together by thick ropes laced through metal dogs that had been hammered into each log. Meanwhile, a wooden dam was erected near the landing, and when the rafts were ready a gate would be opened releasing enough water to flood the river and float several rafts down past the village and beyond it to the Imbyr's junction with the Prut River. From there the logs would travel to Baron Potocki's mill in Yeremeche and the lumber shipped by rail to European markets. Natalya shivered, remembering tales she had heard of harrowing escapes by the men who steered these rafts down the winding Imbyr, and of battles with treacherous rapids that had been known to break the roped and bundled logs apart and hurl the raftsmen into the turbulent waters.

"You will leave at daybreak with the first raft," Vasyl said. When Zhanna protested that the journey was too dangerous, he reminded her that in half a lifetime of rafting, Yevhen had never yet lost a single log or any of his crew. Then he added, "In the village I learned Andronic's friends are watching every track to Yeremeche. If we try to go that way, God knows what evil they will wreak upon us."

Oleksi put his arm around his mother. "I'll be fine, Mama. I've been on the rafts before with my friends. And I am a strong swimmer."

Vasyl unfastened the belt that held his axe and placed them both in Oleksi's hands. "Your great-grandfather gave me this on his deathbed. He wore it proudly all of his life, as did his father before him. Now, it is yours. Use it with honour and only when all else fails, and God will guide your hand."

From the stairwell, Natalya caught the flicker of dismay on Oleksi's face before he ducked his head to examine the gift. She remembered how he had practised throwing a crude hatchet day after day until he could hit his target, always hoping his father would someday allow him to use his special axe. But when Yevhen Hutopila gave *his* son a Berdan rifle that he had secured from a passing Cossack in exchange for a jug of homemade *horilka*, Oleksi had put his own hatchet away and began pestering his father for use of the rifle Vasyl had acquired after his encounter with the bandits.

"And what good is a rifle when there are no bullets?" Vasyl had asked. "Better you stick with the axe."

Now, as he strapped the belt around his waist, Oleksi declared staunchly, "I shall wear it with pride, Papa."

Vasyl nodded in satisfaction then said brusquely, "We must leave. They release the water at dawn and with no moon to guide our steps, it will take most of the night for us to travel to the landing."

Natalya wanted to rush to Oleksi and beg him not to go, but she knew doing so would only result in a switching from her mother. So instead, she went back to bed and lay awake until she heard the dawn birds twittering in the beech trees outside.

There was no one in sight when she crept down the stairs and slipped outside. In the barn the roosters were crowing noisily, and in his small enclosure Oleksi's boar was snuffling the dirt searching for food, but Natalya spared only a glance in their direction as she ran through the gate and down to the intersection between the two main trails. There she turned onto a third trail, almost obscured by long grass, and climbed to a bluff nearly a kilometre from the farmhouse. She had been to this spot many times, having shadowed Catherine and Oleksi on their pre-dawn expeditions to witness the rafts hurtling down the stream far below. This morning only Catherine stood on the bluff, and she said nothing when Natalya joined her.

"Am I too late?"

Catherine shook her head. Her cheeks were wet, but her face showed no emotion as she gazed down at the rocky streambed winding through the green valley. Then suddenly the thin stream trickling between the rocks was transformed into an angry surging mass of frothy water, and Natalya cried out as the narrow end of a raft emerged from around a sharp bend.

"There, Catherine! See!"

As the rest of the raft came into view, she could pick out five men near the narrow end, two of them skilfully working the long oars, steering the cumbersome collection of logs around and between boulders and other obstacles. Behind the oarsmen were three others, and though it was impossible to determine who was who, Natalya guessed that the man standing apart from the others was her brother.

At that moment the raft lurched against a boulder, and the man was knocked off balance. Catherine screamed as he crow-hopped madly from log to log, straying dangerously close to the edge, but just when it seemed certain he would go over, he managed to regain his balance. As he made his way safely to the centre of the raft again, Natalya remembered to breathe. Catherine's arm went around her sister as they watched the raft careen around the next sharp bend and disappear from view.

They stayed to watch two more rafts battle the rapids, and by the time these had passed, the flood had abated and the Imbyr was once again just a small stream trickling through the valley. When Catherine started walking along the track to the farm, Natalya followed.

"Will he be safe, Catherine?"

It was several moments before the older girl responded, quoting one of their father's favourite proverbs. "A strong body and an honest heart will conquer all difficulties, Natalya. Our brother has both." She compressed her lips and set her jaw in the same way their mother did each time a calamity befell the family.

ST. PETERSBURG
June 26, 1914

Through a light curtain of rain Alice glimpsed the golden onion-shaped dome of a church just before the train pulled into the Verzhbolovo Station on the Russian side of the border with Germany and came to a steaming stop, accompanied by the clanging of station bells and whistles. Conversation in the railway car grew hushed and there was tension on the faces of her fellow passengers as they sat waiting rather than rushing to the exits as they had at previous stations. A well-dressed woman next to Alice kept darting nervous glances at the grey-haired man beside her. The conductor had already warned them to have their passports ready, and as Alice dug from her bag the letter she had obtained in Montreal, two grey-and-red uniformed officers entered the car.

"*Pasporta, pozhaluysta!*" they commanded in clipped Russian, German, French and, finally, English. "Passports, please."

One by one they took the documents the passengers held out to them, studied the contents, then, without returning them, moved on to the next person. The grey-haired man surrendered his passport and after flipping through the pages the officer turned to the woman and asked for her papers. Then he told them both to come with him into the station. Obediently, the man got to his feet, but the woman remained seated.

"He has nothing to do with me," she insisted shrilly. "I am travelling alone!"

But the order was firmly repeated and at last, still protesting, she followed.

As the two were escorted from the car the second officer turned to Alice who, after warily eying the sword and pistol strapped to his waist, reluctantly handed over her letter. He studied it for several long minutes during which she scarcely dared to breathe, certain that she, too, was going to be escorted from the train. Instead, he added it to the other documents he held. Panicked by the thought of losing her only legal connection to

Canada, Alice held out a slightly trembling hand and said in Russian, "I would like my passport back, please."

He spared her a brief glance.

"*Pozzhe*," he snapped. "Later."

He moved on to the next passenger and Alice had no choice but to sit and wait. When every passport had been surrendered, the taller of the two officers announced that everyone must wait in the station until they could be transferred to a Russian train. She visited the washroom where she tidied her hair, repositioned her hat and tried unsuccessfully to smooth some of the wrinkles from her grey linen travelling suit. Then, like most of her fellow passengers, she went into the station's restaurant which, unlike those she had encountered during the tedious journey from Hamburg, was bright, airy and remarkably clean. At one end were stalls selling an assortment of pastries, meat and vegetable dishes. Too tired to decide what she might like, she copied the passenger ahead of her and purchased a dish of potatoes and cabbage and a cup of hot tea. Seated by herself at a table for two, she sipped the tea and felt restored enough to tackle the meal, which was surprisingly tasty.

When she had eaten, she looked about the room, searching for the officer who had taken her passport. He was nowhere in sight and neither were the man and woman who had been escorted from the train. Meanwhile, amid the clatter of plates and cutlery and scraping of chairs against the floor, she picked up bits of the conversations flowing around her, though much of it was in languages she could not identify. But at the table closest to her, three men in dark suits spoke Russian and after a while she realized they were discussing the situation in the Balkans.

"Austria will invade Serbia," predicted one of the men, prompting a contemptuous wave of the hand from another.

"Franz Josef is a fool! He should listen to Ferdinand." The rest of what he said was lost in the shriek of a child who had spilled hot tea on himself, and by the time his sobs subsided the conversation had switched to Germany's preparations for war.

"She's increasing the size of her army," said the first man while the second added indignantly, "And charging a war tax when there is no war!"

"Not yet."

The third man shook his head morosely. "What else can Mother Russia do now but increase our own armies?" he asked just as a loud bell clanged outside, summoning the passengers back to the train.

As she grabbed her bag and rose from the table, Alice looked anxiously about for the border guards but they were nowhere in sight.

I'm not going without my letter, she told herself as she followed the three businessmen outside, but on the platform she spotted the two officers handing out documents to each person as they passed by. When Alice approached the officer who had taken her letter, he shook his head and her panic returned.

"I want my letter," she sputtered.

Unperturbed, he calmly directed her to the other officer. Barely able to contain her impatience, she waited as this one doled out passports to three more passengers before finally handing her the letter. It had been stamped on both the front and the back. She muttered a grudging, "*Spasibo,*" and tucked it safely into her handbag before boarding the nearest car, where she found a seat next to a window.

The Russian train ran more smoothly than those in Germany, possibly because the route was straighter, and Alice was able to walk from one car to another for exercise. On none of her excursions did she encounter the woman or the grey-haired man.

After another long day and night, she finally arrived at St. Petersburg.

It was late afternoon, and bone weary and thoroughly sick of trains and confined spaces, she was grateful to escape to the station platform. There, after peering about for several minutes, she spotted a young man holding up a sign bearing her name and anxiously inspecting each new arrival from the train. Obviously not Russian, he was wearing, despite the heat, a wool vest over a collarless, long-sleeved white shirt, grey wool breeches and black boots. Alice had seen people dressed in many different costumes on the train, but none had embroidery that equalled the intricate stitchery on this man's sleeves and none carried weapons like the unusual axe that was strapped to his side. When she identified herself, he bowed stiffly, clicked his heels and said far too loudly, "Oleksi Vasylivich Tcychowski, *Mademoiselle!*" He added something in garbled French, but when it was plain she did not understand, his cheeks reddened and he said more slowly, "I speak not good French, *Mademoiselle.*"

Her father had told her French was the language used most often among the aristocracy of Europe. "I'm not so good at French myself, Mr. Tcychowski," she said in Russian, "though they tried to teach it to me at school."

Visibly relieved, the young man switched to a stilted form

of Russian, but it was much better than his French had been. "The countess has requested that I escort you to her home on the English Quay."

"But where is my brother?" Alice asked. "And my grandfather?"

"They are in Valdai, Miss." He gestured for her to follow him, at the same time shouting to a porter to take her luggage.

"Are they all right?" she persisted. "Tusya was supposed to meet me."

"He is fine, Miss," he said, handing her up to a horse-drawn carriage. "He will explain." And he busied himself directing the porter how to load the luggage onto the back of the carriage.

A short while later, as she tilted the pale green parasol the young man had insisted she needed to protect herself from the sun, Alice leaned back against the padded seat of the carriage and felt life creeping back into her maltreated body. Although the warm air reeked of rotting waste from St. Petersburg's numerous canals, at least she was outside and not crowded by fellow passengers.

Oleksi sat beside her, facing the huge back of the bearded driver, and as the cab clattered along the stone-paved street bordering the Neva River, she asked, "Where did you say my brother is?"

"Your grandfather suffers from a sickness of the lungs, Miss. He goes to Valdai for the cure. In the morning you will travel there."

Alice gazed at the huge stone fortress they were passing. Following her line of vision, Oleksi said, "That is called the Bastille of Russia. It is beautiful, yes?"

Too worried, tired and unkempt to appreciate the magnificence of the building,. she returned her attention to her escort. "How far is it to Valdai?"

"I have been told it is a ten-hour journey by train, Miss . ..."

"Ten hours!"

"... and to the house where your grandfather is staying, many more hours by carriage."

Alice grimaced as the cab turned onto a wide thoroughfare so packed with vehicles of every description that she expected everything to come to a complete standstill at any moment.

"It has been arranged that I shall accompany you and remain until it is time for your return," her companion said, apparently unconcerned with the crush of vehicles.

Miraculously, the motor cars, trams and carriages continued

to move forward while on either side of the street a strange assortment of people vied for space. Women wearing brightly coloured scarves hawked baskets of fruit and vegetables, while shouting hucksters offered everything from songbirds imprisoned in wooden cages to jugs of honey. Adding to the din was the brassy trumpeting of horns from bands performing in parks, and everywhere there seemed to be construction workers hammering and sawing. Once the cab moved aside for a *troika* pulled by three sleek black horses, whose harness was decorated with painted flowers and tinkling bells. Considerably larger than the cow ponies on her father's ranch, these Russian horses trotted in such perfect unison that they seemed a single unit. Less colourful were the horse-drawn trams, most often filled with men in dark suits or military uniforms. Comic relief was provided by the antics of ragged youths gathering dung from the streets while dodging vehicles that constantly threatened to mow them down.

But what Alice noticed most of all were the cheerful faces of pedestrians and passengers alike—a lightheartedness that contrasted with the anxious looks she had encountered in England. She thought of Tusya and sighed. She had been so eager to see her rather headstrong brother again, and now she would have to wait another long day. Misinterpreting her sigh, Oleksi said comfortingly, "God willing, your grandfather will be much better."

"I hope so," she said politely, although she really had no feelings one way or another about him. She supposed it was because she had only met the man through his letters.

As the carriage swung sharply onto a cobbled embankment along the Neva, Alice slid involuntarily toward Oleksi. Hastily moving back to her side, she stared out at the closely packed three-and-four-storey buildings, mostly of stuccoed brick, that lined the other side of the street. Here there was little traffic and only a few couples strolled along the embankment, bright parasols angled cheekily over the women's shoulders, the gentlemen accompanying them dressed in three-piece suits, and the children, when present, wearing clean and obviously expensive clothes.

The cab stopped at a two-storey building, dwarfed on either side by more elaborate structures. Stepping down to the street, her escort held out his hand to help her from the carriage then ushered her up the steps. She was folding the parasol when a young maid in a dark gown, white apron and ruffled cap opened the door.

"*Bienvenue, Mademoiselle,*" she said politely, motioning them to enter.

Once inside the large, dark foyer Oleksi gave her a slight bow. "I shall deliver your luggage to your room, Miss," he said and disappeared out the front door again.

"*Si vous voulez suivre, s'il vous plait,*" the maid said and led the way across the broad foyer toward the open door of a drawing room.

Standing in front of an unlit fireplace was a tall, stern-faced man with a moustache and short scraggly beard and a robust woman in an elegant high-collared black dress. They were studying a small pamphlet on the back of which Alice could see an image that was vaguely familiar, but before she could identify it, the woman became aware of her presence and hastily thrust the pamphlet into the man's hands.

"Yes, Elsa?" she asked sharply.

The maid said meekly, "*Mademoiselle* Alice Galipova, Madam."

Although the maid addressed the woman, it was the man who, having stuffed the pamphlet into his pocket, stepped forward and bowed stiffly to Alice. "*Bienvenue à St. Petersburg, Mademoiselle Galipova. Je suis Feliks Stolin, secrétaire de son Excellence.*" There was nothing welcoming in his voice and his narrowed eyes reminded Alice of a wolf she had once encountered on a trail ride. But there was an arrogance about Feliks Stolin that told her he wasn't the kind of man who would slink into the woods and disappear as silently as that wolf had.

His companion lacked the same composure. With a flustered attempt at a smile, she curtsied and introduced herself as Feliks' wife and the countess's housekeeper, Grusha Stolin. "Your cousin is so very sorry she could not be here to meet you, Miss Galipova..." she began, the words tumbling out in rapid French.

"I am afraid, Madam Stolin," Alice interrupted apologetically, "that my French is ... not very good. I would be grateful, please, if you would speak Russian."

Feliks sniffed contemptuously as his wife obligingly switched languages.

"But of course, you must be utterly exhausted," she said then turned to the maid. "Elsa, go upstairs and draw a bath for our guest."

As the girl hurried from the room, the housekeeper said, "Our countess is attending a banquet at the home of the Baroness

Cervinka. She regrets she will be unable to meet you until your return from Valdai but she begs you to understand that she is garnering support for her hospital." Without giving Alice a chance to respond, Grusha launched into a description of the hospital, which had been converted from a small private school founded by the countess's late father. Annoyance flickered across her face when Feliks interrupted her description by suggesting that she show Alice to her room.

"But of course," Grusha said, as if it was her own idea. "If you will follow me, Miss." With a curt nod to her husband, she led the way up a wide, circular staircase that ended in a long dark hallway decorated with portraits of men and women from a much earlier era. Halfway down the hall, she opened a door and they entered a bright bed and sitting room, its high ceiling ornately decorated with biblical scenes. Elsa was waiting at the entrance to an anteroom where Alice could see steam rising, presumably from the bath.

"I have ordered a luncheon to be brought to you after your bath," Grusha said. "Then you shall nap and after that we will have a long chat, yes?"

The thought of lying in a pool of clean water was suddenly so overpowering that Alice forgot all the questions she wanted to ask, and she scarcely managed to express her gratitude before following the maid into the bathroom.

It wasn't until she was soaking in the soothing water that she remembered the man who had helped her escape from the parade of striking conductors in Montreal. The pamphlet he had given to her was identical to the one the housekeeper had been holding and that Feliks had stuffed so swiftly into his pocket. Alice didn't know what it meant, but she was sure that Feliks was not a man to trust. Sliding deeper into the tub, she closed her eyes and pushed aside her concerns, concentrating instead on an image of the hills surrounding the ranch at Willow Bar Creek. Overwhelmed by exhaustion and homesickness, she began to cry.

ZGARDY
July 1914

As Natalya, bucket in hand, carefully squeezed between the gate post and the gate of the willow wattle enclosure that Oleksi had built for his pig, she was closely watched by the black-and-pink-spotted owner of the pen. She knew he was waiting for just the slightest opening and had he seen one, he would have knocked her aside and gained his freedom as he had done on three other occasions since Oleksi went away. Whether his sudden passion for freedom was a result of being abducted by Farmer Andronic or because he missed Oleksi, she wasn't sure, but she was tired of chasing the animal across the meadow where Oleksi's sturdy chestnut pony, Zirka, was tethered and into the woods. The last time it had happened it was almost dark before she got him back to the farm.

"Not that I blame you," she murmured as she fed him a green apple that had fallen too early from the tree. She scratched the stiff bristles behind his ears and didn't let herself think of the fate that awaited him as soon as her father had a day off from supervising Baron Potocki's logging operations. The pig snuffled her hand for further treats and, finding none, eased his heavy bulk to the ground and rested his chin in the dirt, as if he was just too weary to hold his head up any longer. She knelt beside him, petting his back because she liked the feel of his wiry hair against her hand, then reluctantly got to her feet and, using a small wooden shovel, began scooping the pig's droppings into her bucket. When she'd cleared the small enclosure, she carefully let herself out again and carried the waste to a pile behind the barn.

She was just returning to the yard when Catherine emerged from the barn with the basket of eggs she had gathered.

"There's a broody hen in the loft," Catherine said. "I counted six eggs beneath her."

They were walking past the pump in the middle of the yard

when they heard the sound of horses approaching and Farmer Andronic appeared, riding a bay pony. He was followed by the short, rotund figure of Bailiff Wojcik perched on the white stallion the farmer had been riding the day he took the pig, and then by Lech Wojcik, the bailiff's youngest son, on a Hutsul pony. Dark-haired and handsome even to Natalya, who was not yet interested in boys, Lech's searching gaze found Catherine almost instantly. Her cheeks grew red and she anxiously smoothed her dark braids and then her white shift and apron, straightening the pleats, before raising her eyes to the young man.

Natalya glanced from one to the other then hastened back to the pig's enclosure, which was clearly the object of the two older men's attention. At the same time, while Yuliya and Leysa watched from the porch, their mother, with difficulty, waddled across the yard to greet the men.

"Praised be Jesus Christ, Bailiff Wojcik," she said, crossing herself and smiling. Edging closer to the gate, Natalya scowled and wondered why her mother was treating their enemy as if he were a neighbour coming to visit. Frowning, the bailiff pulled a folded document from his shirt, passed it down to Zhanna and said sternly in Polish, "I have been ordered by the council to collect the pig you have stolen from Farmer Andronic."

"But we have only been keeping the pig safe for our neighbour." She waved toward the pen. "Surely, Bailiff, you can see the pig is not hidden, but out in the open for everyone to see. Is this the act of a thief, or a good neighbour who should be blessed for such service? And see how the pig has grown from the small runt our son saved from the wolves? Merciful Jesus, for such dedicated care do we not deserve to be rewarded with at least a portion of the meat?"

"It is by God's grace only that your thieving son and husband are not going to prison, Madam," Farmer Andronic said as he dismounted, rope in hand. As he strode past Zhanna, he bumped her and would have knocked her to the ground had Catherine not grabbed her arm. Natalya's cheeks reddened with anger and shame. *It is Oleksi's pig, and you are the thief!* she fumed silently.

The pig, as usual, was watching the gate, and suddenly Natalya smiled. Moving quickly, she managed to slide in front of Andronic just before he reached the gate.

"Let me help," she said meekly. "It is always difficult to open."

Before he could agree or object, she released the latch and

swung the gate as wide as she could. Without acknowledging her helpfulness, Andronic stepped through the opening, but as he reached down with the rope, the pig darted between his legs. Knocked off balance, he fell face-first into the dirt and the pig barrelled through the gateway, startling the three horses so that the bailiff and his son were too busy calming them to give pursuit as he headed for the woods.

Regaining his feet, Andronic turned on Natalya, cuffing the side of her head so hard her ears rang. "After him, you little bitch!" he shouted, and fearing another blow, Natalya took off after the pig, with Andronic following close on her heels. By the time they reached the woods, the pig was nowhere to be seen.

"I'll go this way," Natalya said, darting down a trail she knew was not the one the pig had taken, but one that led to a thicket of willows. There she ducked down behind some bushes and waited. She heard Andronic cursing on the second trail, and peeping through some branches she saw that Lech, with Andronic's horse in tow, had followed them. Since the pig obviously hadn't stuck to the trail, the horses were of no use and the two men were forced to go forward on foot, following the pig's tracks. As they disappeared from sight, Natalya crept from the thicket and made her way back to the house, avoiding the yard where her mother was busy pleading with the bailiff, who had not dismounted.

"As God lives, Bailiff," Zhanna implored, "she is only a child! It is not her fault that the pig escaped."

"Even a child must face the consequences of her actions, Madam!" he responded severely.

A loud, piercing squeal drew their attention to the woods, and Natalya slipped into the house unnoticed.

Yuliya and Leysa, who had retreated upstairs where they had a better view of the yard, hung out of the open bedroom window.

"You did that on purpose," Yuliya accused when Natalya entered and came to stand behind them.

"I don't know what you're talking about," she said, rubbing her ear, which still throbbed from the blow the farmer had administered. But she was trembling as she thought about what the bailiff had said. Would she, like Oleksi, be sent away? And if so, where would she go?

At that moment Farmer Andronic, mounted on his horse once more, emerged from the woods. He was followed on foot by Lech, who was leading his horse, and Natalya gasped when she saw, tied to the pony's back, the limp body of the pig, his dangling head encased in a canvas water bag. At an order from the farmer, Lech led his horse and cargo across the field to where Zirka, Oleksi's pony, was standing, and untethering him, climbed onto his back and rejoined Andronic just as the farmer reached the pen.

Andronic jerked his horse to a halt and shouted, "Bailiff, I want that young whelp arrested!"

Catherine, still holding her mother's arm, looked pleadingly at Lech, and for the first time, he spoke.

"Surely you don't want to press charges, Brother Andronic," he said good-naturedly. "After all, we have the pig and it would certainly do your reputation no good if it was discovered that a mere child had bested you."

Andronic glared at him. "No one has bested me," he snarled.

"As God lives, Farmer Andronic," Zhanna pleaded again, clasping her hands together, "Surely you do not want the fate of a child on your conscience!"

The farmer spared her a scowling glance then grunted, "I suppose the girl deserves a whipping, not arrest."

"And I swear to our dear God she will get the most severe whipping I can deliver," Zhanna promised, crossing herself.

"See that you do," Andronic snapped then turned his horse away from the pen and rode with the bailiff from the yard. Lech raised his hat to Zhanna, "I will return your horse this afternoon, Mother," he said, politely adding, "Blessings upon you and your house." Then, with a nod to Catherine, he followed his companions.

As the dust settled in the yard, Catherine helped Zhanna back to the house and Natalya went downstairs to face the whipping that was in store for her. She reached the outside door just as Zhanna, having climbed the last step, suddenly gasped and bent over.

"The baby!" she cried and then groaned in both anguish and pain. "Oh, dear God, it is too soon!"

Natalya ran to her side, but Zhanna pushed her away, and it was Yuliya and Catherine who helped her inside and up the stairs to her bedroom, with Leysa trailing anxiously in their wake.

There was no time to send for the midwife, but Catherine had helped her mother deliver so many other women's babies that she knew what needed to be done. She helped Zhanna to her bed then sent Yuliya downstairs for hot water, ordered Natalya to bring in fresh buckets from the well, and gave Leysa the job of applying a cold compress to Zhanna's brow.

Happy to have something to do and to escape the screams coming from the bedroom, Natalya ran back and forth to the pump in the middle of the yard until she had carried in enough water to last a week. Then she went to the lean-to at the back of the house where firewood was stored and brought in enough wood to keep the stove burning all night long if necessary. Unable to bear the groans and occasional strangled scream coming from her mother's bedroom, she escaped to the barn and began cleaning the horses' stalls. Dusk was settling over the farm when she finished and as she walked wearily back to the house she suddenly realized all was quiet.

Hurrying upstairs, she went to the door of her mother's room where her three sisters were peering down at the baby that Catherine held in her arms.

"Look, Natalya," Leysa said, reaching a hand out to her. "It's a boy!"

Natalya went to them and stared down at the tiny red face peeping from the blanket. He looked perfect and sturdy and beautiful, but instead of being overjoyed as she should have been, she was overcome with grief and it was all she could do not to cry. How close they had come to losing him, and all because of her disobedience.

On the bed Zhanna lay, pale and exhausted, her eyes closed.

"We'll let her sleep," Catherine whispered. Still carrying the baby, she ushered them from the room.

⁂

When he arrived home later that night, Vasyl appeared even more exhausted than Zhanna, who had insisted on coming downstairs to supervise the evening meal. But when he saw his new son, his exhaustion evaporated.

"We will call him Pylyp," he said to his wife, "after your father. It is a strong name and he, praise God, was a strong man. Our new son, God willing, will be the same."

From the curtained bed beneath the stairwell that Oleksi had used before he left and which Catherine had recently taken over, Natalya could see the adoring expression on her father's face as he looked at the baby, and she felt a twinge of jealousy.

Zhanna waited until after Vasyl had rested and the family

had eaten before she told him about the pig. He responded as if it was one of his own children that had been abducted.

"Yurri Andronic is no better than a common thief, and neither is the bailiff!" he roared. "God curse them both!"

"May God have mercy upon us, Husband," Zhanna interjected, crossing herself. "Surely we have had enough trouble with Farmer Andronic and the bailiff."

But Vasyl did not agree.

"Young Wojcik is right, though it sickens me to say anything good of that family," he said. "It is not kindness, but a desire not to look the fool that has stopped Andronic from pressing charges." He looked across the table at Natalya. "Our daughter is a true Hutsul," he said proudly. "She fights for what is hers."

Natalya felt a warmth creep through her that banished her jealousy.

Frowning darkly, Zhanna got to her feet. "Our son is lost to us because of your pride, Husband" she said. "And now you praise our daughter for sinning against God and placing us all in danger." She shook her head and asked bitterly, "Of what use is it to be a Hutsul when we are all rotting in an Austrian jail cell?" Turning to an icon hanging on the wall near the stove, she crossed herself, muttered a prayer for mercy then took the baby from Catherine and began climbing the stairs.

Vasyl sat quietly thinking. Then he sighed wearily, rose and went to stand behind his youngest daughter. Placing a hand on her shoulder he said soberly, "Your mother is right, Natalya Tcychowski. It does no good to anger a dog like Andronic. We would both do well to remember that."

GRANDFATHER GALIPOVA
June 27, 1914

Alice scarcely recognized the tall, sober, mustached young man who met her and Oleksi at the Valdai station. Yet in his penetrating blue eyes, so like her own, and the unruly blond hair that drooped over his forehead, she could still see the undisciplined, mischievous brother who had left their father's ranch two years earlier.

He hugged her. "You shouldn't have come, Ali," he said in English, using his pet name for her, "but, damn it all, I'm sure glad you did!"

When he finally released her, she straightened her suit and hat and, switching to Russian, introduced Oleksi, who was stowing their luggage on the back of the carriage. "He's from Hutsulchynia."

Oleksi bowed stiffly to Tusya and explained that he had only recently been hired by the countess.

"I'm sure she welcomes your help," Tusya responded, extending his hand. "Thanks for seeing my sister safely to Valdai." Oleksi awkwardly shook his hand and went back to stowing the luggage with obvious relief.

The open carriage was not as fancy or as well-padded as the one in St. Petersburg had been but the chestnut pony in the traces seemed sturdy. Alice looked curiously at the wooden arch rising in front of the horse's withers. "What is that?" she asked, pointing to the arch. It was similar to those she'd seen on the *troikas* and cabs in St. Petersburg, though not as ornately decorated.

"It's a *duga*," Tusya said. "Keeps the collar from pushing against the horse's neck." He helped her into the carriage and she couldn't help but smile. At home he would never have been so polite. Once she was safely seated, he turned to Oleksi. "You know how to drive?"

When he nodded, Tusya handed him the reins and climbed in beside Alice. Moments later they were trundling along a dirt road past farmyards with houses, barns and outbuildings of weathered, unpainted wood and rough plank roofs. Each yard was surrounded by a strange-looking fence of tall, willowy sticks crudely woven together.

"How was the trip over?" Tusya asked, drawing her attention back to the carriage.

She made a face and launched into a litany of the miseries she had endured since leaving Montreal. How the *Empress* had rolled so badly she was seasick for most of the nine long, stormy days it had taken to reach England. The tiresome journey to Hull where she had caught a steamer to Hamburg and the long, dreary train ride from there to Russia. She suspected her brother was only half-listening to her tirade, and as soon as it subsided he began asking questions about the ranch. She told him how they had spent the whole of the previous spring and summer clearing and draining a piece of land near a bend in the creek for a new hay meadow, and how old Pete Leroux had been promoted from chuckwagon cook to chef in charge of the home kitchen.

"And Borya?" he asked, and in his eyes she saw a longing that almost brought her to tears. "Is he behaving?"

"That darned stallion hasn't let anyone close to him since you left," she said gruffly. "He's almost as wild as he was when you caught him."

He was silent for several minutes before bursting out, "I want to go home, Alice!"

She reached over to squeeze his hand. "The countess wrote that Grandfather was ill. Is he really bad?"

"Yes, he doesn't have long, but he knows you're coming. He wants to see his only granddaughter before ... ." He turned to stare into the pine tree forest through which they were now travelling. Focussing on some bushes with pale pink blossoms, he murmured, "Cowberries."

"I told Father he should have been the one to come," Alice said crossly. "He claimed he can't come back here, but he wouldn't say why."

The carriage bounced over a rut and Tusya grabbed her arm to steady her.

"That's because our dear father does not like to admit to his mistakes." His voice was bitter. "You know there's a price on his head over here."

She stared at him. "Father?"

Tusya nodded grimly. "From what I've been able to figure out, he was in some student movement that was up in arms over the way the government was handling a famine that was going on. He even wrote an article in the student paper. Said Russia was still stuck in the Middle Ages when it came to farming." They were travelling along the shore of a lake and he pointed to a man poling a crude raft of two hollowed-out logs joined by boards in the middle. He was maintaining his balance by having one booted foot anchored in either log. "Like that. And he said the government had downplayed the summer droughts and winter floods that pretty much destroyed two years of crops. Instead of declaring a famine and saving what little grain they had for the people, they exported it and raised the farm taxes so high the farmers had to sell off their seed grain. While the capitalists got rich from the exports, almost half a million Russians starved to death."

They left the lake and the strange boatman behind as the road continued along the outskirts of another village of unpainted wooden houses. Alice looked out at a group of children playing beside a ditch, laughing as they splashed each other. She had never known hunger and could not imagine what it would be like to face day after day without food or to watch your children waste away and die.

"I don't blame him," she said stoutly. "I would have written that article myself."

"Even if it caused a riot?" Tusya shook his head. "As near as I've been able to find out, Father didn't mean for that to happen, but it did and when it was over, twenty people were dead, including two police officers. The paper's editor and staff went to prison and a warrant was issued for Father's arrest."

They crossed over a wooden bridge where the rattle of the carriage wheels drowned out any chance of conversation. When they were back on the dirt road he said quietly, "Grandfather was teaching history at the same university and, according to one of my professors, everyone had been sure he would be appointed rector. But because of Father's article, he lost all that and just barely kept his teaching position. Six months later, Grandmother died. She had a weak heart and the scandal and Father's departure were just too much for her."

For a while they rode in silence, listening to the jingle of the harness and the strange tune Oleksi was whistling, a haunting melody that saddened her as much as Tusya's story had done.

"So that's why he sent us over here," Alice said resentfully, forgetting that only moments before she had championed her father's actions. "We're paying the debt he owes to his father."

"More than that," Tusya said, but didn't elaborate. Instead, he went back to asking questions about the ranch.

By the time they passed through a forest of scraggly pines mixed with white-barked birch trees, the afternoon was almost spent and when they arrived at the small wooden cottage where Tusya and their grandfather had been staying, stars were beginning to appear in the dusky sky. Climbing stiffly from the carriage, Alice followed her brother into a kitchen brightly lit with oil lamps, where she was greeted with the savoury aroma of cabbage soup. A large, matronly woman whom he introduced as Irinya was dumping a bowl of *perany* into a pot of boiling water.

"Your grandfather rests," she said brusquely. "You must eat and sleep and in the morning you will visit."

Alice compressed her lips. She was in no mood to let anyone else tell her what to do. "I am a nurse," she said crisply, removing her hat and placing it on a chair with her bag. "I will see him now."

❧

The old man's room was off the kitchen. A single oil lamp burned on a bedside table, the flickering light illuminating the face of the ghostly figure who lay propped up with several pillows, his bony fingers clasping the covers as if he was afraid to let go. *They're so smooth*, Alice thought, staring at hands unmarred by scars and calluses. *Not at all like Father's*. Nor were his cheeks weathered by wind and sun. But in Alexandrei Sergeivich Galipova's eyes and in the faint smile he managed when he saw her, she recognized her father.

"You look just like your grandmother," he said weakly.

"It is an honour to meet you, Grandfather," Alice said politely. She sat on a chair beside the bed and, taking his wrist in her hand, timed his pulse. Satisfied by its strength, she slid her hand into his and was surprised by the strength of his grip.

"The honour is mine, my child," he countered then began to cough. His grip tightened, and from the rigidity of his jaw she knew he was in pain. When the cough subsided, she studied him closely, noting his shallow respirations and the dryness of his skin then leaning forward and listening to his chest. With each breath he took, she heard the scratchy sounds of pleurisy.

"I'm afraid I don't do so well in the evening," he apologized. "I will be much better in the morning."

"You should be in a hospital," she admonished.

He closed his eyes, and as she sat silently beside him, she looked about the room, surveying the walls lined with books of every shape and size.

"Grandfather can recite whole plays," Tusya had written to her once. "And he knows everything there is to know about Russian history."

Her father, in a rare moment of openness, had told her that Alexandrei Galipova had been orphaned as a young boy and placed in the home of his mother's cousin General Stanislav Federov, who was the countess's father. When it was clear the boy was not cut out for military life, the general had wanted little to do with him, but he did see to it that he received the best education available in St. Petersburg.

On the bedside table next to the lamp was a tray holding a bowl of watery soup and a glass of tea, both untouched. "Would you like me to feed you?" she offered quietly, but instead of answering, his grip eased and she realized he was sleeping. After a few moments she rose and tiptoed from the room.

※

The room the housekeeper assigned to Alice also branched off the kitchen. It was starkly furnished but the single bed was comfortable enough and she was looking forward to a sound night's sleep. What she had not anticipated was the sun rising just before two in the morning, accompanied by a rather annoying bird that had perched in some bushes outside the room's small window. For the next two hours it serenaded her with a medley of trills, whistles and clicks that chased away any chance of sleep. At last she rose, dressed and went outside to vent her frustration on the intruder. But when she rounded the corner of the *dacha*, as Tusya had called the small cottage, the bird had disappeared, probably into the forest that adjoined the clearing.

Unable to do battle, she walked instead down a worn pathway to a marshy lake and along its shore. The morning mists filtered through the clumps of green and brown reeds, almost obscuring a family of mallards. A gull screamed on its way across the open water that stretched toward a far distant horizon where it met the pale blue sky and a few scattered clouds. There were no hills or mountains here, but Alice felt a kinship with this land, with the water and the ducks and the peaty air, and it was easy to pretend she was standing beside one of the marshy lakes on her father's ranch.

That's where I should be, she thought, *Helping Doctor Bill and practising for the July rodeo, and seeing if Ray Barnes is back from university.* The son of a neighbouring rancher, Ray was always trying to expand their relationship beyond friendship, a prospect that suddenly seemed much better than being stuck in a foreign land for the next six months. For an instant she hated her father and then hated herself for not standing up to him. *Never again,* she vowed, *will I let someone else dictate the path of my life.*

When she returned to the *dacha*, Irinya had prepared breakfast. She waved Alice to the table then brought her a glass of strong, hot tea and a large bowl of *kasha* topped with thick cream.

"My father used to make this," Alice said after tasting the buckwheat porridge, "but it was never as good as this."

The cook grunted noncommittally as she busied herself washing dishes. She did not seem inclined to talk, but when Alice remarked on the bird that had wakened her, she did volunteer that it was probably a nightingale.

After checking on her grandfather, who was sleeping soundly, Alice went back outside where she found Oleksi and Tusya harnessing the carriage.

"Where are you going?" she asked.

Oleksi gently slipped a padded collar over the horse's head. "The countess has sent word that I must return at once," he said. "The Archduke Ferdinand has been assassinated in Sarajevo."

She looked at Tusya, who was positioning the leather saddle behind the horse's withers. "And just what does that have to do with us?"

"The Archduke was heir to the Austrian throne," he explained. "And now Austria has the excuse she's been waiting for to invade Serbia. That means Russia's going to war." There was an excitement to his voice that annoyed her.

"You sound as if it's some great sporting event, Tusya. A competition of winners and losers."

"I suppose in a way it is." He turned toward Oleksi. "We don't have wars in Canada."

Oleksi shook his head. "Then you are blessed with a truly remarkable country," he said soberly. "Nobody wins in a war."

"If there really is going to be war, we need to go home now, Tusya," Alice said urgently. "Before it starts."

About to place the harness on the horse's hindquarters, her brother paused. "And what of Grandfather?"

She met his gaze then looked away.

"He should be in a hospital," she said with greater firmness than she felt. "We can't help him here."

"He wouldn't even survive the journey to Valdai, Alice. And even if we did get him to a hospital, there's nothing they can do for him. The doctors told the countess that all they can do is make him as comfortable as possible."

"Then our staying here won't help him," Alice persisted. "And I'm sure he wouldn't want us to risk our lives doing so."

Tusya brought the harness down so hard against the horse's back that the animal started, almost knocking Oleksi over as he was adjusting the shaft bow. Speaking softly, Tusya steadied the animal, and then with gentler movements he moved the tail to fit the crupper beneath it. At last he stepped away from the horse and stood, hands on hips, facing Alice.

"You're right, Alice. He wouldn't ask us to risk anything, just as he has never asked Father for anything. But he's family." In his anger, Tusya resembled their father in a way Alice had never noticed before. He waved his hand in disgust. "Go and get your things if you must leave. I'm not letting him die alone." Turning his back on her, he helped Oleksi bring the carriage up behind the horse.

Alice's hands fisted as she watched them. "That's exactly what I'll do!" she shouted. Furious with her brother, her father and whatever idiot had killed the Archduke, she swung about and stormed back into the house.

Her grandfather was awake, and as he had indicated the night before, he seemed to be much stronger this morning, his breathing almost normal.

"Do I hear the horse?" he asked as she came to sit beside him.

"Oleksi has to return to St. Petersburg," she said, then had to explain who Oleksi was and why he was leaving. The news seemed to sadden but not surprise him.

"Your brother is right. There will be a war. It can't be helped."

"But why, Grandfather?"

He sighed heavily. "There are many outward reasons, child. Austria wants the land Serbia has. The Serbs, Croats and Slovenes want Bulgaria. The Germans want to have more say in the African colonies and the Mediterranean. Britain wants to own the seas." He paused for a breath then added, "And Russia wants to recuperate from the losses she suffered in her fight with Japan over Manchuria while at the same time keeping Germany in her place."

"How on earth," Alice exclaimed, putting her hands to her temples, "can anyone possibly figure all that out?"

"You don't need to," he said, "because at the root of it all is fear. Each country is afraid of not having enough. So afraid that they have forgotten how to share, and instead, like greedy children, they try to grab everything for themselves."

He began to cough and once again she could see he was in pain. She helped him to sit forward, and when his breathing was finally under control, he leaned back against the pillow and looked at her kindly. "You and your brother should return home, Alice. This is not your quarrel."

As she took his hand in hers, she realized he was very much aware of how alone he would be if they left, but in his expression she read nothing more than genuine concern for his grandchildren's welfare. Unlike her father, he was not a man who would use others for his own purposes, and suddenly she understood why her brother could not leave him.

"We're not going anywhere," she said quietly, patting his hand.

※

In the three weeks that followed, Alice came to be grateful for the time she was able to spend with her grandfather. On his bad days, she saw his courage and perseverance as he gasped for every breath he drew, stoically fighting the knives of pain she knew were stabbing at his chest. On his good days, when his breathing was easier and the pain tolerable, they talked, often about her father.

"Even as a boy, Sergei did not know how to compromise," he told her one day. "He expected right and would not tolerate wrong. If a toy was defective, it was tossed in the flames. If a friend crossed him, he became an enemy. God did not behave, so God was banished."

Alice smiled, feeling a sudden kinship with a deity she had never been allowed to know.

"He could not grasp," her grandfather persisted, "that our task is to accept our fate and endure until the reason is revealed to us. Sometimes on this side of the veil. Sometimes on the other."

On another day he spoke again of war. "It is not all bad," he said, sensing her fear. "With each battle, something is taken and something is left behind. It is God's way of sorting the wheat from the chaff."

One morning his pain was evident and he coughed continuously, despite the herbal concoctions the doctor had prescribed for reducing the phlegm that was smothering his lungs. By late afternoon he was drifting in and out of consciousness. Alice left his side only for minutes at a time, but at suppertime Tusya came in to sit with him.

"Irinya has gone for the priest," he said. "She has supper waiting for you."

Alice started to shake her head then stopped. It was Tusya's right to be there. He was the one who had brought the old man to Valdai and insisted on staying. She rose, and as her brother took her place, she gripped his shoulder.

"Call me if his condition changes," she said softly.

Strangely, although she was hungry, she only stared at the *pareny*, and she was still doing so when Tusya appeared in the doorway. His face was sad but she sensed relief as well.

"He's gone, Ali."

☙☙

The following day they took the body back to St. Petersburg and once again Oleksi met the train. He seemed more confident and gave detailed answers to Tusya's questions about the countess, especially the work he had been doing on her hospital, which was set to open the following week.

"If the countess says something must be done, it is done now," he said.

An hour later, when Alice finally met the countess, she understood what Oleksi had meant. A short, stout woman of seventy, she had a regal manner and the agility of a much younger person.

"I have arranged for your grandfather to be interred beside his parents at the Alexander Nevsky monastery," she said with the assurance of one whose authority is never questioned. "Father Vorobiev will conduct the mass."

They were in the sitting room where Alice had first met Feliks and Grusha, and the countess was standing near the fireplace with Tusya. Alice, seated on a *fauteuil*, felt somewhat overwhelmed, though also determined.

"As soon as the funeral is over, Tusya and I must return home," she said firmly.

The countess was not pleased. "Surely you are not going to abandon me before my hospital opens?"

"We have no choice," Alice said. Ignoring the warning look that Tusya directed her way, she added, "I'm very grateful to you for paying my passage here, and I promise that when I get home I will work day and night until I pay you back."

The countess bristled. "You'll do nothing of the sort, young lady," she snapped. "In Russia a gift is given and forgotten. We will not speak of it again." Then, before Alice could advance her argument, the older woman swept from the sitting room, almost bowling over Feliks who was standing in the doorway. When she was gone, he eased into the room and handed Tusya a letter, then turned to Alice.

"I believe I can secure your passage, *Mademoiselle*," he offered. It was the first inkling of friendliness he'd shown to her.

Alice looked at him suspiciously and she wondered what had caused the sudden shift in his manner.

"Oh, hell," Tusya muttered, drawing her attention. "Father has broken his leg."

"What?" Alice rose to snatch the letter from him. She scanned the pages Sergei had written in Russian, giving only the briefest details of his accident. Apparently he had been riding Borya when the horse stumbled and he had fallen, landing so hard on the corral fence that it splintered, gashing and breaking his leg.

William has me hobbled up so I cannot move, he wrote, *and insists I must stay this way for six weeks. He does not realize how impossible that is!*

"I'll bet Borya bucked him off," Tusya said. "That horse is too surefooted to stumble."

"It doesn't matter," Alice retorted. "Now we really have to get back. If Father tries to walk before that break heals, he could be crippled for life." She turned back to Feliks. Although she didn't trust his motives for an instant, she needed his help. "If you can find us passage, we will be most grateful," she said, emphasizing the grateful part.

He nodded, showing he understood, then bowed slightly and left the room.

<hr>

The memorial began with a day of endless prayers and a continuous stream of visitors, most of them former students and faculty members from the university. The following day the coffin was placed in an elaborate horse-drawn carriage with a domed white canopy and white lace curtains. The countess, Alice and Tusya climbed into the second carriage in the procession and it moved slowly toward the monastery at the southern end of Nevsky Prospekt. The students who were too poor to afford a carriage followed on foot.

Trussed into a heavy black dress the countess had produced

for her from somewhere and squeezed between the countess and Tusya, Alice felt as if she was being smothered, and only the slight breeze caused by their passage kept her from leaping out of the carriage. The warm air was laden with a mixture of odours, fragrantly sweet when they passed by a garden park, mouth-wateringly delicious near the bakeries, and reeking of filth when they went through the poorer districts. Here, dressed in rags, small children with gaunt faces and swollen bellies, and adults, bent and shrunken, many with missing or twisted limbs held out dirty hands for kopeks. When a coin was tossed to them, there was a mad scramble to retrieve it. Shamed by the memory of the bread and sausage and fruit she had eaten for breakfast, Alice tried to look away, but a morbid fascination kept drawing her back to the scene.

No one deserves to live like this, she thought. *It's not fair.*

The countess, who had already developed an uncanny knack of perceiving Alice's thoughts, said firmly, "God gives each of us a role to play in this life, my dear. These poor beggars are here to learn their lessons just as we are here to learn ours. To question their lot is to question the wisdom of our teacher."

"But what if our role is really to help them?" she asked.

The countess sniffed. "There are many organizations that do just that. I myself contribute funds to several orphanages."

Tusya pointed toward a multi-domed cathedral on their left that was fronted by a huge barn of a building and a sidewalk cluttered with small booths, each offering something different for sale—melons fresh from country gardens, oranges from the south. "That is the Haymarket, Alice," he said. "They've got fish from all over the world!"

"I used to take your father there when he was a little boy," the countess added.

Alice could not imagine her father—who found even the tiny settlement of Willow Bar Creek too confining—walking among the crowds that filled the noisy market square.

✿

The mass was held in one of the smallest of the monastery's sixteen churches. As they entered the vestibule, Alice was overwhelmed by the cloying scent of frankincense. Gleaming jewelled icons covered in gold and silver reflected the light of hundreds of candles. A red-carpeted aisle ran from the vestibule to the eastern end of a second room where marbled steps led to a semicircular platform and a wall of icons, in the centre of which were two doors, guarded on either side by a gold candelabrum.

"Are all of the churches like this?" Alice whispered to Tusya. He shook his head. "Many of them are even grander."

As the coffin was brought up the aisle and placed near the platform, the women gathered on one side, the men on the other. In spite of the incense and excess of candles, it was cool and peaceful in the church, and Alice felt herself relaxing as she listened to the soothing voices of the choir, the soft chanting of the priest and the rhythmic jingle of the censer from which even more incense wafted into the room. Unable to understand the mass, her attention strayed to the women around her. Their heads were covered, as hers was, by black lace scarves, and each woman held a candle that illuminated her solemn face as she chanted monotonal prayers, prompted by the white-robed priest and, or so it seemed to Alice, a rather large number of helpers dressed in robes of varying colours.

She tilted her head to observe the sky-blue dome above her and wondered how many workers it had taken to paint the celestial figures in gold and blue and white. And at what cost were the intricately stained glass windows of the nave created and installed or the icons and frescoes that adorned the walls? One of the icon figures reminded her of the street beggars, and she could not help thinking of the meals that could be purchased with the silver surrounding that one small picture. For the first time in her life she began to understand her father's bitterness toward the church.

"Churches and priests! Parasites sucking money from the pockets of the poor!" he had shouted whenever the question of religion arose in their house. He had never forgiven the priest in Kamloops who had refused to marry him and his Methodist sweetheart unless she agreed to raise their children as Catholics, a sin Alice's maternal grandparents would never have forgiven. The argument that had ensued between the young couple almost destroyed their hope of a future together until they finally agreed to be married in a civil ceremony and to keep religion out of their home entirely.

It was late in the afternoon before the funeral moved to the graveside and after even more prayers they returned to the countess's home for a final meal. Saddened by the loss of a grandfather she'd had so little time to know, and exhausted from the day's ordeal, Alice nevertheless felt a surge of hope as the last of the visitors left and she was able to retire to her room.

Now we can go home, she thought happily as she prepared for bed.

But when she inquired the next morning, Feliks confessed he had not been able to find passage with any of the shipping agents in St. Petersburg, and the few trains that were not being pressed into service transporting soldiers and the tools of war were fully booked.

"Do not despair, *Mademoiselle*," he said grimly. "There are still ways to secure passage. It is only a matter of time."

Meanwhile, the countess was busy making arrangements to establish a field hospital that would be ready to be put into service the minute war was declared. Alice helped by rolling bandages and putting the finishing touches on the new hospital. Located on Nevsky Prospekt, it would serve as an auxiliary medical unit that would be available when the larger hospitals in the city were full. It would also provide a base for the field hospitals. Following instructions from the countess, Tusya and Oleksi were signed up to train as sanitars—as orderlies and ambulance attendants were called in Russia.

"What is the point of that," Alice asked her brother, "when we're going home?"

"I have to do something," he said evasively.

Wherever Alice went in the city, she heard arguments about whether Russia should continue to mobilize or try to seek a peaceful resolution to the Serbian crisis, and every day the papers were filled with ominous reports about Serbia's intentions and Germany's warnings that she would mobilize her armies if anyone interfered with the Austro-Hungarians, no matter what they did. Finally, on July 28, Austria declared war on Serbia and on the following day the tsar announced that Russia was mobilizing.

"He has no choice," the countess said vehemently. "Russia has promised to protect Serbia and we shall keep that promise."

That is all the more reason why Tusya and I should leave now, Alice thought but didn't say out loud. She had decided it would be better to secure their passage and then tell the countess they were still set on leaving.

But as if reading her thoughts again, the countess said, "Your brother and Oleksi are proving invaluable in securing supplies for me."

"I'm sure you will find someone else just as competent," Alice said, determined not to be manipulated by the guilt she was feeling.

On August 1, after an especially long and tiresome day, she retired early and was sound asleep when she was roused by the maid tapping gently on her shoulder.

"The countess requests that you join her downstairs, Miss."

Alice stared groggily at the young woman.

"Now?" She peered at the clock on the mantle. "What time is it, anyway?"

"Four o'clock, Miss."

Tusya was already in the grand parlour where the countess sat in her favourite brocade chair like an empress upon a throne. She waited until Alice was seated before announcing solemnly, "I am afraid, my dear Canadian cousins, that Russia is at war."

Alice began to tremble and grabbed her brother's arm to steady herself.

"We have to get home, Tusya!"

He patted her hand, but instead of responding he stared moodily at the flames licking bits of coal in the fireplace.

"If it is your fate to go," the countess said, "you will go. And if it is not, you will stay."

Alice did not go back to bed, and she seriously contemplated not going to the hospital that day. When she did go, she felt as if she was carrying a thousand-pound weight upon her shoulders, and by the time she returned home, she was so exhausted she refused dinner and went right to her room. She was there an hour later when Feliks knocked on her door.

"I have found you passage on the *Dwinsk*," he said, handing her an envelope. "It leaves tomorrow."

She opened the envelope and removed a single ticket. "Have you given Tusya his, then?"

Feliks shook his head. "There was only one passage available, *Mademoiselle*. A diplomat who has been persuaded to stay in Russia. But your brother has told me he does not wish to leave."

"That's nonsense," Alice snapped. "Of course he's going home!"

But when she found her brother in his own room, Tusya confirmed what Feliks had said.

"I'm staying, Ali. I owe it to the countess. I'm going to join the ambulance corps with Oleksi."

"You *owe* the countess?" she shouted. "That's ridiculous, Tusya! You paid any debt you might have had by staying with Grandfather."

Tusya smiled sadly. "I know you don't understand, and that you're afraid. But I can't leave her. She's been like a mother to me ever since I came here. And she looked after Grandfather all those years."

"But Russia is at war, Tusya! Do you have any idea what that means?"

"The countess saved Father's life, Ali."

She stared at him and remembered their father had said the same thing.

"How do you think he got out of Russia?" Tusya persisted. "She used her connections to get him a passport and travel permit and risked going to prison and worse by taking him in her carriage to the border. She even bribed the guards to let him pass into Germany."

"But what about Father?" Alice sputtered.

"He'll be fine. He's got Pete and Doctor Bill. And if you're going back, he'll have you. Besides, it's his damned fault we're here in the first place!"

Tears of frustration stung Alice's eyes, but she knew when Tusya made up his mind, nothing would persuade him to change it. Feeling sick to her stomach, she returned to her room and sat on her bed. Among the thoughts spinning through her head was the memory of a hunting trip she and Tusya had taken with their father. Sergei had been determined that his son would shoot whatever game they came upon, but when he had a four-point buck lined up, Tusya couldn't pull the trigger. If he couldn't even shoot a deer, she thought now, how was he going to shoot a human being? And how could she leave him here alone to face the consequences?

"Damn it to hell!"

Getting to her feet, she snatched the ticket from her bedside table and set off to find Feliks.

ZGARDY

September 1914

At the end of July Austria-Hungary declared war on Serbia and from then on Vasyl began spending even more time at the baron's logging site. Often he would leave early in the morning before the birds began to stir and not return for several days. When he did come home, he would arrive long after dark, his face haggard and bristling with whiskers, his clothes filthy and torn.

"Why is the baron driving you so hard?" Zhanna asked one day in late September.

"Because the Kaiser and Franz Josef need timbers and ties to rebuild the bridges and railroads Russia is destroying," Vasyl explained patiently. There was pride in his voice whenever he spoke of Russia's victories, although he was very careful not to let it show outside of their home. "There is more than one Judas in our village," he had warned his children, "who would report to the Austrian authorities that Vasyl Tcychowski is a Russian spy."

The following morning while they were working in the garden Zhanna complained to Catherine, "Your father is full of foolish dreams. He thinks his son is responsible for Russia's every victory, when we do not even know if Oleksi is alive!" They were pulling beets from the ground and slashing off the tops, which Yuliya and Leysa then hauled to a silage trough close to the barn. The roots, from which most of the dirt was shaken free, were deposited into baskets to be carried to the root cellar.

Nearby, Natalya was minding Pylyp, whose wooden cradle had been placed in the shade of a beech tree. Although the baby was nearly two months old, he was still so tiny he scarcely mounded the blanket covering him, but since he spent most of the day sleeping, she had also been given a second chore to keep her out of mischief—preparing down for quilts. Seated on the ground between two large sacks, she extracted chicken feathers from one sack, plucked the down from the spine then deposited the soft fibre into the second sack. Occasionally a breeze rustled through the beech leaves and teased her with the sweet scent of pine needles roasting in the sun, a reminder of trails waiting to be explored and secret places to be discovered. Only the threat of a switching and the fact that she could eavesdrop on the conversation between her mother and eldest sister kept her from escaping to the woods.

Now, as Catherine whacked all but a few inches of top from the fat beet she was holding, Natalya heard her say, "At church Farmer Andronic was boasting that Russia's armies have been destroyed and the Kaiser will be celebrating the fall harvest in St. Petersburg."

Zhanna sniffed contemptuously. "What nonsense! Only last night your father told me the baron has ordered him to hire more men. He wants to produce as much lumber as he can before the Russian army destroys his mills."

She bent to pull the next beet from the ground just as a loud, cheerful voice called out, "Glory be to Jesus Christ, Mother Tcychowski." She straightened to see the grinning face of the village postman astride his horse. He raised his saddlebag in the air. "You will be most grateful to his holiness, I'm sure, when you see the letter I have brought to you from your son!"

Natalya knew her mother must be overjoyed, but she showed no sign of it as she brushed the dirt from her skirt and plodded forward to greet the postman.

"Glory be to you, Ivan Hawrylak," she said. "It is a long way you have travelled on this great morning our Lord had seen fit to grant us! Come into my poor kitchen and rest your bones while my daughter takes care of your horse."

The ends of Ivan's thick moustache disappeared into the creases of his broad smile. "It is an offer I cannot refuse, good mother," he said as he dismounted, "for I am weary after my long trek, which started before the sun chased all of the stars from the sky above Yeremeche."

Catherine took the man's horse to the watering trough as Zhanna picked up the cradle and led the way into the kitchen. Natalya followed and settled herself discreetly on the bench to the left of the door where she was in the shadows and partly concealed by her father's winter coat, which hung from a peg. From here, as from Oleksi's bed beneath the stairwell, she could observe and hear all that was going on in the kitchen. She loved the rough softness of the sheepskin coat that smelled of wool, sawdust and sweat and made her feel as if her father was close.

While Zhanna prepared a meal for the postman, he sat in

Vasyl's place at the table and rambled on about the aches and pains he had endured on his long ride and how only the thought of a plate of Zhanna's fine *kulesha* and cheese had sustained him. From the size of his very prominent belly, Natalya suspected he said the same thing at every farm and village house he had visited between here and Yeremeche. She stared at the saddlebag resting at his feet.

Why doesn't he give Mama the letter?

But the mail seemed to be the last thing on Ivan's mind. He drank *zentyca* greedily from Vasyl's long-handled wooden cup then smacked his lips. "It is a sad day for the mothers of Yeremeche," he rambled on. "Their homes are threatened and their sons are being slaughtered by the Russian invaders."

The pitcher in Zhanna's hand wobbled as she refilled his cup, spilling the whey onto the table. "The Russians are that near then?" she asked faintly, setting the pitcher down and fetching a cloth to wipe up the mess.

"In Yeremeche the thunder of their cannon fire keeps us awake far into the night, Mother. I tremble to think of what will await me on my return."

"And will they come here, do you think?"

He snorted derisively. "Believe me, there is nothing in Zgardy that would tempt any army to trek so far into these cursed hills! Only a postman with great compassion would sacrifice his bones for such a long and difficult journey."

Oh, for goodness sakes, Natalya fumed silently. *Stop talking and eat!*

However, it was a long time before Ivan wiped a film of whey from his moustache with the back of his hand then lifted his pack onto the table. After digging through the contents, he finally pulled out a thick envelope marred with water stains and a black censor stamp. He pointed to the faded postmark on the front. "Three weeks it has been since your son first sent it on its way," he said, then added meaningfully, "It is lucky Ivan Hawrylak is a man of great discretion. Should someone else who likes to gossip have found out you have a son in the Russian army, your position in the country of her enemy might not be safe."

Zhanna said quietly, "We are in your debt, Ivan Hawrylak, and we will not forget your kindness. Nor will our Lord Jesus Christ fail to notice it. You will surely be blessed for being so honourable a man."

Ivan beamed with satisfaction and finally put the letter into Zhanna's trembling hand. Had it been Natalya's choice, the envelope would have been opened and the letter read before the postman had left the house, but Zhanna would commit no such discourtesy. Instead she walked outside with Ivan and endured more idle chatter until finally the man mounted his horse and started toward the village trail.

As soon as the horse and rider disappeared, all of the girls crowded around their mother.

"Can we open it now, Mama?" Natalya begged.

"Of course not," Zhanna snapped, but there was a longing in her face as she fingered the envelope. "We must wait until your father comes and we will read it together."

Catherine said, "I could take the letter to the logging site, Mama. Papa can read it there and then I will bring it back for you."

Zhanna thought for a long moment. "There might be patrols out," she said. "It would not go well if they found this letter with you."

"I'll be careful, I promise. And I'll take the lookout trail. No one uses it but us because it's so steep."

Still Zhanna hesitated. Then, with a deep sigh, she agreed to Catherine's plan. "But," she warned sternly, "do not make a fuss in front of the workers. If your father chooses to wait before reading the letter, you must simply come back home."

Catherine nodded. "Yes, Mama." She tucked the envelope into the large pocket of her apron and headed for the barn. At that moment a faint cry came from the house and Zhanna hurried inside to nurse the baby. Yuliya and Leysa followed her, and Natalya knew Yuliya's goal would be to scrounge any bread or cheese the postman may have left behind, for she was constantly hungry. Natalya, however, ran toward the barn from which Catherine had emerged carrying Zirka's bridle.

"I'm coming, too," she said as they walked to the meadow.

But Catherine shook her head. "You'll slow me down. I must ride fast if I'm to return before the sun sets. It's better that you stay and help Mama with Pylyp."

"No," Natalya said stubbornly. "I'm going with you or," she warned, her eyes narrowing, "I will tell Papa that you kissed Lech Wojcik when he brought Zirka back."

Catherine's cheeks paled then flushed with anger. "So go ahead and tell, you spying little witch! Giving someone a kiss of gratitude is not a sin." They had reached Zirka and sensing Catherine's distress, he stepped back from the bridle she was trying to slip over his head. She clicked softly and spent several minutes calming him before she tried again. This time she was successful.

"It was Lech's father who sent Oleksi away," Natalya reminded her. "And who made us give his pig to Farmer Andronic."

"Bailiff Wojcik wasn't even here when Oleksi left," Catherine retorted as she secured the bridle strap. "And he was only doing what the village council ordered. Besides, Lech is nothing like his father or his brother Dom. He is gentle and kind and he makes wonderful poems." As if realizing she had revealed more of her feelings than she intended, Catherine's face hardened. Pulling herself onto the pony's bare back, she straightened her skirt around her legs and, tugging on the reins, turned Zirka toward the gate. "Tell Papa if you like," she said coldly. "I am not taking you with me."

☙❦

It was long after dark before Catherine returned to say that their father had sent the letter back unopened, promising he would come the next evening and they would read it together.

"We'll prepare a feast," Zhanna decided, and though she said it was to celebrate the letter, Natalya suspected it had much more to do with keeping them too occupied to pester her about reading it.

They started working at dawn, taking care of the regular chores—feeding the chickens, gathering eggs and firewood—then working on the dinner. Natalya was enlisted to chop dried white *cep* mushrooms, which Yuliya had soaked until they were soft, and fresh beets for the *shukhy* their mother was making. Catherine used the beet greens for *holubtsi* that she stuffed with thin slices of brisket and cornmeal fried with onions and garlic. All the while Oleksi's letter rested on the chest beneath the Russian tapestry.

The evening dew was starting to collect on the grass, and Natalya and Yuliya were fastening the wooden flap over the opening that let the chickens in and out of their small enclosure inside the barn, when they heard the clip-clop-clop of Vasyl's pony on the rocky track. A moment later he rounded the corner. He was dressed in his heavy woodsman's shirt and trousers with a hand axe tucked into its sheath on his belt. Although not as ornately decorated as the one he had given to Oleksi, the blade of this axe was just as sharp and, in Vasyl's hands, just as deadly.

After a hasty greeting, and impatiently waiting for him to dismount, the two girls took Nich, so-named because of his glossy black coat, to the barn. There they removed the thick wool quilts and wooden saddle Vasyl had inherited from his grandfather, stored them in the tack room, then fed the animal and led him into a stall beside Zirka. By the time they returned to the house, the family was already seated around the table.

Only after he had satisfied both hunger and thirst did their father sit back and consent to have the letter brought to him. As he began to read, even the baby, who only moments before had been crying for Zhanna's breast, fell silent.

> *May the blessings of Christ be upon you, my family. I am so far from you and my beloved mountains that each morning brings an ache to my heart.*
>
> *My journey from Yeremeche was long and filled with enough adventures to amuse little sister for two winters at least. It ended with my arrival at St. Petersburg, where I was directed to the house of your countess, Papa. She truly is a lady worthy of her title, and she did not hesitate to welcome me to her home. Under her direction I have been trained as a sanitar along with her cousin, Tusya Sergeivich Galipova, and we are both soon to be dispatched to her field hospital as part of a Russian Red Cross unit.*
>
> *I am sure this is not the kind of fighting you might believe worthy of the son of Vasyl Tcychowski. Only after seeing our wounded comrades suffering in the hospital here, their bodies mutilated and wracked with pain, and knowing their lives were saved only by the courage of the sanitars who carried them off the battlefield, have I come to realize that what Tusya and I are about to do is a noble thing and to be certain I will earn the pride which you have in your only son.*

Vasyl paused as all eyes shifted toward the baby in Zhanna's arms, but no one spoke and after a moment he continued to read.

> *Your insistence that I learn Russian and Polish, Mama, has been a blessing. So many languages are spoken here that it is sometimes difficult to understand what our patients are saying. Tusya grew up in Canada and from him I am also learning both French and English. French is spoken in the countess's home, and Tusya says in the field many of the doctors and nursing sisters speak only English. In exchange, I am*

teaching Tusya our Hutsul language.
They are calling now for us to assemble, so I must bring this to an end. May God in his mercy keep all of you safe.
Your loving son, Oleksi.

No one spoke for several minutes as each member of the family absorbed the details of the letter.

"Thanks be to Jesus he is safe," Vasyl said at last.

Zhanna was not reassured. "That letter is three weeks old, Husband. There must have been many battles since it was written."

Sensing an argument in the making, Natalya said quickly, "Please, Papa, could you read it to us again?"

His expression softened. "I might be so persuaded, little one, if my dry throat was soothed by some of your mother's sweet *zentyca*."

Natalya almost dropped the earthenware jug in her haste to refill his cup and was back in her seat by the time he had picked up the letter once more. But just as he began to read, a loud rapping sounded at the door. For a brief moment a look of alarm passed between the parents. Guests usually arrived during the day and a visitor at night almost always meant trouble of some sort. Handing the letter to his wife, who tucked it under the baby's cover, Vasyl strapped his axe belt around his waist.

"Take the baby upstairs," Zhanna said, dumping Pylyp into Yuliya's arms. By the time they reached the upper landing, Vasyl was opening the door. Yuliya and Leysa disappeared into the bedroom with the baby, but Natalya hid in the shadows of the top step from where she could see her mother and Catherine clearing the last of the dishes from the table. At that moment Lech Wojcik stepped through the doorway. He was followed by two shorter, older men.

"Good evening, Woodsman Tcychowski," the young man said in a deep voice.

Even from upstairs Natalya could hear Catherine's sharp intake of breath and the rattling of the bowls she was carrying.

There was no friendliness in Vasyl's customary, "Welcome to my house, brothers," and he did not ask his guests to sit as he usually would.

As if nothing was amiss, the bailiff's son removed his wool cap, freeing a thatch of dark hair that spilled over his long forehead, and said politely, "Blessings be upon you, Mother Tcychowski."

Lech's greeting was echoed by the other two men, whom Natalya recognized as the bailiff's neighbours. One was a weasel-faced man who worked on the rafts and the other was merchant Grabsky, a short, heavy Polish man who owned the only store in Zgardy. They both had the flushed cheeks Natalya had seen on men emerging from the village tavern.

Vasyl's hand rested pointedly on the head of his axe. "To what do I owe this unexpected visit, Wojcik?" he asked, spitting out the name as if it was something foul.

Lech's bold manner disappeared, and as he nervously fingered his hat, his dark, brooding gaze fell on Catherine, whose face was so filled with emotion that Vasyl's frown deepened.

"Well?" he rapped.

Water splashed from the pan in which Catherine was washing dishes and each droplet hitting the floor jolted the silence of the room.

Then, with the careful speech of one who is trying to appear sober, the weasel-faced raftsman said, "We have come, Woodsman, to discuss a match between this fine young man and your beautiful daughter."

A dish crashed onto the counter and Vasyl tightened his grip on the axe. "Then you have wasted both your time and mine, raftsman," he said, his voice taut with anger. "My daughter is far too young to be considered for any match."

With a hearty laugh merchant Grabsky brushed aside Vasyl's gift of an honourable rejection. "My own daughter is the same age, Woodsman," he boasted, "and already she is wed and swollen with child!" He waved his hand toward Lech. "Here is the perfect match for your daughter, a man with a good future in Baron Potocki's lumberyard and from a respected family, too. Any father in Zgardy would be eager to court him as a son-in-law."

"What other fathers would do is of no interest to me, merchant," Vasyl said harshly. "Had he the fortune of the baron himself, I would not allow a daughter of mine to wed this whelp or any other of the bailiff's litter!"

Zhanna, who had been standing in the shadow of the stove, gasped at the insult. Not only did it break every rule of Hutsul hospitality, it also opened the door for Lech to retaliate with a demand for satisfaction. In a duel with axes, even if they survived, neither man would emerge with his limbs intact.

Natalya had watched Lech's expression shift from hope to disappointment and now to a kind of hurt that reminded her of the bewilderment she had seen in the eyes of animals whose masters treated them badly. His face paled, and though it was clear he knew what was expected of him, Catherine's eyes pleaded with him not to take the next step.

In the end it was merchant Grabsky who pushed forward. Standing squarely in front of Vasyl, his eyes swept the room, pausing briefly on the Russian tapestry. Then he spat on the floor. "It is said in the village, Woodsman, that your son is fighting with the Russians."

Vasyl shrugged. "What of it, merchant? Many of our countrymen are doing the same."

"But not those employed by our good baron," Grabsky said.

The raftsman nodded vigorously, his small dark eyes bright with anticipation. "The baron despises Russophiles."

"Then it is a good thing, brother," Vasyl said, "that I am a Hutsul and nothing more. Or," he asked quietly, removing his axe from its sheath, "are you suggesting otherwise?"

"No, no! Of course not!" the raftsman stammered, backing safely behind Lech.

Grabsky said, "We have come in honourable fashion, Woodsman, and you have responded with the manners of a Boiki serf!" Turning to his companions, he snapped, "We have no further business in this house, brothers."

Natalya gripped the stair railing. She had never seen so much anger in her father's face, and she held her breath as she saw him raise his axe. He stopped, however, when Lech stepped forward and bowed stiffly toward him.

"We thank you for hearing our proposal, Vasyl Tcychowski," Lech said calmly as if nothing untoward had taken place, "and may the Holy Mother bless this house and all within." Then, before Vasyl could react, the young man walked out the door, followed by his companions.

The clomp clomp clomp of their boots on the porch was followed moments later by the soft thud of hooves. Zhanna sank to her knees, clasped her hands around her cross and began muttering prayers. Catherine gripped the counter as if she was afraid to let go and stared at the closed door, her face so white that her eyes seemed twice as big as usual. Vasyl glanced from mother to daughter then walked slowly to a shelf and removed a small jug of *horilka* that was kept for Christmas celebrations. Pulling out the wooden stopper, he took a long drink, recorked the jug and returned it to the shelf. "It is best we put an end to this day," he said at last.

His footsteps were heavy as he climbed the stairs.

ST. PETERSBURG
September 1914

"The Grand Duchess Cyril has kindly agreed to attend our opening," the countess announced to her hospital staff, who were gathered for a final briefing, "so everything—and I do mean everything—must be absolutely perfect!" She stood in front of her small contingent of housekeepers, kitchen workers, two sanitars, four war nurses, two Russian doctors, two civil nurses, and Alice, who also wanted the ceremony to be perfect. This was partly because the countess had worked so hard on creating the hospital, and partly because she would then be more inclined to send Alice to the field hospital where Tusya and Oleksi were serving as sanitars.

When it had operated as a school, the two-storey brick building had contained a long, twenty-bed dormitory on each level. They were graced with high ceilings and oak floors that, although polished, retained scuff marks from the boots of the hundreds of boys who had boarded there over the years. Now these dormitories had been converted into wards with nightstands separating the beds, each with a small icon hanging above it. The upper floor classrooms had been renovated into operating rooms and a room for dressing wounds, while the downstairs classrooms had become reception rooms. The largest of these also served as a small chapel, and it was here that the opening ceremony was to be held.

While the staff scurried off to their respective posts, the countess charged about like a demon, seeming to be everywhere at once, making sure that uniforms were spotless, the beds were impeccably made up, and the pastries and candies she had ordered for the tea that would end the ceremony were ready to be served. Alice followed in her wake, smoothing a slight wrinkle in a bed cover, repolishing a smudged window, and soothing feelings that had been hurt by the countess's abrupt manner.

Just before the appointed hour, the staff lined up along one side of the ceremonial room and a choir gathered in one corner.

Father Vorobiev, in an elegant green and gold robe, stood beside the chapel door. Alice joined the nurses and suddenly realized one of the war nurses, Oksana Starkova, was missing. Taking advantage of the fact that the countess was talking with Father Vorobiev and avoiding the disapproving eye of the matron, Alice slipped out of the room and hurried upstairs to the ward she had been assigned to supervise. There she found the war nurse in tears trying to clean a dark stain from the floor in front of a dressing trolley.

"I dropped a vial of iodine, Sister," she sobbed, "and it won't come out. Matron will dismiss me for this!"

Oksana was a large, blond seventeen-year-old with a freckled face and normally an engaging smile. When they first started working together she had told Alice how her father, a station master, and her mother and siblings, had died when a typhoid epidemic swept through her village near Archangel a year earlier. Without any other family and no real means of supporting herself, she was grateful when a friend of her late mother had contacted the countess, who arranged for her to train as a nursing sister in Petrograd, as St. Petersburg had been renamed after the German language was outlawed in Russia.

"She won't be happy if you aren't in line," Alice said, surveying the glass shards that littered the floor, and the iodine stains on Oksana's fingers. "Now, you'd best dry your eyes and wash your hands. I'll clear away the glass and we'll worry about the stain later."

They made it downstairs and into position seconds before the outside doors opened.

In that instant, the countess was miraculously transformed from domineering overlord to lady of the court, sweeping forward to greet the Grand Duchess. The countess had told Alice how the Princess Victoria Melita of Saxe-Coburg and Gotha had scandalized the Russian court when, having divorced her first husband, she married Grand Duke Cyril Vladimirovich, a first cousin to both herself and the tsar. As a consequence, the couple were banished from Russia, but when the death of Cyril's uncle Alexei placed him fourth in line for the throne, all was forgiven. Now, considering her romantic history and all of the fuss the countess had made about her visit, Alice was surprised to discover the Grand Duchess looked just like any other society woman. Dressed in a simple white gown, with a long-sleeved white overcoat and a wide-brimmed white hat fringed with lace, she chatted with the countess as if they were old friends. She seemed oblivious to the number of officials and officers in full uniform with chests adorned with medals and ribbons who paraded after her.

However, during the half-hour service, while the priest blessed the hospital and the choir sang, Alice was thinking not of the Grand Duchess, but of what she would do about the stain marring the otherwise spotless floor of her ward. As soon as the staff was dismissed and the official inspection of the facility began, Alice and Oksana hurried back upstairs.

"I am doomed," Oksana said mournfully, surveying the stain that had not diminished in their absence.

"Not necessarily," Alice soothed. "If we move this cart just so ... and I stand here," she stepped onto the portion of the stain still visible, "it may go unnoticed."

There was no time to test the plan for at that moment the entourage entered, led by the countess, then the Grand Duchess and finally the matron, Sister Bohdana, a small, wrinkled woman whom Alice was certain must be at least a hundred years old.

After inspecting the beds and nodding approvingly at the icons above the dressing tables, the Grand Duchess turned to exit the room, but as she passed Alice she paused.

"The countess tells me you are from Canada, Sister Galipova," she said in perfect English. "My Aunty Louise lived there for a number of years."

Alice suppressed a smile as she remembered reading that the Duchess of Argyle had hated every minute of her time spent in Ottawa while her husband was governor general of Canada.

"It is a beautiful country, your highness," she said, then added pointedly, "and I intend to return there as soon as I can."

"Well, let us hope that our brothers make short work of these German upstarts so we can all go back to our lives as they were before the hostilities. In the meantime, perhaps you will find time to discover the beauty that Mother Russia has to offer."

With that, she swept past, leaving Alice to wonder if the woman had been comforting or chastising her.

Sister Bodana, who followed in the wake of the Grand Duchess, also paused in front of Alice. "A few drops of ammonia might remove that stain," she murmured before moving on.

When the official inspection was over and each room blessed by the priest, tea was served and finally the Duchess and her entourage departed, along with the countess, leaving Alice and the staff to prepare for the first patients who were to arrive the next morning.

That evening the countess insisted on dining at the rooftop garden of the Hôtel de l'Europe. Surrounded by palm trees and boisterous chatter, Alice brought up the subject of her transfer to the front, but at that moment a gentleman at the next table, encouraged by his companions, jumped to his feet and began singing an aria from *Romeo and Juliette* in a rich tenor.

When the noisy applause that followed the song had died down, the countess said firmly, "Your father has written that under no circumstances are you to go to the front lines, child. But there is much for you to do here in St. Petersburg."

"I am not a *child*," Alice said. "And my father no longer has a say in what I can or cannot do. I agreed to stay here only if I could go with Tusya. If that is not possible, I will find a way to return home to Canada."

The countess smiled. "And how will you finance such a journey?" she asked slyly.

Alice scowled. With the little cash she had left after paying off Feliks, she couldn't afford much more than a night's lodging, never mind passage home to Canada. And even if she had the money, she doubted her cousin's secretary would be willing to find her another ship.

"If you won't send me to the front," she said, "then I will join the Red Cross and go with them."

For several minutes the two women stared at each other, neither willing to back down until at last the countess said, as if it had been her intention in the first place, "I will see what I can do. In the meantime, you will help me at the Federov Hospital."

It was the best Alice could hope for and with a grudging nod of acceptance she went back to her meal, only to be interrupted once more by an actress at another table who was giving an impromptu recitation.

☙❧

As Petrograd was far from the fighting, the little hospital was not overwhelmed with patients, and on her first official morning of duty as ward sister, Alice took the time to show Oksana a more efficient method of redressing a leg wound. The matron stopped by to watch then moved on without indicating whether she approved of the technique or not. As an orderly helped their patient back to his bed, the war sister said conspiratorially, "Some people call matron the Grand Demon but she's really very kind."

"It doesn't really matter whether she's kind or not," Alice

said. "I'm only here for a little while. Then I'm going to the front to be with my brother."

Oksana shuddered. "I don't want to be anywhere near the fighting, though if my brother was still alive, I would probably choose to be with him."

Alice liked the young sister. They were both strangers to Petrograd and they began to meet after their shifts to explore the city. Soon they were also studying together. While Oksana had a natural gift for the practical side of nursing, she was frustrated by the medical language in the textbooks because her village schooling had not included science. Alice, on the other hand, was well-versed in nursing theory and anatomy, but she had to learn the Russian words for every technique and instrument. Helping Oksana provided her with the perfect learning tool, and often their study sessions ended in laughter over an amusing blunder one of them had made.

On the wards the two friends reverted to their roles as supervisor and war sister, but it was an easy transition since they were both conscientious workers. Oksana was so cheerful and gentle that everyone liked her, and because of her honest concern and discretion, patients often confided in her. It was in this way she learned in late September that an English surgeon in charge of the field hospital close to where Tusya and Oleksi were stationed had requested an assistant—preferably one who could translate the needs of his patients to him as well as tending to their wounds.

"It won't get you right to your brother," Oksana told Alice. "But you will be a lot closer than you are here."

Still, it took endless threats and badgering to finally convince the countess that the Petrograd hospital would run perfectly well without Alice's help and that she would be of much more use serving with the *Letuchka*.

"Frankly," Alice confided to Oksana, "I think she would rather have me blown to bits on the battlefield than face another day of my nagging."

Her friend didn't laugh, as Alice intended.

"If I have endangered your life, I shall never forgive myself," she said.

"I'll be fine," Alice soothed.

However, when she arrived at the 250-bed hospital that had been established in a monastery fifteen miles from the front, she wasn't so sure. The artillery on both sides was active that day, and under a deafening cloud of noise came a stream of wounded soldiers, transported in everything from motorized ambulances to mule-drawn carts. Alice's first task, after a hasty introduction to the harried sister in charge, was to take care of minor wounds while the more serious cases were directed to the operating rooms. By the end of the day her white apron was bloodied and she was so tired she could barely eat the soup and black bread she was given for supper. Afterwards, she fell onto the cot that had been assigned to her and was instantly asleep.

The next morning was quieter and she was finally introduced to the surgeon she had come to help. He was an older man with a mustache and a hand tremor that, she discovered, inexplicably disappeared as soon as he began to operate.

There was a special camaraderie among the field hospital sisters, brought on, Alice suspected, by the knowledge that each day could be their last, and that survival could sometimes depend on their ability to work together and comfort each other. "You'll see your brother soon," they reassured her when after a week she still had not been reunited with Tusya. "He drives one of the motor ambulances."

And as if to prove them right, that afternoon Tusya arrived. As excited as a schoolboy on a field trip, he was both pleased and exasperated by her presence. "This is as close as I want you to come to the fighting, Ali."

"Nonsense," she retorted. "If you can work near the trenches, so can I."

But it was almost three weeks before she received a temporary assignment to the advanced dressing station. It came about when she was helping the English surgeon remove a shell fragment from the leg of a student doctor from the same first aid station where Tusya was working. The young man's commanding officer insisted on being in the operating room during the entire surgery and ranted interminably about how his troops were fighting without adequate supplies.

"The ammunition they send from Petrograd is too large for our Russian guns!" he fumed. "What do they expect us to do? Beat the enemy with our rifle butts?"

Alice sympathized with the officer and, much to her surgeon's dismay, suggested she would be happy to be the temporary replacement for the student doctor at his dressing station. The officer was delighted to accept her offer and immediately commissioned his personal sanitar to accompany her to the station, threatening the young man with extinction if she came to any harm.

For the journey, Alice wore a long-sleeved shirt, leather jacket and trousers, and high boots. She had been assigned the outfit when she left for the front lines, but this was the first time she'd worn the trousers and they still felt strange to her. Her first aid pack, bedroll and duffel bag, which contained her uniform, apron and a sturdy pair of shoes, were strapped behind her saddle and bumped against her as the ancient sway-backed mare that was provided for her followed the sanitar's horse.

The first aid station was situated just behind the Russian trenches that lined the eastern side of the Nemunas River, and the route Alice and the sanitar followed wound through a swampy forest of black alder. Trees, still wet from a downpour during the night, dripped onto her head, but it was so peaceful she felt almost as if she was back home, riding along one of the trails in the river valley. From time to time they passed wetlands where tiny islands of marsh grass and soft green and brown mosses sprouted from the dark water. Some of the ponds were covered with lily pads. She breathed deeply, inhaling the musty, earthy odours.

"It's beautiful," she told the sanitar when they stopped for a rest beneath a cluster of alder trees.

"It is also dangerous, Miss," he said. His face was grim as he stared out at the bog. "That mire swallows what it doesn't like." He handed her a cup of tea he'd made in a metal samovar. "At Masuria, the mires ate whole battalions. We could hear the men screaming through the night, but we could do nothing to help." He crossed himself and there was desperation in his face. "I should have died, too, only God wasn't ready for me."

While she was at the field hospital, Alice had heard rumours that a major defeat had occurred at Tannenberg at the end of August. It was said that a feud between two Russian generals had allowed a crucial communication to fall into the enemy's hand. As a result, the Germans were able to encircle one whole army, forcing the Russian soldiers to flee into a swamp.

"The papers reported only a few casualties," she said quietly. "They said the Germans lost more men than we did."

The sanitar shook his head. "I was there, Miss. The enemy lost very few."

As they silently drank their tea, she wondered how much truth there was in any of the war news.

"We must go, Miss," he said when she'd finished. "Two days ago a German plane went down in a swamp about a kilometre from here. A search party went out, but they couldn't find the plane or tell if the pilot had died in the crash."

She got to her feet and brushed leaves and twigs from her pants. "You might have warned me about that earlier," she said tartly, deciding that generals were not necessarily the only Russians who failed to communicate with each other.

He patted the rifle slung over his shoulder. "We are safe, Miss. But we must not stay too long in one place."

She eyed his gun and was not reassured. Although similar in shape to an ancient single-shot Berdan that hung above the fireplace at the ranch, the sanitar's rifle was in even worse shape. The butt was cracked and held together with several wraps of rawhide, the outside of the barrel was pitted and one end of the trigger guard was bent inwards. She wondered if the sanitar even knew how to shoot the weapon.

They rode through more forest and past another swamp, but now instead of enjoying herself, Alice was constantly scanning the woods and trail for signs of the enemy, jumping every time a bird flew up unexpectedly or her horse shied away from an unfamiliar object. She was especially nervous when they rode through a narrow stretch where a dense growth of trees and brush crowded the trail, and she was relieved when the road opened up once more. In the same instant, she caught a flash of movement near a clump of willow bushes on their left, followed by a muffled crack, and saw the sanitar fall sideways from his horse. As a second bullet whizzed past her head, she leaped sideways, landing hard on the edge of the road and rolling down a steep embankment. Digging her heels into the mud, she stopped herself before she reached the bottom, and despite slipping and sliding, scrambled back up to the road. The sanitar, protected by the horses that were milling about, was trying unsuccessfully to crawl toward her side of the road. His right arm and shoulder were bloodied and he was dragging his rifle.

Alice could see no movement from the willow trees across the road as she crawled forward and helped the sanitar down the embankment, but when she went back to remove her pack from the horse, the gun cracked again. She felt a hot burning in her left calf, and as her startled horse leaped forward, she dove back over the bank. Grabbing the sanitar's rifle, she manoeuvred herself along the embankment until she was behind a thick clump of sedge that grew beside the road and from where she could see the willows. She waited and finally, seeing a leaf quiver, held the gun to her shoulder. Bracing her elbows on the ground as her father had taught her, she took careful aim just below the leaf and fired. The whole bush moved violently and then was still. Satisfied that, if he was still alive, the shooter now knew she was armed, she made her way back down to the sanitar.

His coat and the shirt beneath it were soaked with blood. Setting the rifle aside, she pulled away the fabric and saw that while the bullet had penetrated the muscles just below his collarbone, it had missed the bone itself and the subclavian artery. But his face was grey and his pulse was faster than she liked.

"Perhaps God is ready for me now, Miss."

"Nonsense," she said brusquely as she ripped his shirtsleeve free and folded the material into a thick wad. "You're going to be just fine."

He winced as she pressed the wad onto the wound. She wished she had the disinfectant that was in her pack, and wondered if she dared risk exposing herself again to get it.

The sanitar glanced nervously up at the embankment. "Did you hit him, Miss?"

"I don't know." She fastened the wad in place with her scarf. His colour was better and his pulse was slowing, but the bandage she'd made was crude and she didn't know how long it would be effective in stopping the bleeding. "I need to get to my pack," she said. "Do you have more bullets?"

He reached with his good arm for a worn leather cartridge holder attached to his belt and pulled out four shells.

She stared at him. "That's it?"

"I'm sorry, Miss, but sanitars are not given weapons or ammunition. These were my grandfather's."

She tucked three of the bullets into her coat pocket and inserted the fourth into the rifle chamber before climbing back to the clump of sedge. Though she watched for several minutes, there was no movement from the willows. The sanitar's horse had disappeared down the trail, probably, she thought, returning to the first aid station, but her horse was standing beneath an alder tree only a few metres away, and on her side of the road. If she could make her way to where he was standing, she might be able to retrieve the pack after all.

It was a task much easier imagined than accomplished. The embankment was too steep for her to walk along it, and the bog below seemed to have no bottom, the mire oozing over her boot tops as she slogged forward. Her left leg throbbed and she tried not to think of the sanitar's story about the soldiers being swallowed up by the swamp. *It's only a little way*, she told herself. Still, she was relieved when she reached a spot below the alder tree and started back up the bank, which was so steep she kept slipping backwards until she began using the gun butt as a stabilizer. When she finally reached the top, her hands and the rifle butt were thick with clay and she was breathing hard. But the horse was still beneath the tree. Keeping it between her and the willow bush, she climbed awkwardly onto the road, and when no shots exploded around her, she dared to stand. At once the horse jumped backwards, her eyes wild.

"There, there," Alice soothed, wiping her hand on her coat and holding it out for the mare to smell. "I won't hurt you."

She took a slow step forward and the horse danced backwards again, this time exposing her to the road and a man with crazed eyes who stood clutching a revolver that was pointed at her head.

"*Lass die Waffen fallen!*" he shouted, waving the gun toward her rifle.

He wore a uniform coated with mire from the swamp; a scarf wound around his left thigh was dark with blood.

"*Lass die Waffen fallen!*" he screamed hysterically.

Her hands shook as she hastily pulled the rifle strap over her shoulder and threw the weapon on the ground. But the move didn't seem to satisfy him.

"*Lass die Waffen fallen!*" he screamed again, waving the revolver even more erratically. Sweat beaded his forehead and she could see his pupils were dilated. "*Lass die Waffen fallen!*"

"It's okay," she croaked, her mouth dry. "I won't hurt you. ..."

But the words meant to soothe only made him wilder, and she tensed as he aimed once more. She saw him squeeze the trigger, heard the click as it connected with an empty chamber, then saw the man fall forward and land face down in the mud. Protruding from the back of his head was an elaborately carved axe. It was the last thing she saw before her knees gave way and she collapsed.

※

"Ali! Ali!"

Tusya's panicked voice seemed to be coming from a long way off, but when Alice opened her eyes her brother was bending over her. "Dammit all, Ali! What the hell are you doing here?"

She twisted her head and saw Oleksi kneeling beside the German pilot.

"What are *you* doing here?" she countered weakly.

"The horse came in without a rider. We came to find out why."

"Oh my God! The sanitar!" Alice pushed her brother away. Struggling to a sitting position, she pointed to the embankment. "Ivan ... he's wounded ... ."

Tusya hurried down the steep slope to where she pointed. From the corner of her eye she saw Oleksi wipe the blade of his axe on a tuft of grass before he tucked it back into the sheath on his belt, picked up the pilot's handgun and got to his feet. His face was ashen.

"You were lucky, Miss. His Luger misfired," he said, his voice thick with emotion. "He had four more bullets."

He held out his hand to Alice, and as soon as she was standing, he went down the embankment to help Tusya while she hurried to her horse and collected her first aid bag.

Just before dusk they reached a maze of trenches paralleling the riverbank. Ducking low, Alice followed Oleksi, Tusya and the sanitar along an approach-trench that zig-zagged at least a hundred yards behind the front-line-trench—roughly, she calculated, the same distance as one of her father's hayfields back home. At the entrance of another trench, protected by barbed-wire fencing, they went down several steps to a dugout that had been fashioned into a dressing station. Here the surgeon, who looked as if he had not slept in a week, removed the bullet from Ivan's shoulder and dressed the abrasion on Alice's leg.

While Oleksi and Tusya escorted the sanitar back to the field hospital, Alice stowed her bags under one of the cots and acquainted herself with the shelter. Lit by a few flickering candles, and measuring roughly three by five metres, the dugout was walled and roofed with logs and dirt. Between the planks that made up the floor she could see muddy water. A small coal heater burned at one end of the room where there were two army cots and three wooden benches. At the other end of the room was the operating table made of a stretcher fastened to thick poles beside a crude table covered with dressings and surgical equipment.

"We do what we can here," the surgeon told her. "Try to stop hemorrhages and apply patches that will last until the poor buggers reach the field hospital." He glanced about the dim room and added harshly, "It is not a place for a woman."

"It's no place for any human," Alice retorted, "but I won't let you down if that's what's worrying you."

"Tell that to the poor devils we're trying to stitch together when the bombs are exploding around us," he said.

A sanitar entered with their dinner, carried in a string of pots that were wired together. Alice was surprised that the meal of hot soup, hamburger steaks and fried potatoes was better than anything she'd eaten at the field hospital. She was just finishing when Tusya returned with grim news.

"Oleksi and I are being transferred to Ostrolenka," he said.

She gaped at him. "Transferred?"

He nodded, but before the volcano of anger that surged through her exploded, he added, "Only this time you're coming with us. A direct order from the countess."

For the first time since Alice had entered the dugout, the surgeon smiled.

ZGARDY
October 2, 1914

Most beloved parents and sisters,

First, I am well and as fit as when I left you. I cannot say where we are—partly because I do not know this place myself. It is a land of many lakes and every day the rain falls about us in torrents. When we march, the mud sucks us into the earth so that every step is a struggle. The soldiers who go ahead of us suffer most for they must dig the trenches which within an hour are half-filled with water. Our job as sanitars is to collect men whose bodies have been ripped apart by bursting shells and who lie in the mud, screaming for God to grant them a swift and merciful death.

When things are quiet between battles, Tusya and I scrounge supplies for the medical unit and continue our language lessons—a task that tortures my poor brain but upon which he thrives.

Shortly after arriving at our last station I heard of a Hutsul man from Zgardy who was suffering from a head wound. It was Andrukh Vitovskyi. His wound was healing and he will soon to be sent to a POW camp in northern Russia. He believes at least there he will finally be able to sleep without bombs or bullets exploding around him. Since he left Zgardy he has not had a full night's rest.

They are calling now for letters.
May our blessed Lord keep you all in good health.
Oleksi

"What do you think you are doing?" Yuliya rasped, ripping the letter from Natalya's hands and tearing one of the pages. "Now see what you've done!" she accused, shaking the torn page in Natalya's face.

"You're the one who ripped it," Natalya shot back.

But Yuliya paid no attention. "You are surely going to get a switching for this, little sister."

"Leave her be, Yuliya," Catherine said, coming into the room with Pylyp, who was sleeping contentedly nestled against her shoulder. "She just misses Oleksi—as we all do."

Natalya flashed her eldest sister a grateful smile. Catherine had changed since the night Lech Wojcik had come to ask for her hand. She never spoke of that confrontation, but after that evening she spent all of her time tending to Pylyp and helping with the farm and refused to go to the village except for mass. There she cast anxious glances at the section of the church where the Wojcik men usually stood, but Lech was never with his family. She no longer laughed, and she ate so little her blouse and skirt hung on her like empty sacks.

One day after services the barrel maker's wife had told Zhanna that Lech had joined the Polish Legion and was now missing in action.

"Our good bailiff blames your husband for this, Zhanna Tcychowski," Galyna had sniffed. "And why should he not? The chief forester of Zgardy will rue the day he so cruelly smote that young man's pride! Of course," she had added smugly, "had his friends used my services then none of this would have happened at all. Men have never been good at matchmaking."

"You talk nonsense, Galyna Shevchenko!" Zhanna had snapped, but before leaving the church that day she purchased a candle and placed it at the altar of the Holy Mother then knelt and begged for her intervention in whatever evil the bailiff might inflict upon the Tcychowski family.

Yuliya tossed the letter onto the bench. "She can't even read," she scoffed.

Natalya hastily gathered up the pages and tucked them back into the envelope. "I can read better than you, Yuliya!" Her claim was not completely true. She was taking lessons from Father Ishchak with the other children of Zgardy, and she did have a verbal gift for languages, even learning French from her father, which none of her siblings could speak. But her reading skills were questionable, mostly because she preferred to be outdoors rather than inside practising.

"It doesn't matter," Catherine said crisply. "Papa has been summoned to Baron Potocki's estate, and it is your turn, Natalya, to accompany him. You must hurry and dress in your church clothes for he is saddling Nich as we speak."

Yuliya's plump cheeks puffed into a pout. It had been almost a year since she last visited the baron's estate, but she never stopped talking about the bowl of sweets he kept on his desk and which he shared generously with young guests. Then she smiled slyly. "She will not be going if Papa knows she stole Oleksi's letter."

"I didn't steal it!" Natalya shouted, horrified that her chance to have their father all to herself might be threatened. "You are a hateful... ."

Catherine held up her hand. "Yuliya knows it's not true," she said sternly, "and she will not be repeating the lie to Papa or anyone else unless she wishes it known that she ate the *kulesha* Mama was saving for him." Dumping the baby into Yuliya's arms, she swung around and headed for the stairs. "Mama wants you to wear your vest and boots, Natalya, for the sun will set long before you return and it will be cold this evening."

Scarcely able to contain her excitement, Natalya hurried after her and quickly changed into the red and green ribbed skirt and white embroidered blouse Catherine pulled from a chest at the bottom of their bed. Most of the clothes had been passed down from sister to sister, but the multi-coloured woollen vest Natalya put on last was one her mother had made just for her. Finally, after squeezing her feet into boots too snug for her feet, she sat on the bed so that Catherine could braid her hair.

"Be sure to keep it tidy so Papa is not ashamed in front of the baron," her sister warned as she secured the hairdo with a bright green scarf. She had barely tied the knot before Natalya wriggled from her grasp and escaped down the stairs and out the door.

Vasyl was mounted on his horse near the gate, and as she ran toward him, Natalya thought he was the most handsome man in the world with his thick dark hair, bushy brows and mustache. He was wearing his best outfit—leather boots and black woollen trousers, a white blouse Zhanna had painstakingly embroidered, the fine wool vest she had made him the previous winter, and around his neck a bandanna patterned in red and green. Removing his foot from the stirrup, he held out his hand to Natalya, but before she could grasp it, Zhanna made a quick, slightly disapproving inspection of her daughter.

"You'll do," she said at last.

Hastily, before her mother changed her mind, Natalya climbed astride the horse, just behind the saddle, and wrapped her arms around her father's waist. As she squirmed to find the most comfortable spot, he said sternly, "Be still, child, or Nich will take fright and run."

Privately Natalya thought a running horse would be a fine adventure, but she sat as still as she could and gave herself over to the comfort of having her father in front of her. She loved the earthy smell of his shirt, and the jostling to and fro as Nich picked his way over the rocks and down the trail. Where the path was level she could pay attention to the woods and willow bushes on either side, but on steep descents she had to brace herself against her father to ease the chafing of the wooden saddle against her legs, though she was too busy trying to see everything at once to really mind the discomfort. Once, while traversing a ridge, Vasyl remarked that it was a fine day for travelling, and she sensed his satisfaction as he surveyed the golden fields below them and the trees set ablaze with the fiery orange and yellow foliage of early autumn.

Soon they reached the village graveyard and the two-storey wooden church with its planked walls and the *opassania* built around the perimeter to protect it from the rain. As they clip-clopped past merchant Grabsky's store, the barrel maker's shop and the village's only tavern, almost everyone they met paused to tip his hat or wave to her father and call out a greeting.

As they should, she thought smugly. *He is the chief forester, after all.* Pretending the tipped hats and smiles were for her, she nodded majestically to her subjects, including Yuliya's friend Luba Vitovsky, who waved from the steps of the community hall.

They left the village behind and emboldened by her fleeting importance, Natalya dared to ask, "What will you do at Baron Potocki's estate, Papa?"

"I expect His Excellency wants to congratulate me for sending him twice as many rafts as we've ever managed before," her father said proudly, speaking French, as he often did when they were alone. "He will surely be giving me a fine reward for my hard work, and with that, child, I shall purchase your mother a bolt of the finest cloth in the village."

"From merchant Grabsky's store, Papa?"

She felt her father's back stiffen.

"I will not set foot in that store," he said coldly then lapsed into an angry silence that lasted for the rest of their journey.

❧

The Potocki mansion was situated at the end of a forested road almost two kilometres west of Zgardy, and like the forest surrounding the Tcychowski farm, most of the land between the village and the estate was owned by the Polish baron. As she had been on the only other occasion she had accompanied her father, Natalya was awed by the wide beech-lined drive and by the enormity of the three-storied yellow brick mansion with great towers rising from each corner and more gleaming windows than she could count—every one of them larger than the door to the Tcychowski farmhouse.

In the courtyard she jumped to the ground then waited while her father slowly dismounted. Together they led the horse past the wide staircase fronting the mansion's grand pillared entrance and around to the back of the compound where Vasyl tied him to a post in front of a large stable. Gravel crunched beneath their boots as they walked across the yard to the servant's entrance. At his sharp rap the plain brown door was opened by a woman wearing a lacy white cap and a severe black dress protected by a snow-white apron.

"Glory be to Christ, Madam Elsa," Vasyl said in French, removing his felt hat. "I am here to see His Excellency, the baron."

The woman, who had known Vasyl since he was first born and his mother had been working at the manor, was clearly flustered. "I'm sorry, Woodsman, but I've been instructed that his honour is not receiving visitors at this time."

Vasyl drew himself up straighter. "I am here at the baron's request, Madam."

They matched stares for a full minute before the woman gave a slight nod. "Come in then. But wait here while I check with His Excellency."

Leaving them standing in the dark hallway, she disappeared through a pair of ornately carved doors. Natalya stared silently at the polished stone floor and listened to the muffled sounds of activity beyond the closed doors. She felt she knew every inch of the mansion from her father's many stories about his childhood with the baron and his siblings. Her grandmother's position as the Potocki children's nanny had not only enabled Vasyl to join in their activities in the nursery and to eavesdrop on the lessons given by their tutor but had also provided him with an opportunity to explore the building from top to bottom. "It is easy to be invisible when you are small," he told his children—a maxim that had proven useful to Natalya many times.

Suddenly the doors opened and Natalya sucked in her breath as the bailiff's eldest son strode into the hallway. Dominic Wojcik, a tall, smooth-shaven man, dressed in the pale blue uniform of a lieutenant in the Polish army, thrust a thick envelope toward Vasyl.

"You have come a long way for nothing, Woodsman," he said, smugly. "His honour, the baron, no longer requires your services."

Vasyl made no move to accept the envelope. His face was impassive and only the slight thinning of his lips and narrowing of his eyes told Natalya of the shock he must be feeling and the fury that burned within him. "I am here to see His Excellency, not you, Wojcik." His deliberate use of the diminutive "you" was not lost on the soldier, whose own eyes narrowed. As Vasyl moved to step past him, Dominic Wojcik blocked the door with his body.

"That is no longer your privilege, Woodsman."

Vasyl thrust Natalya behind him and resting his right hand on his unsheathed axe, glared at the lieutenant. "Do you dare to stand in my way?"

"Do you dare to move me?" Dominic countered, grasping the hilt of his sword.

Natalya's whole body trembled as he withdrew the long blade from its scabbard, but before he could raise the sword, the doors opened again and the baron stood glowering in the entranceway. A dignified man of medium height with hair greying at the temples, Stefan Potocki was dressed in a blue uniform similar to the one the bailiff's son was wearing, but with embroidered shoulder flaps and a string of medals pinned beneath his left shoulder just above his scalloped pocket flap. His blue eyes coldly surveyed the scene. "What is the meaning of this commotion, lieutenant?"

Swinging about, Dominic replaced his sword, snapped to attention and saluted.

"I was just carrying out your orders, sir, and giving the woodsman his pay."

Barely checking his anger, Vasyl said, "I have been informed that my position as chief forester has been revoked, Excellency. Surely after more than thirty years of service to your family, I deserve to hear this from your own lips and not from an underling still wet behind his ears!"

Even in the dim light of the hallway, Natalya could see the colour flooding Dominic's face.

"This matter is better discussed in my office," the baron said abruptly.

Halfway down another hallway he ushered them into a room furnished with a large wooden desk and leather chairs and lined with shelves filled with books. Dominic followed, but at a stern command from the baron, he placed the envelope on the desk, saluted and withdrew. As the door closed behind him, the baron settled into the enormous leather chair behind the desk and waved Vasyl to a seat in front of it.

Natalya stood as close to her father as the chair would permit, and as if he had not just a moment before interrupted a brawl between his lieutenant and the chief forester, the baron smiled indulgently at her. "This must be the youngest of your daughters, Vasyl. She has grown since her last visit." He pushed a bowl of peppermint candies toward her. "What is your name, child?"

She glanced at her father's face and when he gave a slight nod, she took a single candy from the bowl, imprisoning it in her fist to enjoy on the ride home. Then she tilted her chin upward. "I am Natalya Halyna Tcychowski, Monsieur Your Excellency," she all but shouted, shattering the solemnity of the room.

The nobleman's right brow lifted slightly and his lips twitched as he said to Vasyl. "She has her mother's beauty, Woodsman, but there is much of you in her manner."

"She has spirit, Baron," Vasyl agreed, unsmiling. Then he asked pointedly, "Did our rafts arrive safely at your mill, sir?"

"Yes, yes. They arrived in top condition. But I'm afraid they will be the last logs we'll be cutting for some time."

Vasyl waited.

"The Russians are very near to Yeremeche," the baron said. "By working nonstop at the mill, we were able to saw every log we had into timbers and load them on the last northbound train." His expression darkened. "After that, we burned the mill and every scrap of wood that was left. I leave in an hour to join the Polish Legion in Warsaw." He nodded to the envelope. "I fully expected to have left before you arrived."

Vasyl said nothing, and the tension between the two men increased with every tick of the clock on the nearby mantel.

"A western Ukrainian regiment has been formed," the baron continued, and by the slow and precise way in which he was speaking Natalya had the feeling he was setting a trap with his words. "Most of my workers in Yeremeche have joined this regiment, and I expect the men of Zgardy will do the same. Including your son, Oleksi, yes?" His eyes narrowed slightly as he stared at Vasyl.

For the first time Natalya sensed an unease in her father. He had seen the trap and he was edging around it.

"My son is no longer living with us, Your Worship," he said coolly.

The baron's brow lifted. "Is that so? Then perhaps the

rumours he has joined the forces of our enemies are not idle gossip?"

"That would depend, sir, on who our enemies are. I have not noticed that the Austrians have been particularly good friends to either the Hutsuls or to the Polish people under their command."

"Better than our Russian oppressors, Woodsman. Or do you forget the thousands of Polish citizens who were killed or left to rot in the tsar's prisons during the uprisings?" He leaned forward, his face suddenly alive with passion. "The Austrians and the Germans need Poland's support in this war, and that will give us an unparalleled opportunity to break the chains that bind us! At a crucial moment, we will demand autonomy in exchange for our allegiance, and the Kaiser and Franz Josef will be forced to give it."

"And if Russia wins, sir?"

"Bah! The tsar and that insane priest who leads him and his wife by the nose have lost the faith of their people, and their statesmen scrap like cats in an alley. The tsar will lose this war ... and if he is not careful, he will also lose his country."

"But surely you can understand, sir," Vasyl said guardedly, "that it matters little to a Hutsul man who wins this war. In the end, we will plow our fields and cut our trees as we have always done, and the fruit of our labours will go not to our families but to government treasuries far beyond our homeland."

Annoyance flashed across the baron's face, and as if he were admonishing a child, he said coldly, "There are those who would consider such a statement seditious, Woodsman. You would be well advised to keep such thoughts to yourself. And," he added, his eyes narrowing, "to remove the Romanov tapestry that I am told holds a place of honour in your house."

Natalya sensed a resurgence of her father's anger, but his tone remained respectful. "As you know, Excellency, that tapestry was given to me in gratitude many years ago by your own distant cousin, the Countess Stanislavovna Federov. However, it is only because the image of our blessed Christ and his Holy Mother are woven into its fibres that I hang the gift in a place of honour. Would any true follower of Christ and his teachings have it otherwise?"

The baron's lips thinned. "All the same, there are those who would consider the presence of the tsar's crest in your house an act of treason. Many have gone to the gallows for a less serious offence."

Vasyl rose to his feet. "I am no traitor, sir, but it is to Hutsulchynia that my loyalty lies and to no other."

"If our long acquaintance had not convinced me of that, Woodsman, I would have put an end to our relationship when you brought your bride to this village, for it is well known that her family in Lemberg are Russophiles. In the future, however, it may not be your understanding baron who will judge your actions. This war will bring many strangers to your door, and if you are wise, your Romanov rug will not be visible when they arrive." He picked up the envelope and handed it across the desk. "It is regrettable that our association must end so abruptly, Vasyl Tcychowski, for we have worked well together these many years. When this conflict is over and the true greatness of the Polish empire is shown to the world, perhaps we will join once more in harvesting the bounty of the Potocki forests."

Vasyl's jaw was rigid as he reluctantly accepted his pay. "May our merciful Saviour watch over you, Excellency," he said. Then he pushed Natalya ahead of him and marched from the room as if nothing was amiss. It wasn't until they were outside and he was unfastening Nich's reins that Natalya noticed the trembling of his hands.

FRONT LINES BETWEEN LODZ AND WARSAW
Christmas 1914

An exploding shell rattled the windows of the small brick store that had been transformed into a field hospital, but Alice scarcely noticed the sound. She was too intent on the young man lying on the makeshift operating table.

"My leg, Little Sister," he gasped. "It is on fire! Do please help me!"

The leg he referred to did not exist, and as the ether she was administering took effect, lulling him into temporary oblivion, she suddenly felt like weeping. It had been early morning when she and the tall American surgeon had started the first operation of the day—an abdominal wound that merely needed suturing. That patient had long ago been hauled off to whatever space was available in the two-storey building, but he'd been instantly replaced by a head wound, which was followed by a shattered arm. After that, the surgeries had seemed to merge together in her mind, a grotesque collage of missing limbs, ruptured rib cages, mangled organs, and grotesquely altered faces that beneath the surgeon's hands were somehow rearranged into a semblance of their original order. Daylight had gradually faded from the room, windows were darkened with canvas and lanterns lit, and still the wounded kept coming. Those in stable enough condition to be moved were transferred to the railway station to await the next train to Moscow. The bodies of the unfortunate soldiers who didn't survive surgery were stacked one upon the other in a shed behind the store.

To keep sane, Alice had learned to focus on whatever wound was being repaired and on following the surgeon's orders. She closed her ears to the pleas of men whom they knew would not survive no matter what was done for them, and she avoided the eyes of those patients they did help, especially those with stomach wounds who cried out for water despite being told that a single drink would kill them. But with this patient she had somehow allowed her gaze to stray to his face, and in that instant he became not just another amputation that had to be cleaned up but a young boy who was going to face the rest of his life without a leg.

"Sister!" The surgeon's sharp command broke through her thoughts. "I need more light!" The doctor wasn't very old, but he had a keen eye for assessing injuries and a knack for knowing instantly what needed to be done. He had joined the medical team on the Russian front, he had told her, in the hope of honing his skills as a surgeon, little knowing that there would be no time for honing anything.

Setting the ether aside, she hurried around the table and grabbed the lantern, holding it close to the stump, enabling him to clamp the artery that was pumping the boy's lifeblood from his body. When the suture was secure, he released the clamp and stood back. Grunting his satisfaction with the repair, he then continued suturing until the wound was closed, then allowed her to apply a moist dressing of hydrogen peroxide. This was the only moment he would have to rest before the soldier was carted away, and the next patient was positioned on the table. Alice did not allow her focus to stray again, not even when a patient arrived with clothes so infested with fleas that they swarmed the dressing as fast as she applied it to his wound.

Then at long last the sound of the guns faded and the parade of wounded dwindled and came to an end. When the final patient was removed, the surgeon whipped off his gloves. "Get some rest, Sister," he advised. "Morning will come early."

She nodded and trooped tiredly through the holding area that all day had been filled with wounded men to the outside where she was surprised to see that clean white snow was softly falling, muting all sounds, even the guns that still occasionally thudded in the distance. There was something so simple and pure in the large flakes drifting around her that she paused on the steps to watch them, imagining for just a moment that she was back home on the ranch, with her father seated by the fire inside, smoking his pipe and reading while waiting for his dinner. And suddenly she remembered the parcel he had sent for her and Tusya. It had arrived a week earlier, but she had refused to allow her brother to open it until Christmas Day. They had read the letter, though, which was filled—as all of their father's letters were—with his concern for their safety and his orders for them to stop their foolishness and return home. It didn't matter that Alice had written to him that they were far safer in Russia than on a ship at sea playing roulette with German mines and submarines. He wanted them home.

"We were beginning to think we'd have to celebrate Christmas without you!" Tusya's voice boomed from the sidewalk where he and Oleksi were waiting.

"We had to pay the restaurant owner extra to stay open until you got there," Oleksi said. "But if you don't hurry, his doors will close!"

"Then what are we waiting for?" Alice asked, her hunger being far more acute than her exhaustion. Hurrying down the steps, she put a hand through each of their arms and together they walked along the street to a dingy building that was even drabber on the inside. Still, it was warm and the aromas of cabbage and cake surfaced above less appealing odours. By Alice's reckoning, the owner was somewhere between fifty and eighty years old. His grey beard and mustache covered most of his face, and he was bent over as if there was a great weight upon his shoulders. He reeked of raw, over-ripe onions, and as he led them to a dark table close to the kitchen, he wiped his hands on an apron that hinted at a bygone whiteness. But moments later when he placed three steaming bowls of soup in front of them, Alice would not have cared if he were an ogre and his apron had been covered in blood. Without waiting for the soup to cool, she scooped up a spoonful of cabbage and meat, blew on it briefly and stuffed the whole lot into her mouth.

"Oh, Lord. I swear I have never tasted anything so delicious," she groaned.

She chewed slowly, savouring the flavours. By her second bowl, her hunger was appeased enough for her to pay more attention to her companions. They both seemed even more exhausted than she was, for while she had been working in the relative shelter of the surgery, they had been outside in the cold searching for the wounded amid the rubble of bombed-out buildings and in the trenches that had been dug down the middle of outlying streets by the German rearguard as they tried to slow the Russian advance and protect their own soldiers' retreat. Tusya's unshaven face was black and creased with stress, and Oleksi was sporting a wound above his right eye where, he told her reluctantly, a piece of shrapnel had tried to end his life. But when she asked for more details, Tusya interrupted.

"No talk about work," he ordered. "This is the holiest night of the year, remember?"

Alice snorted. "And since when did that mean anything to you?"

"It doesn't," Tusya said. "I just want to forget the war for a few hours."

Oleksi regarded them curiously. "You don't celebrate Christmas?"

"Our father is an atheist," Alice told him. "Only way my mother could get him to participate at all was to call it a solstice celebration. That way she could give us presents just like our friends were getting."

"For my family, Christmas is the most special day of the year," Oleksi said sadly. "This is the first time ever I shall not be with them."

Tusya held out his spoon on which a large chunk of dark meat rested. "Anyone care to guess what strange flesh this is that so flavours our soup? A well-aged mule? Last year's mutton? Or ... ," he grinned wickedly at Alice, "perhaps a two-legged animal?"

She frowned and lowered the spoonful she was about to eat. "That's not funny, Tusya."

Oleksi contemplated the restaurant floor. "There *does* seem to be an absence of rats in this establishment."

Tusya put the meat in his mouth and chewed thoughtfully. "Mmmm, no, I think not, my friend. It is more like ... ."

"Horse," Oleksi said around his own mouthful. "Most definitely it is horse meat."

"You're right!" Tusya nodded vigorously. "Perhaps the one we saw rotting this morning, just two streets from here."

An image of the horse flashed into Alice's thoughts, but she refused to let it linger.

"Sorry, gentlemen," she said, finishing her soup and tipping her bowl to show it was empty. "You're too late to ruin my appetite. And you will not, Tusya Galipova, be rewarded for your rudeness by mooching my uneaten dessert as you did at home." To prove her claim, she reached for a thick slice of currant cake from a plate the old man had brought to their table.

As she took a huge bite, Tusya's eyes narrowed. "Then I suppose it won't matter to you what unappealing alternative our host might have used in place of currants for that cake?"

"Not in the least," she said defiantly though she chewed more slowly.

"It matters not to me," Oleksi said, reaching for his own slice of cake. "So long as it fills the belly."

Acknowledging his defeat, Tusya raised his glass of tea and

said solemnly, "Merry Christmas, my friends!"

The other two raised their own glasses.

"We should go to midnight mass," Oleksi said. "Tonight we need God's blessing."

Alice shrugged. "What can it hurt? There is not much else to do."

Her brother yawned. "We could sleep."

"Sleep if you want to," Alice said. "I'm going with Oleksi."

In the end, all three of them walked down the street to the large domed church that Alice was surprised to find filled with worshippers. Soldiers bundled against the cold. Two Red Cross sisters dressed as Alice was in black veils with large red crosses sewn onto the front of their black capes. Dazed and bedraggled refugees. Old men in frayed wool coats and soiled foot wraps. Ragged children who gazed wide-eyed at a nativity scene that had been set up near the altar and clung to the aprons of women whose shapes and faces were all but obscured by their shawls and headscarves.

Although not so grand as the one in Petrograd, even this small church possessed an opulence that, given the poverty of the congregation, seemed wildly out of place. At the altar stood a white-robed priest, flanked by two young boys wearing surplices over their coats and each holding an oil lamp. Alice was sure their hands must be freezing, for it was almost as cold inside the church as it was outdoors, and yet the boys, like the rest of the worshippers showed no sign of discomfort as they listened in rapt attention to the priest's address. She could not understand the words, but she sensed the meaning as those around her prayed and wept and finally rejoiced at his message.

The sermon seemed to have a profound effect on Oleksi as well. He crossed himself many times during the service, and his voice was vigorous and sincere during the congregational responses. When the choir sang, their haunting voices resonating throughout the whole church, his eyes glistened with tears.

"My sister Catherine sings at our church," he whispered after one particularly beautiful hymn. "If I close my eyes, it is as if I am in Zgardy with Mama and Papa and even pesky little Natalya." His voice broke, and without thinking Alice slid her hand into his and squeezed. She was disconcerted by the warmth that flooded through her from touching him and by the adoring expression that crossed his face when he looked down at her.

They were all three quiet on the walk back to the hospital and the building next door where the nursing sisters were quartered.

But before Tusya and Oleksi left for their quarters in the ruins of a warehouse, Alice insisted they come inside to open the package from Canada. It contained heavy woollen socks and scarves for her and Tusya and several bars of sweet chocolate.

"Here," Alice said, presenting her overlarge socks to Oleksi. "You will need these more than me, for I'm not slogging through snow and mud."

"And this from me," Tusya said, passing him a bar of chocolate.

Oleksi stared at the gifts. "But I have nothing for you."

"You have already given us a fine gift," Alice said. "That beautiful service and music will stay with us forever."

"She's right," Tusya said then added quickly, "not that you'll get me into another church any time soon."

"Don't be too sure of that, my friend," Oleksi said. But he accepted their gifts and he and Tusya went off to their own quarters, leaving Alice to her bed and a deep, dreamless sleep that ended far too soon for her liking.

ZGARDY
May – September 1915

"Russia is doomed," the postman declared triumphantly one afternoon in early May. "The Kaiser's battering ram is slamming through the Grand Duke's defences like a harvester through a field of rye. Already Gorlice and Tarnów have fallen and Przemysl is sure to be next. How could it be otherwise when most of Russia's munitions are stockpiled in Murmansk waiting for the ice to melt? Who can win a war without weapons?"

Ivan Hawrylak had arrived with his mailbag while Zhanna was preparing a late lunch for her husband, who had just returned from a two-day journey to the molfar's spring grazing camp. As was the custom in many Hutsul communities, sheep were pastured for most of the year in the higher alpine meadows under the care of the village molfar, who periodically sent one of his assistants to deliver milk and cheese back to the villagers. Vasyl had used the bonus he received from the baron to purchase an additional eight sheep, bringing the size of his herd to twelve, and having nurtured them through the winter, he insisted on accompanying them to the molfar's camp.

Reluctantly embroidering the sleeves of a new blouse, Natalya was seated on the porch, where she could see the two men through the open window and hear everything they said. Unlike the precise stitches her mother and sisters created, hers were large and loopy and she was forever piercing her thumb with the needle because she was paying more attention to the conversation than her sewing.

"I have heard otherwise, brother," her father said as he mushed some *brynza* with his knife then spread it over a wedge of *kulesha*. "Just last week our barrel maker returned from Yeremeche to say that the Russians had almost reached the Hungarian plains."

"That was last week." Ivan snorted, stuffing his mouth full of *brynza*.

"Then it is not true?"

"Mmmph-mmmph." Ivan washed the cheese down with a swallow of *zentyca* before explaining. "All winter the Kaiser sent men and artillery to help our Austrian brothers, and now they're bombarding the Russians nonstop. It is said they have enough shells and artillery to level the whole of the Carpathian Mountains!" He peered regretfully at his empty plate. "This was a tasty snack, Mother Tcychowski. Your *brynza* is truly the best I have eaten."

"Then you must have some more, Postman," Zhanna said politely, serving him another large portion.

"Of course, the Kaiser needs the Hungarian plains to feed his armies," Vasyl mused, absently pushing his still-untasted *kulesha* around his plate.

Ivan nodded in agreement. "It is a good thing for you, Vasyl Tcychowski, that Zgardy is far from any railroads. In my travels I have seen whole villages burned to the ground by the retreating armies and farmsteads ransacked for provisions. They are even dropping bombs from airplanes!"

Vasyl pushed his untouched meal aside. He had not been the same since his visit to the baron, and like Catherine, there was a sadness about him now that never seemed to go away. "And still our young men are taken from us," he said bitterly. "Just this week two of our village boys were buried in far-away graves without a proper funeral."

Having finished his lunch, Ivan heaved himself from the bench, reached for his sack and pulled out a worn envelope. "Well, it is fortunate that this comes from the north where the fighting is not so intense, and it is proof your own son is alive and well."

Natalya pierced her finger as she leaned forward to see the envelope, and before she could stop it, a droplet of blood landed on the white sleeve. Hastily scrubbing it with a bit of spit, she discovered she had stitched both sides of the sleeve together.

☙❧

When the postman departed, Zhanna and her daughters gathered at the table where Vasyl read Oleksi's letter aloud, sometimes with difficulty for the lines were crammed close together, and some words had been blacked out by the censor. Every inch on both sides of the page was filled.

> *My dear family. May God have been merciful and kept you all well and safe from the blood and misery of the battlefields where so many brave men have fallen. Only by His grace am I alive and whole! I have even found a new friend, Alice Galipova, sister of Tusya, of whom I have written before. They are distant cousins to your countess, Papa, and Alice is very much like our Catherine. Sometimes she tells me stories of their home near the Rocky Mountains of Canada, which sounds much bigger than our blessed Carpathians.*

"Alice is a Catholic name," Zhanna said approvingly then frowned. "But it is not right that he should be so familiar with a stranger. Father Ishchak would not be pleased."

"Oleksi is a young man," Vasyl said impatiently. "It is natural he should be interested in a woman." He continued with the letter.

> *Just before our present assignment, we were posted to Petrograd and were granted several days leave. Tusya, who has a gift for gaining access to anywhere he pleases, treated me and his sister and her friend, Oksana, to endless tours of gardens and markets and even a night at a theatre where men and women dance like the sprites in the old molfar's stories. On our last day we visited the Hermitage Museum, which stands next to His Imperial Majesty's Winter Palace. Inside were rooms with ceilings higher than the peak of our roof, where to look upward is to glimpse at what heaven must be like. From floor to ceiling were paintings of holy scenes so beautiful that I was compelled to kneel before them, especially those which I knew from Father Ishchak's gospel readings. Many of them, Papa, are like the grand tapestry that hangs in our home.*

Natalya cringed at the mention of the tapestry that was the source of the ongoing quarrel between her parents. The quarrel had grown more intense after she and her mother had listened to Galyna Shevchenko telling the women at church about the Talerhof prison that had been established in the Austrian Alps. "Whole families have been imprisoned there," she had said ominously. "They are given no shelter and barely enough food to keep a mouse alive." She gave a slight but significant nod in

Zhanna's direction. "That's what happens to Russophiles these days."

"Then it is a good thing we are all loyal Hutsuls," Zhanna had shot back. But the comment had worried her, and as Vasyl read the last lines of Oleksi's letter, she scowled at the tapestry.

"Father Ishchak says we are committing the sin of pride, Husband, by keeping that tapestry on the wall. He has asked us to remove it, and yet there it hangs, inviting the wrath of our Lord to rain down upon this house!"

Vasyl's temper flared as it always did when the tapestry was threatened. "In my home I say what hangs and what doesn't, Wife!" he snapped. Then, pushing away from the table, he grabbed his hat and axe belt and stormed from the house, slamming the door behind him. It was not until many hours later, when Natalya and her sisters were preparing for bed, that he returned smelling of beer and stumbling about the kitchen as unsteadily as Pylyp, who was just learning to walk.

While Vasyl dismissed Zhanna's predictions that they would all be sent to die in the Talerhof prison as nonsense, Natalya wasn't so sure, especially when she saw Bailiff Wojcik glowering at her father during Sunday services.

Yuliya, who openly agreed with their mother that the tapestry should be removed, said, "The bailiff blames us for what happened to his son."

The girls had been hunting for mushrooms and Catherine stopped dead in her tracks. "What do you mean?"

Ignoring Natalya's warning frown, Yuliya began to repeat the conversation she and Natalya had overheard while they were cleaning the church the previous afternoon. "Galyna Shevchenko says Lech Wojcik isn't dead."

"She doesn't know anything," Natalya interrupted. "She is just repeating gossip."

But Yuliya would not be shushed. "She said his face was burned and his lungs were ruined by poisonous gases, but he's alive."

Catherine's face had gone white and she hugged her mushroom basket to her chest. "Where is he now?" she asked faintly.

"Galyna said he has gone to live with his grandparents in Warsaw." Finally becoming aware of Catherine's shocked face, she finished lamely, "He has married a widow ... with two children."

Catherine stared unseeingly at her basket of mushrooms. "His beautiful face is burned?"

Leysa, who could not bear to see any of her family hurting, said quietly, "Everyone knows Galyna's stories are much bigger than the truth."

Catherine was not consoled. After they returned home, she disappeared for several hours, and when she came back just before dinner, her eyes were red and swollen.

Natalya's concern for her sister was soon replaced with a much greater worry. In late May an Austrian patrol arrived in the village, led by a cold-eyed commander who demanded to be taken to the upland meadow. There he confiscated the villagers' sheep and all the cheeses the herders had made that were supposed to be divided among the owners of the flocks in their care. After the Austrian patrols left the area, the molfar retrieved twenty sheep he had hidden in a ravine surrounded by woods.

"It was the meadow sprites who warned our molfar that the Austrians were coming," said the barrel maker, "and it was they who guided him to the secret ravine."

When Yuliya repeated this story at home, Vasyl snorted contemptuously. "No doubt it was the molfar's watchmen who warned him of the Austrians, daughter. And knowing that a patrol was bound to show up someday, he would naturally have planned a hiding place."

Zhanna, pointedly ignoring her husband's answer, crossed herself and announced, "Of course, it was our dear Lord who guided him, and it is His Holiness we should thank for this blessing."

At a meeting in the village hall, it was decided that the remaining flock would be divided according to the number of sheep in each owners' original herd. Vasyl was allotted two pregnant ewes.

A few days later when Boris Vitovskyi was helping Vasyl to plow a new cornfield on a slope behind the barn, they noticed the bailiff had stopped his horse on the road to observe them. "It was our good bailiff who led the soldiers to the molfar's camp," Boris told Vasyl quietly.

Natalya, who was bringing a bucket of water to the men, glanced nervously at the bailiff. Had he not been so dangerous, she might have laughed at the comic figure he presented—a round, goblin-like man whose short, thick legs were barely capable of straddling his sleek white stallion, which, according to village rumours, had been a permanent gift from Farmer Andronic after they had confiscated Oleksi's pig.

"The smaller the man, the bigger his horse," Vasyl commented when the bailiff finally rode on toward the village.

"Wojcik thinks he is master of us all," Boris said bitterly.

Vasyl shook his head. "He will not fare well when the Russians return, brother."

"Perhaps. But until they do, no one dares to touch him because he is a distant cousin of Governor Von Beseler. If even a hair on his head is harmed, the whole village will be burned to the ground." He spat contemptuously. "But even a governor can't protect him forever. Our molfar has cursed him and it is only a matter of time before he is destroyed."

Despite his steadfast belief that the Russian forces would soon return to the mountains, Vasyl was so disturbed by the bailiff's visit to his farm that he went the next day to the molfar's camp and collected his two ewes, along with their offspring.

"Less than half a morning's ride from here is another meadow," he told Zhanna. "The trail leading to it is known only to a few, and certainly not to the bailiff. I will take our sheep there and Natalya and Yuliya can stay with them."

Zhanna was horrified. "You would leave our daughters alone on an isolated meadow!"

"Would you rather we starved because the soldiers have taken our sheep?"

"Sheep can be replaced, Husband. Our daughters cannot."

They argued long into the night and, listening from her bed, Natalya prayed that her father would not give in. *I should like to spend my days on the meadow,* she decided, *and let someone else do the washing and mending and cleaning.* Not that she had much hope. Since losing his position as chief forester, her father had surrendered most of the family decision-making to her mother, and now, instead of ending the argument with a stern verdict, he was defending his position.

"The girls will be fine, Wife. Natalya is far more at home in the woods than in the house and she has the wits to keep them both safe, I promise you."

Zhanna wasn't convinced and the argument was still raging when Natalya fell asleep. In the morning she learned of the compromise her parents had worked out. Yuliya and Natalya would take the sheep to the meadow each morning but return to the farm in the evening.

"What good that will do is beyond me," Vasyl complained at breakfast. "The sheep will be skinny and tough from travelling back and forth, and if the soldiers come at night, they will surely find them."

But on this Zhanna would not budge, and though he grumbled that his wife was not the master of the household, Vasyl accepted her conditions. The following day, toting a package containing a thick wool blanket and an equally thick cape, he rode to the molfar's camp, returning late in the afternoon with a large dog as white as winter snow.

"His name is Savruk," he said as Natalya knelt and wrapped her arms around the dog, which immediately licked her face. "He cost more than I intended to pay, but the herder says he is as fierce as a wolverine when defending his charges."

"But think how much food it will take to feed such an animal!" Zhanna objected. It was the same argument she had used a year earlier when Vasyl wanted to replace their last dog after it was killed by a pack of wolves.

With a touch of his old spirit, Vasyl said with indisputable finality, "He will keep our daughters safe."

Yuliya hated the idea of going to the meadow. "Leysa is much better with animals than me," she insisted.

Afraid of her own shadow, Leysa had trembled at the idea, but she need not have worried.

"Your sister's health is too fragile," Vasyl said firmly. "*You* and Natalya will go, and Savruk will protect you."

"A dog won't save us from a band of murdering Cossacks!" Yuliya wailed.

"Perhaps not, daughter, but he'll warn you of their coming in plenty of time for you to hide where they'll never find you."

Natalya suspected that being so far from the meal table troubled Yuliya more than murdering Cossacks, but she kept that thought to herself.

Just after dawn the next morning they crossed the small horse paddock that separated the farm from a grove of beech trees and set out on a faint trail that only Vasyl could see. The girls were on Zirka, with Natalya in front handling the reins and Yuliya holding tight to her waist, while their father rode Nich. Sitting proud in his saddle, Vasyl's shoulders were straight and there was a cheerfulness in his whistled commands to the dog, who was herding the sheep ahead of them.

"It's good to see Papa happy again," Natalya said.

"He's just pleased he's getting the better of Bailiff Wojcik," grumbled her sister. "He won't be so happy when he finds his daughters murdered and his sheep roasting on a Cossack fire."

It took almost an hour for them to reach the meadow, which was really little more than a small clearing among the trees. It was the result, Vasyl said in response to Natalya's question, of a fire that had swept through the mountains more than a hundred years earlier. For some reason, no trees had grown back on this spot.

"The molfar says such clearings were made by the evil wood nymph *Niavka* dancing with her friends," Yuliya said quietly so Vasyl could not hear her. "They dance so fast no one can see them, but they make the sound of the wind and that's how you know they're present."

Natalya laughed. "Papa says such stories are nonsense," she said, refusing to allow superstition to cloud her happiness. Like all the village children, Natalya had listened to the molfar's tales of the meadow nymphs whom, he said, were really the souls of young girls who had died unnatural deaths and who considered the alpine meadows their own.

They rode across the meadow, leaving a dark trail in the dewy new-green grass and she guided Zirka around a cluster of blueberry bushes dotted with tiny white blossoms. At the far edge of the clearing where she could hear the rush of running water, they dismounted. She ran toward the sound and discovered a small stream meandering through the trees. Her father's sharp command brought her back to the clearing, and for the rest of the day she and Yuliya helped him build a crude shelter near the trees. Constructed of poles he lashed together and slanted toward the ground, it was supported at one end by a beam anchored to a pair of sturdy trees. The roof was reinforced with branches and clumps of sod, and an opening was made for smoke to escape.

"It's like a hill," Natalya said when it was finally finished. Even their mother's thick wool rug hanging over the entrance blended with the colours of the meadow.

"If it rains, you will stay dry," her father said. "And if the weather is too bad for you to come home, it will be a safe place to spend the night."

They returned to the meadow the following morning and this time he taught them how to whistle commands that would direct Savruk to move the sheep one way or another or to hold them in position until he was given a second command to release them.

After that day, they went alone, but Vasyl was always up to see them off just after daybreak, making sure Zirka was properly saddled and that they had enough food to last for several days and a blanket to keep them warm.

"If the weather is bad, do not try to come home," he warned them again and again. "Savruk will keep you and Zirka and the sheep safe. And when you do come home, always leave the woods with the greatest of caution. If there are strangers about, you must take the sheep back to the meadow."

"I hate it here," Yuliya complained the first morning they arrived at the meadow alone. Now almost sixteen and twice the size of Natalya, she was so plump she found it hard to get on and off the horse, and she jumped at every unusual sound or movement. "Daryna Hutopila says *bohynias* hide among the trees and steal children, so we must always stay together."

"But there's no grass left," Natalya argued on their third day, waving her hand at the stubble close to the shelter. "If the sheep are hungry when we bring them home, Papa won't be pleased."

"That's what Savruk is for, little sister. He will take them further out into the meadow, but you must stay here. Or," she warned, "I shall tell Papa you are disobedient and he will send Leysa instead."

"And I shall tell him you repeat the molfar's stories as if they are true," Natalya retorted. But only when she was bribed with a larger share of their lunch did Yuliya give in, and from then on Natalya was free to explore the meadow and the woods and the stream. When she tired of exploring, she played with Savruk, whistling commands and delighting in the power she had over him and the sheep.

Several times during the summer there were storms that forced the girls to stay the night in the shelter. The first time it happened, even Natalya grew uneasy as darkness descended. But although the winds howled in the trees and the rain beat down upon their shelter, it remained sound, and after the first time, she wasn't afraid. Their father always arrived first thing in the morning to bring them food and make sure they were safe, and one night he arrived before the storm hit and stayed with them.

Still, their mother continued to fight against her daughters being on the meadow, and in September when the nights began to get colder and the storms came more frequently, she argued repeatedly that it was time to bring the sheep down for good.

"Even the molfar will be bringing his herds back soon," she

said, "and Father Ishchak is asking why the girls are missing school."

But Vasyl remained firm. "The Kaiser's armies have been fighting hard and they are hungry," he insisted. If they find our sheep, they will take them and we will starve. Until the snows come, Yuliya and Natalya will go to the meadow."

Late one afternoon in mid-September a storm worse than any other descended unexpectedly, pelting the clearing with an icy rain and winds so wild that the shelter wobbled beneath their assault. Natalya was torn between wishing her father would come and praying he would not venture onto the treacherous trail.

"I've taken Zirka deeper into the woods," she told Yuliya, who was huddled on their makeshift bed of spruce boughs, "but we need to get the sheep inside."

"It's the *Niavka!*" Yuliya whimpered. "They want us to leave!"

"It is a storm, sister, and nothing more."

Still, Yuliya didn't move and finally Natalya rounded up the sheep herself, bringing them all inside the shelter.

"I can't move with them in here," Yuliya complained. "And they're all wet!"

Natalya tried to fasten the rug more securely over the entranceway, but the thick woven material kept blowing inward and the girls were soon as soaked as the sheep. Outside, lightning flashed and thunder cracked like a thousand rifles above their heads. Frightened by the noise and unaccustomed to the enclosure, the sheep refused to settle, fidgeting and bumping the walls and each other with such force that Natalya was afraid they, and not the wind, would knock the shelter down. Only Savruk, crouched in front of the doorway, kept them from charging out into the rain. As the night fell and the clearing grew dark, the flashes became even more terrifying, transforming shapes that were innocent by day into hideous demons, until even Natalya grew afraid. Clutching the cross her father had carved for her, she muttered every prayer she could remember.

All through the long night the storm raged, roaring through trees and making even the ground beneath them tremble, and only when the first feeble light of dawn began easing the darkness away did the wind calm and the rug over the door stop flapping at them. It was then that the girls finally slept.

When Natalya woke a few hours later, the rain was still falling and in the dim light of the shelter she could see the two lambs shivering beside their mothers.

"You need some warmth, poor things," she murmured, crawling out from under the blanket. Savruk rose and shook himself, then followed her outside. They went first to Zirka, who seemed to have weathered the storm even better than they had, although he was skittish and jumped at every unusual sound. She led him back to the meadow, where she collected some dry scraps of wood she'd placed under a log, then returned to the shelter and lit a fire just outside the entrance. When the embers were glowing, she brewed a pot of peppermint tea.

Yuliya pushed aside one of the sheep that was resting on her makeshift bed. "I'm hungry," she complained, wrapping the damp blanket around her and accepting without thanks the hard piece of *kulesha* Natalya handed her along with a mug of tea.

"Papa should come before long," Natalya said, peering outside where Savruk had settled himself just beyond the fire. Zirka had found his own shelter beneath a pine tree. But the hours crept slowly past with no sign of their father, even when the rain eased and finally stopped.

Knowing the sheep needed food to stay warm, Natalya shooed them outside and followed them onto the meadow, running through the sodden grass in her bare feet. In the afternoon she ventured into the woods to explore the stream that had been transformed into a muddy torrent, tumbling boulders and sweeping broken limbs along its path until they disappeared into a steep ravine. She was absorbed in the sound of the water crashing against the rocks far below her, when she suddenly heard Yuliya screaming from outside the shelter. Racing to the edge of the meadow, she heard the loud rumbling from the sky that had so terrified her sister.

"Get the sheep!" Natalya shouted.

While Yuliya whistled for Savruk to bring the sheep to her, Natalya ran into the meadow and grabbed Zirka's halter, pulling him into the woods just as an airplane appeared above the treeline.

The double-winged machine was very much like one that had landed in Andronic's field the winter before the war. Along with all of the other villagers, the Tcychowski children had hurried to the field and watched open-mouthed as the baron had stepped from inside the monster. After that Father Ishchak had shown them pictures of airplanes and tried to explain the principals of flight, but to the children of Zgardy the plane was as magical and fearsome as any of the molfar's tales.

Unlike the pale yellow plane that had landed in Andronic's field, this aircraft had the black cross of the German army painted in the centre of a white circle on the underside of the wings and on the tail. The plane roared across the meadow, flying so low Natalya was sure the pilot would see them, then rose into the sky and disappeared in the direction of the village.

"It's gone," Yuliya breathed.

Still, it was many minutes before the girls ventured out of the woods.

"We must go home," Yuliya said fearfully. "It might come back."

Natalya glanced nervously at the sky. The clouds were gathering once more, threatening another storm.

"Papa will be worried if we stay," she agreed, and they both hurried to the shelter to gather their things.

They were on the trail less than an hour later, with Savruk herding the sheep in front of them. Natalya leaned forward in the saddle as she carefully guided Zirka along the rough track that led down the mountainside.

"That pilot was probably lost," she said over her shoulder then added, "I hope he crashes into a mountain!"

Yuliya, riding behind the saddle, gripped Natalya's waist so tight she could scarcely breathe. "No, he was searching for sheep," she insisted. "We must tell Papa we can't take them to the meadow anymore."

"That's silly, Yuliya! He couldn't even see us in the trees."

"Yes, he did. He tipped his wings to us."

"He was just turning. Didn't he fly off as soon as he passed over us?"

"That's because he saw us, Natalya."

Knowing no amount of talking would convince her sister otherwise, Natalya changed the subject. "I wonder why Papa never came like he did after the last storm?"

"Because he doesn't care about us," Yuliya pouted.

Their path, which at first followed the creek as it gradually descended through the trees, now skirted the edge of a cliff from where they could see the stream as it tumbled down into a deep gorge. On previous trips, the girls had discovered that from this point, if there was no fog, they could also see the road that led from their farm to the village. Today it was almost obscured by the mist rising from the falls, and neither girl gave the road a second glance until a flash of movement caught Natalya's attention.

"Look!" she cried, reining Zirka to a stop and whistling to Savruk to hold the sheep in place. She pointed to the spot where she'd seen the flash. "There!"

Barely visible through the mist was a large troop of soldiers riding hard toward the Tcychowski farm. In the lead riding a large black horse was an officer wearing a spired helmet and beside him was a small figure on a sleek white stallion.

"The bailiff," Natalya breathed, suddenly more terrified then she had been at any time during the storm.

EASTERN FRONT BETWEEN GRODNO AND MINSK
Early September 1915

All through the month of August, as the Russian army retreated from a massive German offensive, the mobile medical unit made do in tents and old barns and once in a dilapidated grain shed that leaked and threatened to collapse whenever a shell landed within a mile of it. But in September the dressing station had been set up in the coach house of what had once been the summer mansion of a leather factory owner in Lida, ten kilometres north of the estate. While the shelling in a previous battle had reduced the mansion to rubble, the coach house had remained intact and was a welcome relief to the dressing station staff.

Alice liked it because it remained cool even in the heat wave they had been enduring for the past two days. Late on the third morning, during a brief lull in the stream of patients flowing in and out, she took a cup of lukewarm tea and a slice of black bread outside. Sitting on a bench, she leaned back against the wall and stretched her legs out in front of her, letting the sun warm her skin. She was half asleep when a young sanitar approached.

"These are for you, Miss," he said, handing her two folded pieces of paper. Then he swung about and marched toward the field of tents where the soldiers and sanitars were bivouacked.

Alice unfolded the first sheet and recognized Tusya's untidy scrawl. As she read his message, her heart began to pound.

> *Sorry, Ali, but Oleksi and I have just received orders to pull out. Can't tell you where we're going or when we'll be back. Be safe and I'll see you soon!*
> *Love, Tusya.*

Her hands trembled as she opened the second letter. Oleksi's script was in perfect alignment with the page, each letter a work of art, each word carefully planned.

My dear Alishka. The sun has just risen and with it have come orders that Tusya and I must leave immediately. They do not tell us where we are going—only that it will be some time before we return. Nor will they allow us time to bid you the farewell you deserve. You will be anxious, I know, but please do not fear. I will care for Tusya as if he was my own brother, and when our mission is fulfilled, we will both find you. Until we do, be safe and strong.
Your own Oleksi.

She stared toward the line of tents that had swallowed the sanitar. It was almost noon and her brother and Oleksi would be well on their way by now.

It's not fair! She wanted to scream the words to release the lump lodged in her throat. Then she thought of the men lying inside the coach house, most of them suffering indescribable pain, some with missing limbs, others with disfigured faces and wounds that might never heal. Not fair? Hell, nothing was fair in this bloody, brutal war. Nothing was planned. Nothing made sense. People came and went and suffered and died, and the only thing that was predictable was that the misery wouldn't stop.

"Damn it to hell!"

She reread Oleksi's letter. What had he meant by signing it *"your own Oleksi?"* Was it simply the comradely salutation of a good friend? Or was it something more?

In the past year they *had* grown very close, but always as a threesome with her brother.

"Our very own Triple Alliance," Tusya joked.

And it was true, she thought, folding the letter. They were always there for each other. Comforting Oleksi after he had risked his life to save a boy who died before reaching the dressing station. Covering for Tusya when he was late returning from a wild night at a village tavern that was supposed to be off-limits to the troops. Many times the only thing that got Alice through a heart-wrenching shift or an awful night of shelling was knowing her brother and friend were close and that she would soon be able to cry on one or both of their shoulders.

Through it all, Oleksi had acted as a brother, teasing her as Tusya did and protecting her from the unwanted advances of his fellow soldiers. And although there was occasionally something very un-brotherly in the way he looked at her, and in the way her heart raced when he touched her, neither of them had ever spoken of their feelings. A tacit agreement not to spoil what they had.

I should have shown him I wanted more! That he was more than a friend to me, she fretted. *What if he doesn't return? Do I go through the rest of my life never knowing the feel of his lips or the touch of his flesh against mine?*

The door to the coach house opened, interrupting her brooding, and a sanitar said politely, "They're waiting, Miss."

She sighed heavily, tucked the letters into her apron pocket and slowly got to her feet. Forcing everything from her thoughts except the task at hand, she returned to the dressing room and began unravelling the temporary dressing that had been wound about the shattered foot of a soldier who could not have been any older than twelve. In each fold of the dressing was a cluster of lice, covered in the young man's blood.

A week later, by which time the dressing station had moved to another small village twenty kilometres to the east, Alice received orders from the hospital command to return to Petrograd.

"Your cousin is gravely ill," the doctor in charge of the medical unit told her when she protested that she could not leave until Oleksi and Tusya came back. "She needs you in Petrograd."

"What's wrong with her?" Alice asked suspiciously, not trusting her cousin's motives.

"The message only says that she is ill and you must come at once."

"But how can I possibly leave when we're so short-handed here?"

"We have a student arriving this afternoon," the doctor said firmly. "She has been on the front for the past six months and I'm told she is very competent."

Alice still suspected the countess's illness was merely a ruse to remove her from the front, and although she did not wish her replacement any ill will, she fervently hoped the new nurse would somehow fail to show up that afternoon. *Maybe for once this bloody war will work for me.*

But when the young student arrived, she proved to be both dedicated and knowledgeable. The following morning, Alice, still protesting that she was needed at the station, gathered her things and climbed into the sidecar of the motorcycle that was to take her to the nearest train station. For the rest of the day she and the driver bumped past ragged columns of refugees, some with their worldly goods piled high onto carts that were pulled by weary horses or mules or oxen, some carrying everything they owned on their backs. Old men and haggard-faced women, many with babies in their arms and several emaciated children in tow, plodded forward as if they were sleepwalking. Parallel to the refugees were long columns of soldiers, transport trucks and horse-drawn ambulances, all going so fast no one dared to slow down lest they be run over. Once she saw an old man fall from the back of a wagon, and before he could move out of the way the wheels of an artillery wagon had crushed him deep into the mud. She cried out to her own driver to stop, but he simply manoeuvred around the spot and kept moving. By early evening they reached Minsk and, feeling both relieved and guilty for leaving her post and thoroughly exhausted, she boarded a night train for Petrograd.

ZGARDY

September 1915

"We've got to go back to the meadow!" Yuliya cried fearfully. "They won't find us there."

But Natalya was already digging her heels into Zirka's flanks. "No! We have to warn Papa!"

The path down from the ridge was steep, and despite her urging, the horse picked his way carefully until the trail finally levelled out. As they approached the beech grove, she pulled Zirka to an abrupt halt and whistled to Savruk. The dog immediately circled his charges and brought them back to the denser woods, and when she whistled the "hold" command, he crouched in front of the small herd, his eyes fixed on the leading ewe. Now, so long as Savruk was there, the sheep wouldn't move.

"One of us should stay with them," Yuliya said, nervously eyeing the trail to the farm as if she expected the soldiers to come riding down it at any moment.

Natalya jumped to the ground. "You stay. I'm going to warn Papa!" She started running through the trees, and Yuliya slid from the horse, hastily tying the animal to a small fir sapling.

"Wait! I'm coming with you!" she cried.

When they reached the edge of the paddock separating the woods from the farm, she grabbed Natalya's arm.

"Remember, Papa said we should make sure there's no one about!"

Although Natalya wanted desperately to run forward, she reluctantly altered her course, creeping southward through the willow thicket along the eastern end of the field until she found a spot where they had a clear view of the farmyard.

At first everything seemed so peaceful that had she not seen the soldiers from the bluff, Natalya might have thought nothing at all was wrong. Her father was perched on a ladder working on the roof, and they could hear the rat-tat-a-tat of his hammer as he fastened a shake in place. A few chickens roamed about the yard and she saw Catherine disappear into the barn with the basket she used for collecting eggs.

Then suddenly the ground trembled and the calm was shattered by the thunder of galloping hooves as twelve mounted soldiers rounded the bend in the road and splashed through the muddy gateway.

Pulling his horse up sharply in front of the porch, the officer shouted a series of commands, too rapid and distant for Natalya to understand.

Their father, having come down the ladder, marched toward the porch. He stood tall and straight, his hand resting on the butt of the axe strapped to his waist, and he showed no fear as he faced the officer and roared so loud the girls could hear every word, "What is the meaning of this?"

Ignoring him, the officer issued another sharp command and all of the men, except the one issuing commands and Bailiff Wojcik, dismounted. Fixing bayonets to their rifles, they jogged forward in groups of three, one group into the house, another to the granary and a third to the barn. The tenth soldier stayed with his commander by the porch. Only when his men were dispatched did the officer address Vasyl. Natalya could not hear what he said, but she saw the bailiff gesturing wildly, pointing first at her father and then at the house. Her heart almost stopped when the soldier on the ground pointed his rifle at her father. The officer and the bailiff dismounted and marched into the house, followed by Vasyl, with the guard's bayonet poking at his back.

Natalya started forward, but her sister grabbed her arm and pulled her back.

"They have guns," she cried. "There's nothing we can do!"

Afraid that Yuliya's hysteria would give them away, Natalya forced herself to stay put, but it seemed to take forever before the officer stomped back outside, clearly furious with the little man who followed him.

"You waste my time, Bailiff!" he shouted. "A blanket on the wall is not a Russian symbol!"

A soldier stepped from the house with a bulging sack that he set on the ground, while a second soldier came out with another sack, and a third carried a stack of blankets Natalya recognized as ones her mother had woven to sell in the village. Behind them came Vasyl and the soldier with the bayonet. Zhanna followed, her hands clasped pleadingly toward the commander.

When they were all outside, the officer dismissed the soldier guarding Vasyl and mounted his horse once more. While the bailiff struggled to do the same, the three men who had gone into the granary came out with several full sacks, which they proceeded to fasten to their mounts.

Natalya watched helplessly, sick to her stomach, but not daring to move. If the soldiers discovered her and Yuliya, they might also discover the trail and follow it to the sheep.

Suddenly, they heard a raucous squawking of chickens and a piercing shriek, and in the next instant a grinning, thickset soldier emerged from the barn with Catherine, kicking and screaming, imprisoned in his arms. Vasyl roared something unintelligible. Whipping out his axe, he ran forward, refusing to stop when the soldier who had been guarding him shouted, "Halt! Halt!"

Again Natalya tried to break away, but Yuliya tightened her grip and forced her to the ground, straddled her so the younger girl couldn't move.

"Let me go, Yuliya!" She tried to wriggle free and at the same time watch what was happening in the yard. As the soldier raised his gun, a shriek rose in her throat, but before it reached her lips Yuliya's hand closed over her nose and mouth. Unable to breathe and with the meadow slowly spinning about her, she heard a shot ring out and saw her father fall. As if in a dream she watched Catherine break free of her captor and run to her father, reaching him at the same time their mother did. She saw them turn him over and her mother cradle his head in her lap. Overwhelmed by blackness, Natalya went limp. Yuliya jerked her hand from her mouth, though she continued to pin her to the ground.

"Stay still, Natalya," she begged in a hysterical whisper.

Gasping for air, Natalya realized the squawking in the barn had stopped. She raised her head and saw the remaining two soldiers emerge with Nich bearing the pack saddle that was laden with more bulging sacks. At a sharp order from the officer, the men assembled near the porch where the pile of blankets and even more sacks were added to Nich's load.

When all of the soldiers had mounted, two torches were set aflame, and the troop circled the yard, tossing one torch into the barn and the other onto the roof of the house. Then they galloped through the gate and disappeared the way they had come. The pounding of hooves gradually faded, the sound replaced by the crackle of burning wood, and Yuliya's sobs as she finally released her sister and began running across the field, shouting, "Papa!"

Natalya scrambled to her feet and ran forward, but midway across the farmyard she froze. Dreamlike, she watched her mother rising from the ground and heard her scream, "He's dead! God have mercy on us! They have killed my husband!" Behind her flames were igniting the interior of the barn, but the torch that had been thrown onto the roof of the house had rolled off before causing any damage and was smouldering on the wet ground. From the open doorway Leysa, with Pylyp bundled in a blanket, peered anxiously out. With tentative steps, ready to flee back inside at the least provocation, she crossed the porch and sank down onto the top step, clutching her baby brother in her arms.

Zhanna started to run toward her but halfway across the yard stopped and returned to her husband's body where she sank to her knees, her clasped hands reaching imploringly to the grey skies.

"Mother of Christ, I beg you, show some mercy!"

Yuliya dropped to the ground beside her mother and Catherine and grabbed Vasyl's hand. "Papa!" she sobbed. "Get up, Papa!"

Forcing herself to move closer, Natalya stared down at her father, whose sightless gaze was fixed skyward, his face contorted in everlasting fury. He wouldn't want them to be staring down at him, she thought. He would want them to do something. "We have to stop the fire," she said. "We need some buckets ... and sacks."

Her sisters didn't move and her mother continued to beg her saints for mercy.

"It's Papa's barn, Mama!" Natalya pleaded. "We can't let it burn!"

Zhanna stopped praying. The crackle of burning wood grew louder and as some of the smoke pouring from the barn washed over her, she got to her feet. "Yuliya, go to the house," she said in a voice that grew more commanding with each word, "Get a blanket to cover your father." When Yuliya didn't move but continued to wail over her dead father, Zhanna grabbed her daughter's shoulder and pulled her to her feet. "Go to the house," she repeated in a voice as cold as ice, "and get a blanket to cover your father. Then you must help carry water to the fire."

By the time her mother finished speaking, Natalya was already halfway to the well in the middle of the farmyard. Alongside an empty bucket was a small container of water. Her hands shaking, she poured this into the shaft to prime it and began pumping madly, and by the time Zhanna arrived with two more buckets the one Natalya had placed beneath the spout was full. Zhanna grabbed a full one, thrust an empty bucket under the spout, and ran toward the barn just as Catherine ran up with two more buckets. Duplicating her mother's actions, she grabbed the now-full bucket and headed for the barn. Natalya was filling one of the remaining buckets when Leysa approached carrying Pylyp in a large basket. Setting it down close to the well, she grabbed the third bucket and ran after the others.

In the yard, Yuliya covered her father with a rug then hurried to the pump where Natalya had filled the fourth bucket.

"You pump and watch Pylyp," Natalya told her. "I can run faster."

Without a word, Yuliya took over the handle just as their mother returned. Grabbing the full bucket, Natalya raced to the barn.

The heat near the door was intense for the torch had landed in a bed of straw in Nich's stall and already the half wall separating it from Zirka's stall was being consumed by the flames. Now they hungrily licked the posts on either side, the tongues of fire flicking toward the ceiling and the tack room wall. Catherine was slapping at the flames on the posts with a wet burlap sack, but the burning hay prevented her from going into the stall, and though Natalya emptied her bucket into the enclosure, the water only reached the edge of the fire, as did her mother's bucketful. Tossing her bucket aside, Natalya grabbed a rake, reached into the stall as far as the heat would allow, raked out a mound of burning straw then dragged it through the door and into the yard. Meanwhile, having put out the fire attacking the posts, Catherine was beating back flames that were consuming the tack room wall, but as fast as they were extinguished in one area, the flames rose hotter and fiercer in another, luring the sisters deeper and deeper into the barn's interior.

Realizing the fire had spread higher than either of them could reach, Natalya snatched a bucket from Leysa and started up the ladder to the loft.

"No!" Catherine screamed. "Stay below, Natalya!"

"It's getting into the loft!" Natalya shouted back and crawled through the open hatchway. The floorboards in the loft were tinder dry and covered with last year's hay. If they started burning, there would be no stopping them, and if she was up there when they caught fire, she might not have time to escape. But she didn't let herself think of this as she ran through the blinding smoke to where she could see sparks rising from cracks beside the upper edge of the tack room wall. Here the floor was already so hot that steam rose as she dumped her water over the boards. Then she raced back to the opening where Catherine had just arrived with a new bucket.

"The water comes through the cracks," Catherine cried. "It's putting out the fire where I can't reach."

Natalya grabbed the fresh bucket and ran back to the spot where she'd poured the first, and from then on they raced back and forth, Catherine hauling a full bucket up the ladder, taking the empty one down and exchanging it for another full one from Zhanna, while Natalya raced across the loft and poured the water over the floorboards and down any crack near the fire. Her arms ached and her legs grew rubbery, but she didn't dare stop until finally Catherine appeared with no bucket at all.

"It's out, Natalya."

Not quite believing her, Natalya went back to the spot where she'd thrown the water and felt the floorboards. They were warm and wet but no longer steaming. Slowly she crossed the loft and climbed down the ladder and she and Catherine stood together staring at the blackened remains of Nich's stall and the charred wall of the tack room and the ceiling above it.

Zhanna and Leysa ran into the barn with fresh buckets then stopped and gaped at the steaming timbers. And a moment later Yuliya, with Pylyp in her arms, joined them. They looked at each other, their faces black, their hair and clothes wet and filthy, but in their eyes, a triumph. Then, overwhelmed by exhaustion and despair, Natalya began to shake, and as she grabbed Catherine's arm to keep from falling, she realized her sister was having the same reaction.

Tears streamed down Natalya's cheeks. "We did it, Papa," she whispered, looking toward the rug-covered body in the yard.

Her mother frowned. "It was by our Lord's grace alone that the fire was extinguished." She dropped to her knees amid the ashes and began another series of prayers thanking God for sparing them and saving the barn. At last she rose and turned to her daughters. "The people from the village will be here soon. We must tend to your father before they come."

Natalya remained in the barn and glared after her mother as she crossed the yard with Catherine, Yuliya and Leysa following dejectedly behind. *God didn't put out the fire! We did.* As soon as the thought was out, Natalya wished she could take it back. Of course God helped them. How else could they have done it?

Afraid of the retribution her impure thoughts might bring down upon her and her family, she hastily crossed herself and said three Hail Mary's in rapid succession.

The yard was empty when she finally left the barn. It was raining again, bringing an early dusk that created deep shadows in the yard, and as she walked past the paddock, she suddenly remembered that Zirka and the sheep were still in the woods with Savruk.

There was scarcely enough light for her to see and she was forced to pick her way along the trail. Her fears of encountering an Austrian soldier magnified each rustle of leaves and scraping of branches and, when an owl hooted from a limb high above her, it was all she could do not to flee. Only the thought of the animals, alone and untended, pushed her forward, and she wished again that she had not been so hasty in denying God's help earlier. At last she heard Savruk's low growl of warning, the soft bleating of a lamb, and Zirka's impatient snort. The sweet smell of his sweat guided her to the horse where she clumsily untied his reins and tried to climb onto his back. But, spooked by the darkness, he kept moving away until she grabbed his mane and used it to pull herself up high enough to get her foot into the stirrup and from there wriggle onto the saddle. Then she whistled to Savruk to take the sheep home and nudged Zirka to follow, letting him find his own way.

The long, sad notes of a *trembita* greeted her as she emerged from the forest. Candlelight shone from the windows of the house, illuminating the white kerchiefs that had been hung in the openings to signify that someone inside was dead.

Unsaddling Zirka, she left him in the paddock and secured the gate, and while Savruk herded the sheep into their willow wattle enclosure between the barn and the house, she carried the saddle to the tack room. The barn was filled with the acrid smell of wet, charred wood, but Natalya lingered there. She didn't want to be with the villagers who had so often criticized her father's ways, or to listen to her mother saying harsh things about him. But he would want her to be there and so at last she left the barn and walked slowly across the yard and into the house.

As she feared, the kitchen was filled with villagers, including Yevhen Hutopila, who had just arrived and was placing a small loaf of *kulesha* on the table that was already laden with an assortment of food.

"The soldiers left us very little," he apologized to no one in particular, "but at least they did not burn us out. We've brought what we could spare."

Near the stairwell, long planks had been placed between two chests then covered with the tapestry, and on this rested a white pine coffin. Natalya remembered how, as a small child, she had watched her father carve his favourite flowers and designs on the box. "Who is it for, Papa?" she had asked and when he said it was for himself, she had burst into tears and beseeched him not to die.

"Everyone must die eventually, little one," he had said. "Of course, I don't intend to do so for a very long time."

"Then why do you build it, Papa?"

He had patted her head comfortingly, and she recalled how big and protective his hand had been, and how warm and gentle it felt against her hair. "It is the Hutsul way, Natalya. What will happen tomorrow is always a mystery and a wise man prepares for all possibilities."

She hadn't been consoled then, and she wasn't now as she watched Father Ishchak, dressed in white, walk solemnly about the room rattling the bells of his censer from which incense wafted. His balding head was crowned with a white brocade mitre embroidered in gold, and his monotonal chant, filtered through his wispy mustache and beard, seemed to mesmerize the villagers who were seated on benches near the coffin. There was not enough room for everyone and periodically someone would rise to give those standing a chance to rest. The person about to sit would blow on the bench before sitting so he or she didn't crush her father's soul should it have decided to occupy that space.

Closest to the coffin sat her mother, her hands clasped and her eyes closed as she rocked back and forth chanting prayers in unison with the priest. Catherine, resembling a wilted flower whose season had passed and not at all like the stalwart woman who had fought the fire in the barn, sat nearby with her head bowed in either weariness or prayer. Curled on the floor beside her were Leysa and Yuliya, their eyes puffy from the tears they had shed, their arms entwined and Pylyp asleep on Leysa's lap. Natalya yearned for the comfort they were giving each other, but she did not feel a part of them. Torn between her need for comfort and a lingering resentment toward her mother, she finally sat on the floor beside her and rested her head against Zhanna's legs. After a while the gentle rocking and soft chanting lulled her into a deep sleep.

Vasyl's funeral was held in the early hours of the morning at the little church in the village. Normally, Natalya loved the small, weather-worn building that was so plain on the outside, yet so bright and beautiful on the inside. She thought of it as a giant treasure box lined with blue and white and filled with gold. Of course, most of the gold was merely paint on wood, but the majesty of the altar, the images in the stained-glass windows, which came alive when touched by the sun, and the blood-red carpet stretching the length of the nave never ceased to thrill her. Except on this day.

Her father's coffin rested on the carpet and the grey skies outside brought only the dimmest light into the room crowded with mourners. Even the incense, which usually comforted her, hung heavy in the air. She tried desperately to concentrate on the liturgy, but her thoughts were filled with her father's stories and the horrifying realization that never again would she hear them from his lips or see him gazing proudly at the Romanov tapestry as he told how he had saved the countess and their village.

When Zhanna had heard the soldiers ride into the yard, she had hastily hidden the tapestry beneath the mattress of the girls' bed. Doing so, she told them later, had probably saved them all from being sent to the Talerhof prison camp, and she insisted the tapestry be buried with her husband where it would never again be a threat to their lives. "It has brought nothing but grief to this household," she declared.

But for once Catherine had spoken up. "No, Mama. The tapestry is Papa's legacy. It stands for everything he believed in and his spirit will not rest if it is buried with him."

When Natalya and Leysa added their own tearful pleas, Zhanna had relented. "But after the funeral," she said, "you had best keep it from my sight. If I see it again, I shall burn it!"

No one seemed to know quite what to do when they returned home after the funeral. Catherine and Natalya dismantled the plank table that had held the coffin and helped the others clean the house. The sheep were milked and the garden tended. The daily tasks helped them cope, and as one day trudged after another, the pain in Natalya's heart began to ease. She found herself pretending everything was as it had been before the war, that her father and Oleksi were at the logging site and would soon be home. Only when she went to the barn and saw the burned-out stall was reality forced upon her. Averting her eyes, she would hurry past the charred posts and climb to the loft to check on a broody hen the soldiers hadn't found that was sitting on a clutch of eggs.

One day almost a month after her father's death, she was just returning from this chore when she saw two riders approaching the gate. Her heart began to pound as they drew closer and she realized they were soldiers. But their uniforms were khaki-coloured, not grey, and there was something familiar about the dark curly hair beneath the lead soldier's cap. And suddenly a scream tore from her lips.

"Oleksi!"

She started to run toward him then changed her mind and charged up the steps. "Mama! Mama! Oleksi has come!"

Although Catherine, Yuliya and Leysa immediately crowded onto the porch, their mother didn't come out of the house until Oleksi and his companion had already dismounted. Even then, she moved slowly, almost reluctantly, across the porch and stopped at the top of the steps. She didn't smile or speak as she gazed down at her son.

Unable to restrain herself any further, Natalya brushed past her and leaped to the ground, landing next to Oleksi. But she stopped short of hugging him, not entirely sure how to greet the stranger her brother had become.

He, too, seemed unsure of his new role. "You've grown, little sister," he said, then turned uncertainly to their mother.

Zhanna's face held no welcome. "Why do you come now?" she demanded bitterly. "Why do you come when it is too late?"

His face reflected his bewilderment. "Too late for what, Mama?"

Natalya glanced at her mother then said quietly, "The Austrians killed Papa, Oleksi."

He swallowed hard. "Mama?"

Without being obvious about it, his companion moved closer to his side. He was taller than Oleksi and he had blond hair and compassionate blue eyes.

Quietly Natalya told her brother about the soldiers and their father's death. As he listened, Oleksi's right hand went to his axe, which he slowly withdrew from its sheath. "I had his axe," he said, his voice strangled as he ran his fingers over the carved handle. He ducked his head and swiped the sleeve of his tunic across his eyes. As he did so, Natalya saw his temple was creased by a deep, jagged scar. Behind her, she heard her mother cry out, "God forgive me, you've been hurt, Oleksi!" And suddenly she was down the steps, engulfing him in her arms and sobbing uncontrollably.

To combat her own tears, Natalya focussed on the stranger. "I'm Natalya," she said.

"Yes. The little sister." He managed a slight smile. "I've heard many stories about you." The way he said it made her suspect that those stories were not flattering, but before she could make a retort, he held out his hand and said gently, "I wish we were meeting under happier circumstances, Natalya. I am your brother's friend, Tusya Galipova."

She took the hand briefly, liking his firm grip, then pulled away. "Your horses must be thirsty," she said. "I'll take them to the trough."

※

That night Oleksi told their mother that he and Tusya were on a scouting mission to determine the strength of enemy strongholds in the Carpathian Mountains.

"You are spying?" Zhanna cried. "But you are sanitars!"

Natalya had been resting on Oleksi's bed beneath the stairs and had fallen asleep, but their voices wakened her and she felt a sudden tightening in her chest. She had seen posters the Austrian soldiers had placed on the door of the church and the village hall warning that anyone caught spying or giving shelter to a spy would be shot. Trembling, she moved to the end of the bed where she could hear her brother more clearly.

"I volunteered, Mama. I thought I might get a chance to visit you and Papa ..." His voice broke and he paused before adding, "Tusya wouldn't let me go alone, and since I know this area and we both speak the language, we were signed on."

Zhanna moaned softly. "Mother of God, you have endangered us all."

"No one's ever going to know we were here," Oleksi reassured her. "And Tusya and I are leaving tomorrow afternoon ..." The rest of his words were drowned by Zhanna's prayers and after a few minutes Natalya heard her brother walk to the door and go outside. Peering around the corner, she saw her mother kneeling with her back to the stairwell. Taking advantage of the moment, Natalya slipped upstairs to join her sisters in her own room.

The next morning, Natalya was up at dawn and anxiously watching the trail that led to the village and the road to Yeremeche. Every wisp of dust caused her to start and her ears were soon aching from listening so hard for the sound of riders. She didn't dare to show Oleksi the meadow where she and Yuliya had tended the sheep as she had planned, and she found no opportunity to tell him all of the things she had learned since he had left. Then, just before lunchtime while she was filling a bucket with water from the pump, she saw him go into the barn. With a quick glance at the trail, she set her bucket by the pump and followed him, and when she could not find him in the lower half of the barn, she started up the ladder to the loft. She stopped when she heard voices and peered over the edge of the opening. Oleksi and Catherine were seated on the loading platform at the farthest end of the room, not far from the nest of the broody hen. They were gazing out at the mountains and the corn field and were so intent on their conversation that they didn't hear Natalya hide herself behind a mound of hay near the hatchway she had just climbed through.

Oleksi was in the midst of an enthusiastic description of Tusya's sister, Alice, whom he declared had hair the colour of rich honey and eyes that mirrored the sky.

When he paused for a breath, Catherine asked in a worried voice, "This Alice—she and Tusya come from Canada, yes?"

"Yes. From a place called British Columbia," Oleksi said, pronouncing the words with difficulty. "Their father was given his land for free—an estate so immense it takes two days and a fast horse to ride from one end to the other! She never stops talking of this place." His voice grew sad. "She is just like Papa's countess."

"You sound as if you love her very much," Catherine said.

He nodded vigorously. "When I am away from her, it is like a whole part of me is missing." His voice grew hesitant. "She wants me to come to Canada, Catherine. She and Tusya tell me their government will give land to anyone who comes there. Just as the posters said in Father Ishchak's reading room."

"But Canada is a whole world away, Oleksi. We would never see you!"

He leaned toward her. "But if I had such an estate as her father, you could come and live with me," he said. "You and Mama—it would be big enough for all of us."

In her hay mound, Natalya felt a new fear knotting her stomach. *Leave Zgardy? Leave Papa's grave?* She could not bear to think of it.

"It sounds wonderful," Catherine said, "but you know Mama would never hear of leaving our farm."

He straightened and stared out at the hills. "No, I don't suppose she would."

They were silent for several minutes before Catherine said in a low voice, "The one I love is lost to me."

"Yes," he said, putting his arm about her shoulder, "I came home thinking to show Papa how much I have learned, and instead I find him murdered!"

There was a long silence and then Catherine said, "Papa's death is my fault, Oleksi."

"*Your* fault?"

"It's my fault the bailiff brought the soldiers here," she said. "I encouraged Lech Wojcik to ask Papa for my hand, and when he did, Papa sent him from our house in shame."

Oleksi withdrew his arm from her shoulder. "My god," was all he managed to say.

"I love him, Oleksi, as you love your Alice Galipova."

"It's not the same! He's the son of our father's murderer ... "

"But Lech is nothing like his father!"

"He's a Wojcik," Oleksi said, rising to his feet, "and that makes him our enemy."

"No! He is gentle and a poet and he loves me!"

The floor vibrated as Oleksi stomped across the loft, and when Natalya dared to look again, he had disappeared through the hatchway.

At the other end of the room, Catherine, still seated on the loading platform, wept softly. Natalya yearned to comfort her, but to do so would reveal that she had heard secrets not ready to be shared. So instead she watched and waited and at long last her sister stopped crying, got to her feet and walked dejectedly across the loft.

In the silence that lingered after Catherine disappeared down the ladder, Natalya heard the hen clucking in disapproval. But the grunts and rustling that accompanied the sound were made by something far bigger than a hen. Instinctively, she ducked back behind the hay.

"You might as well show yourself, little spy," a man's voice said, and she lifted her head to see Tusya standing behind the chicken's nest.

"I was checking on the hen," she said haughtily. "*You* are the one who is spying."

"Ah, but it can hardly be called spying when intruders come to your bedroom and wake you from a deep sleep, now can it?" He brushed hay from his trousers and retrieved his greatcoat from a dark niche between the hay and the corner.

"You could have let them know you were here."

"If I had, they would not have said those things that needed saying." She eyed him dubiously as he shook the coat. "Not that I am opposed to spying, little Natalya. Much can be learned in the shadows, and that which is learned can often be of use in desperate times. Unfortunately, what we hear is not always pleasing to our ears."

She scowled at him. "Oleksi was cruel to Catherine. She can't help who she loves."

"Your brother takes honour very seriously ... and a lot of men would be dead if he didn't."

Her eyes widened slightly but her scowl remained. "He still doesn't have to be so cruel."

"He's angry. I'm sure even you say things you don't mean when you're angry."

Natalya thought of the barbs she had often directed at Yuliya. *But that's not the same,* she told herself. *Yuliya is always mean.*

Oleksi shouted from the porch that it was time to go and suddenly Natalya remembered her original purpose in coming to the barn.

"I have to say good-bye!" she said, scrambling toward the ladder.

☙❧

Catherine did not reappear, even when Oleksi and Tusya were mounted and riding from the yard, but as they disappeared around the bend she came running across the paddock calling out Oleksi's name. When she drew close, Natalya pointed to the empty track, and her sister sank down onto the steps where her mother and siblings were gathered. Zhanna surveyed her with a mixture of resentment and pity. "Our Lord has spared us, daughters, and we must not let his beneficence go to waste." She nodded at Natalya. "Now that Oleksi has gone, you and Yuliya must take the sheep back to the meadow and keep them there until I send for you."

Yuliya's eyes grew wide. "Stay there, Mama?"

"Bailiff Wojcik knows we have sheep," Zhanna said sternly. "Should he discover they are not with the rest of the village flock, he will bring the soldiers back. For now it is better we keep them hidden."

Natalya lifted her chin. "We will keep them safe, Mama," she said then swung about and marched to the barn to harness Zirka. *At least today there's no storm,* she thought. But, she realized dismally, there also was no Papa to rescue them if anything went wrong.

PETROGRAD
November 1915

"I refuse to be dressed up like a Christmas doll!" Alice said. She thrust aside the gown the countess's personal maid had laid out for her. "You promised to keep me on the front with Tusya."

The countess cast a significant glance toward the closed door to her bedroom.

"I trust you," she said, her voice low but firm. "You have been to the trenches and you know what shipments are getting through and what aren't."

"That's exactly why you should send me back, cousin." Alice lowered her voice to match that of the countess. "So I can continue to keep track of the supplies."

"And what good—" The countess broke off, hit by a sudden spasm of coughing. Alice helped her to sit and held her until the spasm passed, then brought a glass of brandy-laced water to her lips. After a few small sips, the countess leaned back against the pillows. "What good will that do if there is no one to direct shipments at this end?" she asked weakly. "I need you to find out where and why our supplies are being diverted. General Banketik is in charge of medical transports, and his wife is hosting tonight's dinner to raise funds for soldier's relief. I have been assured that the general will be present."

"But Tusya would be much better at such things. He's so good with languages and he knows how to get information from people without them even being aware he's interested."

The countess shook her head. "Tusya is too valuable where he is."

"Wherever *that* is," Alice said bitterly. Since her brother and Oleksi had left on their secret mission she had received only a few terse messages that said nothing more than that they were alive. She picked up the gown. "I've never worn anything so grand, Countess! I'll probably trip and fall the first time I try to move."

"Which is exactly why you are going to put that gown on now, my dear," the countess said, suppressing a smile. "So you can practise moving about without falling."

"And I don't know a thing about proper etiquette."

"You are a bright and observant young woman. Just imitate what everyone else is doing and you'll be fine." She began to cough again and by the time she recovered, her face was grey with fatigue. Afraid that another spasm would send her into heart failure, Alice reluctantly gave in.

She spent the rest of the day practising sitting, standing, walking and curtsying while dressed in the beautiful gown. Although the red satin skirt draped loosely from a waistline just below her bosom, it was so tight around her ankles that it threatened to trip her at every step, and she had already snagged the delicate weave of the matching chiffon tunic.

"The Baroness Cervinka's daughter wore it at last year's fête and she left it behind when she went to England," the countess said, adding smugly, "It suits you much better than it did her, my dear."

Alice bit her tongue to keep from retorting that it did not suit her at all and resolutely continued to practise until late afternoon when a woman arrived to fix her hair.

"I can fix it myself," Alice lied, planning to fashion it into a simple French roll. Instead, the hairdresser teased and bullied her straight, golden locks into curls and piled them precariously on top of her head, all the while muttering a continuous stream of Russian curses under her breath.

"My hair likes to be free ... like me," Alice said when the elaborate hairdo collapsed, provoking a fresh string of blasphemy that lasted until the last curl was firmly pinned in place. She grimaced at her reflection in the bedroom mirror.

"Why do I feel like Marie Antoinette about to eat cake?"

Later that evening she discovered that copying the manners of the other guests at the dinner party, especially when she could not understand half of what they were saying, was even more daunting than moving about without falling or destroying her hairdo. Although her French had improved since her arrival from Canada, not everyone spoke that language with the same accent or fluency, and once when she thought she had made an appropriate comment, her listeners responded with raised brows and uncomfortable laughter.

At the dinner table, thanks to her cousin's manipulations, she was seated next to the grey-bearded General Banketik, whom she privately labelled Sir Garlic Breath. The old soldier was so grossly overweight that he had trouble breathing, and he gasped between sentences that were longer than a few words. Most of his talk was of his adventures on the front lines, in which she feigned interest.

"It is not often," he wheezed, patting her hand, "that someone so beautiful truly understands what it is like to look death in the face." He stuffed a forkful of trout smothered in béchamel sauce into his mouth. "My brave fighters would follow me to hell and back," he bragged then began to cough, spewing flecks of fish and sauce in all directions. While Alice discreetly wiped away the bits that had landed on her cheek, he continued as if he had not been interrupted, "Each one would lay down his life in an instant should I ask it of him."

How a man in his condition could even mount a horse, never mind command a battalion, Alice didn't know, and she was annoyed because his battle descriptions always neglected to include the plight of his soldiers. Not once did he tell how they were forced to endure weeks of standing in the icy waters of their trenches, wearing lice-infested uniforms they'd been forced to take from the bodies of their dead comrades, and with boots—when they were available—that were so worn they barely held together. Or how those who were wounded went untreated because medicine and equipment had not arrived. But she gritted her teeth, and instead of telling him he was a foolish old windbag, she said sweetly, "It must infuriate a conscientious man like yourself to see your poor troops suffering from want of medical supplies. Which I am sure is completely due to the incompetence of clerks who've never come close to the fighting."

"It does! It does indeed infuriate me!" he declared loudly, pounding his fist on the table. "I despise incompetence!"

His vehemence startled the other guests into silence. Feeling their stares, Alice's cheeks grew warm and even the general seemed slightly embarrassed. He cleared his throat noisily and took a large gulp of mineral water, which she suspected had been spiked with *samogon*, a bootlegged form of alcohol that had replaced vodka after the tsar outlawed the sale of all spirits at the beginning of the war. As the talking slowly resumed around them, the general examined her keenly. "And what, my dear, does someone as pretty and delightful as yourself know about the bunglings of Russia's supply clerks?"

"Not anything close to what you must know, General," she said, "but my cousin has discovered several discrepancies in the supplies reaching her own field hospitals." As the countess had instructed, Alice carefully listed the missing supplies. By the time the meal ended, she had secured the general's promise that transports to the field hospitals would now be his first priority and the chief clerk at the supply depots would be ordered to give her any information she requested.

※

Over the ensuing weeks the dinner parties became easier to bear, and Alice soon became a favourite, not just of General Banketik, but also of the Baroness Cervinka and her friends who adopted her as their "little Canadian *émigré*."

What did not become easier were her battles with Feliks Stolin. He had not forgiven her for returning the ticket on the *Dwinsk*, although she suspected he had sold it for much more than he had paid, and, except in the presence of her cousin, he treated her with rude disdain.

The countess, however, would hear no ill spoken of her secretary. "Grusha has devoted her life to the Federov family. She and Feliks are the most loyal servants we've ever had."

"But he won't let me anywhere near the account books," Alice said. "There might be something in them that will help me find out why supplies are missing from our shipments."

The countess patted her hand. "But I've already asked Feliks about that, my dear, and he insists there is nothing in the records that will help you."

"Well, if he's so trustworthy, why isn't he searching for the missing supplies so I can return to the front?"

"My dear, he's hardly the sort that could mingle in proper society," the countess exclaimed. "And it is there that you will find the solution to our dilemma, not in my secretary's ledgers. I can't imagine that you would even understand them."

Alice didn't remind her that she had been managing her father's accounts since she was fourteen, but she did keep pressing her cousin and finally the countess gave in.

"Only to stop your pestering," she said. "But do try not to offend Feliks. We truly would be lost without him."

However, even with permission from the countess, Alice was unable to get anywhere close to the account books. Whenever she approached the secretary's office adjoining the downstairs parlour, he would inform her of a luncheon or a soiree or some other affair that he had arranged for her to attend. Finally one morning after breakfast, she gathered a stack of waybills she had obtained from the Petrograd Medical Supply Depot, knocked sharply on the thick oak door of the office and entered without waiting for permission. Closing the door behind her, she strode to the desk and said firmly, "I need to see the account books."

He shook his head. "This is not a good time, *Mademoiselle*. You are expected for tea with the matron of the Red Cross Hospital in one hour."

"On the contrary, having sent my regrets to the matron, I have the whole day free. You, on the other hand, must go to the Vitebsk Station. The countess has asked that you personally inspect the supplies General Banketik has arranged to be sent to our hospitals. She wants you to ensure that everything we have ordered is included in the shipment."

Feliks leaned back in his chair. "Since you were the one who arranged the shipment, it would be more prudent for *you* to carry out the inspection."

Meeting his stare, she asked with a calm she was far from feeling. "Then shall I inform the countess that you refuse her request?"

For a long moment the ticking of the clock on the fireplace mantel behind the desk was the only sound in the room, but in the end it was he who looked away. In tight-lipped silence he closed the cover of the account book, inserted it into a drawer of the desk, which he then locked, and got to his feet. As he went to step past her, Alice held out her hand.

"The key, *Monsieur* Stolin." She nodded pointedly at his pocket.

A dark flush rose above his beard and at last he pulled out the key and threw it onto the desk. Then he left the room, slamming the door behind him.

Alice stood for several minutes before she walked slowly around the desk and sat in the still-warm highbacked chair. After unlocking the drawer, she withdrew the first of two account books, this one bearing the title "Field Hospitals" written in dark, Cyrillic letters.

For the next two hours she carefully checked each waybill against Feliks' entries in the ledger and then consulted a railroad map the supply clerk had also given to her. In every case where supplies had gone missing, the initials "MB" were penciled beside the entry, and the shipments had been routed through a complex series of stations where the supplies were transferred from one train to another. One shipment of morphine that could have gone directly from Petrograd to Minsk had instead been detoured south to Moscow, then even further south to Kaluga before being transferred to a northbound train bound for Viazma where it was sent on a westbound train to Minsk. It was between Kaluga and Minsk that two cases of morphine had been lost. The order for the complex route was in the same handwriting as the ledger entries.

While it was true that shipments were often routed to avoid conflict areas, on the date of the morphine shipment the train line between Minsk and Petrograd had been clear. This she knew because it was the day she had returned from the front, and she had travelled along that route.

Setting aside the hospital record book, she removed the second ledger, titled "Household Accounts" from the drawer. Here she found precise details of the countess's personal income and expenses and discovered, among other things, that her cousin's income came from a small pension and rents from a number of properties within the city.

Disappointed that she had found no discrepancies in either account book, Alice closed the ledger, but when she tried to return it to the drawer it would no longer fit. The cause was a thick envelope that had fallen forward from the back of the drawer. Within it, wrapped in a sheet of paper, was a wad of twenty, fifty and one hundred-rouble notes. On the paper was written: *The enclosed is a donation to the Federov Hospital fund.* There was no name or date on the paper, but the envelope was addressed to Feliks Stolin, and it was postmarked Viazma.

Returning to the hospital account book, Alice looked for an entry that would explain the cash. She was still looking when the door opened and Feliks strode into the room. His gaze went immediately to the cash lying on the desk, and though she was sure she detected a flicker of alarm in his eyes, it was gone in an instant. In a stiff, expressionless manner he said, "My wife wishes to know if you will be taking tea with the countess in her suite."

Alice glanced at the clock on the mantel and was surprised to discover that it was almost four.

"Yes," she said, "but first I have some questions about the accounts." She nodded toward the cash. "I cannot find any record of these monies in the ledgers."

"That is because there is none."

She waited, but he did not elaborate. "And why is that? Or must I ask the countess?"

He shrugged. "The money arrived yesterday. I simply have not had an opportunity to record the transaction and take it to the bank."

Her right eyebrow lifted slightly. "Two-thousand roubles is an excessive amount of cash to have just lying about with no record of its existence."

"It was hardly lying about," he snapped, adding in a more even tone, "If you remember, that drawer was securely locked."

Alice smiled. "Then I can expect to find the entry in the journal when I check it tomorrow?" She pulled one of the waybills from the stack and pointed to the routing instructions. "This is your writing, is it not? Surely you must know that such a complicated route increases the chances that supplies will go missing?"

"Of course, you are not a true Russian, so you cannot be expected to understand our distribution system." He waved his hand dismissively, but there was something in his voice and expression that made her glad there was a desk between them. "It is why such things should be left in the hands of those who do."

"Nor am I a bee," she said, "but that won't stop me from discovering where they hide their honey." She opened the ledger and pointed to one of the pencilled initials. "What does this 'MB' mean?"

"It means nothing."

"And yet it is beside every entry in which supplies have gone missing."

"Enough!" he hissed, banging his fist on the desk. Leaning forward, he thrust his face within inches of her own. "Your meddling endangers the countess!"

Her heart pounded erratically, and his breath on her cheek sickened her. Still, forcing herself not to draw back, she met his stare without blinking, and at last he straightened.

"If there are discrepancies in the shipments," he said coldly, "I promise it will be the countess who is incriminated, not I." Turning abruptly, he left the room, and only when the door closed behind him did Alice's heartbeat settle back to a normal rhythm.

☙❧

The office of the chief clerk of the Petrograd Hospital Supply Depot was a dingy, windowless room, the air stale and all the lesser-used surfaces coated with dust, but everything within the office appeared to be organized. Cabinets were boldly labelled, as were the ledgers arranged on the shelves, and the desks were tidy, including two being used by younger clerks, one of whom was deftly manipulating the wooden beads of an abacus. Even the chief clerk was tidy, his face and head shaved smooth. He was a dour little man, but he was eager to help.

"Losing supplies is a black mark against all of us here at the depot," he said mournfully.

Alice pulled the waybills from her bag and set them on the counter. "The ones for the shipments with missing supplies are on top, but I'm afraid I didn't find out very much. Except that someone with the initials 'MB' might be involved."

The chief clerk, who had begun shuffling through the papers, muttered the initials to himself. Then he smiled. "Mikhail Ivanov Bobronski! He is the chief medical officer with the Tolchnov Regiment. My daughter is one of their field nurses."

"A doctor? Well, I suppose that would make sense, diverting medical supplies to your own unit." She didn't bother to hide her disappointment that Feliks was not involved in some nefarious scheme, but the chief clerk didn't seem to notice her reaction. He was studying the waybill for the morphine shipment.

"They may have been diverted, but not to Doctor Bobronski's unit." He tapped the waybill with a bony forefinger. "The day this shipment went missing, they were down to their last few vials of morphine. My daughter called and pleaded with me to send them a fresh supply at once. Fortunately, it only had to travel to Viazma."

Alice stared at him. "But Viazma is where our supplies went missing." It was also, she remembered, the postmark on the envelope of cash.

He fingered the rest of the waybills, muttering to himself once more. Then, scooping up those with missing supplies, he hastened to the only unoccupied desk. After studying a thick ledger for several minutes and comparing entries with the information on the waybills, he said triumphantly, "Every one of the missing shipments coincides with a troop transfer. Whoever is responsible would know that the station would be chaotic at these times, making it much easier to interfere with a shipment."

"And a chief medical officer stationed in Viazma would certainly be aware of when troop transfers were about to happen!" Alice smacked the counter with the flat of her hand, causing the two junior clerks to look up. "We must report this to the authorities!"

For the first time, the chief clerk looked uneasy. After glaring at the junior clerks, who hastily returned to their own work, he closed the ledger and, clutching the waybills to his chest, returned to the counter. In a voice too low for anyone except Alice to hear, he said, "A chief medical officer has much influence. To make accusations against him could cause ... difficulties."

"But soldiers are suffering horribly because the medical units can't get supplies!" Alice protested, lowering her voice to match his own. "We have to speak up."

The clerk shook his head. "It is better that we simply make sure the shipments are no longer routed through Viazma."

Alice protested again but soon realized that the man's fear was much greater than his compassion. And without his help there was no way she could support any accusation against the doctor or Feliks.

※

The following morning Alice met Oksana for a walk along the banks of the frozen Neva River.

"I know that Feliks is involved, Oksana. But if I go to the authorities he'll see to it that the blame falls directly onto the countess. And he's devious enough to get away with it."

"At least you made him donate that money to the hospital."

Alice smiled, remembering the furious expression on the secretary's face when she insisted on checking for the donation entry in the hospital journal. They paused to observe a group of children skating on the ice below.

"You must be careful of him," Oksana warned. "He sounds like a very dangerous man."

"Don't worry. I'm a Canadian citizen. He can't touch me."

Oksana shook her head. "Do you really think there are no foreigners in Russian prisons?"

"I suppose that was a bit naïve," Alice agreed as they began walking once more. "But there has to be some way to stop him!"

"At the hospital when something goes wrong, we tell the matron," Oksana said sympathetically. "She always knows what to do."

"Well, in this case, I don't have a matron to tell," Alice said then suddenly stopped. "Or do I?" She gave her startled friend a hug. "Oksana, you are brilliant!"

A few nights later, wearing yet another of the gowns discarded by the Baroness Cervinka's daughter, she attended a dinner being held in General Banketik's honour. Seated on a tiny sofa that barely held two people, the old soldier was listening to a particularly talkative young countess describe a séance led by the priest Rasputin.

"We saw the holy man transformed before us," she gushed. "His eyes glowed like embers from a hot fire, and then he spoke and his voice! Well, no one who had ever met Count Venovich could deny it was his voice coming from the holy man's mouth!"

"Well, well," General Banketik said politely, although he had previously told Alice he considered the priest an unholy fraud. "What a privilege to witness such a scene!"

Alice suppressed a smile and waited patiently until the countess finally rose to greet a "dear friend" who had just arrived. As Alice slid into her seat, the general said gratefully, "I thought I should go mad listening to her ramble on about that insufferable man!"

A waiter brought them glasses of *faux champagne* and Alice used the interruption to change the subject.

"Do you know, General," she said, as if she were disclosing a great secret, "that everyone connected to my cousin's hospitals calls you the tsar of the field hospitals?"

"Oh, tush, my dear!" he chuckled, with a wave of his hand and a nervous glance around. "Such a comparison could get me in trouble with His Excellency."

"All the same, sir, I can't help but think someone as important as yourself would carry great weight with those in charge of drafting soldiers for the front."

"Well, that I do, indeed, my dear! It just so happens my wife's brother has command of that department here in Petrograd." He gave a conspiratorial wink. "I've sent him the names of more than one agitator who found the trenches a suitable grave for his seditious ideas."

"Well, I'll tell you, *Monsieur* General, if I had that kind of influence, there's one person I'd love to see getting a taste of the front lines."

He stuffed a *blini* piled high with caviar into his mouth and chewed noisily. "And who might that be?"

Pulling slightly away lest he start to cough, Alice said with feigned reluctance, "My cousin's secretary, Feliks Stolin."

The general swallowed, then emptied his champagne glass in a single gulp. Immediately, one of the servers took his glass and replaced it with a full one.

"Feliks Stolin .... hmmm. I believe I've heard his name mentioned ... not sure where. Supply depot, perhaps?" He moved so close his sweaty cheek brushed hers and she was showered with a garlic mist. "And what has this Stolin fellow done that has so outraged you, hmmm?"

"Well ... I cannot prove this, but I'm very sure he's responsible for diverting some of our medical supplies to places other than our field hospitals."

"Indeed?" His heavy brows drew together. Then he squeezed her hand and graced her with a leer. "Well, my dear, you might have more influence than you think."

"You are a naughty one, sir," she said. "But if that is true, those soldiers who follow you so bravely will be grateful."

At that moment dinner was announced, and with relief she rose to her feet and headed for her place at the table—pausing discreetly to wipe the general's sweat from her cheek. She was pleased to find herself seated far away from him.

∽◊∾

A week later Alice returned to the countess's house after a brief visit with Oksana to find Grusha waiting for her in the foyer, her face flushed with fury.

"It was *your* doing!"

Alice removed her cloak. "I don't know what you're talking about, Grusha. What is my doing?"

"My Feliks has been conscripted," the housekeeper hissed. "And we both know why. You've been out to get him ever since you arrived here!"

A mixture of relief and consternation flooded Alice. "It's far more likely, Grusha, that Feliks was caught stealing," she said crisply. "And if that's the case, you can count your lucky stars he was sent to fight and not to the tsar's prison."

Grusha drew her immense bulk into an outraged huff. "Feliks is a hero to Russia, not a thief," she snapped. "He gives relief to those our emperor has forgotten."

"By taking from soldiers who are out there risking their lives for them?" Alice found the image of her cousin's secretary as a Slavic Robin Hood almost laughable.

"Is that why you think the Russian soldier fights? To save little children starving in the streets?" Grusha shook her head. "You are a stupid foreigner!"

Swinging about, she stomped off to her own quarters leaving Alice both angry and disturbed. She thought of the soldiers she'd seen on the street that day, all of them with rows of little photographs of Princess Tatiana pinned among the medals on their chests, signifying that they had donated many times to her fund for bread and clothing for the war-ravaged people of Poland. Grusha was ridiculous, of course. Feliks was a petty thief, and nothing would convince Alice otherwise. But as she climbed wearily to her own room, she thought also of the beggars she encountered every day who were dressed in rags that could not possibly keep them warm and crying for scraps of bread just to get them through another long cold night on the streets.

ZGARDY
Summer 1916

Bailiff Wojcik did not come again to the Tcychowski farm, but the Austrian soldiers remained in the village until the early summer of 1916 when a second Russian advance pushed them westward again. Fearing revenge for having revealed the location of the villagers' sheep, the bailiff and his wife went with them.

"When Kaja Wojcik looked back and saw her house in flames along with all of her beautiful furniture," Luba Vitovsky reported at school the next day, "her shrieks could be heard throughout the whole village! Of course, it was the molfar's curse that did it."

Yuliya repeated the story to her mother.

"Bailiff Wojcik sinned and the Lord punishes all sinners," Zhanna said, contemptuously dismissing the notion that the molfar had anything to do with the bailiff's departure. But she also remained convinced the disasters that had befallen her own family were a divine retribution for Vasyl's pride in the tapestry and his connection to the Russian countess. Terrified that even worse would happen if she and her children did not make suitable amends, she now insisted that they not only submit to prayers several times a day, but also do penance by fasting for trespasses both real and imagined.

"She only does it so we won't eat as much," Natalya said in the shelter one afternoon when she and Yuliya opened the meagre supply of *kulesha* and cheese their mother had sent with them to the meadow.

Yuliya snatched the food pack from her hands. "It's wrong to say such things about our mother," she scolded and thrust an icon of Christ on the cross close to her sister's face. "You must repent or God will see that you burn in the darkest pits of hell!"

Natalya pushed the icon away. "You're not Father Ishchak."

Yuliya tightened her hold on the pack. "If you don't repent, you will get no food!"

"Keep it then," Natalya said indifferently and, ducking her head, she went outside.

Savruk crouched near the shelter, his eyes fixed on the sheep grazing nearby. During the winter Zhanna had been forced to trade one of the mature ewes and the young ram that had been born the previous spring for grain and corn, but in late March the two remaining ewes had lambed and already their offspring had almost reached full size.

Natalya adjusted her scarf and squinted at the cloudless sky. It was going to be a warm day and fishing in the cool woods suddenly seemed a much better alternative than picking berries on the meadow or tackling the bag of mending their mother had sent with them. From behind the shelter she collected her father's old fishing rod that she had found in the barn a week earlier. Although she had tried it out several times since then, she had not managed to catch anything so far.

Today will be different, she told herself as she dug up a handful of worms and stuffed them into the pocket of her apron. She gave Savruk the order to stay then followed the creek to a small pool where she had often seen trout swimming in the shadows. Carefully threading a worm onto the hook as she'd seen her father do, she surveyed a spot near the middle of the pond where the water slowly circled a large rock.

"Watch for eddies," her father had told Oleksi once when the two of them were planning a fishing trip. "That's where trout like to rest and feed."

But as Natalya cast toward the small whirlpool, her worm flew in one direction while the hook and line fell in a tangle about her feet. Frowning, she wove the hook more carefully into another worm, and tossed it out again. This time it landed close to the eddy and as it disappeared beneath the surface she felt a tug on her line. An instant later a sleek brown trout leapt from the water.

"I've got you!" she cried, but she was too slow in pulling the line taut, and the fish dislodged the hook and swam away. Disappointed but determined, she kept trying and finally near midday she felt the satisfying tug once more. This time she managed to set the hook and keep the line taut as she worked the trout close enough to flip it onto the shore.

She tried again and again but the light was already fading from the forest by the time she was able to land a second trout. Satisfied she had enough for dinner, she returned to the meadow.

Savruk barked his relief at her return, but Yuliya was furious.

"You haven't milked your sheep!" she shouted.

Natalya shrugged. "No matter. I'll do it now."

Setting her fish down, she grabbed her milking bucket, crouched beside the ewe that she usually cared for and expertly squeezed out at least a third more milk than Yuliya ever managed to get from her sheep.

"That's only because you've left her so late," Yuliya grumbled.

Without answering, Natalya poured the milk into one of the jugs they had brought from home and set the container in the creek where it would stay cool.

It was dark when she fixed a small fire outside the shelter, and by the flickering light of the flames cleaned the trout, feeding the intestines to Savruk. Threading one of the fish onto a beech switch, she held it over the coals to roast.

Yuliya sat on the ground in front of the shelter and scowled hungrily at the cooking fish.

She can starve for all I care, Natalya thought, but after inhaling the sweet, savoury odours of the trout as it cooked, she stole a glance at her sister. Everyone in the family had grown thin over the winter, but Yuliya had seemed to suffer more from hunger than anyone. Sometimes the pain in her stomach had been so bad she cried herself to sleep.

Natalya sighed. *I suppose Yuliya cannot help being Yuliya any more than I can help being Natalya*, she decided, and pulling one of the fish away from the coals, she held it out to her sister.

❦

Although Zhanna was afraid the soldiers would return and find their sheep at home, she was even more afraid of offending God by keeping her daughters from church. Her compromise, after consulting with Father Ishchak, was to have the girls return home every Saturday night so they could attend services on Sunday and collect their school lessons for the following week. At daybreak on Monday they would go back to the meadow.

One Sunday after attending morning mass, Zhanna worked in the graveyard tidying the graves of Vasyl and her babies while Catherine, Yuliya and Leysa attended choir practice led by Lydiya Vitovskyi. In a small, stuffy backroom next door to the choir room, Natalya helped give catechism lessons to the younger village children, while Pylyp, now two years old, played on the floor. Tired from her week on the meadow, she struggled to stay awake as Father Ishchak's wife droned out biblical stories against the backdrop of the choir. Only Catherine's voice, rising sweet and clear above the other singers, kept Natalya from falling asleep.

"Our daughter has a voice that angels would trade their wings to hear," her father had once said. The older Catherine grew and the sadder her life became, the more feeling she seemed to impart into her songs, and on this day the full weight of her sorrow wrapped itself around Natalya with the haunting chorale of "With the Smoke of Fires."

> "*Forever a crown of thorns has grown into our brows
> As a monument to your anger ... .*"

When they returned to the farm, Natalya changed her clothes and went outside to hoe the garden. The spring had been cold and wet, but with the long sunny days of early summer, the greens, peas, carrots and beans were flourishing, and the tops of the swollen beetroots were now rising up from their earthy beds. In the corn field that Boris Vitovsky had helped her mother plow and reseed, the husks were beginning to fatten. Even the four chicks hatched by the hen in the loft had matured and were now laying eggs of their own.

"Mama worries the soldiers will return," Catherine said when she and Natalya were shelling peas for the evening meal. "No matter what task she is working on, her eyes go constantly to the road, and the sound of horses passing is enough to make her tremble."

"Are you afraid, too?" Natalya asked studying Catherine's drawn features.

Her sister shrugged. "Fear is for the living," she said with unaccustomed bitterness. Then she managed a wan smile. "Of course I am afraid. But it will not help our mother to show this, will it? So I think only of what we must do today."

Natalya snapped a pod. "If the soldiers come again, I'll kill them!"

※

The following morning Natalya, who usually arose before anyone else, found her mother already in the kitchen preparing a large pot of *kasha*.

"Come, daughters!" she called, and when they were all seated at the table she scooped lavish portions of the porridge into their bowls. Ignoring their astonishment, she launched into a story that made Natalya wonder if her mother had crossed the line between reality and insanity.

"Last night, my children, I was visited by the Angel Gabriel!" She smiled benignly at them all, even Yuliya, who was stuffing *kasha* into her mouth as if she might never get another chance to eat. "In a dream he came and instructed me to build a cellar."

"But Mama," Cathcrine said carefully, "we already have a cellar and it is empty."

Zhanna nodded emphatically. "A cellar that can be easily discovered, yes. This new cellar shall be hidden in the woods. The angel showed me exactly where it will be!" With glowing eyes she explained how the angel in her dream had taken her to the grove of beech saplings where Natalya and Yuliya had hidden when their father was killed and told her that within that grove she was to build a cellar disguised as a mound of rocks and sod.

"So eat well, because today we are going to work very hard."

As soon as breakfast was over and the dishes cleared away, they gathered tools and trooped across the paddock to the beech grove and set to work. While Catherine and Yuliya helped their mother pull and dig saplings and brush from the ground, Leysa watched over Pylyp who, now that he was walking, was constantly getting into mischief. Natalya's job was to haul away the debris, cutting and stacking anything that could be burned next to the house and dumping the rest over the edge of a small cliff.

The day was warm and Yuliya soon grew tired of swinging the heavy pick. Once, after almost falling backwards when the root she was tugging suddenly gave way, she said crossly, "Surely we don't have to fear the soldiers now that the Russians have driven them from Zgardy."

"One army is no different from another," her mother said, twisting a stubborn sapling free from its hold. "When men go to war, God is chased from their hearts. They are hunters and killers, and all who cross their paths are mere stones to be trodden over as they stalk their prey."

The bitterness in her voice silenced Yuliya's complaints until midmorning when she began moaning of the hunger that gnawed at her stomach. But it was well past midday before

Zhanna agreed to stop for a brief lunch of *kulesha* and cheese.

As the day wore on, they grew progressively more scratched, bruised and exhausted, but by dark they had cleared the site. Setting their tools aside, they trooped wearily back to the house where Leysa, who had returned earlier, had soup and freshly baked *kulesha* waiting. The next morning they rose early and were back working before the sun touched the meadow.

While Zhanna, Catherine and Yuliya tackled the digging, Natalya continued to cut wood and haul branches away.

"Nothing must remain to show we've worked here," her mother insisted. "And no one—not even Father Ishchak—must know what we are doing!"

By midmorning Yuliya's complaints were getting almost too tiresome for Natalya to bear, and she was glad to escape with Zirka, who was laden with bundles of branches cut to burnable lengths. She removed the bundles and was stacking the wood in the lean-to at the back of the house when Zirka lifted his head and snorted. In the same instant she heard Savruk barking in the paddock where he was guarding the sheep.

Heart pounding, she straightened her apron and her scarf and, leaving Zirka tied to the lean-to, hurried to the front of the house.

A bedraggled horse stood near the steps where a haggard, unkempt man sat with his elbows propped on his knees. His chin rested in his cupped hands and hid part but not all of the raised scars disfiguring the right side of his face. A patch covered his right eye, but his profile was familiar, and Natalya's hand flew to her mouth as she recognized Lech Wojcik.

She thought instantly of the cellar they were building, and then of Catherine. Somehow she had to keep him away from both! But Leysa would soon be coming with Pylyp to make lunch and her mother, Catherine and Yuliya might come with her. Especially, Natalya thought, if they heard Savruk barking. She whistled at once for the dog and as he raced to her side she signalled him to stop barking and follow behind her.

Lech straightened at her approach and a relieved smile touched his lips. "I thought everyone was gone."

Savruk growled low in his throat and she signalled again for him to stay quiet.

"They *are* gone. There's only me. They won't be back till long after dark."

He arched his left brow. "Natalya, yes?"

She nodded curtly.

"You have grown up." His gaze flicked past her to the yard

where, except for a pair of dragonflies chasing each other over a tired clump of white daisies, nothing moved. "I was hoping ... ." He held both hands out, palms up, as if reaching for something he couldn't quite see. "I wanted ..." He gave a defeated wave and said wearily, "I would like to leave a note for Catherine."

Natalya toed the grass with her sandal. She didn't want him to write a note to anyone, especially not to Catherine. But neither did she want him to linger.

"Do you have paper?" he prodded. "A pen?"

Clamping her lips together, she edged past him up the steps and disappeared into the house. A moment later she returned with her mother's writing tablet, a bottle of ink and a pen.

"I have chores to do," she said as she handed them to him.

"Please, do not let me stop you. I will write the note and then find you."

But she did not dare to leave him alone or to have him wandering about in search of her. "I'll wait."

Sending Savruk back to the pasture, she settled herself on the grass below the steps and contemplated him as he frowned down at the paper. From the front his face didn't seem quite so deformed, and from the left side he was as handsome as ever. And there was still a lost look about him that she had to harden her heart against by reminding herself he was a Wojcik, and Wojciks could never, ever be trusted.

At last he dipped the pen into the ink, tapped it against the edge of the bottle, and using the porch as a table, began to write. Without being obvious, Natalya glanced toward the paddock and the beech grove beyond it. *God, please don't let them come home now!* She jumped every time she heard a sound, but he was so engrossed in his letter he didn't seem to notice. She wished he would write faster and not pause so long between sentences. What could he possibly have to say that took so many words? When he filled one page and moved onto a second, she cringed. Paper was precious and used only for letters to Oleksi, but she feared any objection she made would take even more time.

At last, having filled the second page, he set the pen aside and when the ink had dried, he folded both sheets of paper carefully and handed them to Natalya.

"Give this to Catherine as soon as she returns," he begged. "Please."

Hoping a visual lie was not as great a sin as a verbal one, she nodded and was relieved when he got to his feet. Still, he didn't immediately head for his horse.

"Would you have some water?"

She raced inside and filled a cup from the water bucket on the counter and returned. He drank without a pause then handed her the empty cup.

"I'll be off then," he said reluctantly.

As he mounted his horse she thought she heard voices near the far edge of the paddock, but Lech must not have noticed because he turned his horse slowly about and rode from the yard. As soon as he was safely through the gate, Natalya grabbed up the writing supplies and carried them into the house, putting them away just as someone clomped up the steps to the porch.

"So there you are," Yuliya said accusingly as Natalya met her at the door. "Idling about the house while we work ourselves to death on the cellar."

"I was getting a drink of water," Natalya said, terrified her sister would see the outline of the letter she had tucked into her apron pocket. "I have to finish unloading Zirka."

Her mother, Catherine and Leysa, with Pylyp in tow, were climbing the steps when she hurried outside. Muttering the same excuse she had given Yuliya, she hurried past them and around to the lean-to. There she read what Lech had written.

> *Dearest keeper of my heart and soul, how I have yearned for you, and how grey my life has been without your light! So much has happened since I was ordered from Zgardy by my father, and you may have heard that I have married. It is a loveless match arranged for convenience and nothing more. How could it be anything else, when my heart is yours?*
>
> *I am here for three days at the request of the baron who wishes me to take care of some critical matters on his estate. I pray ... if you love me still ... that you will come to me there. I believe we were meant to be together, that apart we are mere shadows of ourselves, halves that are ever-seeking to be reunited. If this is your belief as well, we shall find a way, my love, to be together.*
>
> *My soul waits for you.*
> *Your own always and forever, Lech.*

"Natalya?" Catherine's voice preceded her, giving Natalya just enough time to stuff the letter into the woodpile before she faced her sister.

"Is anything wrong, Natalya? You seemed very upset when you went past us."

"Nothing's wrong," Natalya said as she added more wood to the pile. "I just wanted to finish this task."

"We heard Savruk barking," Catherine persisted, "and Mama thought she saw a horse and rider rounding the corner when we came into the yard."

Natalya shrugged. "Perhaps someone passed by while I was in the house." She tried to sound reassuring. "I wasn't feeling well, so I stopped a moment to rest. I'm sorry."

Instantly concerned, Catherine put a hand to Natalya's forehead. "Don't be sorry. If you aren't well, you should rest."

Ashamed of both the lie and of hiding the letter, Natalya could scarcely bear to look at her sister.

"I'll be fine, Catherine." She untied the horse's rope. "I'll just put Zirka in the paddock and come in for lunch."

Catherine observed her for a moment then nodded and, to Natalya's relief, headed back around the house.

⁂

The pit, when it was finished two days later, was waist deep, but twice as long and wide. Four large beech trees that Catherine and their mother had felled and which Zirka hauled to the clearing were cut into corner posts and cross beams. Lined with poles and covered with sod, the roof protruded less than a metre above the ground, yet the cellar below was roomy enough for Zhanna to enter, although she had to bend almost double to do so. And when the sod was covered with leaf litter and the entranceway hidden by transplanted willows, the cellar blended into the natural lay of the land.

Zhanna surveyed it critically. "It will do," she said. "We will put half our harvest in the cellar beneath our house, and half in this one."

There was an assurance about her that had been missing ever since their father was killed, and as they walked slowly back to the house, Natalya felt some of that confidence seeping into her own heart. They were going to survive.

She did not allow herself to think of the letter that was now buried beneath several loads of wood in the lean-to. She had not yet found the courage to destroy it.

PETROGRAD
September 1916

The countess was close to bankruptcy. As Alice probed deeper into her financial affairs, she discovered that her cousin had sold many of her income-producing properties in order to fund the Federov Hospital. Fortunately, it was now being financed through donations from Baroness Cervinka and her friends, but there was not enough left in the countess's personal estate to cover all her household expenses.

"We cannot afford Grusha's wages," Alice told her. "And I can manage the household as well as she does."

But her cousin was firm. The rest of the staff could be let go, but the housekeeper would stay.

"I won't cook and I won't clean," Grusha said disdainfully when she was informed of the changes. "Those are not my jobs."

With some difficulty, Alice found a cook willing to work for little more than her meals and lodging, and Ludmila, the scullery maid, pleaded to be allowed to stay on under the same conditions as she had no place to go. Within weeks, however, their attitude had shifted from gratitude to resentment, and although she had no way of proving it, Alice suspected Grusha was behind the transformation.

"Everyone seems upset these days," Alice complained to Oksana one afternoon in early September. "Even at the dinners I attend. The smiles are there and the chatter is as ridiculous as ever, but under it all I sense uneasiness." They were working together again, Alice having been called to help with a rush of wounded soldiers who had arrived that morning from the front.

"You're not imagining it," her friend said. "There is much anger everywhere. People are hungry and tired of the war. They ask for bread and peace and the tsar gives them empty speeches." She smiled encouragingly at the young man the sanitars had just carried to the dressing table and began unwinding the filthy dressing that was wrapped about the stub of his leg. The gangrenous stench had prepared both sisters for the black, pus-filled wound underneath, and though she tried to keep her face impassive, Alice winced when she saw how far the infection had spread. There was nothing that could be done now except clean the wound and keep the boy as comfortable as they could for the little time he had left.

"They ran out of disinfectants at the field hospital," Oksana said grimly.

That afternoon Alice walked home because the streetcars were on strike. She took Marata Street, which was quieter, past the five-domed Vladimirskaya Church and down Ghorkovaya Prospekt to St. Isaacs. Normally, it was a delightful walk over picturesque canals and past well-groomed gardens, but today there were piles of garbage everywhere as the street workers were also on strike, and outside every bakery were long lines of people hoping desperately that there would be something left when they got to the counter. By the time she reached the countess's house, she was so despondent she almost missed the telegram that had been placed on the console in the hallway.

> *Granted 10 day leave STOP Petrograd Tues 11 STOP Tusya*

Alice read the lines twice before she allowed herself to believe them. Then, realizing that she had only one full day to prepare for their visit, she rushed upstairs to change and to tell her cousin the good news.

❧

On Tuesday afternoon Alice hastened to the kitchen to ensure the wild goose she had helped the cook prepare earlier that morning was still simmering in a vegetable-laden broth. It had been a long time since such delicious odours had emanated from these quarters, and she sent a mental thank-you to her father for the ten Canadian silver dollars he had sent her. By flashing one of the dollars under the nose of the butcher, she had convinced him to set the goose aside for her. A second coin had bought her a basket filled with potatoes, onions, garlic and carrots and a precious loaf of bread, and a third had been exchanged for enough kopeks to encourage the cook to stay sober for most of the day and for Ludmila to help her clean the house.

Satisfied the meal would be ready in time for her brother's arrival, she went upstairs to change into a dinner gown.

When Tusya and Oleksi arrived an hour later, Alice had to stifle a cry of dismay. Dressed in ragged uniforms, they looked gaunt and exhausted and smelled as if they hadn't bathed in the five months since she'd last seen them. Forcing back her tears, she frowned at them and, wrinkling her nose in distaste, fanned the air with her hand.

"You two would attract flies in a blizzard," she complained. "Has the army suddenly run out of water?"

Tusya turned to Oleksi in astonishment. "Tell me, my good friend, do you know this pretentious peacock?"

Oleksi peered at Alice then shook his head. "Could it be we have entered a public house by mistake?"

Alice was unable to prevent the embarrassed heat colouring her cheeks. "I'll have you know this dress belonged to the daughter of Baroness Cervinka! Not that you two louts would be expected to know the difference."

"Louts, is it?" Tusya arched his eyebrows. "Then perhaps Oleksi and I shall take ourselves to a place where we are welcomed and not scorned."

"Good luck finding that in your condition!" She inclined her head toward the stairs. "There's a bath waiting and clean clothes have been laid out in your rooms."

Oleksi audibly inhaled the aromas drifting from the kitchen. "I, for one, would not mind trading my cargo of fleas and filth for a hearty meal."

Tusya agreed, but as they headed for the stairs, Alice placed a hand on Oleksi's arm. "I'm sorry about your father," she said quietly. Their eyes met and she felt like weeping at the anguish she saw in his.

"As am I," he said stiffly. Then he gave her hand a gentle squeeze and followed her brother. She stood for a long moment until the warmth of his touch was gone then hurried into the kitchen to check the stew.

Grusha had grudgingly agreed to serve the meal, partly because she was promised even more kopeks than the cook and charwoman had received but mostly, Alice suspected, so that she could eavesdrop on any conversations in the dining room.

When Tusya and Oleksi reappeared an hour later, bathed, shaved and dressed in the dinner suits Alice had laid out for them, they were astonished to find only two places set at the table.

"I must attend a dinner at the home of General Banketik," she said regretfully. "The whole party is then attending a ballet performance at the Mariinsky Theatre."

Her brother wagged his head. "Ooooh-la-la! Dinner *and* the ballet." He made a face at Oleksi, who was hungrily eying the bowl of stew Grusha was setting on the table, alongside part of the loaf of bread.

Alice felt her temper rising, but she waited until the housekeeper had left the room before she turned on her brother. "Don't think for one minute, Tusya Galipova, that I enjoy sitting for hours listening to that drunken old fool."

Oleksi looked at her solemnly. "Then why do it?"

She splayed her hands. "I have no choice. The countess is too ill to campaign for her hospitals and the only hope we have of getting the funds and supplies we need is to make sure those in command remember why the hospitals are important."

"Doesn't seem to me like you're having much success," Tusya said. "Our surgeons have been operating without ether because the last shipment was waylaid."

Alice remembered the young man she had treated two days earlier. She glanced at the door and switched to English, speaking slowly for Oleksi's benefit. "Thanks to General Banketik, the supply line should start to improve," she said and quietly told them how she had managed to stop Feliks from sidelining the shipments.

"Why didn't you just report him to the police?" Tusya asked.

"Because I'm sure he was paying off the police. He said if I made a fuss about it he would see that the countess was blamed for any shipments that went missing. Besides, I couldn't upset her. She trusted Feliks and the shock of his betrayal could have brought on a heart attack." She glanced again at the door. "Grusha is pretty certain I am behind his banishment to the front lines."

Tusya snorted. "She's fortunate both she and her husband aren't in prison right now."

"That's not how she sees it," Alice said. "And the alarming part is that they both have strong connections with the Bolsheviks."

She broke off as a sturdy knocking sounded on the dining room door. Grusha entered, glared at all of them and said, as if she were issuing a rebuke to a staff member, "Your carriage has arrived, *Mademoiselle*."

When General Banketik learned that Alice's brother was in the city, he immediately sent one of his staff to the countess's residence with a carriage and two tickets to the ballet. Unfortunately, the seats were in the main audience section. From there, Tusya and Oleksi could see everything that happened in the general's balcony box, including his clumsy advances toward Alice. What they could not see was the skill with which she fended off those advances. Still, she was relieved when the performance was over and eagerly hurried to the foyer where they were to meet her.

Oleksi stood out among the people milling about the large lobby, and when she caught sight of him, Alice's heart skipped a beat. But as she drew closer, she saw his face was dark with anger.

"Your general is an animal with no honour."

Relieved that General Banketik had been called away as soon as the ballet ended, Alice said soothingly, "He's just an old man trying to be young." She nodded to a woman she had met at one of Baroness Cervinka's parties, then led the way through the crowd to the broad courtyard outside the theatre.

"Where's Tusya?" she asked, surprised he was not there waiting for them.

Oleksi's frown deepened. "He went off with a woman who was seated next to us." Grimly taking her arm, he escorted her to a long line of carriages, and helped her into the one that had been designated for them. As he settled into the seat beside her, he shook his head. "I don't understand Russian morality. Women flaunting themselves at men like tavern harlots. You're worse than the Poles!"

Alice's cheeks grew warm. "Are you implying that I am immoral?"

He shrugged. "The way you allowed that old man to be so familiar with you, what else can I think?"

His words were like a lash across her face.

"You could trust that I am a lady of good character and sound judgement," she said cuttingly. Moving as far from him as the small carriage would allow, she stared out at the dark canal they were passing. The evening was cool and the lamps bordering the embankment illuminated the mists drifting up from the water. Except for the clop-clopping of the horse's hooves on the stone pavement, the carriage was silent.

When they reached the countess's house, Oleksi jumped out and offered his hand to her. Alice ignored him and climbed down by herself. She entered the house and slammed the door in his face. Halfway up the stairs, she realized he wasn't coming in. Running back down, she flew to the entranceway and opened the door, but there was no one on the steps or on the street. Both Oleksi and the carriage had disappeared.

※

The effects of overindulgence and lack of sleep were evident in Tusya's unshaven face and bloodshot eyes, and he was in no mood to listen to Alice's complaints about his friend.

"Don't be so harsh, Ali," he groaned, holding his hands to either side of his head. "The poor man's father was killed by the Austrians and as far as he's concerned, his favourite sister betrayed the family." He explained how Catherine and Lech's love affair had caused Vasyl Tcychowski's death. "It hasn't exactly put him in a tolerant frame of mind."

"Well, if he wasn't such a stick-in-the-mud, he'd realize that his sister didn't betray anyone. She just fell in love," Alice said, pushing aside her breakfast tea. She had spent most of the night listening for Oleksi's return and only in the early hours had she drifted into a restless sleep. "So when is our self-righteous friend coming down to breakfast?"

Tusya shrugged. "He's not here, and near as I can tell, his bed hasn't been slept in."

Alice's spirits sank even lower. "Where would he have gone?"

"I have no idea," he said, "but he'd better return soon because we have to leave on the 2:30 train."

"Leave?" Alice stared at him. "Please tell me you're not going on another secret mission."

"No, we're finished with that business. Only reason we volunteered was so Oleksi could see his family."

"But you have a week's leave!"

"I know, but we forfeited it in order to transfer to a field hospital that is closer to Petrograd. Our orders came last night before we left for the theatre. We're heading for Dvinsk—just south of Riga." He leaned forward, his forearms resting on the table. "I'm worried about you, Alice. You need to go back to Canada and take the countess with you."

A movement in the hallway caught her attention. Putting her fingers to her lips, she walked quietly to the entrance where she was certain she saw a black skirt disappearing into an adjoining room. Closing the door, she returned to her seat and once again spoke in English.

"We both need to go home, Tusya! This isn't our war."

"But it is," Tusya said. "Russia is our ally. Besides, even if I'd gone back to Canada, I would still have had to fight."

"In any case," Alice said regretfully, "the countess is far too weak to travel. There's no way I can leave her alone."

He grasped her hand. "You may have to, Alice. There are stories going about ... enough to make at least some of them believable. In one company, the troops not only refused to obey their commander's orders to advance but pulled him from his horse and threw him head-first into a village well."

Alice thought of General Banketik. As repulsive as he was, she couldn't bear to think of him dying in such an undignified manner.

"The tsar's soldiers have been no less brutal, Tusya. Last week the Cossacks charged right into the middle of a peaceful demonstration, bayonetting women and children along with the men." There was silence between them and then she said, "Until things settle down here, I cannot leave the countess."

❦

Oleksi did not return to the house until it was almost time to leave for the train, and he stayed only long enough to collect his gear. He did not acknowledge Alice, stoically ignoring her on the short journey to the station. There, fighting tears, she hugged Tusya and promised to send word if she needed him. Then she moved close to Oleksi, who was standing stern-faced on the platform. Speaking loudly so she would be heard over the din of engines, the clatter of trollies and the shouted farewells of departing passengers, she said, "In this war, my friend, we are sometimes forced to do things that in normal times would not make us proud. But you wrong me, Oleksi, when you say I am immoral. It would be a lot easier on you and everyone else if you let a little bit of grey into your life, instead of insisting that everything must be black or white."

His chin lifted and although, from the pulse throbbing in his cheek, she knew he was affected by what she said, he made no response and still refused to look at her.

"For all that," she added, her throat tight, "I care for you just the way you are."

A whistle sounded and Tusya said, "We'd better get aboard, brother, or we'll be marching to Riga!"

He gave Alice a final hug, and the two men hurried toward the troop car they were to board. She watched them in a blur, no longer able to check her tears. Every part of her wanted to rush after Oleksi and wrap her arms around him, and it took more willpower than she'd ever exerted to stand her ground as he stepped onto the train. Then suddenly he swung around, leapt back to the platform and ran to her, taking her in his arms and crushing her against his chest so tight she could feel his heart beating beneath his vest. Finally he kissed her, his lips rough against hers, sending a current of longing through her veins. A second whistle blew and with an anguished groan, he pulled away and ran for the train as it started from the station. Clambering aboard, he turned and shouted, "I love you, Alishka Galipova!"

"And I love you, Oleksi Tcychowski!"

In a rush of smoke and steam, the train lurched around a dark corner and was gone.

ZGARDY
October 1916

A series of chilling, drawn-out howls and Savruk's warning bark pulled Natalya from a deep sleep. She could hear Zirka snorting and pawing nervously where he was picketed just outside the shelter.

"They're too close," she said, throwing off her blanket. "We need to check the sheep."

The wolves howled again and Yuliya huddled deeper beneath her own cover. "I'm not going out there! Savruk will take care of them."

"And who will take care of Savruk?" Natalya pulled the curtain aside and stepped into the darkness, almost stumbling over one of the sheep that the dog had herded close to the shelter. She helped him hustle them inside and closed the curtain on them. Next she set about rebuilding the fire to keep the wolves away from Zirka. Then, with her blanket wrapped around her, a hatchet in her hand and Savruk crouched at her side, she sat with her back against the shelter and stared out at the darkness.

It's getting too dangerous to stay here, she thought as she listened to one particularly drawn-out wail. *It's time to pack everything up and go home for the winter.*

They left early the next morning and Natalya was surprised their mother made no objections when they arrived home.

"It is freezing harder each night," Zhanna said. "Better you are home before the snows come. And it's time you returned to school."

While Yuliya was delighted to be back in the house where it was warm and there was plenty of food, Natalya quickly escaped outdoors. Having cleaned the barn and completed every chore she could find to do, she began collecting wood to add to the pile that now almost filled the lean-to. As she worked, she tried not to think of Lech's letter hidden beneath the farthest row. She had meant to destroy it as soon as the new cellar was finished, but by the time there was an opportunity, her mother and sister had completed the pile and added a second row in front of it and there was no way she could take the piles apart without prompting questions she didn't dare answer.

When the lean-to was finally full, Natalya carried a load of wood into the house. A fish soup, made from her latest catch, was simmering on the stove and Catherine was slicing hot *kulesha* at the table. Pylyp was playing on the floor near the stove and their mother, Yuliya and Leysa were upstairs sewing.

"It's going to freeze again tonight," Natalya predicted, dumping her load into the wood box and removing her shawl. "The sky is clearing."

"It is a good thing you are no longer on the meadow," Catherine said. "You would ... ." She broke off as Savruk started barking in the yard.

Through the window they saw a white streak flash through the gate and out onto the trail leading to the village. A moment later an ancient grey mare ridden by a thin, unshaven officer with a bandaged forehead came into view. Behind him limped a ragged company of mud-spattered soldiers, some of them carrying stretchers bearing wounded men.

"Mama!" Natalya cried.

As Catherine lifted Pylyp from the floor, their mother raced downstairs. She was followed by Yuliya and Leysa.

"You two take Pylyp to your room," Zhanna ordered, grabbing her son from Catherine and thrusting him into Leysa's arms.

"There are eleven men, Mama," Natalya said as she watched the troop struggle through the gate. The men's uniforms were all different and she could not tell to which army they belonged.

Her mother pulled her from the window. "Go with your sisters!" she ordered sharply just as one of the men uttered a loud curse followed by an anguished yelp. Natalya wrenched her arm free, ran out the door and raced past the soldiers to the white dog writhing in the dirt.

"Savruk!"

Despite his pain, Savruk was struggling to rise from the ground but his hind legs could not support his weight. She stared horrified at the muddy boot print staining the dog's white coat.

"What have you done to him?" she shrieked, and dropping to her knees, she hugged the dog's head to her chest.

The officer leading the ragged troop rode up to the steps where Zhanna stood brandishing a broom and shouting, "Leave us be!"

He said with cold authority, "Your house is hereby requisitioned by the Imperial Russian Army, *kulak*. You have one half-hour to gather your things and leave."

Zhanna continued to wield her weapon until the one of the soldiers in the lead raised his rifle and pointed the barrel at her head.

"But we have no place to go!" she cried, lowering the broom.

"One minute has already passed." The officer nodded to the men carrying the stretchers. "Take them inside."

Although the two patients wore thick woollen greatcoats, they were shivering and they moaned incoherent prayers as they passed. When one of them feebly reached out, his hand filthy and covered with sores, Zhanna drew back then hurried into the house after them and began shouting orders to her daughters.

From a place far beyond herself, Natalya watched the officer dismount and saw Yuliya and Leysa emerge from the house, their arms laden with clothes and bedding from which protruded poorly hidden strings of garlic and onion, a sack Natalya knew was filled with dried beans, and a wreath of herbs that always hung near the stove.

"Take them to the barn," Zhanna shouted after the girls. "We will make our beds in the loft."

From the doorway, the officer ordered his men to carry their patients upstairs.

As Catherine, with Pylyp in one arm and a full basket in the other, ran down the steps and across the yard, Zhanna called sharply to her youngest daughter.

"Natalya! You must help!"

The urgency in her voice forced Natalya to her feet. "I'll be back, Savruk!" she promised and, racing to the porch, grabbed a basket her mother had filled with more food and covered with candles and clothing.

In the barn Yuliya was perched partway up the ladder to the loft and handing blankets through the hatch to Catherine. Trying to ignore Savruk's whimpering, Natalya lifted her burden to Yuliya, but just as her sister's fingers closed over the handle, the dog gave another anguished yelp and then was silent. Letting go of the basket, which Yuliya barely saved from dropping to the floor, Natalya raced from the barn.

Savruk lay where she'd left him, but now there was a red slash across his throat and his blood was spilling onto the ground. A young soldier, who appeared to be about the same age as Oleksi, wiped the blade of his bayonet on the dog's coat.

"His hip was broken," he said gently in Ukrainian. "He would only suffer." Then he rose to his feet and went inside the house.

Numbly, Natalya held Savruk's warm, limp body in her arms, not caring that his blood was soaking her blouse and skirt. From somewhere far away her mother called, but Natalya couldn't respond. She rocked back and forth mumbling, "Savruk, Savruk, Savruk ... ." As if saying his name would make his blood once again flow through instead of from his veins, would bring him back to life, would prompt him to raise his head and gently lick her hand. "Savruk, Savruk, Savruk ... ."

Darkness fell and a bright, full moon rose above the trees, while in the field the ewes called softly to each other. Then the barn door creaked open and soft footsteps approached.

"We will bury him in the paddock, Natalya," Catherine said.

Gradually Natalya stopped chanting and stared at the two shovels her oldest sister carried. Minutes passed, and then, still holding Savruk tight in her arms, she allowed Catherine to help her to her feet, and stagger with her load through the darkness to a moonlit corner of the field. Like a sleepwalker, she gently laid the dog in the grass and took up a shovel, forcing the blade into the stiff clay soil.

Natalya didn't cry at the burial, nor later when she sat near the fire pit someone had dug in Nich's burned-out stall. Arms wrapped tight about her knees, she watched the shifting shadows that haunted the darkest reaches of the barn. In one corner they touched the sheep milling about. Did the ewes sense, she wondered, that their protector was gone? Did Zirka know that Savruk had been killed? Was that why he was stomping and snorting in his stall? Or was he just disturbed by the presence of the grey mare who was sharing his small space?

A movement brought her attention back to the fire. Her mother bent over a pot of vegetables suspended on a tripod above the flames, gave a quick stir then straightened and said in a voice that failed to be reassuring, "Our Holy Mother is watching over us, children. We have this fine barn ... " She stopped as the outer door rattled open and along with a rush of cold air, the young man who had killed Savruk emerged from the darkness. In his arms he carried the Russian tapestry. As if motivated by a single thought, Zhanna's four daughters stepped back into the shadows.

"I found this beneath a mattress, Mother," he said, laying the rug at Zhanna's feet. "It is better that my comrades do not see it."

She frowned. "And why would such a tribute to his Imperial Majesty offend his soldiers?"

"Times have changed, Mother, and there are many among my brothers who believe that His Majesty has betrayed them." He removed his woollen toque and said softly, "Russia is not the same as it was when your Oleksi joined the ranks of His Majesty's service."

She sucked in her breath. "Who are you?" She leaned forward to peer into his face. "How do you know Oleksi?"

"I am Veniamin Michaelovich Kyrylenko, Mother," he said, thumping his chest with his fist. "And I am only here today because your son—when no other would dare—came onto the field where bullets were flying from every direction and carried me to safety."

"And you know where he is now?"

He shook his head. "I don't even know where my own company is. None of us do." With a wave of an arm he indicated the men occupying the farmhouse. "We have had no food for days and two of my comrades are suffering from typhus."

Zhanna stepped back from him, her eyes wide with alarm. "Typhus? You are sure?"

He nodded. "Yes. It is the reason we stopped here rather than pushing on to find our units." He hesitated then in a rush explained that the officer leading their small brigade had agreed to guarantee the family's safety if she would cook and help to care for the men who were ill.

"He is a man of honour, Mother. He will keep his word."

"A man of honour would not throw a widow and her children out of their home, Mr. Kyrylenko."

Natalya followed her mother's gaze as she surveyed each of her daughters standing in the shadows. Although thin, Catherine was still a beauty and so was Yuliya, with her golden sheen of long, wavy hair and deep blue eyes. Even fragile Leysa was fully a woman, and small as she was for a thirteen-year-old, Natalya had noticed men looking at her in a way that plainly said she was no longer a child.

"Tell your commander," her mother said at last, "that I accept his terms."

Veniamin nodded then gave a slight bow and left the barn, carefully closing the door behind him.

After morning prayers Zhanna called a family meeting.

"I will need Catherine's help in the kitchen," she said, inclining her head toward her eldest daughter, who was holding Pylyp, "but the rest of you must stay well away from the house."

Yuliya eyed the pot that had held the previous night's soup. "But what will we eat, Mama?"

"There's kale in the garden and beans and corn in the baskets. And there should be some eggs this morning. You can use two of them."

"I can catch some more trout," Natalya offered.

"No," her mother said sharply. "You are never to go out alone!"

"But, Mama ... ."

Zhanna held up her hand, silencing Natalya's protest. "God watches over us, daughters, but men are men, and soldiers do not always obey their commanders." Her stern gaze encompassed all of them. "No one goes out alone, and no one," she added, turning to Yuliya, "goes near the hidden cellar ... no matter how hungry you might be."

She wrapped her shawl around her shoulders. "Yuliya will be in charge," she said then headed resolutely to the door. Catherine handed Pylyp over to Leysa.

"Take good care of him," she pleaded.

There was much to do in the barn. As soon as they milked the ewes, the sheep and horses had to be taken to the paddock and their quarters cleaned. The loom that had been dismantled and stored in the loft earlier that fall was moved to a far corner and the girls then bundled straw and wove it into crude sleeping mats that they placed close together on the floor. Below the loft, near the fire pit, they fashioned an old sled into a table and arranged candles and the baskets of food. As Natalya worked, she tried to keep her thoughts away from Savruk, but by late afternoon the barn walls were closing in on her. She felt as if she couldn't breathe and was nearing panic until Leysa agreed to go with her to check on the animals.

"You and Pylyp should come, too," she told Yuliya, who was standing just inside the doorway, her gaze fixed on Veniamin as he carried an armload of wood to the house.

"Do whatever you wish," she said absently. "Just stay together."

In the meadow Natalya gathered a handful of summer daisies that were still blooming near the fence and placed them on the mound marking Savruk's grave.

"He was a good dog," Leysa said kindly, adding the flowers she had gathered.

Clearing her throat, Natalya dusted the dirt from her skirt. "He's with Papa," she said stoutly then set about searching for the last of the field mushrooms, trying all the while not to think of how much more fun it would have been with Savruk romping at her side.

It was long after dark when Zhanna and Catherine returned to the barn. As they stepped into the light of the fire, Natalya's hands flew to her mouth and both Yuliya and Leysa gasped.

"Your hair, Mama!" Yuliya cried, staring at the shaven heads of her mother and sister.

"It was the lice," Catherine said quietly. "We had to shave our heads because of the lice."

Unaware that anything was wrong, Pylyp toddled happily toward them, crying, "Mama! Mama!"

Instantly, Zhanna drew back.

"Do not let him come near us," she said, so sharply that Pylyp was startled and began to cry. Leysa picked him up and as she attempted to soothe him, her mother explained in a gentler voice that she did not want to contaminate them with typhus. "Catherine and I will sleep in the tack room."

As Pylyp's wails subsided, Leysa asked worriedly, "But will you not get sick, Mama?"

"No. I had typhus when I was a child."

"And Catherine?" Leysa persisted.

For a moment their mother was silent. Then, her voice resigned, she said, "We shall all pray for your sister."

Natalya shivered and Catherine gave her a comforting smile. "Don't worry, little one," she said softly. "I am strong, and Mama won't let me near the soldiers."

But Catherine wasn't strong at all, and Natalya knew if one of the sick soldiers needed assistance, her sister would never refuse to help him.

A cold, unsatisfying breakfast convinced Yuliya that a fat trout for their dinner was worth the risk of venturing into the woods. As soon as the chores were done, the four siblings set off for the small pool where Natalya had caught fish two days earlier but, though she fished all morning, she caught only one small trout.

"One fish is better than none," Lcysa said optimistically as they walked back along the trail. "We can make another soup!"

Yuliya frowned. "And this one won't go to the soldiers."

Natalya was trying to think where she might find a better fishing hole and was so lost in thought as she rounded a bend in the trail that she almost collided with Veniamin.

"Whoa, there!" he cried, putting a steadying hand on her shoulder.

He wasn't a tall man, nor did he seem particularly strong physically, but his grip was firm and in his face Natalya could see an honesty that invited trust.

"That's a fine catch," he said, nodding to the fish she was trying to hide behind her back.

"It is for our dinner," she said pointedly, pulling away from him.

But Veniamin was no longer paying any attention to Natalya or the fish. Instead he was staring at Yuliya who, in turn, couldn't seem to take her eyes from his face.

"Forgive my *little* sister," she said in a very un-Yuliyish voice. "I'm afraid she is a wild child with no manners."

"Unlike you, Miss," he said, his face reddening.

Natalya glowered at both of them.

"We're not supposed to talk to the soldiers," she reminded Yuliya then swung on her heel and walked away. When she realized no one was following her, she stopped and looked back. Leysa's face was troubled as she gripped Pylyp's hand and watched Yuliya and Veniamin, but it was the loop of wire in the young man's hand that caused Natalya to retrace her steps.

"Is that a snare?"

Veniamin nodded.

"How does it work?"

Yuliya frowned at her. "Why must you be so rude?"

"It's no matter," he said. He held the wire out so they could see that it had been threaded through a second but smaller loop then fastened to a long stake. "I've planted three of them already and I was just about to set this one over there." He nodded toward a faint trail just visible under a clump of willows. "If I'm lucky, a fat rabbit or two will come past here tonight."

"Snares are forbidden in these woods," Natalya said primly. "The rabbits belong to Baron Potocki and no one is permitted to hunt them without his permission."

Veniamin shrugged and pointed to the trout in her hand. "I expect that fish must also belong to the baron, and yet you are taking it home." He walked toward the willows with Yuliya and Natalya following close at his heels.

Leysa gripped Pylyp's hand so tightly that he cried out. "We are not allowed ... ," she began, but when it was clear that neither of her sisters was listening, her voice trailed away. Reluctantly she followed the others but stopped a safe distance away from the willows and stood like a butterfly perched on a petal, ready to take flight at the slightest hint of danger.

Dropping to their knees beside a clump of bushes, Natalya and Yuliya watched Veniamin grip the stake and force it into the ground until the loop hung just a few inches above a slight indentation in the ground that he explained was a rabbit trail. Getting to his feet, he helped Yuliya to hers, holding her hands much longer than Natalya thought was necessary.

"If you would like to come with me tomorrow morning, I'll share my catch with you," he invited.

She nodded slowly, lost in his gaze.

"We'll *all* come," Natalya said.

As they walked back to the farm, Veniamin told them he was from Kiev, where his parents owned a restaurant. "My father makes the finest *verenyky* in all of the Ukraine!"

"Your father cooks?" Yuliya exclaimed.

"All of my family cooks. And when I return from the army, I, too, shall open a restaurant."

He left them at the edge of the field and headed for the house. For a moment Yuliya stood gazing after him. "You would never go hungry if you owned a restaurant..." she said dreamily.

※

As soon as her mother and Catherine had departed the next morning, Natalya crawled quietly from her bed. Taking special care not to disturb her sleeping siblings, she climbed down the ladder. It was warm beside the fire, which had been carefully banked so the coals would last. Natalya sat on the makeshift bench and wound long strips of cloth in a herring-bone pattern around each foot, securing them just below her knees. Fitting a pair of leather slippers over the bindings, she wrapped a shawl about her shoulders and slipped outside.

At the corner of the barn she peeked out at the field. Veniamin was standing facing the barn, but she didn't think he had seen her. *He is probably waiting for Yuliya*, she thought. *He doesn't know how she hates to rise early.* Stepping back, Natalya flattened herself into the small niche created by the corner joints and covered her mouth so her breath in the icy morning air did not give her away. When she ventured another peek, he was disappearing into the woods. She glanced toward the house, but there was no one else about, and praying that her mother and sister were not watching, she hurried after the soldier.

The frozen grass in the paddock crunched beneath her feet, but when she reached the trees there was no frost. There were also no footprints to tell her which of the several trails available Veniamin had taken.

Savruk would have known, she thought glumly as she peered at the carpet of leaves littering the forest floor. But there were no clues that she could see and finally she set off along the trail they had taken the previous day. She walked slowly, searching for signs of the young man's passing, and was so intent on the ground that she almost revealed her presence when she rounded a bend and came upon the soldier contemplating an empty snare. Ducking behind a tree, she watched him turn the stake over in his hand.

"You escaped this time," he grumbled out loud, "but I'll get you yet, my friend."

He reset the trap and continued down the trail, pausing to check two more snares, neither of which had been disturbed. When he reached the one by the willows, the stake was bent and a small rabbit dangled, unmoving, from the wire loop. Expertly he released the animal and tucked it under the belt of his tunic, reset the snare and started back along the trail. Natalya hid until he passed then hurried silently after him.

Although she expected him to head directly for the farmhouse, just a few yards from the meadow he suddenly broke away from the main path and made his way along a fainter trail that she knew would lead him to the grove of beech saplings and the hidden cellar. Anxiously she followed closer than before, almost crying out when he came upon an unshaven, grim-faced soldier savagely stabbing his bayonet into the sod they had placed over the hidden cellar. Natalya was sure this was the soldier who had kicked Savruk.

As she hid behind a clump of willows, Veniamin strode forward.

"You're not likely to find mushrooms there, brother!" he called out jovially.

"There's something queer about this place," the man grunted. "Looks like it's been cleared."

As he jabbed again at the mound of dirt, Natalya breathed a prayer of thanks for her mother's insistence on piling so many layers of sod over the roof.

"Doesn't look queer to me," Veniamin said easily then opened his coat to reveal the rabbit fastened to his belt. "But I have a trap set nearby for another, and I'll thank you not to be scaring the game away before it has a chance to sample my wire neckerchief, brother. A fine rabbit will surely sweeten the stew the old mother is preparing for us."

"A fine lamb would sweeten it even better," the soldier responded grumpily but with less vigour than before. "A single rabbit will not go far among twelve men."

Veniamin tucked his catch back under his belt. "Tomorrow will produce more—if my snares are left undisturbed."

When the older soldier continued to probe the ground, Veniamin added with a knowing look, "Besides, I've heard a rumour there is a tavern in the village with a large store of *horilka*."

"*Horilka?*" The man licked his lips. Removing the bayonet from his rifle, he wiped the blade on his pants, tucked it into a sheath attached to his belt, and followed Veniamin back toward the main trail. As the soft thud of their steps receded, Natalya crept from behind the willows. She was sure Veniamin had said he had only set four snares, but she began checking every game trail leading to the little clearing, looking for the snare he had warned the other soldier not to disturb. When she failed to find it, she walked slowly back to the paddock.

A storm was brewing, darkening the sky and bringing an early dusk to the farm, and by the time the soldiers returned from the village, abusing the night air with their raucous songs of war and love, a sharp northeast wind had come up, chilling everything in its path. As the evening progressed and the farm was cloaked in darkness, the songs disintegrated into shouted insults and accusations. Peeking through a crack in the wall near Zirka's stall, Natalya was relieved when she finally saw her mother and Catherine hurry across the yard, the wind whipping at their shawls. They were almost to the barn when Veniamin suddenly emerged from the shadows, causing both women to cry out in alarm.

"I'm sorry to frighten you, Mother," he said quietly, "but I wanted to warn you to bar the doors tonight. I will be close by, but there is little I can do against so many."

Zhanna crossed herself.

"You are a good man, Veniamin Kyrylenko," she said gratefully. "Our Lord will bless you for your kindness!"

Too afraid to even consider what damage so many drunken men could inflict upon her family, Natalya hurried from the stall just as her mother and sister entered the barn.

"I'll help," she told Catherine, and together they lifted a heavy wooden bar into slots on either side of the door. It would not stop a determined assault but Natalya was comforted by the thought that it would give them some time to prepare should such an attack occur.

In the loft, icy gusts whistled through the cracks in the walls, chilling everything they touched, and though Pylyp, Leysa, Yuliya and Natalya huddled close together beneath a pile of blankets, they still shivered. The haunting notes of a shepherd's flute eventually soothed Pylyp to sleep, but the others lay awake listening in alarm to the ever-increasing noise from the farmhouse. Amid the shouts and laughter they could hear glass shattering and wood splintering, and occasionally from the yard came the thuds and curses of men fighting. Once someone pounded against the barn door and a drunken voice shouted, "Come out, you whoring *khokhols!*"

"Let's burn 'em out!" yelled another.

Terrified, the three sisters clutched each other, until they heard Veniamin's reassuring voice cajoling the soldiers to return to the house where it was warm and they could get another drink.

As their voices receded, Natalya could hear her mother down below feverishly thanking God for their deliverance.

It was close to dawn before the raucous activity ceased and silence gradually descended over the house and yard. Only then did the family sleep.

One of the sick men died on the fifth day after their arrival, and by then three more of the soldiers had become ill, including the commander. As their companions began to fail, Father Ishchak was summoned to the farm to administer last rites and to pray for those who were still alive. When a second soldier died, the Bolshevik soldiers decided that the priest's prayers were useless and having heard of the molfar's powers, summoned him to the farm. But despite being plied with all of the potions and spells in the wizard's arsenal, a third soldier died and the molfar too was sent packing.

"As if he could undo what our Lord has ordained," Zhanna scoffed.

Since the tavern had run out of alcohol, there were no more drunken parties, but Catherine told her sisters that there were now five soldiers lying in the beds and on the floor, all rambling deliriously as they feverishly relived childhood traumas or battlefield nightmares. Two more graves were filled before any of the sick men began to show signs of recovery. By then both of the young sheep had been butchered and eaten, and most of the vegetables and corn were gone from the cellar beneath the kitchen. At night, Zhanna's prayers grew longer and more passionate as she pleaded for mercy from saints Natalya didn't even know existed.

Meanwhile, Veniamin continued to tend his traps, and although they were often empty, one morning he caught three fat rabbits. That evening the soup Yuliya made for the family was thick with meat.

"Where did this come from?" Natalya asked suspiciously.

Yuliya flashed a triumphant smile "You are not the only one who can find food, little sister," she gloated and refused to say anything more. After that, Natalya began to notice that often when she was engaged in a task she couldn't leave, Yuliya would slip away from the barn and when she came back she was cheerful in a way she had never been before. Sometimes she even sang as she worked.

As Yuliya's happiness grew, Leysa's diminished. She seemed always afraid and spent more and more time with Pylyp, keeping the little boy amused and safely away from the soldiers. At mealtimes she ate less than a bird, and had become so thin she seemed to Natalya to have more bones than flesh.

"You must eat, Leysa," their mother admonished her one

night then said sternly to the others, "If there is meat in the pot, the largest serving must go to your sister!" But more than once in the days that followed, Natalya saw Leysa giving her share of their dinner to Pylyp.

The deciduous trees around the farm gradually shed all of their leaves and the nights grew increasingly cold. The upper slopes were white and every storm was now accompanied by snow flurries. Although the ground at their level remained bare, Natalya knew it was only a matter of time before winter set in for good. She dreaded the thought of having the soldiers camped in their house until spring, for although the commander had recovered, his control over the men was weakening. Twice Catherine had narrowly escaped assault as she worked in the kitchen, and only the broom Zhanna wielded had made the soldiers back down.

"There will come a time when neither Mama's broom nor Veniamin will stop them," Yuliya predicted gloomily.

Then one morning they woke to strange, muted noises. Natalya hurried down the ladder and peeked outside at a world blanketed by snow and large flakes falling thickly. On and around the porch the soldiers were gathered, all dressed in their greatcoats and wool hats, their packs and weapons strapped on their backs. Suddenly the commander, who stood at the top of the steps, gave an order and two men marched toward the barn.

Natalya scurried up the ladder and woke Yuliya. Together they watched as the barn door creaked open and Veniamin and another soldier entered. As soon as she saw who it was, Yuliya climbed down the ladder and Natalya followed.

"We're leaving," Veniamin said quietly. "The lieutenant wants to be out of the mountains before the trail to Yeremeche becomes impassable."

While the other man led the old mare from the stall and began saddling her, Veniamin collected the pack saddle from the wall and took it and a blanket to Zirka.

"You're taking our Zirka?" Natalya exploded.

His face registered shame as he looked past her to Yuliya. "I have no choice. We need him to carry the sheep and other supplies."

Hatred surged through Natalya. Because Zirka was familiar with Veniamin, he stood calmly and trusting as the pack was positioned on his back. He had no idea he would soon be in the hands of men so cruel they would kill a dog just because it annoyed them.

"You are evil," Yuliya cried. "You leave us with nothing!"

"*Nitchevo!*" the other soldier said with a dismissive gesture of his hand. "It could have been much worse. It is only because of him that they have not harmed you."

Veniamin's eyes begged her to understand. "The snares are still in place, Yulishka," he said softly. "I'm sure the one in the willow thicket will have a fat prize for you this morning. Your sister knows the spot."

Natalya's cheeks reddened. He had known all along that she was following him!

"Where will you go?" Yuliya asked, as if in shock.

"With God's blessing, I will be with my family in Kiev before St. Nicholas Day." He touched her cheek then led Zirka from his stall. As they passed, Natalya reached her hand out to the horse's neck, feeling his warmth and the stiff bristles of his hair for the last time. Then he was gone.

A quiet descended over the farmstead after the soldiers left, and although the clouds remained grey and forbidding, the snow stopped falling. Stunned by the loss of their horse and the sheep, Natalya made her way to the house, but as she entered the once-cheery home, she wished she had stayed in the barn. The sour smell of sweat and vomit and something equally vile that she could not identify pervaded every room. The beautiful pine floors were muddy and gouged with burns from cigarette butts that had been ground into the wood and every wall was mutilated where knives and axe blades had been buried in them.

Catherine and Zhanna sat unmoving at the table laden with breakfast remains.

"Mama?" Natalya said hesitantly. "Can we come back now?"

Her mother stared as if at a stranger.

"Mama?" Natalya repeated, gently gripping her shoulder.

Zhanna's gaze fell to her daughter's hand then slowly she drew herself together and got to her feet. "First we must clean," she said wearily. "Go and collect Yuliya to help, but tell Leysa to keep Pylyp in the barn."

Everything in the house that could not be boiled clean or scrubbed with a solution of lye and water was burned in a bonfire outside and for most of the day the air was filled with the rancid stench of scorched feathers from pillows thrown on the fire. The wash boiler was set up over a second fire and all of their blankets and clothes were boiled then hung to dry in the house or on the line outside where they froze almost instantly. Finally, the bathing tub was carried to the porch where they could remove their clothes and bathe without recontaminating the kitchen. Natalya, who was in no rush to expose herself to the cold evening air, offered to collect more water for the pots heating on the stove.

"And I'll get more wood," Catherine said.

"Then I'll have the first bath," Yuliya declared. As she started to undress, Zhanna reached for a pair of shears she had set on the bench.

"First we must cut your hair, daughter."

Yuliya stared at her in horror. "No, Mama!"

"There is no other way." Zhanna motioned her to a stool. "Lice hide in hair."

As the scissors cut through her thick, golden braid, tears flowed down Yuliya's cheeks. "I'm glad that Veniamin has gone," she sobbed. "I could not bear for him to see me this way."

She was in the tub and still sobbing when Natalya returned with the water.

"Has Catherine not come back?" she asked.

Her mother shook her head. "You should go help her," she said, "then you must have your bath."

Natalya hurried around the house to the lean-to where Catherine was standing with Lech's letter in her hands and tears streaming down her cheeks. Natalya tried to speak, to say something that would explain the letter, but she couldn't get the words past the lump in her throat.

"Why?" Catherine choked, staring at her. "Why is it here?"

"I was afraid," Natalya managed at last. "I didn't want you to go away."

"When?"

"In the summer ... when we were building the cellar." Trembling, she clasped her hands. "Please don't hate me, Catherine."

Her sister ran a finger over the words on the first page, caressing them. Then she folded the pages, tucked them into her pocket and gathered an armload of wood. In an emotionless voice that was more frightening than her tears, she said, "I must help Mama."

Natalya watched her go, and then because there was nothing more she could do or say, she loaded her own arms with wood and followed.

In the morning, Catherine and their mother rebuilt the outside fire beneath the washtub. While they boiled the clothes that had been discarded the previous evening, Yuliya and Natalya went to the secret cellar and with picks and shovels, dug out the entrance and squeezed inside. The dark enclosure smelled musty, but the vegetables in the bins Zhanna had made were as firm as when they had pulled them from the ground, and the girls quickly filled their basket.

"You take them to Mama," Natalya said. "I'm going to check Veniamin's snares."

Yuliya shivered. "That's fine with me. It's too cold out here!"

It *was* cold, and the scarf Natalya had wound around her shaven head failed to keep her warm, but being outside and away from the house was preferable to being with Catherine. She had not spoken to Natalya since she left the lean-to and was so quiet with everyone else that their mother grew worried.

"You have worked too hard, daughter. Today you should rest."

Instead, Catherine spent the morning scrubbing clothes and ironing dry those that were still hanging from the previous day.

Natalya tried not to think of her as she trudged through the snow to find Veniamin's traps. In the end she was only able to locate two of them, including the one in the willow bushes which, as he had predicted, contained a fat rabbit.

Perhaps when she sees this, Catherine will forgive me, she thought as she trudged home. But when she entered the kitchen, her mother was gently helping Catherine up the stairs.

"She fainted," Yuliya said gravely. "She has the fever."

A moment later their mother came down for a basin, which she filled with hot water and a handful of herbs from a wreath that hung on the wall. "Natalya, bring more water from the well and then gather some willow bark," she instructed brusquely. "Yuliya, you must boil the rabbit with plenty of garlic and onions, and when Natalya returns, brew the willow bark into a strong tea."

She looked at Leysa, who was seated near the window where she was transforming one of Vasyl's old shirts into a shift for Pylyp who, though still small for a three-year-old, was outgrowing most of his clothes. He was curled up on the bench beside his sister, sound asleep.

"Keep him warm," Zhanna said. Then, basin in hand, she hurried back upstairs.

Pylyp was still asleep when Natalya returned with the willow bark, but the blast of cold air that swept into the room with her woke him, and he let out a piercing scream. Leysa dropped her sewing and tried to pick him up but he screamed again and kicked and twisted in her arms.

Zhanna appeared at the top of the stairs. "What's wrong?" she demanded, but it was clear she already knew, and her legs seemed to wobble as she stared down at the little boy struggling to free himself from Leysa's hold.

"He has the fever, Mama," she said.

※

For Natalya, the next two weeks were a blur of pumping and carrying water from the well to the house, making willow bark tea, and emptying bedpans as Catherine and Pylyp fought their way through fever and delirium. There was no time for checking the snares, and she and Yuliya were able to make only two more trips to the cellar. Like a frail shadow, Leysa went from bed to bed placing cool cloths on feverish foreheads, changing sweat-drenched blankets and offering comfort and prayers. But when Yuliya also succumbed to the infection, Leysa seemed to wilt, and by nightfall she too was battling the fever.

Slowly Catherine began to recover, though she was still too weak to do more than toddle a few feet from her bed, and a few days later Yuliya's fever began to abate, but Pylyp and Leysa seemed only to get worse. Then one morning Natalya woke feeling more exhausted than when she had gone to bed. Believing she was just tired from caring for the others, she forced herself to get up and go outside to collect more wood and water. But she had no appetite for breakfast, and by mid-morning she was so weak she could scarcely walk up the stairs to the bedroom where her head suddenly exploded with pain. She fell to her knees and crawled onto the mat she'd made for herself on the floor. She could not remember ever hurting so much or feeling so cold, and despite the blanket she had pulled tightly around herself, she shivered uncontrollably. Then the chills gave way to fever and her whole body seemed to be on fire. She heard herself cry out, but it was as if the cries came from someone else, and she was only distantly aware of her mother and Catherine lifting her from the floor and laying her on the bed beside Yuliya.

Days and nights merged into a whirling sea of ice and fire and pain and horrifying visions, most often of her father running and then falling into mud that was soaked with Savruk's blood and of Catherine looming over her asking, "Why? Why? Why?" Once, she saw the savage image of a snarling wolf staring at her with cold blue eyes and another time Father Ishchak was praying over her. But he soon swirled away as everything did, leaving her writhing in pain.

Then, as inexplicably as they had arrived, the visions and the pain and the fever and chills vanished. Waking in the early hours one morning, Natalya stared at the small window in her bedroom and marvelled at the leafy patterns imbedded on the frosty glass. She tried to sit so she could survey the rest of the room, but she could only manage to turn her head. Yuliya was seated beside the bed, her face thin and pale but relaxed in sleep. Natalya mumbled a prayer of thanks that her sister had survived, and as she did so, Yuliya's eyes flew open.

"Natalya?" She put a cool hand on Natalya's brow. "We thought you were going to die!" She turned and called, "Mama!"

Natalya scarcely recognized the gaunt woman who came to the doorway. Her mother's head was partly covered with a scarf, but the spiked hair that showed was snowy-white and her face was so creased with wrinkles that she resembled one of the village grannies. She stared down at Natalya as if her daughter was a ghost.

"Thank God!" she whispered. Crossing herself, she knelt beside the bed and immediately began giving thanks to the Holy Mother.

Hearing the commotion, Catherine came in, carrying Pylyp. She, too, was thin and drawn, but it was in Pylyp that Natalya saw the greatest change. He had the face of a little old man with hollowed cheeks and sunken eyes. When Catherine placed him beside her on the bed, the little boy didn't clamber over her as he would have before, but clung instead to Catherine's hand. Even when Natalya whispered his name he paid no attention to her.

She peered past her sisters and mother. "Where is Leysa?"

No one answered, and with a feeling of dread, Natalya repeated her question.

"She's gone," Yuliya said at last, tears wetting her cheeks. "Leysa died the night you became ill."

"Our sweet angel is with God and your Papa," Zhanna

said softly, running worn fingers over Natalya's brow. "She is at peace."

Natalya's attention shifted back to her little brother and once again she called his name, this time louder.

"Pylyp?"

Catherine put a protective arm around the boy and said gently, "He can't hear you anymore, Natalya. Pylyp is deaf."

PETROGRAD
January 1917

Alice heard Grusha admit General Banketik into the foyer, but because she didn't think the old general would want her to witness his struggle up the stairs, she waited for him in a bedroom she had converted into a small drawing room next to the countess's suite. The fact that he was making such an effort had compelled the countess, against Alice's advice, to leave her bed for the first time in weeks and to dress for the occasion.

"If the general's message is of such great import that he must deliver it in person, then I shall certainly *not* be greeting him in my boudoir!"

Now, dwarfed by the white brocade Empire armchair that she had once filled snugly, she clutched the thick woollen shawl protecting her shoulders.

In the fireplace beside her, a single flame licked at a small mound of coal dust that Alice had foraged from the empty coal bin, much to Grusha's dissaproval.

"There are citizens on the streets with no food or warm clothing," she had scolded. Over the winter the housekeeper had grown progressively bolder, speaking her mind, disappearing for hours—occasionally for whole days—and neglecting her duties. Dust was evident everywhere, linens went unwashed, and meals were always late as the two servants she was supposed to be supervising repeatedly abandoned their posts.

But the countess still refused to consider Alice's suggestion that they dismiss the housekeeper. "This is not the time to make enemies," she said. "And Grusha is having a difficult time with her husband fighting at the front."

Privately Alice wasn't even sure Feliks had remained at the front because twice she had seen Grusha in the market speaking with a man who, from behind, looked very much like her cousin's former secretary. But on both occasions, before Alice could move closer to confirm her suspicions, the two had ducked into the crowd and disappeared. Nor did Alice think her cousin was telling the exact truth. Whenever Grusha was in the room, the countess seemed uneasy, almost as if she was afraid of the housekeeper.

Having tried unsuccessfully to fan some life into the fire, Alice got to her feet just as the door opened and the general limped into the room.

"Forgive me, Madam," he wheezed, pausing to mop his red face with a handkerchief before giving the briefest of bows. "It has been a while since I climbed such a mountain!"

"No forgiveness is necessary, General Banketik," the countess said graciously. "It has been many months since I tackled those stairs myself." She waved to the sofa. "Please be seated, and my cousin will bring you a refreshment."

As he limped to the sofa and collapsed onto the cushions, Alice poured a generous portion of vodka into a glass, and his eyes widened when she presented it to him. "It is from before alcohol was banned," she explained quietly. "We've been keeping it for a special occasion."

He gulped most of it down in one swallow then smacked his lips and bestowed a grateful smile on her. "You have saved my life!" Resting the glass on his knee, he said, "We missed you at last night's dinner, my dear. There were two of the British delegates from the conference that I wanted you to meet."

Alice had briefed the countess on the inter-allied conference that had for weeks been the centre of discussion in the grand parlours of Petrograd where diplomats from France, Italy and England were being entertained. Much of the talk was about the newly opened railroad from Murmansk on which the delegates had travelled to the city. Everyone believed that the conference—and the new rail line—would not only relieve Russia's financial dilemma but also eliminate food shortages and the inability to transport vital supplies that were currently stockpiled in Archangel and Vladivostok. At her cousin's urging and hoping to secure more medicine and equipment for the field hospitals, Alice had already approached several delegates but she regretted not being able to speak with them again at the dinner.

"I'm sorry, General Banketik, but as you know, I've been helping at the Federov Hospital when they're short-handed. Yesterday a train came in from Riga with more wounded than they anticipated, so they asked if I would work an evening shift." She didn't tell of her terror that Tusya or Oleksi might have been among the wounded, nor of the relief that almost overwhelmed her when one of the patients had given her a scribbled note from her brother saying that he and Oleksi were safe.

"The dinner went well, I trust?" the countess asked.

"It did indeed!" He swallowed more vodka then cleared his throat and, with a significant glance at the closed door, lowered his voice. "I am sure, Countess, that your cousin has kept you informed of the dilemma facing Mother Russia, hmm? I fear our people have lost faith in the tsar. Discord increases each day between His Imperial Highness and the Duma and between the progressives and leftists in the Duma itself. Even his own family is turning against the tsar, furious over the banishment of the Grand Duke Dimitri to the Persian frontier and the illegal searches of their houses!"

The countess nodded. "Alice has told me about the lineups outside the bakeries," she said. "The newspapers, such as they are, say the shortages are the result of striking workers who won't unload wheat from railcars and bakers who refuse to bake." She shook her head in disgust then spread her hands out, palms up. "But surely, my dear General, discord has always been a part of Russia's temperament. We squabble and complain and walk away in a fit of temper, but when we are needed most, we rise to the occasion and fight to the death for our country and our tsar."

"I am afraid, dear Countess, that today few Russians will even bow to the tsar," the general said, then lowered his voice even more so Alice had to lean forward to hear him. "I have seen a dispatch from a commander in Galicia. The number of soldiers deserting is growing, and disarray within the high command is causing fatalities and hardships on the front lines that no soldier should have to endure. Ninety-five thousand men lost at Riga because they had no artillery support and the wounded left to freeze because there was no Red Cross to attend them!" He shook his head despairingly. "And how does our esteemed interior minister, Protopopoff, deal with this crisis? Why, he locks himself away to consult with the ghost of that crazy priest, Rasputin, who tells him the strikers and riots must be squashed, not reasoned with!"

He leaned back and swallowed the last of the vodka in his glass. As Alice hastened to refill it, the countess said quietly, "I can see, sir, that you are distressed. But I wonder at your purpose in delivering such dismal news to an old lady who can do nothing to change the course of these sad events."

"It is true, my dear, that you cannot affect a change. I doubt anyone can at this point. Our country is about to explode in a revolution of such proportions that it will not be extinguished without the loss of many, many lives ... and I fear that anyone connected to the Romanovs will be in grave danger—yourself included." He leaned forward once more. "Yesterday I spoke with two gentlemen from the British contingent to the conference. They are willing to secure passage for the two of you on their ship, which is to leave from Murmansk in a fortnight's time."

The countess arched her brows. "Desert Russia in her hour of greatest need? You would shame me, General!"

"And of what good will you be to Russia, dear Madam, if you are dead?"

Alice shuddered, remembering the day the mounted soldiers had charged into the crowd of protestors. It was not difficult to imagine those victims lashing back against their oppressors, and whether it was true or not, she and her cousin would be included in the ranks of the rulers.

"The general is right, Countess," she said quietly. "You should leave the city."

"I should, hmm?" The countess arched her brow. "And you, dear cousin, will travel with me, yes?"

Although there wasn't a day when she didn't ache to be back home in Canada, Alice reluctantly shook her head. "I will see you as far as Murmansk, yes. But I cannot leave Russia without Tusya."

"Just as I thought." The countess nodded to the general. "You are very kind, my friend, to be so concerned about us, but we will not be bullied into leaving this country by a sorry lot of rabble rousers. Our tsar will succeed, as he always has, and this whole nasty business will soon be just another page in the history of Russia."

The general sighed. "I do wish that were so, Madam."

He did not try to persuade her further. It was well known that the countess never changed her mind once it was made up. Instead, he spoke of the conference itself and even managed to amuse her with a story of how the British ambassador, having failed in all attempts to secure coal for his embassy, was astounded one day to see several wagons of coal being unloaded by Russian soldiers and carried into the house of a well-known actress.

"Of course," the general added with a smug laugh, "any good Russian would agree with the wisdom of keeping a voluptuous woman warmer than a stodgy Brit!"

Although Alice laughed politely, she could not help thinking that the Russian workers whose loved ones were succumbing to the cold would not share the general's opinion. Their outrage, she was sure, would be even greater than that of the British ambassador.

When the general left an hour later, Alice followed him downstairs. "Are Tusya and Oleksi safe in Riga?" she asked.

He said kindly, "They are alive today. But you know what it is like at the front, my dear. No one is safe for long." He studied her face for a moment. "Of course, I could have your brother and his friend transferred to Archangel. Not much is happening there and should they need to leave the country quickly, they will be in a good position to do so."

Alice could easily imagine her brother's outrage if he discovered that once again she was interfering in his orders, and as if sensing her dilemma, General Banketik patted her shoulder. "Do not worry, my dear. I am travelling to Archangel myself in two days time to review our hospital there. I shall simply arrange for your brother's unit to accompany me."

She smiled gratefully and pushed away her misgivings. *After all, she told herself firmly, a promise to a father easily trumps a brother's fury.* She didn't allow herself to think of how incensed Oleksi would be to find out he was obligated to the general.

On the afternoon of Thursday the 8 of March, Alice attended a tea given by the Baroness Cervinka and most of the conversation was centred on the dance that Princess Radziwill was giving on the following Sunday. As she listened to the chatter, Alice wondered if General Banketik might have been mistaken about the threat of a revolution. Surely, she thought, these people who were so closely connected to the royal family would know if such a danger existed. And if they knew, how could they possibly appear so unconcerned?

But as she travelled back to the English Quay in the baroness's automobile, she encountered procession after procession of demonstrators marching and singing the Marseillaise. She had seen similar demonstrations over the eighteen months since she returned to the city, but today the participants were determined and fearless as they shouted, "Down with hunger!" It was even more surprising that there were no Cossacks charging into their midst.

When she voiced this observation, the baroness's chauffeur said daringly, "The soldiers are beginning to realize they are brothers to the people."

The following day, as she was reading to the countess, Alice heard gunfire, and when she went to the kitchen for their evening meal, she found the cook and Ludmila in tears and Grusha in a black mood.

"The cavalry fired on the people," the housekeeper said bitterly, "for no greater crime than asking for bread to feed their starving families."

Alice was disturbed by the government's response. Was the emperor, like the ladies at the baroness's tea, truly so insensitive to the plight of his subjects? She would have loved to ask her cousin what she thought, but since the countess had developed a raspy cough and was running a slight fever, she decided it was better that she didn't know what was happening beyond her doors.

Over the next two days the demonstrations continued and more than once the crowds were attacked by soldiers and police. As before, they killed women and children as indiscriminately as men. Yet through it all life in the city went on as if nothing was amiss. On Sunday while on her way to the Federov Hospital, Alice saw restaurants filled with people and on the streets young boys passed out leaflets for a ballet at the Mariinsky Theatre that evening. It was so normal, in fact, that she readily agreed when the hospital matron asked if she would work again the next day.

"I don't like to leave the countess," she told Oksana, "but this is the only way I can get her the medicine she needs."

Recently promoted to supervisor, Oksana was as caring and popular with the patients as ever, but with the rising threat of violence in the city, worry lines often creased her forehead and she didn't laugh as easily as she once did.

"Just be careful," she warned. "I have heard that tomorrow there is to be the biggest demonstration ever."

The countess no longer had a fever, but she was so weak that she needed help going in and out of the bathroom, and she seldom had any appetite. That night she was unable to eat more than a few spoonfuls of the thick *borscht* the cook had made for dinner.

"You are a dear girl to take care of me like this," she said, patting Alice's hand. "Your grandfather would have been very proud of you."

Alice slipped an extra pillow behind her so she would breathe easier.

"It's the least I can do," she said gently, "after all you've done for my family and for so many others."

When her cousin finally drifted off to sleep, Alice found the scullery maid in the servant's quarters and gratefully slipped her a kopek for looking after the countess during the day while she was working at the hospital. "There'll be another kopek tomorrow if you do the same."

"Yes, Miss," the woman promised, but there was a gleam in her eye when she saw the money that made Alice wonder if rewarding her was such a wise idea.

"Just don't let Grusha know."

"I won't, Miss. Madame Grusha is not here anyway. She has been away since early this morning."

Why am I not surprised? Alice thought grimly as she made her way to her room.

※

The next morning the trams were still not running, so Alice walked the four kilometres to the hospital. It was dark and cold, and having forgotten her gloves, she shoved her hands in her pockets as she made her way along streets so quiet the only sound was the crunch of snow beneath her boots. In such a peaceful setting it was hard to imagine the turmoil of the previous days until she started across the first bridge and was stopped at a barricade manned by a company of armed soldiers. They demanded to know who she was and where she was going before they let her pass. Standing around fires nearby, their fellow soldiers were engaged in loud arguments about whether they should join the people or remain loyal to their officers. At a second checkpoint the arguments were so heated that she began scanning the streets and alleyways for escape routes.

She kept as close to the buildings as she could and was uneasy whenever she had to cross an intersection where there would be no shelter if firing started. More than once she wished the expansive boulevards she had once admired were not quite so wide. As she approached a bakery near the hospital, she heard the murmur of voices from a bread line that, although it was not quite six o'clock, was already two blocks long. Standing three and four abreast, the queue was orderly and she sensed an unaccustomed atmosphere of hope. One attractive woman with a bright red scarf and a saucy grin stood with a small child, whom Alice guessed to be about four years old.

"We're going to get bread, Miss," the child called out excitedly. "Today there will be bread for everyone!" A loud cheer greeted her announcement and soon everyone was chanting, "Bread for all! Bread for all!"

Caught in the excitement of the moment, Alice smiled and raised her fist in an encouraging salute as she hurried past. She was still smiling when she entered the hospital.

Oksana greeted her with relief. "Every bed is filled," the young sister said. "There was more shooting and the surgeon has been working through the night."

Alice went at once to her ward and was soon too busy to think about what was happening outside. Then, just after eight, the sound of shouting drew her and several of the patients and sisters to the north-facing windows from where they could see a crowd advancing down Liteiny Prospekt. They were shouting and waving red flags and banners, and just as Alice was wondering where the soldiers were, she realized that the troops had joined the demonstrators.

"We've won!" shouted one patient who had been stabbed by a bayonet during Saturday's protests. "The people are free!"

"Back to bed, you," Alice ordered crisply before the man ignited a revolution on the ward, "or you won't be alive to enjoy your winnings."

A few hours later they heard machine guns firing and within moments new victims were arriving with bullet wounds and broken bones and stories of being bayonetted, shot or trampled when they were caught in the battle between the soldiers and police.

"The police have machine guns everywhere," one man exclaimed as Alice dressed his shoulder after a bullet had been removed. "Even on the rooftops! But our soldiers will have them off soon enough."

Just as a sanitar helped him lie down on a makeshift bed in the hallway, the next patient was brought in on a stretcher, a young child accompanied by a sobbing woman with a red scarf. Alice stared down at the battered, unconscious face of the little girl she'd seen in the bread lines and was consumed with a fury she couldn't contain.

"What in God's name happened to her?"

"We was just crossing the street," the mother wailed, gripping her daughter's right foot, which was the only part of her that was not bleeding or bruised. "I thought it was safe! But the automobiles come and they was filled with soldiers with guns firing. We run as fast as we could but one of the automobiles hit her. She was tossed up and landed in front of a horse that couldn't stop!" She pleaded tearfully, "You've got to save her, Miss! She's all I got left!"

Ashamed of letting her anger interfere with her job, Alice said gently, "We'll do everything we can. I promise." But as she assisted the surgeon in repairing the damage, she knew nothing would help the child. The wounds to her arm and upper body were so deep, ragged and dirty that if the damage to her internal organs didn't kill her, the infection that was sure to follow would. Still, when the child was out of surgery, Alice made sure there was a bed for her and insisted that extra food be brought for the mother. By late afternoon the little girl was awake and there was no sign of fever. Alice wanted to see her safely through the night, but she didn't dare leave the countess alone for that long.

"I will check the child during the night," Oksana promised.

The matron frowned when she saw Alice preparing to leave. "You should stay here tonight," she said. "It is not safe on the streets."

"I have no choice," Alice said, pulling on her cape. "But I'll try to come back in the morning if my cousin is well enough."

There had been no gunfire for the past hour, and now the dark streets, lit only by the fires of burning buildings, were filled with exultant crowds celebrating the victory of the people. Still, as she followed a group onto the wide expanse of Nevsky Prospekt, she couldn't stop thinking of how the little girl had been mowed down, and she was trying to determine the exact spot where the accident had occurred when she heard the rat-ta-tat-tat of a machine gun from somewhere behind her. Bits of snow flew up close to her boots and people around her began to scream and run in all directions, some falling to the ground and crawling forward on all fours. Without thinking, Alice ducked low and ran, zig-zagging, to a small street vendor's booth where she dove into a snowbank just as a spray of bullets hit the side of the stall.

She landed on something soft, but her heart was thundering so loudly in her ears, it was a moment before she realized she was lying on top of another person. She didn't dare move until the machine gun had been silent for several minutes and neither, apparently, did the person beneath her. With a growing dread, she cautiously moved her hand over the greatcoat covering the body, along the back to the shoulders and neck where her fingers plunged into a wet gaping hole where a head should have been. She screamed and yanked her hand back and forgetting about the bullets, scrambled to her feet and began running wildly down the dark sidewalk, not knowing or caring where she was going. Close to exhaustion, she finally escaped into a small garden, its lawn piled high with snow. Collapsing onto her knees, she shoved her hands, sticky with blood, into the icy pile.

"I hate this place!" she screamed, sawing her hands back and forth in the snow until they were raw, trying to get them clean. "I hate this cruel, god-forsaken country and these cruel, god-forsaken people!" She pounded the snow with her fists. "I want to go home!"

Suddenly she felt strong hands beneath her arms, lifting her to her feet.

"It isn't safe here, Miss." In the darkness she peered into the face of the young cadet helping her. His voice was gentle but he was clearly terrified. "You need to go someplace safe."

He led her from the garden onto the now-quiet street and, after learning that she was going to the English Quay, told her the best route to take to avoid any more fighting. "Don't stop, Miss. Just keep going and you'll be safe."

Numb with shock, she stumbled forward, down the streets he had suggested, following crowds over the bridges so she wasn't questioned at the barricades and, as she had that morning, keeping as close to the buildings as she could. Drawing closer to the English Quay, she could see the dome of St. Isaac's Cathedral, partly obscured by smoke from the smouldering ruins of what had been a police station while flames from what she was sure was the Astoria Hotel lit up the night sky. Immune to the screams and explosions echoing around her, she detoured along the north side of the Catherine Canal to avoid gunfire near the Mariinsky Palace and city hall, crossed over the Moyka Canal, and almost sobbed with relief when she turned onto the English Quay. Here there were no crowds, no explosions, and from what little she could see in the dark, the houses had not been harmed.

The front door to the countess's house was unlatched and slightly ajar. She closed it quietly behind her and stood listening for a moment. There was no sound of movement. Surmising that any intruders had probably left the building, she called out softly, "Grusha?" Receiving no answer, Alice felt her way into the office, where a candelabra and matches were kept on the mantle above the fireplace. She lit a single candle and, shielding the flame with her hand, slowly climbed the stairs to her cousin's suite.

The countess was lying on the floor and moaning softly, and Alice hastily set the candelabra on a dresser and knelt beside her.

The old lady was shivering, her pulse was weak and thready and her breathing had a raspy edge, but a quick inspection showed there were no broken bones.

"I tried ...," she said weakly, "... bathroom ... couldn't wait ... ."

Alice ran a soothing hand over her cousin's forehead. "It's okay. You're going to be fine now," she soothed. Collecting a wash cloth and a basin of cold water from the bathroom, she set it on the floor. As she removed the countess's clothes and cleaned her as best she could, she talked quietly about the hospital and how well the staff were working together. Then she dressed her cousin in a flannel nightgown and lifted her onto the bed.

"You must eat more, Cousin! You weigh next to nothing," she said reprovingly as she tucked a down comforter around her patient.

The old woman opened her eyes and with surprising strength, gripped Alice's hand. "You are a blessing, child."

But Alice did not feel like a blessing at all. She felt drained and confused. How could you hate a country that produced people with the dignity and caring of her cousin, and the courage and compassion of the young cadet who had helped her? Yet how could you not hate a people so busy shooting at each other that they run down an innocent child and ruthlessly cut the head off of some poor soul who was probably doing nothing more than bringing bread home to his family?

From the window facing the Neva she saw that several buildings across the river were in flames. How, she thought despairingly, could a people be so bloodthirsty and compassionate at the same time?

ZGARDY
November 1917

"Russia's falling apart," Ivan Hawrylak said as he looked disappointedly at the watery soup Zhanna had served him along with a small slice of *kulesha*. "The tsar's been under arrest since he abdicated, Prince Lvov has resigned and Brusilov's lost his job. They blame him for failing to win back Galicia last summer—but what can a general do with no supplies and an army you can't discipline?" He ate the bread in a single bite, talking all the while. "Now the Bolsheviks are negotiating with the Kaiser for peace. If they're lucky, they'll get an armistice before the Germans take Petrograd."

"What does it matter?" Zhanna asked, wearily turning to the icon of the virgin mother and crossing herself. "God is angry and until his anger subsides, the killing will go on and soldiers will continue to steal our food."

She had been able to feed her family from the secret cellar after the Russian soldiers had left, but the summer of 1917 had been rainy and cold, and although Yevhen Hutopila had again helped her to plough and seed her fields, the harvest was poor. Now she was scrambling once more to make their provisions last through another winter.

Ivan drank his soup and wiped his mouth with the back of his hand. "I begin to think there will never be an end to the fighting, Mother. Today our children are back to learning German in their classrooms. Tomorrow maybe it will be Romanian. Who can tell?"

Natalya, who was sitting near the stove fashioning a new snare to replace one that had been broken, remembered her father telling the baron that it didn't matter much who was in charge because most of what they earned went to the government anyway. She didn't mind the new language lessons Father Ishchak was required to give and was already able to speak a few sentences in German. What she did care about was the number of people who were trapping in her territory. More than once she had found blood and tracks indicating that someone had robbed her trap, and she was now forced to take elaborate precautions to hide her snares and her routes through the woods.

In his usual way, before he departed Ivan produced a letter. It was not, as Natalya had hoped, from Oleksi, but from Veniamin and addressed to Yuliya, who had gone to the village with Catherine and Pylyp.

At least one of us will be happy, Natalya thought.

She finished the new snare, and as soon as the postman left, she headed out to set it in a clump of willows near the stream where she'd seen a number of rabbit tracks, but no sign of human activity. On her return she checked the snares she'd set out the previous afternoon and in the farthest one, which she had set along the trail to the meadow, she found a fat rabbit. She smiled as she stuffed the frozen carcass into the canvas bag Veniamin had left behind and which she had altered by adding a shoulder strap, enabling her to wear it slung across her chest, hidden by her shawl.

The rabbit would make a wonderfully rich stew, and perhaps Catherine could fashion a hat from the hide for Pylyp. Although he had completely recovered from the typhus, the little boy tired easily and could never seem to get warm. More than a year had passed since the Russians had left, but Natalya still found it hard to believe Leysa was gone. Her empty place at the table seemed to shout at them at every meal, and there was no laughter anymore, not even from Pylyp. Catherine barely spoke to anyone—especially not to Natalya—and even Oleksi's last letter, received three months after it had been sent, had been full of despair. He could not say where he was, but he described the chaos around him and gloomily predicted that the war would never end.

> *Mostly, I worry about my dear Alishka, for I have had no word from her and the situation in Petrograd is not good. I fear for her safety, yet neither Tusya nor I are allowed to leave our posts to help her.*

Natalya hitched the bag over her shoulder and began slowly walking toward the farm. Would her family, or what was left of it, ever be together again, she wondered? Would their cellar ever be full as it was when her father was alive?

Engrossed in her musings, she rounded a bend in the trail and almost ran into the muzzle of a sleek chestnut horse.

"Whoa!" the rider shouted angrily, pulling the horse up short, and Natalya gasped as she recognized Dominic Wojcik. His left arm was enclosed in a sling, and a white dressing, partly hidden by his Austrian officer's cap, was wrapped about his forehead, but his eyes were as hard and cruel as they had been on the day he drew his sword on her father at Baron Potocki's mansion.

"You're a Tcychowski, yes?" He made it more of a statement than a question.

Natalya had heard of his return to Zgardy and of how, having saved the baron's life during a battle, he was now convalescing on the baron's estate. And she knew she should step aside and let him pass, but she couldn't move.

He gave a short laugh. "Ah, yes, the feud continues, does it?" There was such bitterness in his tone that her eyes widened in surprise. Her scarf had fallen away from her shoulders, and he nodded at her bag, plainly visible and bulging with her catch. "In that case, I should confiscate the booty you have poached from the baron's lands."

Furious with her carelessness, Natalya pulled her shawl tight, covering the bag. "I haven't poached ... ."

He shrugged. "It would be easy enough to prove. Your tracks will lead directly to your snares, I'm sure."

She was caught as securely as a rabbit in one of her snares, and the harm that Dom Wojcik could do to her and her family was worse than she dared to imagine. Still, she couldn't bring herself to move out of his way. If he wanted to pass, he could go around her.

As if reading her thoughts, his lip curled slightly. "Pride is an expensive indulgence, young lady. One for which your father paid dearly. He thought he was better than the rest of us because a silly Russian whore gave him a rug."

"You're a liar!" Natalya shouted. "The countess is a great lady and it is a tapestry, not a rug!" As soon as the words were out, she realized her mistake, and so did Dom Wojcik. His eyes narrowed speculatively.

"Rug or not, it is still a symbol of our enemy. And to possess such a symbol is treason."

Her legs felt as if they would no longer hold her up, and she clutched her shawl tight to hide the trembling in her fingers. "It was buried ... ," she managed through dry lips, "... with Papa."

He laughed shortly. "A wise decision, though I should think that burning it would have been the better option. Fortunately for you, I'm not interested in depriving a family of their dinner.

But be warned—I may not be in so generous a mood should I encounter you again with the baron's game." He nodded curtly, clicked his tongue and, edging his horse into the brush, rode past her.

※

Natalya did not tell her mother or sisters about the encounter, but she was so shaken by it that she went back to the baron's lands only to collect her traps, and thereafter began setting them in the woods and meadows east of the farm. But there were few rabbits in this area, and as the winter grew colder, her snares yielded fewer and fewer catches. The produce stored in the cellars dwindled as Zhanna tried to make up for the lack of flour and fat by increasing the vegetables in her stews, and during the long dark nights Natalya could often hear Pylyp crying softly from hunger pains gnawing at his stomach. Yuliya didn't cry, but from the way she tossed about, Natalya knew that she, too, was suffering.

The worse their circumstances grew, the more Zhanna went to the church to pray and to confess even the slightest of possible sins, and though her prayers produced no concrete results, she always came home in stronger spirits.

"God has a plan," she insisted. "And when he sees that we are truly penitent, it will be revealed."

"If he does have a plan," Natalya muttered one day, "it obviously does not include the Tcychowski family!" Privately she thought any deity who needed to have every prayer repeated to him three times was possibly too thick to plan much at all.

Yuliya said primly, "That remark, sister, could earn you an hour on your knees." But she did not go to Zhanna with the tale as she might have in other days. Since meeting Veniamin, Yuliya's moods had become unpredictable, swinging from despair to elation, depending on how long it had been since she last heard from him. On this day, having recently received a letter from Kiev, she was too happy to be mean.

Natalya began travelling farther from the farm each day to find new runs, often climbing icy cliffs or crawling along downed trees of questionable durability that bridged deep ravines. Once she came upon an old farm surrounded by woods, but with a sizeable field bearing a number of rabbit tracks. Beyond the field was a small cottage that seemed to have sunk partway into the ground, a few outbuildings and a dilapidated old barn.

Although a thin tendril of smoke curled skyward from the cottage chimney, the farmyard seemed to be deserted, and Natalya was trying to decide whether or not to set a snare in the field when a movement near the barn caught her attention. A moment later a woman came into view, her back bent beneath the weight of a bulky sack. A black scarf covered her head and she glanced furtively in all directions before setting her burden onto the ground next to a half-collapsed lean-to at the back of the barn. As the woman straightened, Natalya recognized Crazy Maryska.

The molfar's wife had become a legend in the village. Natalya had long ago heard the story of how, in the late stages of pregnancy, Maryska had been walking with the molfar along a high cliff when suddenly the ground gave way and she fell into a steep, rocky ravine. By the time the molfar reached her she was not breathing, but of course, being a molfar, he immediately began chanting one of his spells while at the same time massaging all of her limbs, and miraculously brought her back to life. Still, she lost the baby she was carrying, and a few weeks after the accident she began having fits. They were never predictable but seemed to be more frequent when the moon was full or when she was upset about something.

"It was the molfar's fault," Galyna Shevchenko had whispered knowingly when she told the story. "He brought her back to life with his spell, but he made a mistake and she suffers for it."

"Nonsense!" Zhanna had scoffed. "I saw many such cases at the hospital in Lemberg. She was not dead at all. She was simply unconscious."

Nevertheless, Maryska was seldom seen in the village, and since the molfar was more often on the alpine meadows tending the village sheep, few people ever visited his farm. In fact, it was located such a long way from the village and reached by such a difficult route that neither the Austrian nor the Russian soldiers had discovered its existence.

Realizing that this must be the molfar's farm, Natalya watched the woman drag her load into the lean-to and emerge a moment later with only the sack. But instead of walking lightly, as one might expect from someone who has just been relieved of a heavy burden, she staggered forward, arms flailing and fell heavily toward the barn, her head striking one of the butt joints at its corner. As she slumped to the ground, Natalya raced across the field.

"Maryska?"

The woman moaned and Natalya rolled her gently onto her back. Foam trickled from her mouth, but there was no bleeding.

"Mother Maryska?"

The molfar's wife stared up at her, uncomprehending.

"Are you all right, Mother Maryska?"

She nodded slowly then said hoarsely as if in a daze. "I must have fallen."

"Yes, you did." Natalya eased her into a sitting position. "Can I get you something?"

"No ... no ... ." She swivelled her head then grasped Natalya's hand, her eyes suddenly fearful. "Please! My husband must not find me here!"

"I haven't seen him. Trust me." Natalya helped her stand then supported her while they walked slowly around the barn and across the yard to the house. It was warm inside and as she helped remove Maryska's outside wraps, Natalya realized the woman was tiny and so thin that her bones were almost visible beneath her skin. It was also evident that she had wet herself.

"I'll make you some tea," Natalya offered, "while you clean up."

But Maryska hobbled to a chair beside the table. "My husband cast a spell on me," she complained tearfully. "If I go where I am not allowed, he makes me fall and piss myself. That way he controls me."

In a storage room lined with shelves filled with sacks of grain and more tinned food than she had ever seen, even in Merchant Grabsky's store, Natalya found a crude clay teapot and a jar of fennel seeds mixed with the stems and dried leaves of the plant. She put some into the pot and filled it with water from the kettle on the stove, then searched about for some cups.

"The villagers say your husband is a kind man," she said, finding a somewhat-clean cup among a pile of dirty dishes.

Maryska's beady eyes followed her every move. "He believes he is being kind, and he thinks he is keeping me safe. But how am I safe when I keep falling down?" She accepted the cup of tea and held it between her hands, warming them, and nodded toward a corner of the room where a large loom stood. "Blankets," she complained. "He wants me to make blankets. Night and day. Day and night. But the wool is filthy. Some of it must be washed over and over and still it is filthy." She looked around carefully then leaned close to Natalya and whispered, "I hide the worst of it in that shed. He thinks it has all gone into the blankets!" She leaned back, cackling at her cleverness.

Natalya stared at her. "You hide wool in the lean-to?"

Setting her cup on the table, Maryska snorted derisively. "He's a man. What does he know about blankets?"

"But what if he finds out?"

"He won't. He never goes there." Her eyes grew wary and she clutched Natalya's arm in a painful grip. "You'll not tell him?"

"No, I won't tell him." Natalya pulled her arm free. "But for how long have you been doing this?"

Maryska stared into her cup as if the answer might be floating alongside the fennel seeds that had escaped from the pot. "Two winters!" she said finally. "That's when he stopped using the lean-to for wood. Built a new one next to the house." She nodded toward the door. "You'd better go now. He won't like it if he finds you here."

It took Natalya twice as long to return home and by the time she arrived, her arms and back ached from the burden she carried.

"What is this?" Zhanna asked as her youngest daughter staggered into the kitchen and deposited the large, smelly burlap sack on the floor.

"That, Mama," Natalya panted, "is food."

"It smells awful!" Yuliya complained, holding her nose as she stared down at the sack.

Even Catherine's face showed interest when Natalya described her experience at the molfar's farm.

Yuliya gasped. "You *stole* from the molfar?"

"I didn't steal," Natalya said. "I have an arrangement with Maryska. The molfar is always bringing home grain and flour that people give him for his services, and for the blankets she makes and he sells. She has far more food than they will ever use, and she'll trade some of it to me for any blankets we make from this wool."

Zhanna inspected the bundle, her expression shifting between hope, disbelief and disapproval. "*Help* from a molfar?" She crossed herself and muttered a prayer.

"Not from the molfar," Natalya insisted, afraid her mother would refuse this opportunity. "From God, Mama! Remember, you said he had a plan? Surely he was the one who led me to the molfar's farm?"

A cough drew Zhanna's attention to Pylyp, who was curled up with a blanket on a small bunk above the stove. She stared at him then sighed. "We will need lots of water. And we'll move the loom into the house."

PETROGRAD

June – December 1917

In early June, for the third time since February, the sanitars and cleaning staff went on strike, leaving the sisters to clean up the wards as well as care for their patients.

"Every time they want a holiday, they go on strike," Alice grumbled as she and Oksana put clean sheets on the bed of a patient who had just been discharged. "I thought the new order was supposed to end all of that nonsense."

Oksana fluffed the pillow and covered it with a clean case. "But they haven't stopped the war, and when there's war there's no food. The people are tired of eating words."

"I don't blame them," Alice said as she snugged the bottom corners of the blanket she had placed over the sheet. "It's hard to tell these days which is longer, the bread lines or the speeches. Of course, they aren't just protesting the war or the lack of food. This morning I passed a parade of women demanding the right to participate in the new government. And," she added as they moved on to the next bed, "you won't believe who was leading them."

"Who?"

"Grusha Stolin!" Alice grinned at her friend's astonishment. "You should have seen her! Dressed in a greatcoat that had belonged to some general—she was like a huge tank knocking anyone aside who got in her way."

"A greatcoat in June?" Oksana shook her head. "How could she stand it?"

Alice shrugged. "Grusha thinks she's invincible now that she's got the local soviet behind her."

It had been three months since Grusha and Feliks had presented the countess with an expropriation order from the Justice Ministry for the house and all of its furnishings. Technically, the house was to be used as a base for the Domestic Workers' Union, and the countess was to be compensated for any financial losses.

In reality, half a dozen of Grusha and Feliks's relatives were living on the premises, and the countess had not received a single kopek from the ministry or the union.

"I suppose it is no worse than what our Imperial Majesty and his poor family are facing under house arrest," she had told Alice the previous afternoon. "I can imagine Her Highness's distress with her children just recovered from the measles and that dear little boy so fragile! Why King George has so callously refused to offer him asylum until this mess is cleared up, I just can't imagine. They are first cousins, for goodness sakes!"

"The king is probably afraid the socialists in England will start rebelling and he'll face the same fate as the tsar," Alice had said. She felt little sympathy for the empress who had shown such poor judgement in championing Rasputin or for the tsar who was so weak he let his wife overrule the advice of his family and military advisors. But she did feel badly for the children.

Oksana stripped the soiled linen from the mattress. "Is Grusha still letting your cousin stay in her suite?"

"She has no choice. The order specified that they could not move her out. But I came home last night and found all of my things in the hallway and a new lock on my door. So I've moved into the countess's wardrobe closet. Without her gowns—which she doesn't need anymore—it's big enough for the small bed and a dresser that I found in the attic."

"That's an outrage!" Oksana fumed, snapping a clean sheet over the bed to release the folds.

"That's what the countess called it," Alice said, "but I told her it's a good thing because now I can keep an eye on her during the night. And since neither of us will be wearing her gowns any more, I'll be able to sell them for enough to keep us going for a while. Not that they are worth much. With so many noblewomen fleeing the country with little more than the clothes on their back, gowns are selling for next to nothing. Even the Baroness Cervinka has gone."

To her credit, before the baroness left, she had visited the countess and made a feeble attempt at persuading her to leave as well. But it was evident that the countess was in no condition to travel anywhere, and she continued to believe that the old order would survive. "There is still an army loyal to the tsar," she had insisted between coughing spells. "When the people see how these socialists have ruined our country, they will cry for his return!"

Oksana glanced quickly around to ensure that no one was

within hearing distance. "They are wise to flee," she said. "Your Grusha has much power, and she has many spies among the servants belonging to her union. It is said that she has a file on every person in the Justice Ministry."

"I'm not surprised." Alice gave the pillow she was covering a final pat before placing it on top of the covers. "Apparently we have to continue paying her and the cook and charwoman, even though they're not doing anything for the countess. In fact, I still have to slip Ludmila an extra kopek so she'll take care of her while I'm working." She shook her head. "But to be honest, it's Feliks who worries me more. He's drunk most of the time, and when he's not fighting with Grusha, he's raging against the countess and me for destroying his life. Thankfully, the walls to her suite are thick enough to block most of the noise."

It was tea time and having finished the beds, they walked downstairs to the empty dining room where there was a samovar of hot water. Alice made two cups of tea and brought them to a long table. "I'm sure Feliks is back to his old tricks," she said, "selling medical supplies on the black market. I caught him with a bottle of cognac the other day that must have cost a fortune. He shoved it into a drawer as soon as I walked into the office, but he knows I saw it." She shivered. "He frightens me."

"He's the kind of man who will destroy the good things promised by the revolution," Oksana predicted. "He puts his own greed before the needs of our country."

Alice couldn't imagine how anything good could ever come to a country where little girls stood in bread lines with bullets flying around them, just to get enough bread to barely keep them alive, and where people were lined up against a wall and shot without the benefit of a trial. Since the night of the revolution she had felt a growing despair, fuelled by nightmares in which headless men chased her down dark streets and machine guns fired at them from every corner. Now she never went outside without checking the rooftops first for snipers.

"It's no wonder my father never wanted to come back to Russia," she said bitterly. "There's nothing here *but* greed and brutality." She stared at the tea leaves in the bottom of her mug. "I wish I'd stayed home!"

Oksana looked at her sadly. "If you had, you'd never have met Oleksi ... or me."

Instantly ashamed of her self-pity, Alice patted her friend's hand. "You're right," she said. "I'm just a little homesick. I haven't heard from my father since before the revolution and the last time I heard from Tusya was that note the injured sanitar brought me a month ago." Crumpled and water-stained, the note had been almost illegible, but she had been able to make out that he and Oleksi had been posted to Ekaterinadar, a small city in southern Russia, about a hundred and fifty kilometres from the Black Sea.

※

By July the strikes and demonstrations had become a daily occurrence and as the tension escalated in the city, so did the frequency of Alice's nightmares. One warm night she woke in a sweat and realized the machine guns she had heard firing were not just in her dreams. Without switching on a lamp, she hurried in the darkness to the open window. From there she heard guns firing again.

There were no street lights, and it was impossible to determine how far the fighting was from the house or who was involved. She thought of the last time there were riots and buildings were bombed and realized that the countess's house could easily be targeted by pro-government forces as it was now the headquarters for the Domestic Workers' Union and the home of a Bolshevik leader.

I should move her to some place safer, Alice thought. *But where? And how could I get her there?*

She made her way to the countess's bed and stood listening to the old woman's raspy breathing. It was no different than it had been the previous evening. Trusting that she would continue to sleep, Alice quietly let herself out of the suite and crept down the hall to the servant's stairwell that led to the kitchen. Here it was even darker than the countess's room, and as she navigated past the work table she bumped into several objects, including a stack of pots she barely saved from clattering to the tiled floor. When she crashed into the shuttered door of a broom closet, she knew a door to the outside would be just a few feet further along. She breathed easier when she opened it and stepped onto a wooden platform that led to an alley behind the house. Between the row of houses across the alley, she could see the dome of St. Isaac's cathedral. She could also hear more gunfire, but it was coming from the direction of the Nevsky and nowhere near the English Quay.

Satisfied that all was well for now, Alice started back to the kitchen, but as she carefully closed the door behind her, she heard heavy footsteps and saw a flicker of light coming down the stairwell. Without thinking, she ducked into the broom closet and pulled the door shut just before Grusha stomped into the room. A moment or two later Feliks stumbled down the stairs after her. "What are you doing, woman?"

"If they come here, we need to defend ourselves!" Grusha said.

Alice heard the clatter of metal on metal, and peering through an opening in the shutters she saw the housekeeper select a long-bladed knife and a kitchen hatchet.

"We wouldn't need to defend ourselves if you and your bitch friends had kept your mouths shut!" Feliks's words were slurred, and Alice could see he was clumsily fanning the air with a glass half-filled with liquid. "You've ruined us, you stupid woman!"

Grusha rounded on him furiously, the hatchet clutched in her fist. "It was that Canadian bitch who ruined us! Now you are nothing but a useless drunk!"

"A drunk!" Alice winced as Feliks's glass crashed against a wall. Fists clenched, he lurched toward his wife. "You viperous ... ."

"Don't you dare!" she hissed, slashing the hatchet at him and stopping his advance. Her voice neared hysteria. "You have shamed me with all the chances you've pissed down the toilet!"

He eyed the hatchet uneasily and sidestepped, so the work table was between them. "That bitch is going to pay for what she did to me!" he whined. "There's ways."

"Of course she will pay, you stupid man! But not tonight. Not while the countess lives." Shifting both weapons to one hand, she grabbed the candle with the other and started back up the stairs. "I owe the old lady that much."

"You string them up," Feliks said as he followed her, "and you peel their skin away ... ."

Alice didn't realize until their voices faded away that she had been holding her breath. She let it out in a rush then grew so dizzy she had to grab the door frame to keep from falling, and it was several minutes before she felt capable of navigating through the dark kitchen again. She paused just long enough to grab one of the knives Grusha hadn't taken, but as she started up the stairwell she was sure every creaking step would bring the housekeeper and her husband charging forth, weapons in hand. When she finally reached the countess's suite and secured the thick door behind her, she was bathed in sweat.

❦

With the arrival of troops from the front who were still loyal to the provisional government, the latest uprising was quickly subdued and within a week the Bolshevik leaders who were blamed for starting it had fled the country. Grusha and Feliks were seldom around then disappeared altogether, and the house began to feel almost like a home again. Even the countess seemed to notice the difference.

"It was all the fault of that hideous Lenin creature," she declared. "The papers say he's really a German spy just here to cause trouble!"

"Well, he's out of the country now," Alice soothed, "and with the Stolins lying low, I feel a lot safer leaving you with Ludmila."

❦

In August a large delegation from the American Red Cross arrived in Petrograd and it was rumoured that they had brought with them a railroad car of medical supplies. The following afternoon a young American army officer arrived at the Federov Hospital with a packet of letters from Alice's father.

"He was very persistent, ma'am," the young man said. "Seems he read in one of your Canadian newspapers that we'd be coming here so he sent a letter to every delegate hoping one of 'em would get to you." He paused, a little embarrassed then added, "But I'm afraid we had to open 'em, just to make sure there wasn't nothin' that might compromise our mission here."

Although she wanted to read the letters immediately, Alice restrained herself and insisted that the young man join her and the matron for tea, mostly so they could quiz him about the medical supplies.

"I know you folks think we brought along a whole carload," he said, "but it wasn't nearly that much. And most of what we brought's already been turned over to your Russian Red Cross, but I'll see what I can do about getting you some stuff."

When he left, Alice found a quiet corner and read her father's letters one by one. There were five in all, each one filled with short anecdotes about the ranch. How the government was paying him to raise extra cattle for the war effort. How most of the hands had gone off to fight, leaving him with just a few old-timers and a Native family to run the ranch. How his leg gave him trouble when it rained. He ended one of the letters with:

> *I know it is much worse for you and Tusya, Alishka.*
> *Russia is not a land for the weak even at the best of times. From what I read in the papers, it is even worse now. I fear for you both and a thousand times a day I curse myself for sending you on this impossible journey.*

His last letter contained a five-dollar gold coin and Alice almost sobbed when it fell into her hands. She remembered the day he brought it home, just two years before she left for Russia.

"It's for luck," he had said, placing it in a cedar box on the mantel above the fireplace. "So long as I have this gold, I will not be broken."

She traced the tiny maple leaves clustered around the Canadian coat of arms on the coin. Until recently, she had not ever thought of herself as truly Canadian. She and Tusya had grown up speaking Russian with their father, eating western food with a Russian twist and reading Russian books their grandfather had sent to their home. At school they were referred to as the "Ruskies," or as "bohunks." But since coming to Russia, the difference between herself and the people around her had grown increasingly apparent. She wasn't Russian, and she wasn't English or American, as she was often referred to by her Petrograd friends. She was Canadian, and as she held the coin in her hand she was overwhelmed with a yearning for the land of her birth.

The following day a box filled with dressings and syringes and medications, plus a large package for herself, was delivered to the hospital. Much to Alice's relief the package contained a carton of digitalis for her cousin. In an accompanying note, the officer apologized for the small amount of supplies he was able to gather. A few weeks later he came in person to say good-bye. "The whole delegation's leaving," he told Alice. "It's getting too hot here, politically speaking, because it doesn't seem like your President Kerensky's gonna be able to hold on much longer. And we got enough to do cleaning up this mess with the Germans."

Although he had given Prime Minister Kerensky the wrong title, the officer's predictions about the provisional government proved to be frighteningly accurate. First Kerensky had failed to end the war and stop the food shortages, and then, in order to launch yet another offensive, he reintroduced the death penalty for deserters at the front. But in Alice's opinion their most foolish decision was to order the arming of the Bolsheviks and release their leaders from prison in order to combat the threat of a takeover by General Kornilov's anti-communist army.

"The Bolsheviks are never going to give back their weapons," she predicted to Oksana one afternoon in late October. "And now that the Cossacks are under control, they're going to go after the government."

They were in the dressing room counting supplies, and Oksana sighed as she surveyed the pitiful number of dressings they had left. "Maybe that's not such a bad thing," she said, "if it brings an end to these shortages."

"It won't be good if the Bolshevik leaders are anything like Grusha and Feliks," Alice countered.

Later that evening as she walked homeward along Nevsky Prospekt, she wondered if her predictions might have been wrong. The people on the street seemed unusually merry, and every restaurant, bar and nightclub she passed was overflowing with customers. Near the Alexandrinsky Theatre she heard one couple lamenting that, because both it and the Mariinsky had sold-out performances, they would have to find some other form of entertainment. Even the countess was in a cheerful mood and ate most of the soup Alice had brought home for her dinner. As a result, they were both stunned when Oksana telephoned the next morning to say that during the night Bolshevik troops had quietly taken over the main bridges and other crucial infrastructure within the city, including the Central Bank and power stations.

"You'd better stay home today," she advised. "Just in case."

Though there was no gunfire during the day, that evening they heard the battleship *Aurora*, which was anchored near the Admiralty, firing on the palace, from which machine gun fire was returned. Through the long night as she lay waiting for a shell to fall on the house, Alice thought about the new regime. Would it be better than the provisional government? Would there suddenly be an end to poverty and hunger as the Bolsheviks were promising? Or would the fighting and the starving and the hurting just keep going on and on? And as dawn lightened the room, she began to despair that she would ever again see her father and the ranch. She wasn't even sure if she would ever see Tusya or Oleksi again for there had been no further word from them during the long summer and fall.

At mid-morning Alice went downstairs to get hot water for the countess's morning tea and found the cook and Ludmila talking earnestly in the kitchen. Their conversation ended abruptly when she walked into the room, and neither was able to meet her gaze as they mumbled, "*Dobroye utro.*"

She looked at them curiously. "Is everything all right?"

"Oh, yes, Miss!" Ludmila said, nodding vigorously. "We just ... well ... ." Her face reddened and she said in a rush, "Grusha and Feliks are back, miss."

Alice wasn't surprised. She carried her teapot to the samovar and turned the spigot, allowing hot water to drain into the pot.

"Was anyone hurt in the shelling last night?"

"No, Miss," the cook said. "The ship was firing blanks."

The countess was relieved when Alice relayed the news to her. "There's been enough killing," she said with finality. "Perhaps now these people can get down to running the country the way it's supposed to be run." It was the first time she had wavered in her belief that the tsar or a member of his family would eventually be reinstated as the supreme leader of Russia.

Thinking she would find out more from Oksana than the servants, Natalya decided to risk another shift at the hospital. There she learned that the Red Cross sisters from England and Canada were returning home. When she phoned the Anglo-Russian Hospital to confirm the story, a Canadian sister urged her to leave as well. "You might have Russian blood, but as a Canadian citizen you're still a foreigner. You could find yourself in prison ... or worse."

Oksana echoed the Canadian sister's warning as they sat at the sister's desk, taking advantage of a momentary lull on the ward to update their patients' charts.

"We're to be assigned a new matron and doctor," she said. "They might not even permit you to work here."

Alice finished a note about the condition of a young soldier's foot when she had changed his dressing that afternoon.

"And what about you, Oksana? How is it any safer for you?"

"I am Russian!" Oksana said proudly. "And thanks to your cousin, I have a profession." She smiled and patted Alice's hand. "The communists may have conquered the tsar, but they haven't conquered disease. So long as people get sick, they will need sisters. I will be fine."

"Well, I'm not abandoning the countess," Alice said. "She wouldn't last a day with the Stolins in her house. And I'm not leaving Russia without Tusya!"

Oksana closed the chart she had finished and reached for another. "Grusha has powerful friends, Alice. Even in our union she is feared."

"Which is why I've got an emergency pack here." Alice nodded to a cupboard where she had hidden a backpack left behind by a soldier and which she had filled with emergency supplies. "If I have to leave in a hurry, my Letter of Request and everything I need is all ready to go."

※

In December the temperature plunged and twice Alice came home to find the countess shivering in her chair, unable to get herself back into bed. The second time it happened, she developed a chest infection and a fever.

"I'm staying home today," Alice told her firmly, but the countess shook her head.

"If you don't work, you won't eat. Go. There is nothing you can do for me here."

But Alice stayed home for the remainder of that week. Only when the countess's digitalis supply was exhausted did she return to the hospital.

"I'll work just today," she told herself. "I'll get the medicine and some more soup."

Fortunately it was a quiet day and there were few patients on her ward.

"Why don't you go home early?" suggested Oksana when she arrived for her evening shift. "I'll cover for you."

Alice accepted gratefully and after collecting the medicine and a canister of soup, which she concealed beneath her cape, she hurried home. In the foyer she met Grusha, who frowned at the bulge under Alice's cape.

"Stealing again from our poor dying soldiers, hmmm?"

"It is scarcely stealing," Alice said tartly, "since it is from the countess's own hospital."

The housekeeper's frown darkened.

"It is the *people's* hospital now! And you would be wise to watch your tongue. Even my kind nature has its boundaries." She clamped her lips in tight disapproval and swept past Alice, almost knocking her from the step. Then she stopped. "It is only because of the work Catherine Stanislavovna has done for the soldiers of Russia that I do not turn you over to the authorities," she added before disappearing down the stairs.

A high-pitched wheezing greeted Alice as she entered the countess's suite. The room was dark, partly because she had left the windows shuttered and the drapes closed to try to keep the room as warm as possible and partly because the electricity was off once again. Dumping the soup flask on the fireplace mantel, she groped her way to the dresser where she found the stub of a candle and a box of matches. Lighting the candle, she carried it to the bed and in the dim light saw that her cousin's face and hands were swollen to twice their normal size, and though she kept trying, she couldn't speak.

"I ... I ..."

Placing a candle on the only table left in the room, Alice slid her arm behind the old woman's shoulders and eased her forward so she could pile extra pillows behind her back. "Shhhh," she soothed. "You're going to be fine."

The wheezing eased slightly, but the countess's pulse was very weak and irregular.

"I should get the doctor," Alice muttered under her breath, but she doubted one would come. And in her heart she knew there was nothing now that anyone could do for her cousin.

She dug the packet of pills from the pocket of her cape, but when the countess tried to swallow one, even with the help of a glass of water, she choked and began to cough. When she finally recovered, she was so exhausted that she collapsed against the pillows. Alice held her thin, icy hands and contemplated the fireplace. She had already burned every scrap of extra furniture she could find, and since there was no hope of getting any other fuel for a fire, she had covered the opening with blankets to stop the drafts coming down the chimney. It helped a little, but not enough to keep the countess from shivering.

To distract her, Alice collected the huge bible from the top of the dresser and began to read aloud. After a while the old woman's breathing grew a little quieter and, finally, she slept.

So many pages, Alice thought, studying the tome in her lap. Then she looked at the fireplace again. *If I could just get her warm, even for this one night, she might at least die more peacefully.*

She used Genesis to start the fire. As the flames licked the crumpled paper, giving off a smidgeon of warmth, their light flickered about the room, dancing along the wall and onto the wooden dresser. With a pyromaniacal gleam, Alice charged toward it and pulled out the bottom drawer. Dumping the undergarments and scarves that filled it onto the floor, she used the butcher knife she had taken from the kitchen to hack the drawer into pieces. Crouched on a small woollen rug in front of the tiled hearth, she fed the pieces one by one into the blaze and by the time she started on the second drawer, the room was a little warmer and the countess had stopped shivering.

The uppermost section of the dresser was divided into two smaller drawers, and Alice was about to put the first one into the fire in a single piece when she heard a sound from behind her. She swung around and saw the countess staring in horror at the glowing coals in the fireplace.

"What ... have ... you done?"

"You were shivering," Alice said.

"You ... must ... stop!"

She was so agitated that Alice set the drawer on the hearth and hurried to her side.

"I won't burn any more. I promise. I just wanted to get you warm."

But the countess would not be calmed. Her hand jerked spastically toward the drawer and she kept trying to speak, only the words that came out of her mouth were unintelligible. Tears filled her eyes.

"You want the drawer?" Alice asked suddenly and the hand jerking grew more frantic. "You want me to bring it here?" She retrieved the drawer and set it on the comforter. The countess's gnarled hand thumped the bottom panel, and in that instant Alice understood. Retrieving the knife from the hearth rug, she worked one side of the drawer free and as she pulled it away she saw that there were actually two bottom panels with a two-inch gap between them. Carefully, she lifted the top panel free and saw, nested on a red felt mat, four toggle buttons made of some dark wood. Each was about a half-inch in diameter and an inch and a half long. As she picked them up one by one, she realized that two were heavier. The countess pushed at one of these with her swollen hand.

Alice examined the circular grooves decorating one of the toggles and found an almost imperceptible seam around the centre. She tried to pull the two halves apart, and when that didn't work, she twisted them and finally discovered that she could unscrew one from the other. As they parted, three glistening stones fell onto the bedspread. She stared at them in disbelief.

"Diamonds?"

The countess grasped Alice's free hand and finally managed a word that wasn't gibberish, "Yours!" Then she collapsed back against the pillow and tried again to speak. "Father ... Voro ... ." Her voice faded, but Alice understood.

"I will get him," she promised. "I'll go right now."

She returned the diamonds to the toggle button, tucked all four wooden buttons into her cape pocket, set the knife on the mantel and placed the little drawer onto the coals in the fireplace. Easing the door open, and closing it behind her, she made her way down the stairs, praying all the while that she did not meet Grusha again. But the house was uncommonly silent, and she slipped through the kitchen and outside without meeting anyone.

A light snow was falling as she hurried down the quay to St. Peter's Square, and though the clock on the corner said that it was just past eight, there was no one on the street. Unfortunately, there was also no one at the church except an elderly priest who said guardedly that Father Vorobiev was unavailable. When she told him she was there on behalf of the countess, he relaxed enough to promise that as soon as the Father returned he would give him her message.

Alice was only vaguely aware of the continued lack of commotion when she re-entered the house, and it wasn't until she reached her cousin's suite and saw the door partly open that she realized something wasn't right. Heart pounding, she cautiously opened the door wide enough to peer inside. The candle still flickered next to the bible on the table, and embers from the burned drawer glowed on the hearth, but there was no movement from the countess and no wheezing.

Dreading what she would find, Alice stepped into the room. Too late, she felt a movement behind her and before she could react, a heavy arm encircled her neck.

"We have accounts to settle, Alice Galipova!" Feliks hissed drunkenly in her ear. Pushing her in front of him, he kicked the door shut with his heel, then thrust her away from him with such force that she landed on her knees on the small rug fronting the hearth. When she swung around to face him, she was staring into the long barrel of a police revolver. He swayed slightly and the gun wavered in his hand.

From the corner of her eye Alice could see the end of the mantel and the knife she had used earlier to take the drawers apart. If she could just reach it! But Feliks had seen the knife, too. "Try it," he dared. Then he straightened and said harshly, "You fucked Feliks Stolin, whore! And now that your bitch of a cousin is dead, Feliks Stolin is going to fuck you!"

He began waving the gun about so wildly that she was afraid he would discharge it without even intending to. Hoping to distract him and buy herself time to think, she asked contemptuously, "And what will Grusha have to say about such a stupid plan?"

His eyes gleamed. "My bitch of a wife and her friends have gone to a rally for their new masters, the Bolshevik bastards!"

"And you," Alice mocked, "being so much wiser than they have stayed at home?" She edged imperceptibly backwards.

He stepped forward, one foot now on the little carpet, and waggled the gun at her. "I am not stupid," he rasped. "I know about the diamonds. I was with the old lady when she had them removed from her rings!"

Again Alice slid backwards until she was completely off the carpet and onto the hearth tiles. Obviously revelling in her fear, he stepped closer. "I know they are hidden somewhere in this room! And you are going to tell me where they are."

Trying not to think of the four wooden buttons she had shoved into the inner pocket of her cloak, Alice straightened slightly and gave a brittle laugh. "So which are you planning, Feliks Stolin? To rape me or rob me of something I don't possess?"

"Perhaps both," he said slyly, but at that moment a noise below them made him turn his head toward the door.

It was the distraction she had waited for. Bending quickly she grasped both sides of the carpet, braced her knees against the floor and yanked the rug toward her. Already off-centre, he fell backwards, arms flailing, and as he crashed to the floor, his gun flew across the room to land behind the little table on which she had set the candle.

"Bitch!" he screamed.

Alice abandoned her quest for the knife and crawled after the revolver, knocking the table over in her haste. But just as her fingers touched the butt of the gun, he grabbed her cloak and dragged her backwards, at the same time snatching the knife from the mantel and stabbing at her. Twisting free, she kicked upwards, landing her boot in his midsection. Cursing and stabbing wildly at her, this time he managed to bury the blade in her right calf, and she sucked in her breath as pain surged up her leg. Pulling the knife free, he slashed downwards again, but by kicking with all of her strength she knocked him to one side then, grasping the gun, scrambled to her feet. He lurched forward, both hands clasped about the knife, and plunged it toward her chest. In the same instant, she pulled the trigger.

His face distorted in a grotesque mask of surprise, horror and disbelief. As he fell forward, she stepped back and the knife clattered to the floor. Blood spurting from his mouth, Feliks collapsed beside it. She knelt and still clutching the gun in one trembling hand, felt for a pulse, but there was none. Feliks was dead.

Suddenly she became aware of a crackling sound and turned to find that the overturned candle had rolled across the floor to the windows, igniting the heavy velvet drapes and then the window sashes. Dropping the gun, Alice seized the rug and began to beat at the flames, but they were already attacking the pelmets and the crown mouldings, which were too high for her to reach. Her eyes burned and she was soon gasping from the smoke filling the room. Finally, giving up on the blaze, she stumbled to the bed. The countess had obviously died before Felix arrived and her face was strangely serene. "I'm sorry," Alice choked, taking both lifeless hands in hers, "but I have no choice."

She gently kissed the hands then let them go and staggered, coughing, to her own little room. After grabbing as many clothes as she could carry, she made her way to the door and escaped into the hallway where she put down her load in order to check her leg wound. It was bleeding but no ligaments or tendons had been cut and she bandaged it with her head scarf then fashioned her clothes into a bundle she could carry. By this time smoke from the fire was seeping under the door to the countess's room, and as she peered down the long corridor, she wondered if Feliks had been telling the truth when he said that everyone had gone to the rally.

Limping down the hallway, she pounded on every door she came to and shouted. "Fire!"

There was no response, and satisfied that the upper floor was empty, she escaped down the servant's stairs to the kitchen and made a quick check through the rest of the lower floor. In a small room near the library that had been converted into a sleeping room for Ludmila she found the scullery maid in bed asleep. "There's a fire, Ludmila!"

As soon as the maid scrambled from her bed, Alice ran back to the kitchen where she let herself out through the side door. It was still snowing and her earlier footsteps had already been filled in, but when she peered around the side of the house, she could see the snow hadn't stopped people from gathering on the quay. They stood staring up at the flames and smoke pouring from the countess's window. In the distance she heard the clang of firebells, but fortunately no one was in the alley and she hobbled away unnoticed.

※

It seemed to take forever to reach the hospital, partly because she kept to the shadows and only crossed bridges where there were plenty of people about and partly because she was forced to stop several times, overcome with dizziness and the pain in her leg. She almost cried with relief when Oksana met her at the hospital door.

"Mother of God, what happened?" She took hold of Alice's arm and helped her down the hallway to the surgery.

"Feliks attacked me," Alice groaned. "My leg ... it's bleeding ..."

Oksana helped her onto the examining table.

"Lie down," she ordered when Alice started to remove the makeshift dressing. "I'll do it. You tell me what happened." Her face was impassive as she carefully cleaned the wound and listened, but when the story was finished, she said, "I told you it wasn't safe for you to stay in Russia."

"I couldn't leave the countess," Alice said, then winced as Oksana applied disinfectant to the wound.

"It's going to need stitches," she said firmly. "I'll get the doctor."

Alice grasped her arm. "No! He'll report it."

"He won't if I ask him not to." Oksana blushed. "I mean ... he's really kind ... ."

"I see," Alice said knowingly. She struggled to a sitting position to examine the wound. It was deep and if she didn't get stitches, she knew it would continue to bleed. She sank back against the pillow. "Fine. But I hope you know what you're doing."

The doctor was new and Alice had never met him, but it was immediately clear that he adored Oksana. And as she had promised, he didn't question Alice's story of stumbling into a sharp object while walking home. Nor did he comment on her soot-stained clothing. As soon as he had stitched the leg, he quickly excused himself, leaving Oksana to apply the dressing.

"It is good that you shot Feliks," she said as she wrapped a sterile bandage around Alice's calf, "but what will you do now?"

"I'm going to Ekaterinadar," Alice said with more determination than she felt. "I'm going to find my brother. And then I'm getting us the hell out of this bloody country!"

When the dressing was finished, Oksana disappeared into the wards, and when she reappeared several minutes later, she had Alice's backpack and a Red Cross bag that contained medical supplies, a thick wool blanket, and a canteen of water. She also handed her a heavy woollen cardigan.

"It will keep you warm," she said, then held out a small packet of ten-rouble notes, "And this might be enough for a train ticket to Moscow."

"No," Alice protested. "I can't take your money."

"You must," Oksana said then shrugged. "Your Canadian coins will give you away. Besides, it is not much and it loses value every day." She pushed the bank notes into Alice's hands. "When you return to your Canada, you can send *me* silver dollars."

Alice suddenly felt like crying. "I won't forget this, Oksana. Not ever."

Oksana wrapped her arms around her friend in a bear-like hug.

"And I won't ever forget you, Alice Galipova."

ZGARDY
Spring 1918

Two winters had passed since Catherine had found Lech's letter in the woodpile, but Natalya's betrayal remained an impervious wall between them. Whenever Natalya broached the subject, Catherine would develop a headache or invent an urgent task that had to be completed. Sometimes she just walked away without a word.

"She'll never forgive me," Natalya said glumly to Maryska as they sat one April afternoon in the molfar's kitchen drinking peppermint tea. "She hates me."

Maryska hacked a chunk of *brynza* from a wedge she had set on the table and stuffed it into her mouth. She didn't chew the cheese, but sucked on it and mashed it with her tongue. After she swallowed it down, she smacked her lips. "It is the first *brynza* made this season," she said. "My husband wants it to cure until the fall, but the cheese is better when it's first made. Not so bitter." She picked up her cup and slurped a mouthful of tea, then plunked it back on the table and peered at Natalya. "You killed her dream. What do you expect?"

"Her dream killed Papa," Natalya retorted, wondering why she had ever confided in the molfar's crazy wife. "*I* should hate *her*."

"My husband hates me," Maryska cackled. "I killed his dream when I fell." She pushed the wedge of cheese toward Natalya. "Eat, girl. You're all skin and bones. Won't get a husband if you're all skin and bones!" She clutched her bosom, pushing her breasts up. "Men like big tits."

"There aren't any young men left to be husbands, Maryska. Only soldiers who come and go. And now the war's over, not even many of them." She swirled her tea around in her cup, watching the peppermint leaves whirl and settle again in the bottom. "Besides, I like to do as I please. If I had a husband, I'd have to stay in the house and cook and clean."

"Not if you're crazy," Maryska said then cackled again.

Natalya hid a smile. She had grown to like this strange old woman who, she had discovered, was not crazy at all though she did everything she could to make people think she was. But having learned that it was better not to acknowledge Maryska's cleverness, she changed the subject.

"I have three more blankets," she said, pulling them from her pack.

Maryska examined the fine weave and the colourful patterns that Catherine had incorporated into the blankets.

"Your sister's spirit is healing. Her weaving is getting better."

"She does seem happier these days," Natalya said. "Not with me ... but sometimes she sings while she works."

"But my husband is beginning to notice that some of the blankets are different," Maryska complained.

Natalya looked at her anxiously. Her mother had only just begun planting their garden and until those crops matured, they needed the grain and beans she acquired from the molfar's wife.

"I will tell her not to be so perfect," she offered quickly.

"No need," Maryska chortled. "I just tell him the bad ones were made when I was suffering from his curse." She heaved herself up and hobbled to the pantry, returning with a small bag of corn.

"It is not much," Natalya observed, making no move to take the bag. "Half what you gave last time."

"That is not my fault. People pay my husband less and less. And Merchant Grabsky gives next to nothing for the blankets."

"Still, I could get as much sifting through the stubble in Farmer Andronic's field and save myself half a day's walking over the mountain."

Maryska shook her head despairingly. "If I give too much away, my husband will find out. If he finds out, he will be angry. You do not want to witness such anger!"

"I don't want to witness my family starving," Natalya countered.

In the end, she settled for the small bag of corn, some pouches of seed, a few beets, dried and wrinkled with age, and two dozen potato eyes that she carefully wrapped in her scarf before putting them in her pack. When she left, Natalya knew Maryska would return the uneaten cheese to a crock, which she would hide in the storeroom where the molfar wouldn't find it.

Zhanna was not pleased with the small amount of corn Natalya brought home, but she was happy with the seed pouches and potato eyes. "We will plant them tomorrow," she said, prompting a groan from Yuliya who, even though she was now eighteen, still hated working in the garden.

The next morning they were up at dawn and digging in the garden before the sun rose, not stopping for lunch until it was high in the sky. Halfway through their meal, Natalya glanced out the window to see Ivan Hawrylak trudge through the gate.

"The postman is here!" she exclaimed

She followed her mother onto the porch in time to see Ivan limp up the steps. He was much thinner now, his clothes were tattered and stained, his muddy boots sported several holes, and his back was bent beneath the load of his mail bag.

"It pains me to ask this, Mother," he lamented as he followed Zhanna into the house and dumped his bag on the floor, "but I must be paid the postage before I can deliver your son's letter into your hands." He pulled an envelope from the bag and waved it in the air as he settled himself on a chair.

Zhanna, having brought to the table the pot of *borscht* she had made for their lunch, paused in the act of ladling a portion into a bowl.

"Then you have wasted a journey, Ivan Hawrylak," she said wearily. "For there is no money to be had in this village for food, never mind for postage that has already been paid. And even if we found a coin, by the time you returned to Yeremeche it would be worth nothing! I can give you a prayer for your soul and some *borscht* that remains from our dinner. Nothing more."

A sound drew Ivan's attention to the corner where Catherine was working the loom while Pylyp sat on the floor beside her. Oblivious to the sounds around him, the boy played with a collection of miniature wooden farm animals that Vasyl had carved when Catherine was just a baby. On a bench beside her was a blanket she had just finished.

"You could pay with that fine blanket, Mother," Ivan said hopefully, "for mine has worn too thin to keep the cold night air from chilling my old bones."

"I'll pray for your old bones," Zhanna retorted, "but a letter from my son will not keep hunger from my children's bellies as those blankets will."

He clutched Oleksi's letter in a grimy fist. "Surely one blanket would not be missed," he wheedled, but Zhanna stood firm.

"I offer you soup and a prayer—nothing more."

Ivan's shoulders slumped. "You drive a hard bargain, Mother," he said at last, "but a starving man is in no position to barter."

As he placed the letter in her mother's hand, Yuliya asked desperately, "Are you sure that is all there is for us, Postman?"

"To get even one letter is a miracle of God, Miss," he said reprovingly. "Mail delivery is a sorry business these days. Even if the post makes it through the fighting, bandits are everywhere. I have heard of postmen being murdered, their bags looted of all valuables and discarded. Sometimes what is left of the mail is rescued before it is ruined by the weather, and sometimes it is not." He leaned over and patted Yuliya's hand. "Do not be sad, Miss. It could well be that the next time Ivan Hawrylak comes to your door, there will be another letter."

Despite her disappointment, Yuliya was as eager as the rest of her family for word from Oleksi, and as soon as the postman left, they gathered around the table. Zhanna read aloud his single-page letter.

> *I do not know where I will be, dear Mother, when you receive this. Tusya and I are shifted about at the will of whoever is in charge of our unit—a condition that changes like the wind. Russia's war with Germany has ended, but no matter where we go, there is still chaos. The Reds fight the Whites. The Whites fight the Greens. Comrades who fought with us one day become enemies the next, and the stench of death is everywhere. Often I wonder if those we save might be better off with God, spared of the agonies of starvation and grief they find when they return to their homes.*
>
> *It is a hell, Mama, that we have tried a hundred times to leave, but always as we are about to depart, someone else appears in our compound with a leg half gone or a face festering with an untended wound, and behind that poor wretch come a dozen more. Our ambulance is a horse-drawn cart more suited to a farmer's field than a medical unit, and because there is only one doctor and a sister, we sanitars are forced to provide care that we've not been trained to give.*
>
> *Only the thought of reuniting with my sweet Alice*

keeps me going from one day to the next, and yet I suffer agonies of doubt for we do not know if she is alive or dead, in Russia or back to Canada. We know only from a soldier who had been at the hospital in Petrograd where she worked that she left St. Petersburg more than a month ago after our beloved countess died in a fire. Please say a prayer for her, dear Mother, for seeing her once more is my single hope in this dark, dark night!

As their mother finished reading the letter, Natalya glanced at Catherine. Oleksi never referred to her or gave any indication that he had forgiven her and his letters usually made her cry. But today she was defiant, not sad.

"He should join the Bolsheviks," she said.

There was a moment of shocked silence, then their mother rose from the bench, reached across the table and slapped her face hard. "Don't ever let me hear such blasphemy in this house again," Zhanna hissed, towering over Catherine. "Now get down on your knees and pray to our Holy Mother to forgive you!"

Catherine raised her hand to her cheek and tears flooded her eyes. "No!" she shouted, and before Zhanna could react, she had pushed away from the table and run from the house.

Natalya and Yuliya gaped after her then stared at their mother.

"We will pray for your sister's soul," Zhanna said, crossing herself. "And then we will go back to the garden and hope that she has not cursed our crop before the seeds are even in the ground."

May arrived with a burst of warm weather, a fat rabbit in one of Natalya's snares and a surprising visitor to the Tcychowski farm. Veniamin Kyrylenko arrived accompanied on foot by Yevhen Hutopila and Father Ishchak. He was dressed in the kind of fine wool suit that Merchant Grabsky sometimes wore, but he walked with a pronounced limp as he led two horses into the yard, one saddled and the other loaded with bundles.

"Glory be to Jesus Christ, brothers," Zhanna greeted the men as they approached the porch. "My home welcomes you."

With obvious reluctance, Veniamin looked away from Yuliya, who stood behind her mother.

"Glory be to you, Mother Tcychowski," he responded politely, then having secured the horses to a post, he removed two of the smaller bundles from the packhorse, and with his companions followed Zhanna into the kitchen.

"Yuliya and Natalya, take your little brother upstairs, and Catherine, prepare some tea for our guests," she said firmly then waved the men to the table. "Please, gentlemen, make yourselves comfortable."

As Yevhen and Father Ishchak sat with their backs to the window, Yevhen gave the traditional Hutsul blessing, "May all your sits be good, Widow Tcychowski." Then he nodded toward Veniamin. "We bring you gifts from our good friend, Veniamin Kyrylenko."

As if in a trance, the young man had remained standing in the middle of the room, staring after Yuliya.

"Veniamin?" Yevhen repeated.

"Yes...yes!" Veniamin stammered as he thrust the two bundles at his hostess. "For you!"

Zhanna's eyes widened when she opened the larger parcel, revealing a round loaf of dark rye bread. Watching from the top step, Yuliya gasped, for such a loaf had not been seen in their home since before Vasyl was killed.

The second bundle held a small sack of salt.

Yevhen said, "That Veniamin has managed to transport these gifts and many more all the way from Kiev without being robbed or murdered is a testimony to his resourcefulness and courage, Mother."

Zhanna touched her finger to the salt and brought it to her lips. "Your friend's courage, brother, was demonstrated two winters past when he kept the soldiers from harming my daughters. And the snares he left for my daughter have spared us from starvation many times over."

Yevhen nodded enthusiastically. "Then we are agreed that he is a worthy husband for your daughter Yuliya, yes?"

Yuliya's fingers tightened around a stair rail as her mother feigned surprise at the proposal.

"As my late husband, may his soul rest in peace, would say, it takes much more than courage and resourcefulness to make a good marriage. A man's background must also be carefully considered."

A sound near the stove drew Natalya's gaze to Catherine, who was glaring down at the teapot as she filled it with hot water. Was she remembering, Natalya wondered, how their father had spurned Lech's proposal because of *his* background? Or was this just more of the anger she had harboured since her quarrel with their mother, which had never been settled but rather ignored.

Father Ishchak cleared his throat, commanding everyone's attention.

"I have questioned this young man thoroughly, Mother," he said, "and I have discerned that he comes from a decent family in Kiev. By all accounts, they have proved themselves both respectable and resourceful for their restaurant has remained open throughout the troubles."

"Bless you, Father," Zhanna said reverently, "but if my late husband were here, may his soul rest in peace, he would surely ask how such a thing is possible. It is said that Kiev has changed hands many times."

"And so it has, Mother," Father Ishchak agreed. "In fact, when Yuliya first confided that Veniamin had serious intentions toward her, I wrote to a bishop I know in the parish where Veniamin's family worships. In a letter he sent with this young man, he assures me that the Kyrylenkos are famous for their discretion and their restaurant has become a meeting place for all sides. It has, he says, been nicknamed Little Switzerland."

On the stairs Yuliya hissed at Natalya, "I told you he's rich!"

Natalya shrugged. "What of it?" she asked indifferently, although inwardly she was cringing. Yuliya already considered herself a step above her siblings; with a rich husband she would be insufferable. "Besides, Mama may not give her consent."

"Of course she will," Yuliya snapped, but she had lost some of her confidence when she resumed watching the scene below.

"I will never see my daughter if she lives in a place so far from Zgardy," Zhanna fretted, pacing the floor and wringing her hands.

"That is so," Father Ishchak said comfortingly, "but she will be well cared for. And there is always the post ... ." He broke off as Veniamin suddenly leaned forward and whispered something in his ear. When the young man straightened, the priest stared down at the table in silent contemplation while everyone in the house held their breath. Finally he said, "Veniamin has made a magnificent offer, Mother. He has invited you and your children to come and live with them in Kiev. His parents have a house with many apartments, one of which, he assures me, they would be happy to share with you."

Natalya's stomach tightened with sudden fear.

No, Mama! she pleaded silently, as she watched her mother's face. Rather than rejecting the proposal immediately, Zhanna seemed to be seriously considering the idea, and Natalya suddenly remembered that her mother had lived in a city before she was married. Certainly not one as large as Kiev—which Father Ishchak had once said was older than any other European city and many thousand times bigger than Zgardy—but a city nonetheless.

Zhanna sank down onto the bench opposite the men.

"My parents, may they rest in peace, died in the city of Lviv," she said in a hollow voice, crossing herself, "when the Germans came. If they had lived in the country, they might have escaped."

"Perhaps," Father Ishchak agreed then said gently, "but your Vasyl was also not so fortunate."

Zhanna nodded slowly. Clutching the cross that hung from her neck, she closed her eyes and mumbled a prayer.

At the stove, Catherine stood, teapot in hand, as if frozen in place. For her, leaving Zgardy would be the end of any lingering hope she might have of ever seeing Lech Wojcik again. Natalya doubted her sister would survive without that hope.

Even I would die in the city, she thought. *And to live in a house ruled by Yuliya? Never!*

She glanced at Yuliya, who was frowning down at the group in the kitchen, and realized that even she was not happy with this idea.

When her prayers were ended, Zhanna said, "Our Lord shall surely bless this young man's generous offer, Father, but such charity is not needed here. My late husband, may he rest in peace, has left me with this farm, and it is here that I belong, close to all that was dear to him and to my precious babies who rest eternally in the sacred ground of our church."

Yuliya's face relaxed into a smile, Natalya almost shouted with relief, and Catherine resumed her tea-making.

"As to the marriage," Zhanna continued slowly, causing Yuliya to clutch at the rails once more, "I believe my husband would want me to give my consent."

❧

Being the centre of attention was a role Yuliya assumed with imperious ease. Seated at the table, she accepted the battered enamel teapot from Catherine as if it were made of the finest porcelain, and in a manner more suited to a countess in the former tsar's court, she poured mint tea into the chipped stoneware cups that Natalya had placed before her and handed them out to the men.

But it was Veniamin who garnered the most attention when he announced that their wedding must take place in four days.

Zhanna's hands flew to her face. "Four days to plan a wedding? But there is so much to do ... and how am I to feed the guests? I have not even a drop of *horilka*, and no flour or yeast to make a proper *korovai*!"

Yuliya helped herself to a thick wedge of the rye bread from the loaf that Zhanna had set out for her guests, and of which they had politely taken only a small portion. "There is no need to fuss, Mama! I am sure Veniamin will provide all that we need."

"The groom providing the bride's wedding feast?" Zhanna crossed herself. "Your poor father, may he rest in peace, would never forgive me."

"The groom is providing nothing, Mother Tcychowski," Veniamin said. "The food is a gift from my parents, who are most distressed that they could not travel with me for this wedding. Sending these gifts is their way of being part of the ceremony, and it would cause them much pain if they were refused." With no hint of falseness, he added humbly, "Besides, such gifts could not begin to compensate you and your family for the tragic cost of the hospitality you extended to me and my brothers when we last visited."

As both Father Ishchak and Yevhen murmured their agreement, Natalya looked at Pylyp, who was now playing quietly beside the stove, close to Catherine. Was there enough food in the whole world to pay for his lost hearing, she wondered. Or for Leysa's death?

Zhanna slowly shook her head. "Such acts were not of your making, Veniamin Kyrylenko, and I do not hold you to them. If it was not for our Lord's mercy and your brave intervention, I would have lost much, much more from that encounter." As Yuliya opened her mouth, Zhanna raised her hand. "Enough, daughter. I will accept these gifts, but only because I understand the remorse of parents unable to attend their own son's wedding."

☙❧

Veniamin did not return to the village with the matchmakers but stayed to unload his packhorse. After carefully inspecting the supplies he'd brought, Zhanna turned to her youngest daughter. "Before dark, Natalya, you must check your snares and see if we can at least provide a fat rabbit or two for our feast."

"I'll help," Veniamin offered.

"And I as well," Yuliya said, stepping in front of her sister.

"No, Yuliya," Zhanna said firmly. "You and I have wedding garments to make."

While they discussed the bridal gown, Natalya gathered her pack and headed outside. Her sister's enraged protest followed her. "A blanket for a wedding skirt, Mama? I would never live such a thing down!"

Veniamin was waiting with the horses. "I won't get very far walking," he said.

Natalya climbed onto the pack horse.

"How did you hurt yourself?" she asked as they rode from the yard.

He grimaced. "On our way out of the mountains. Some of the men wanted to kill the lieutenant and a few of us wouldn't let them. In the ruckus I went over a cliff and landed on my knee." Unexpectedly, he grinned. "The good part is that it got me out of the service. No one wants a soldier who can't march."

They rode to her trapline in a fraction of the time it would have taken Natalya to walk, but there were no rabbits or even squirrels in any of her snares.

"So many people set traps over the winter that there are hardly any animals left," she said as she contemplated the small game trail where she had set her last trap. "Only in the sheep meadow, but I don't dare go there anymore."

"Too many wolves?" Veniamin asked.

"Not the kind you mean," she said then quietly told him about her encounter with Dom Wojcik. "I haven't told Yuliya, and I trust that you won't either. She'll tell Mama and that will be one more worry for her."

"Well, I saw a place on the trail to Yeremeche that was promising," he said. "Too far to walk ... but we could get there easily on the horses."

"I don't go on that trail," Natalya said. "It isn't safe for a woman alone ... ." He nodded in understanding. "But you aren't alone now, so why don't we try it?"

The last time Natalya had been on the trail to Yeremeche was when she was seven years old and had ridden to the neighbouring village with her father. It had seemed much bigger then, the trees taller, the cliff trail narrower and the drop-offs more steep and deadly. Now that she was fifteen years old she found herself enjoying the ride and was almost sad when Veniamin led the way off the track to follow a faint game trail, forcing them to duck under low branches and plough through a willow hedge until they came to a small clearing. Dismounting, they walked the perimeter and finally stopped when she spied a mound of rabbit pellets. Here she placed one of her snares. At Veniamin's suggestion, she placed a second near a blueberry bush, and a third close to a rotting log at the far end of the clearing.

Dusk was already falling when they started for home and it was almost dark when they approached the farm. As they came to the crossroad, Natalya glanced down the trail to the village just in time to see a rider on a white horse disappearing around the bend. Her heart skipped a beat. She was sure it was Dom Wojcik's horse, but she was also sure the rider was not Dom Wojcik. She had not seen him for months and it was rumoured in the village that he had rejoined the baron's regiment.

Terrified of what she would find at home, she urged her horse to a trot, prompting Veniamin to do the same and together they raced through the gate. But when she burst into the house, there was nothing unusual except for Yuliya's grumbling about the dinner preparations, which included none of the food Veniamin had brought.

"No one's been here since you left," Zhanna said in response to her query. "Why do you ask?"

Natalya shrugged. "I just thought I saw some tracks," she lied, thankful her mother was too busy to question her answer.

Veniamin glanced at her curiously.

"Of course you will stay for dinner," Zhanna invited, but he shook his head

"I have promised to dine with the Hutopila family, Mother, since I am staying with them and they are standing in for my family. Instead, I shall come early tomorrow for some of your delicious *kulesha*, yes?"

As he was leaving, Catherine came in from outside carrying two buckets of water. Her cheeks were flushed and she was smiling as she set her load down.

"You were gone a long time for a little water," Zhanna grumbled. "I should be sewing and instead I am making soup."

Catherine gave her a hug. "Well, I'm back now, Mama, so you go and sew while I finish the supper."

Natalya studied her sister then went upstairs to Pylyp, who was peering down at them through the railing.

I'm not about to disturb whatever is making her happy, she told herself. *Not ever again.*

※

Ever since Vasyl's death and the bailiff's ignoble departure from Zgardy, the villagers' attitude toward the chief forester's family had grown more tolerant, especially after Zhanna had helped Father Ishchak set up a soup kitchen at the church to feed the poorest families in the community. With the exception of Farmer Andronic and his friends, almost everyone else in the village had been invited to the wedding and they were so eager to share in the preparations that the day after Veniamin's proposal the Tcychowski house was filled with women all talking at once as they prepared the kind of food none of them had seen for many years. Natalya's stomach growled with hunger spawned by the savoury tang of *borscht*, flavoured with a rabbit she and Veniamin had found in their snares that morning and by the mouth-watering aroma of *korovai* baking in the oven. For this occasion the braid on top of the bread was decorated with two bread doves, and as soon as it came out of the oven, they would be surrounded by a forest of pine tips adorned with colourful bits of wool and shiny pieces of paper.

In the afternoon, while Zhanna worked on the wedding skirt, Yuliya tried to persuade Catherine to alter Vasyl's wedding shirt so it would fit Veniamin, but her sister refused.

"The bride must make her future husband's wedding shirt," she said firmly. "It will bring misfortune to your marriage if I were to do the sewing."

Instead, she and Natalya took Pylyp with them to the village hall where other villagers were preparing it for the wedding reception, scrubbing walls and floors and windows until not a speck of dust or dirt remained. On the walls and ceiling they fastened fir bows, periwinkle vines and spring flowers, and in one corner an altar was set up, laden with the best icons in the village and tented with a white, embroidered runner donated by Lidiya Vitovskyi. Benches lined the sides of the room and a space was cleared in another corner for the musicians. A long table was placed at one end of the room for the *korovai*.

To enable him to share in the preparations, Natalya took her little brother into the woods to gather flowers and periwinkle vines for the bridal wreath. Although he was still small for a child who was almost four years old, Pylyp was losing the gaunt fragility that had plagued him long after he recovered from his battle with typhus. She watched him carefully unravel a vine, following it to the root where he gently detached it from the main stem. He was like their father in that way, gentle, yet persistent and observant. Already he could understand much of what was said to him, simply by watching how people's lips moved, and he mimed what he wanted to say.

She smiled as he dumped an armful of vines at her feet and raised his hands, palms up, as if to say, "What next?"

"Well," she said, making a small wreath from a few of the vines, "if Papa were alive, he would present a wreath to Yuliya and touch her head with it three times." She demonstrated the movements. "But since Papa is gone and Oleksi is not here, it's up to you, little brother, to perform this ceremony."

Pylyp nodded solemnly and when she handed him the wreath, he mimicked her actions perfectly.

"He's a very bright lad," a voice said behind her.

Natalya swung around to see Veniamin watching them.

"Of course he's bright," she said crossly, annoyed that she had not heard his approach. "Why would he not be?"

As usual Veniamin ignored her petulance.

"He would do well in a school for the deaf," he said. "There is a very good one in Kiev."

"We have a school in our church and he's doing just fine. We all are," she added pointedly.

"Still, it's a shame to limit a youngster's future to one small village," he said good-naturedly. He tousled Pylyp's hair then swung about and sauntered back toward the hall.

Natalya studied her brother.

He's just fine, she told herself. *Everyone in Zgardy loves him. One day he'll marry and bring his bride to the farm and they'll raise a whole new family. That is how it was meant to be*!

But as he carefully crafted an exact replica of the wreath she had woven, Natalya felt a twinge of doubt. Suddenly she wasn't so sure if the future she envisioned for her brother was meant to be or even what she wanted that future to be.

☙❧

In the evening four of Yuliya's friends arrived at the farm to share her last evening as an unmarried woman. Although Zhanna would not permit any of the baked goods or *borscht* to be eaten, she did allow Yuliya to serve black currant tea, along with small portions of rye bread and some *bryndza* that Veniamin had sent with them from the village. Gathered around the table, the girls retold legendary wedding stories and sang melancholy songs, most of them centred on the impending loss of Yuliya's girlhood and her new life as a slave to Veniamin's family.

Just before dark the groom arrived and the party took on a merrier atmosphere.

"When Veniamin and Yuliya break the *korovai* tomorrow," Luba Vitovsky teased, "Yuliya is sure to get the greatest piece."

"And that will make her head of the family," one of the others chimed in.

Yuliya pretended to scold them, but it was clear she was in favour of such a concept.

Veniamin said slyly, "If she is the head of the house, then she must wear my trousers. I will be a very rich man if I don't have to buy her dresses."

Natalya grinned wickedly. "And Yuliya will have to work all day and night in the restaurant."

"Ha! I will be too busy having babies," Yuliya countered with a saucy gleam in her eye.

"That never stopped Mama from working," Natalya responded, drawing a scowl from her sister. But before Yuliya could retaliate, Luba changed the subject.

"Is Catherine going to sing at the wedding?"

Yuliya nodded then swivelled her head. "Where *is* Catherine?"

"Maybe she's checking for eggs," Natalya suggested.

"She's been gone since before Veniamin arrived," Luba worried. "Is there something wrong with her? She's been missing a lot of choir practices."

"Catherine never seems to stop working," Veniamin said easily. "If my Yuliya has half her energy, she will soon be running our restaurant single-handed."

Yuliya blushed and slapped his hand, effectively distracting everyone from the subject of Catherine. Then she talked about what a grand city Kiev was and how famous Veniamin's family were.

"Even Father Ishchak has heard of them," she said proudly.

Natalya flashed Veniamin a look of gratitude and quietly slipped away from the group and went outside, but there was no sign of her eldest sister anywhere in the yard or the outbuildings.

Oh, Catherine, what are you up to? she wondered as she finally headed back to the house.

She rejoined the group just as Yuliya was presenting Veniamin with his wedding shirt. Snowy white with Zhanna's delicate embroidery panelling the front in shades of orange and red, the garment was supposed to reach to the groom's mid-thigh area, but since Veniamin was much shorter and thinner than their father had been, it reached to his knees instead. The sleeves were also too long, but unwilling to face the arduous task of taking them apart, Yuliya had simply fastened ribbons around them that, when tied, produced a balloon effect from elbow to shoulder. Still, Veniamin wore the shirt with pride and smiled adoringly at Yuliya as if she'd given him the world's greatest gift.

***

The sun shone brightly through the bedroom window the following morning as the sisters gathered in their room to help Yuliya dress and braid her hair with flowers and bright red strands of wool. Catherine had woven similar red strands into the blanket that her mother had transformed into a skirt, giving it the ribbed contours of a traditional Hutsul garment, and the blouse and vest that Zhanna had worn on her own wedding day fit Yuliya perfectly. Around her neck was a chain of yellow violets and the wooden cross Vasyl had made for her. Even Natalya had to admit that her sister was at that moment quite lovely. She would never have Catherine's ethereal beauty, but for this day her blonde hair shone like gold and her midsummer-blue eyes were bright with happiness.

Surveying her daughter, Zhanna nodded approvingly. "You need only one thing more." Sunlight glinted on the blue and amber stones of the metal cross as she removed it from her neck. "Your father found these stones in the streams that flow through Zgardy. He ground and polished them and then pressed them into a wooden mould and poured hot metal around them. Then he polished them again. On our wedding day he presented it to me." She caressed the stones then lifted the chain over Yuliya's head so the metal cross nestled beside the wooden one. "It is worth nothing to the rest of the world, but it is the most precious thing I have to give, Yuliya. So long as you wear it, your home and the people who love you will always be close to your heart."

Tears filled Yuliya's eyes. "But, Mama, what will you have in its place?"

Zhanna patted her daughter's hand. "I have a cross my father gave to me before he died. I will wear that."

"Your cross is a symbol of Papa's love, Yuliya," Catherine said quietly. "It should remind you always that *true* love never dies."

"Nonsense!" Zhanna snorted. "It is a symbol of God and his love. Men's love shifts with the wind."

Yuliya crossed herself then brought the cross to her lips. "You are right, Mama. It was God who brought Veniamin to me, and it is God who will make him stay … not love."

Catherine turned away from them and pulled on her own skirt, which she had carefully washed and mended, and her blouse, which was even more intricately embroidered than Yuliya's. Watching her, Natalya wondered what it must feel like to love someone with the depth that her sister loved Lech Wojcik. A love that had survived more then four years of absence and a lifetime's worth of sorrow.

Surveying her youngest daughter, Zhanna said, "Natalya, your hair as always is flying in all directions like a wild goose. Sit and let me braid it properly. And Catherine, when you are dressed, you can see to Pylyp."

Their mother was the last to dress, and though her skirt was worn and faded, she had scrubbed her old blouse and bleached it in the sun until it was whiter than snow, and on her head she wore a garland of wildflowers Pylyp had made especially for her.

"You're like the countess in Papa's story, Mama," Natalya said, and though Zhanna scoffed at her foolishness, the sudden colour in her cheeks showed she was pleased by the compliment.

The sound of voices in the yard brought the family to the porch where they found Veniamin waiting with his two horses, their bridles decorated with flowers and ribbons. He was accompanied by Yevhen Hutopila and several other villagers who had arrived on foot.

Dismounting, Veniamin removed the ornate hat he had borrowed from Yevhen, and bowed to Zhanna.

"Glory be to Jesus Christ, Mother Tcychowski!"

"Eternal Glory to God, Veniamin Kyrylenko," she responded.

At her nod, he handed the reins to Yevhen, strode up the steps and took his place beside Yuliya. With bowed heads, they stood before Zhanna as she recited a long prayer then crossed herself and blessed them both. As she finished, a disturbance near the door drew all eyes to Pylyp. Wearing a hat smaller but identical to Veniamin's, and dressed in an embroidered white wool vest and blouse, and a bright red sash into which he had inserted a small hatchet, he was a miniature replica of his father. In his hands he carried the bridal wreath. With a shy smile he walked to Yuliya and held out the flowers. Obligingly, she bent forward, enabling him to perform the ritual as Natalya had instructed, touching her forehead three times. As he extended the wreath a fourth time, Yuliya took it and placed it on her head, then gathered the boy in her arms.

※

The wedding itself took place at the church, which had also been decorated for the occasion. Despite her recent promise never to fall in love, Natalya felt a twinge of envy as she watched her sister and Veniamin exchange vows, both so filled with happiness that even the saints along the walls appeared to be smiling benevolently upon them. The choir sounded better than Natalya had ever heard them, and when Catherine sang a special hymn in Yuliya and Veniamin's honour, her voice rose so clear and beautiful that there was no other sound in the church. The bride and groom's eyes were moist before she finished.

At the end of the service, the couple mounted their horses once more. Followed by a parade of villagers, and accompanied by musicians playing lively tunes, they made their way to the hall where they rode beneath an arbour that had been fashioned out of fir boughs.

Once inside the hall, the music grew even more exuberant. The couple welcomed each guest, and Veniamin began the wedding toasts, lifting a small cup of *horilka* in honour of his wife's family, drinking all but a third of the portion and tossing the rest over his shoulder. Then he refilled his cup and presented it to Yevhen Hutopila who, as his best man, offered the next toast in the same manner.

When the drinking ceremony was finished, the bride and groom were presented with an undecorated *koravai*. After each had individually peered through the hole, they held the bread together and looked through the centre in unison, symbolizing that as a couple they were now heading in the same direction. Contrary to Luba's prediction, when the couple broke the bread, Veniamin held the biggest share. Knowing Yuliya's gift for always getting the largest piece of anything served, Natalya suspected her sister had wisely restrained herself on this occasion.

The first wedding dance was the *arkan*, which was performed by the men and, among other complicated steps, required progressively wilder acts of kicking and stomping of heels on the floor—moves that Veniamin could not possibly perform with his bad knee. Instead, he watched from the sidelines and applauded with the other guests when the stomping rose to such a crescendo that the hall shook. When the *hutsulka* began, however, he insisted on leading the dance with Yuliya and although Natalya knew he must have been in great pain as he whirled her sister about the room, his face reflected only his delight in sharing this moment with his bride.

Veniamin was not, however, able to share the wedding night with Yuliya for she had insisted on observing the local custom of the bride spending a final night in her childhood home.

"We will be together for the rest of our lives," she told Veniamin. "Tonight I must be with my family."

Exhausted from her three-day marathon of cooking and organizing the wedding, Zhanna retired to her bedroom early with Pylyp while her daughters gathered in the room they had shared all of their lives. From beneath the covers of their bed, Catherine retrieved the Romanoff tapestry and hung it over the dark window, placing candles on the floor so the flames illuminated the golden threads. Seated before it in a semi-circle, they each lifted a cup with a small portion of *horilka* that Yuliya had salvaged from the dinner party.

"We will drink to Leysa," she said solemnly. "May she be rejoicing in the arms of our Lord."

Catherine touched the cross with her cup. "May you be in a place of peace, little sister," she said quietly.

Natalya wanted to say something profound but all she could manage was, "Please kiss Papa for me, Leysa." Then, to stop herself from crying, she downed the alcohol in her cup, choking as it seared her throat. It calmed her as its warmth spread through her body.

Yuliya plunked her empty cup on the floor and held out her hand so the candlelight sparkled on the wedding band Veniamin had placed upon her finger that morning. "Yuliya Kyrylenko," she said wonderingly, gazing at the ring. "Wife of Veniamin. Soon to be citizen of Kiev."

"Are you afraid?" Natalya asked.

Yuliya shook her head but then gave a shaky smile. "A little," she admitted. "What if Veniamin's family doesn't like me?"

"If they are anything like Veniamin, they will adore you," Catherine said firmly. She began unbraiding Yuliya's hair, removing the wilted periwinkle blossoms.

"But not if you're bossy and grumpy," Natalya warned as she pressed the flowers between the pages of a small bible—Yuliya's wedding gift from Father Ishchak.

"Without you around I won't have a reason to be grumpy," Yuliya retorted.

"It's strange," Catherine said sadly as she brushed Yuliya's hair, "but I thought I would be the first one to marry."

"I'm never going to marry," Natalya declared. "I won't have some man bossing me about. And besides, there's no one in the village that I like."

Yuliya bent forward slightly as the brush was tugged through the waves made by her braids. "Of course you will marry," she said with her old impatience. "When the war is over, there will be plenty of men asking for your hand."

"They can ask all they want," Natalya said. She closed the bible and set it on the nightstand beside their bed. "I don't have to accept."

"You will if Mama has anything to do with it," Yuliya predicted.

Catherine paused her brushing. "If you are in love, Natalya, nothing will stop you from marrying." It was the first time she had said anything so personal or caring to her since she had found Lech's letter in the woodpile, and it made Natalya want to weep.

Yuliya tossed her head so her hair swished softly in the air. "Love is all well and good, but it doesn't keep your belly full or your bones warm when the wind whistles about your bed." She rotated her ring several times around her finger then said in a conspiratorial tone, "I heard some news today.... from Vira Shevchenko."

Catherine snorted. "That is not surprising. Vira gossips more than her mother, but much of what she says is not true."

"Well, this time her gossip has the ring of truth, sister. She told us how her father had to deliver two new barrels to the baron's estate yesterday, and ..." She paused dramatically. "And he saw Lech Wojcik there."

The brush jerked in Catherine's hands and Natalya felt suddenly sick.

Yuliya continued blithely as if nothing was amiss. "Vira said Lech's wife ran off with a soldier and took her children with her. She said it was because Lech was drunk all the time. Now he's come to manage the baron's estate."

The room grew silent and as if suddenly realizing something was amiss, Yuliya said apologetically, "I wasn't going to tell you because I thought it would only make you sad. And it has, hasn't it?"

Catherine shrugged. "It is nothing to me. Why should it be?" She set the brush carefully on the table and walked to the door. "I'm going to check the stove," she said, though the fire had gone out many hours earlier.

As her steps receded down the stairs, Yuliya's brow furrowed and she shook her head. "I should not have told her."

"Better she hears it from you than Vira Shevchenko." But as Natalya took down the tapestry and replaced it under the bed, she thought about the expression on Catherine's face when Yuliya revealed her secret. Her eldest sister had been already well aware of Lech Wojcik's return to Zgardy.

WESTERN RUSSIA
December 1917 – November 1918

Alice stared unseeingly at the frozen fields and lakes outside the train's frosted window pane. The clickety-clack of the train's wheels had a mesmerizing effect that helped to alleviate her discomfort as she jostled to and fro on the hard wooden bench. She was crowded against the side of the car by an elderly gentleman with a ragged goatee, who was squeezed in turn by a woman wearing at least three dresses, their hems of varying lengths just visible beneath her thick woollen coat.

At each stop her fellow passengers, including the overdressed woman, filed out of the crowded car to stretch their legs and collect hot water for their teapots. Bundled in her thick nurses' cloak, Alice remained hunched forward in her seat, her mittened hands tucked into the sleeves of the thick sweater Oksana had given her. Her wounded leg throbbed, her toes ached with the cold, and her stomach clamoured for food, but she could not bring herself to move.

At their third stop, as the old man got to his feet, he said politely, "You should walk about, Sister. You will get frostbite if you don't move. Hot water will do much to warm you."

He was right, she thought. If she didn't move, she would freeze. And her leg would stiffen.

She sighed, slid to the edge of the bench and pulled herself upright. Wincing at the pain even that small movement caused, she forced herself to take a step, and then another, down the aisle and the two stairs to the platform. She saw that the old man was standing in a line, waiting as one by one those ahead of him filled flasks or buckets or tin cans from the spigot of a huge metal samovar. She rummaged through her pack, pulled out a metal cup and sprinkled some tea leaves in the bottom. When it was her turn, she filled it with hot water, then limped to the far end of the platform where a huddle of women were selling food—chunks of greyish bread, small packets of beechnuts, and some kind of charred meat on wooden skewers.

"I would suggest the *shashlyks*," the old man said, pointing to the skewered meat. "They are less likely to be contaminated." He had followed her across the platform, and now he stood watching keenly as she asked the women the price of their offerings. Without a ration card, a skewer was forty roubles. Besides the diamonds that were hidden once more in the buttons Alice had carefully sewn onto her cape as ornaments, and the five-dollar gold coin from her father stitched into her brassiere, she had only one rouble left from the money Oksana had given to her. With it she could have purchased a packet of beechnuts, but she knew the old man was right. They could easily be carrying typhus or cholera.

"I guess I'm not hungry after all," she said, noting the disappointment in the old man's face. *He was probably hoping I would share*, she thought sadly as she walked back to the train.

Their car was even more crowded as new passengers joined those already squeezed into the compartment. They seemed to have come from all parts of Russia, and in most faces was the stoic resignation that Alice had become accustomed to as part of the Russian persona. But there were a few who stood out, including a young mother cradling two toddlers on her lap. Her clothes spoke of better days, and she kept glancing nervously at a man in a dark suit who stood at the end of the aisle. Arms folded, he scrutinized every movement the passengers made and every person who entered or left the car. Feeling as nervous as the woman seemed to be, Alice pulled the hood of her cloak forward and turned her head to the window, avoiding his gaze.

At a station several stops farther along, a young boy held up the hot water line as he attempted to fill a rusted tin can, only to have the hot water seep out from a crack where the tin's side seam had separated. After a few moments, the crowd behind him grew restless and several shouts of "Throw it away!" and "Move on!" were accompanied by a volley of threats and curses.

Alice felt sorry for the boy and was about to give him her cup when two old soldiers marched onto the platform, one of them brandishing a machine gun, and both wearing red stars pinned just above the brims of their conical wool hats. Her stomach tightened as the taller soldier, whose lined and battle-scarred face was clean-shaven and more severe than the other, grasped her arm and pulled her from the queue.

"Come with us, Miss," he said crisply.

"Why?" Alice cried, trying to wriggle free. "I've done nothing wrong!"

"Please, Miss!" the second soldier pleaded in a high-pitched voice. "Don't make me shoot!" His eyes, just visible through the bushy strands of his full-facial beard, were wild and the barrel of the machine gun bobbed up and down in his shaking hands. The people around her scattered and, realizing how dangerously close he was to pulling the trigger, Alice stopped struggling. The soldier thrust her ahead of him, and as she staggered away from the line that was already re-forming, she saw the old man staring studiously at the ground. Had he reported her, she wondered? Or was he just afraid he would be next?

She stumbled and almost fell as they stepped off the platform, but the soldiers didn't slow down. Half-pushing, half-pulling, they forced her along a second railway track that led away from the town.

Am I being arrested? Am I to be shot?

Remembering Feliks' talk of skinning people alive, she shuddered and desperately scanned the barren, snow-covered stubble fields that stretched to distant horizons on either side of the track. There was no place to flee, no place to hide.

Soon they detoured onto a siding that led toward a lone cattle car, and as they drew closer the tall soldier called out, "We have a sister!"

The car's side door slid open. Inside a number of men lay on the floor, all sporting bloodied bandages. They were being tended by a man who was bundled against the cold in a thick coat. On his sleeve was the unmistakable red cross of a medic.

Alice's heart thumped wildly.

It isn't me. It's a sister they want!

Almost gratefully she allowed her abductors to lift her into the boxcar where the haggard-faced doctor shouted, "Did you bring supplies?"

The taller soldier pulled the Red Cross bag from Alice's shoulder. The doctor tossed out the canteen and blanket then flicked his hand disgustedly at the small amount of medical supplies inside and threw the whole thing to the floor.

"What good is this?" he screamed hysterically.

Alice knelt beside the man lying closest to her. His forehead was bloodied and a deep gash swept from above his left eye to his hairline. She turned to her captors.

"Get us some water! Quickly!" she ordered then retrieved her canteen and bag and turned to the doctor. "There are sutures in the bottom box. I'll set up for you."

She swabbed the wounded man's forehead with disinfectant

and by the time she had the needle, sutures and forceps ready on the blanket, the doctor had regained enough composure to kneel beside her and begin suturing the wound.

"I have worked all night . . ," he mumbled, "no supplies … so many dead … ."

"You have help now," Alice reassured him. "You'll be fine." Then, as he sutured the first man, she moved to the second.

※

Hours later when the eight wounded men had been stabilized, they were transferred with the doctor onto the next train to Moscow while her two wardens frogmarched Alice onto a westbound train. This coach was even more crowded than the one she had taken from Petrograd, and the jolting of the wobbly wooden bench on which she was squeezed between the two men made it impossible to relax. She yearned for sleep but every time she closed her eyes she would be startled awake by a sudden bump or the screech of rusted brakes. The machine-gun-toting soldier had no trouble dozing, and even when the train jerked to a halt, as it did frequently, and sent him sprawling onto her lap, he would merely straighten himself up and resume snoring.

"Denyan could sleep in the middle of a ball-shrivelling battlefield," said his companion, who told her his name was Dmitri.

Too tired to respond, Alice sat huddled over her pack and bag and tried not to think about how cold and hungry she was, or how her leg throbbed with every clack of the wheels against the track.

※

Sometime during the darkest hours between midnight and dawn they disembarked at Vitebsk. Sandwiched between Dmitri and Denyan and pelted with an icy wind and whirling snow, Alice fought her way to a schoolhouse that Dmitri said was being used as a temporary barracks for their Red Guard unit. All she saw when she stumbled inside the unheated building were several long rows of cots whose snoring occupants didn't stir as she was led past them. Near the back of the room she was assigned a cot of her own and given a blanket that she was too exhausted to inspect for lice or any other contaminant before she collapsed onto the straw mattress and slept.

When she awoke ten hours later, it was daylight and her two chaperones were standing guard over her bed.

"We did not want you to be bothered by any piss-brained louts," said Dmitri.

She clutched her covers to her chest and, recognizing the blanket from her bag, realized that one of them must have covered her with it in the night.

Denyan, whom Alice was discovering was the more polite of the two—despite his machine gun—said hopefully, "If you come now, Miss, we can still get breakfast."

Her mouth tasted foul and her aching bones yearned for a long, hot bath, but since she wasn't likely to get one, she tucked her own blanket back into her bag, hoisted it onto her shoulder and followed the Two Dees, as she decided to call them, to the dining hall. This room was filled with long plank tables set between narrow benches. It was cold and the breakfast was nothing more than a thin slice of hard black bread and a bowl of watery soup with a single piece of indefinable meat and something resembling shredded beets, but Alice was grateful. She ate quickly, afraid she would be ordered to move on before she was finished.

After breakfast her escorts delivered her to a large brick building where the Russian Red Cross had set up a temporary hospital.

"You are to work here," Dmitri said. "We will come for you when the horse dung they call dinner is served in the barracks."

Alice wondered why they thought she would remain at the hospital once they were gone, and as if reading her thoughts, Dmitri held up a folded document.

"My passport! How ... ?"

Denyan smiled sheepishly. "You sleep soundly, Miss."

"We will give it back to you," Dmitri said, "when the revolution is safe!"

"Right." She clamped her hands on her hips. "And just how many lifetimes do you figure that's going to take?"

"It will be soon, Miss!" he said, his eyes bright with enthusiasm. "By the time the orchards blossom there will be bread on every Russian table, the war with the bastard Germans will be over and every peasant will have his own land! The Russian people will be free and you will be allowed to go back to your Canada."

"But I could be arrested if I'm stopped without my passport."

She grabbed for the document, but Dmitri held it beyond her reach. "You are safer with no passport than you are with this," he said, tucking it safely inside his coat. "Foreigners are no longer welcome in Russia."

"Don't worry, Miss," Denyan consoled her, "if you are with us, you will not be arrested."

"And if you are wounded or killed?" she demanded. "What then?"

"Oh, we don't fight, Miss," Dmitri said confidently. "I drive the ambulance and Denyan tends the horses."

Alice stared at Denyan's machine gun. "But what about that thing?"

"I've only shot it once," he admitted, "and that was at an oak tree." He grinned sheepishly. "I missed."

As she watched them march back toward the barracks, Alice thought of the gold coin in her bra. *I can buy my way out of this situation*, she mused. According to Dmitri, Vitebsk was located at the confluence of the Dvina, Vitba and Luchesa rivers, roughly four hundred kilometres west of Moscow. If she followed one of them to a larger centre where she would be less noticeable, perhaps she could board another train and resume her journey east. It was a wild idea and completely unworkable, she realized. With her injured leg, she could never make such a journey, and even if she could, the rivers were sure to be heavily guarded. She scanned the street. The sidewalks of the little town were filled with peasants and soldiers and grim-faced men dressed in dark suits who carried an air of officialdom about them. Any one of them could arrest her without reason.

Or with a reason, she thought dismally as the image of Feliks lying on the bedroom floor among the flames flashed through her mind. Heaving a sigh, she turned and painfully climbed the steps to the hospital.

෴

As 1917 drew to a close and the new year began, the Two Dees dragged Alice from one dreary posting to another. Her home became their horse-drawn ambulance, which had actually started out as a motorized truck with an expansive front end. When they were unable to get parts or gasoline to keep it running, they had ripped out the engine and drive train, reduced the size of the cab and expanded the box so they could carry more patients.

"Nikolai and Alexi don't go fast," said Denyan, caressing the neck of one of the two draught horses that pulled the wagon, "but they don't break down either."

When Alice questioned the wisdom of naming the horses after the deposed tsar and his wife, Dmitri explained it was just Denyan's way of reversing roles. Earlier that morning the two had painted over the word "Russian" on the Red Cross sign on the side of their truck and replaced it with the word "*Soviet*."

"We should not need it for much longer," Dmitri said. "As soon as the treaty is signed with Germany, we shall all go home."

⁂

As predicted, the treaty was duly signed in Brest-Litovsk in March, officially ending the wars Russia was fighting with both Germany and the newly formed Ukrainian Republic, but the medical unit was not disbanded. Instead, it was pressed into service supporting Leon Trotsky's Red Army brigades.

"Communism will not be safe until those worm-infested, cabbage-headed anarchistic Cossacks and the piss-rotting Ukrainian separatists have been brought into line!" Dmitri exploded when Alice challenged his earlier promise that she would be free by the time the orchards blossomed. "Until then you are safer with us."

As they continued to move, now to the east, now to the south, and sometimes to the west, but always within the territories under control of the Red Army, Alice lost track of the towns and villages where their temporary hospitals were located. They all seemed the same to her—dirty, snow-covered streets in the cold weather that became muddy quagmires in the spring. She plodded through each day, waking, eating, working and sleeping, feeling always alone, an alien amongst her co-workers, who treated her with a reserved politeness that never strayed into anything closer.

"They hate me," she complained to Dmitri one night as he walked her back to her sleeping quarters.

"It's not you," he said kindly. "They are afraid to be friendly. You are British, and they know the bastard Cheka are watching you."

"I'm Canadian," Alice retorted, but she knew that wouldn't make any difference to Lenin's secret police force. Stories were circulating of people they had arrested who simply disappeared or, worse, were tortured in ways that would have delighted Feliks Stolin. She studied Dmitri curiously. "So, am I hearing disenchantment with your precious communist system?"

"If it wasn't for the piss-headed counter-revolutionaries, there'd be no need for the rat-infested, viper-ridden bastardly Cheka," he growled. Then he patted her shoulder. "Just keep working hard and don't make a fuss, Miss Alice. And stop questioning the patients."

It was easy not to make a fuss, but Alice couldn't keep herself from asking every patient she treated the same two questions—had they been to the south and had they ever heard of two sanitars named Tusya and Oleksi. Unfortunately, the answers were always negative, and had she been allowed time to dwell on her situation, she might have given in to the despair that was always on the edge of her consciousness.

❧

Throughout the spring and summer, the Bolshevik government faced growing opposition, most of it centred around their failure to provide food for those who were starving and their demands on the peasant farmers to surrender their grain for little or no compensation. While the peasants were happy to confiscate grain from the rich farmers, known as *kulaks*, they preferred to distribute their bounty among their own hungry villagers rather than send it on to central committees. Lenin responded by extending the designation of *kulak* to include anyone who refused to surrender their harvests and declaring war on what he called these "rich bastards and known bloodsuckers!"

Alice's grandfather had told her how Russia had once been farmed by serfs who were ruled by their landlords and not allowed to leave their farms without permission. To survive, they would farm two tracts of land, the most fertile tract for their landlord, the lesser one for themselves. In the mid-1800s, serfdom was abolished, and the less fertile land was turned over to peasant communes, but the landlords retained the prime pastoral lands and forests. In order to graze their animals or cut firewood to heat their homes during the long cold winters, the peasants were forced to pay rents that gradually grew so high they had to seek employment elsewhere in order to pay them.

Dmitri's description of *kulaks* was only slightly less dramatic than Lenin's.

"Pus-eating maggots feasting on the flesh of their brothers!" he said one day as they passed an iron gate leading to one of the larger farms in the area. "The weasel-hearted cowards have spent the war stealing even more land, and instead of fighting for Russia the slime-encrusted vipers have raised the price of grain. Workers in our mills and mines and factories starve because they can't afford even a slice of bread for their tables and freeze for want of firewood." He spat again and lapsed into silence, but from the expression on his face, Alice suspected the tirade was still running through his head.

As they rode along in silence, she thought of her father's ranch at Willow Bar Creek and of the long years when he had worked night and day to turn the wild, forested lands he'd been granted into a ranch that would provide for him and his family. Even now he fought an ongoing battle with winter storms and summer droughts and diseases that sometimes wiped out half his herd. Yet there were those in the community who envied him, and ranch hands who complained their wages were too low and that everything had come too easy for Sergei Galipova.

Denyan patted her hand. "There are many good *kulaks*, Miss. And there are many villagers who would give their lives defending them."

The grim result of Lenin's edict was evident one hot afternoon as Alice and her escorts made their way along a country road, having been ordered to report to a newly established medical unit some distance east. Suddenly they were forced to pull off the road to make way for a food detachment hauling four wagons filled with golden grain, and guarded by a company of Red Army soldiers. A few versts further along, on the outskirts of a small town, Denyan halted the horses once more. In horror, Alice stared at a long wooden gallows from which hung five men, their hands tied behind their backs, their bodies bloated and their lifeless faces covered with flies. The executions must have been carried out the previous day, for the smell was almost unbearable, and Alice buried her face in her scarf, hiding not only from the stench but also from the horror.

"What kind of animals would do such a thing?" she fumed when they were finally clear of the site. For once Dmitri had no answer.

Denyan said sadly, "The people are afraid, Miss. They see only their hunger and their babies dying and they need to believe someone is to blame. If the *kulaks* have food and they don't, well then, our leaders must be right and the *kulaks* must be at fault. In the winter, when they are truly starving, they will find out they were wrong." He pulled the horses to a standstill near a grove of aspens growing along the edge of a small stream. "Tonight we will camp here. Tomorrow we will report to the commander."

Dmitri, who usually directed their affairs, made no response. Grim-faced, he climbed down from the wagon then strode off toward the trees. Denyan tended the horses then made a fire and lit the samovar, while Alice stuffed beneath the coals half a dozen cobs of corn they had taken from a farmer's field earlier that day. As she waited for them to cook, she wondered if the corn had been planted by one of the executed *kulaks*. She gazed down at her hands. They had been smooth once and her nails trimmed and manicured. Now they were dry and rough and her nails were as ragged as her dresses. She was only twenty-two years old, but she felt closer to a hundred, and she suspected she looked that age as well.

At least I'm not hanging from a gallows somewhere, she told herself sternly, but wasn't comforted. Like the peasants, she wanted someone to blame, though in her heart she knew there was no single cause for the insanity that had been unleashed on Russia. If there was anyone to blame for her circumstances, it was herself for stubbornly insisting she had to fulfill a promise that no one, most of all her father, would ever have expected her to keep.

A movement near the trees caught her attention and a moment later Dmitri emerged, his shoulders slumped and a weariness in his steps. He did not come immediately to the fire, but climbed into the ambulance. When he emerged and dropped back to the ground, he held a document in his hand. He handed it to Alice. "My conscience will no longer allow me to keep this, Miss," he said sorrowfully. "You are free to go wherever you wish. Denyan and I will not stop you."

Alice fingered the passport. She should have been elated, but instead she felt bewildered and abandoned. "But ... where will I go?"

Dmitri shook his head. "I don't know, Miss."

Denyan stirred the coals. "You could stay with us, Miss," he said, "until you find your brother."

She saw a hopefulness in his eyes, and she realized that

somewhere in the months and months they had travelled together, she had grown very fond of these two old soldiers. Now the thought of leaving them was not something she could bear. At least not alone.

"Then that is what I shall do," she said quietly.

❦

On a cold wet morning in November 1918 the medical unit was stationed at a Red Cross tent camp on the outskirts of Bakhtin, a farming village north of Orel. Several kilometres away, a skirmish had taken place in the night between the Red Army unit to which they were attached and a division from Nestor Makhno's Black Army, which Dmitri referred to as a bloodthirsty horde of bandits. Heavy casualties had resulted from the battle, and the Two Dees' ambulance was called into service.

"You'll be safe, Miss," Dmitri assured her as they prepared to leave. "The director here is from the same estate as Denyan and me. He's promised to watch over you."

It rained in the early morning hours and Alice's boots, which now sported several holes where the leather had worn completely through, were soaked and muddy by the time she reached the warehouse that had been converted into a temporary hospital. Squishing up the steps, she stepped past two figures huddled next to the door—a woman with tangled filthy hair and dark, sunken eyes who cradled a little boy on her lap. His skeletal limbs poked from a ragged shift that barely covered his bottom, and his gaunt face was flushed with fever. A yellow discharge oozed from a wound on his left foot. As Alice stepped past them, the woman grasped her leg.

"Please, Miss," she begged in a raspy voice, "help my son! Have mercy on a little boy!"

The doctor frowned when she brought the two inside, and the commissar in charge, a woman whose bulk and manner reminded Alice of Grusha, stormed over to them.

"Outside!" she ordered the woman, pointing to the door. "You cannot come in here!"

Alice stepped between the mother and the exit. "I just want to clean the boy's infected foot," she said.

The commissar shook her head. "No! Dressings are for soldiers who fight for Russia. Not beggars."

"Then I shall make my own dressing."

"No!" The commissar thrust her index finger repeatedly toward the door and shouted, "Out! Out! Out!"

Finally Alice led the woman outside and down the street to the train station where she used water from the public tap and a portion of her scarf to clean the wound. Wishing she had some disinfectant, she bound the boy's foot with another piece of scarf, and knowing it would do little good, advised the mother to repeat the process at least twice a day. When Alice handed her the rest of her scarf to use as bandages, and the small slice of bread she was saving for her lunch, the woman grasped her hand and kissed it.

"*Spasiba! Spasiba!*" she cried.

Alice pulled her hand free and hurried back to the hospital, aware that several of the villagers were watching her. They were clearly angry as they whispered and pointed from her to the mother and her son.

"You are late for your work," the commissar said coldly when she re-entered the building. "You will have to make the time up."

That day, not even the doctor spoke to her unless it was absolutely necessary, and she was given only those tasks no one else wanted to do, cleaning patients who had messed themselves and bathing those who were newly admitted and covered with lice. By the time she went back to the barracks it was long after dark, and she spent the night dreaming about insects crawling over every part of her body. In the morning she was more exhausted than before she'd gone to bed.

In the mess tent Alice did not mind being a pariah because it generally meant she could eat in peace since no one wanted to sit near her. As she carried her single slice of black bread and her cup of hot tea to one end of the long plank table, the sanitars who had been eating there jumped up and, grabbing what was left of their own meals, hurried out of the tent. At the far end of the table a Cheka agent with a face as severe as his long black leather coat eyed her in a way that made her stomach tighten with fear. Since the attempted assassination of Lenin in August, special punitive brigades had terrorized the countryside, torturing and executing thousands of citizens without trial, often for no other reason than an unsubstantiated rumour that they had expressed doubts about the regime. As a foreigner, Alice was more vulnerable than anyone else in the medical unit, and she knew it was only because of Dmitri and Denyan's support that she had so far escaped the inquisition.

The door opened and as a gust of cold air flooded the room, she shivered then felt a rush of relief as Dmitri strode into the tent. He was clearly furious, but after an uneasy nod to the Cheka agent his face became impassive. Avoiding Alice's gaze, he collected his own breakfast and took a seat halfway along the bench.

Her hands trembled as she forced a piece of bread into her mouth and slowly chewed it to a pulp, swallowing it down with a gulp of tea. She wasn't hungry, but having given yesterday's lunch to the boy's mother and then missing dinner, she knew if she was going to get through another long day, she had to eat something.

The tent flap opened and a second Cheka agent entered and hurried over to the first, who, after a whispered conversation, rose to his feet and left the tent. When it was clear they weren't coming back, Dmitri moved closer to Alice.

"Have you gone crazy in the head?" he hissed. "What kind of cabbage-headed idiot who is trying not to be noticed helps an outcast in front of the whole pissing village?"

Alice swallowed hard, realizing she had not only endangered herself, she had also inadvertently endangered the Two Dees.

"The boy's foot was badly infected," she said defensively. "How could I turn my back on him?"

"You think you did him a favour?" It was an accusation more than a question, and one Dmitri contemptuously answered for her. "The sepsis would have been a quick death. Now he will starve slowly. Or freeze."

"But why the bloody hell must he starve, Dmitri? Surely the villagers could help him. Or we could give him food!"

He gripped her shoulders and gave her an angry shake, barely controlling his rage. "What food? There's scarcely enough for our unit, and even less for the villagers. Will you have them take food from the mouths of their own starving children to help the flea-infested spawn of a traitor?"

She winced and tried unsuccessfully to break free of his painful grip. "What do you mean?"

With a gesture of disgust, he pushed her away from him. "When the Whites came through here, they were rounding up Bolsheviks," he said in the deliberate way one might talk to a child sorely in need of a lesson, "including the boy's father. They said they'd burn the house if the woman didn't tell where her husband was hiding. So she told them and they burned her house anyway."

"But that is not the little boy's fault," Alice protested. "And surely losing her husband and her home is punishment enough."

"There were five other village men hiding with her husband," Dmitri said grimly. "They were all hanged in the village square. For that there is no forgiveness. The woman and her boy will starve, and that will serve as a warning to others." He propped his elbows on the table and buried his head in his hands. "The trouble is what to do with you now. Denyan and I must take a patient to Kursk ... "

"I'm sure I'll be fine," Alice said, aware that it was a wish more than a surety. "And you said the director would protect me."

"Not anymore," Dmitri said miserably. "That piss-for-guts coward has washed his hands of you." He lifted his head and stared at the table. "There are a lot of patients from last night, so they will need your help. You should be fine until we return and by then Denyan and I will have a plan." He got to his feet. "Just don't create any more trouble," he ordered before he strode out of the tent.

"Don't worry," she muttered under her breath. "I won't even look at anything that doesn't have Bolshevik stamped all over it."

It was a short-lived promise, however, for she had just started walking along the road toward the hospital when someone hissed at her from behind a shed. She glanced about and since no one else was on the street, she dared to come closer then froze as she recognized the mother, this time without her little boy. Her bony hands grabbed Alice's cape and pulled her behind the shed.

"Do not go to the hospital, Miss," the woman pleaded. "They wait for you near the steps."

Suspecting this was simply a hoax to get her to attend to the boy again, Alice wrenched her hand free. "Who waits for me? And where is your son?"

The woman said with no emotion, "He is dead. And now they will kill me."

Alice stared at her helplessly. "I'm sorry. But I can't help you ... ."

"Nobody can help me, Miss. I am already dead. But you do not deserve to die for helping me."

Alice surveyed the frozen fields stretching beyond the road. There was nowhere for her to run. No place for her to hide. Her knees felt suddenly weak and she leaned against the shed for support. What could she do?

"There was talk, Miss," the woman said, "at the train station. Some soldiers spoke of a brigade coming to Kursk from the south. There is to be a battle against the Ukrainians."

Alice stared at her.

"But Russia isn't at war with the Ukraine ... ."

The woman shrugged. "I do not make sense of what they say. I heard you ask about units from the south. So I tell you and my debt is paid." She began hobbling toward a wooded area.

"I could give you money," Alice said desperately. "I have a coin ... it would help you get away ... ."

The woman kept walking. She was ready to die and for one bleak moment Alice envied her. Then she shook herself and turned back to the tent camp. She was halfway along when she heard a loud yell, followed by several shots coming from the direction of the temporary horse corral that had been erected behind the tents. Her heart pounded as she slowly pressed forward, keeping close to the tents. There was more shouting, and suddenly three mounted Cheka soldiers charged past, one of them riding Alexi.

Oh, please, no! She hurried around the last tent and saw Dmitri kneeling over a man on the ground by the corral.

Nikolai snorted anxiously at Alice's approach, but it was the fallen man who commanded her attention. Denyan lay on his back, his right eye swollen shut, his beard coated with blood and even more blood soaking a bandage Dmitri was applying to his chest.

"Here, let me," Alice said, kneeling beside him. Pressing the padded cloth hard against the bullet wound just below his shoulder, she managed to stop the bleeding. "It didn't hit his lungs," she told Dmitri.

"They shot him," he said in a stunned voice. "They said we had no right to have two horses when one would do."

Denyan said weakly, his eyes filling with tears, "I tried to stop them, Miss. But they took Alexi and my gun."

"We have to get him to the hospital," Alice said, sliding her hand under Denyan's back, probing for, but not finding, an exit wound. "The bullet has to come out."

Dmitri shook his head. "He was shot by the Cheka. They won't touch him at the hospital."

"It is all right, Miss," Denyan said kindly. "I have made my peace with God. I am ready to go."

"Nonsense!" Alice frowned as she tried to think of what to do. "I can stabilize him," she said finally, "and stay with him while you collect your patient and we can take them both to Kursk. The staff there won't know who shot him."

※

Three days later, Alice, dressed as a peasant with her face half-hidden by a heavy black shawl, stood dejectedly near the boarded-over doorway of what had once been a men's clothing store. She was waiting for Dmitri, who had gone to the local Red Army headquarters to obtain the travel papers he needed to transport Denyan back to Bakhtin. With the bullet safely removed from his shoulder, the old soldier had recovered enough to travel.

"But why to Bakhtin?" she had asked, horrified at the thought of returning to a place where the villagers hated her. "Why not some other posting?"

Dmitri, who had aged by at least a dozen years since his friend had been shot, manifested the resigned stoicism she had seen in so many peasant faces. "If we do not return to Bakhtin they will say we have stolen the ambulance from them. For that, we will all be shot."

Alice suspected they would all be shot anyway, but she didn't press the point because she was still hoping to find Tusya and Oleksi. But after three days of begging for information from any Red Army soldier who looked the least bit friendly, she was overcome with despair. All she wanted now was to go home and wrap herself in the peace and safety of her father's ranch.

She watched a hunched old man pulling a primitive sled on which lay a small body wrapped in a soiled cloth shroud and her despair mounted. It had started to snow again and great white flakes were slowly cleansing the shroud and muffling the street sounds in a silence broken only by the slush, slush of the sleigh's runners against the snow.

Why is there only one person with this body? she brooded. *Is there no one left who cares that a child so small has died? Where is the mother? The sisters and brothers? And why ... why do I feel nothing?*

It was this last thought that bothered her the most and prompted her to step from the protection of the doorway and follow the old man to the end of the street. When the sled disappeared through the gates of a cemetery, she stopped.

What the hell am I doing?

Suddenly remembering Dmitri, she started back toward the boarded-up store. She walked quickly, but not so fast that she would attract attention, and was so intent on searching for Dmitri's tall frame among the pedestrians that she did not notice a man stepping from an alleyway until she bumped his shoulder.

"Careful where you are going, Little Mother," he said in a voice so familiar that Alice swung around. She gasped as she recognized the axe strapped to the man's waist. Her gaze swept over his thin frame and the stress lines furrowing his brow and cheeks and she found herself staring into the blue eyes that had haunted her dreams for the past two years.

"Oleksi? Oh my God! Oleksi!"

Equally stunned, he gaped at her in disbelief. And then she was in his arms.

"Alishka! Mother of God! I thought you were dead! My Alishka!" he cried, repeating her name over and over as he crushed her to his chest and rained kisses on her hair and her face and finally her lips. Then gently removing her scarf, he studied her. "You are even more beautiful than I remembered," he marvelled and Alice forgot that her hair was sheared close to her head, that her skin was dry and rough and that even the bulky peasant dress couldn't hide her thinness. For in that instant she *felt* beautiful.

But the moment passed as swiftly as it had come, replaced by a more alarming thought. She pushed away from him, fear clutching her heart. "Where is Tusya?"

"He's safe—he's safe! Do not worry, my love. Your brother is well."

"Oh, thank God." She sucked in her breath, overwhelmed with relief and an inexplicable urge to cry.

"Come," he said gently. "I'll take you to him. He's waiting for me at a tavern near the river."

"A tavern?"

"It is not what you might think," he said hurriedly. "We don't go to taverns to drink but to get information. A soldier from Petrograd told us about the fire. He said you had survived it, but he didn't know where you had gone. Since then we ask if anyone has been recently to the hospital on the Nevsky, and if they've seen you."

Tears filled Alice's eyes. "I checked the posts," she said, "at every village, but your name was never on them."

"Probably because we were coming from the south and you from the north." Holding her close to his side, he said, "Let us go and find your brother and relieve his mind. It has been all I could do to keep him from heading off on his own with no passport or papers to hunt for you."

Matching her step to his, she started walking then pulled up short.

"Dmitri! I have to go back—he will be terrified if I'm not there to meet him."

Oleksi scowled. "Who is Dmitri?"

Alice laughed. "You'll see," she said, pulling his hand. He came reluctantly, and they arrived at the store to find an agitated Dmitri tearing at his hair.

"I thought they had taken you, Miss!" he cried, grabbing her arms and shaking her. "You promised you would wait here!"

"It's all right, Dmitri," Alice soothed, freeing her arms just in time to stop Oleksi from reaching for his axe. "I've found Oleksi!"

⁂

The tavern, located on a side street, was in a building dingier than any of those around it, and in front of its dark green door stood the largest man Alice had ever seen. Dressed in the uniform of a Red Army officer, his massive arms folded forbiddingly across his chest, he eyed everyone entering the lane suspiciously. After questioning Oleksi thoroughly and accepting a wad of bills tucked discreetly into his hand, he allowed him to enter with Alice and Dmitri.

Folk music from a fiddle and dulcimer greeted them as they made their way single-file down a narrow cement staircase to a dark, smokey basement room. An odd assortment of men, most in uniforms from various armies, stood or sprawled on benches at tables laden with glasses and saucers filled with cigarette ashes. Almost drowning out the music were the laughter and loud voices fuelled by the illegal vodka being sold for gold, jewellery, ration tickets or whatever else the customers had for collateral. Alice followed Oleksi through the crowd and as her eyes adjusted to the dim light, she finally saw Tusya seated at a table near the bar. Like Oleksi, he was thinner and there was a darkness in his eyes that spoke of horrors even worse than she had witnessed. He didn't recognize her until she uncovered her head.

"Alice?" He leapt from the chair and grabbed her shoulders, staring at her with a mixture of joy and disbelief and looking so much like her father that she had to put her hand to her mouth to keep from crying out. But she couldn't stop the emotion of two long years from pouring out, and as tears streamed down her cheeks, she buried her head in the wool of his coat.

"I want to go home, Tusya!" she sobbed. "I want us to go home!"

"We will, Ali," he said hoarsely. "Now we will go home."

When they had both recovered and they were all sitting around the table, he told her the same story Oleksi had of how they had been transferred from one unit to another. "We tried to find you," he said, keeping his voice low so they would not be overheard. "But we couldn't get away. They confiscated our papers after the revolution."

Alice glanced at Dmitri, who ducked his head apologetically.

"What is important," she said, "is what we do now."

She gave them a brief account of the countess's death and her escape from Petrograd, and Dmitri told them about the trouble she had caused in Bakhtin.

"I don't dare to go back there," she said. "And I don't dare go anywhere near Petrograd."

Oleksi took her hand in his. "You won't have to," he said, then with an uneasy glance at Dmitri, lowered his voice even more and said in English, "We have a plan."

Tusya leaned forward. "We helped an English doctor get out of Ekaterinadar. He's connected with the International Red Cross, and if we can make it to Gdansk before he returns to England in May, he will help us find passage on a ship bound for Canada."

Alice shook her head. "But Gdansk must be more than a thousand miles to the north ... "

Oleksi nodded. "Yes, but now that the war is over, we hear it is possible to travel there by train—but first we have to get across the border."

She stared at him. "And you, Oleksi? You ... ." At that moment she saw him stiffen and realized the atmosphere in the room had changed. There was no more laughter and the talk had become muffled. Suddenly the musicians launched into the chorus of The Internationale, and everyone in the room began singing the chorus.

Eto yest nash pslednij
I reshitelney boy
S Internacionalom
Vospryanet rod lyudskoy

The fear around her was contagious, and with trembling fingers Alice slid her scarf up to hide her hair and as much of her face as possible, just as two Cheka agents stepped into the room. No one looked at these men directly, but she knew everyone was aware of their every move. Beside her, Oleksi's hand moved almost imperceptibly toward his axe.

One of the agents held his hand up to the musicians, who instantly stopped playing, and the room grew so quiet that the pounding of her heart sounded like a drumroll in Alice's ears. The agents stood surveying each person in the room, and for a long moment in which she did not even dare to breathe she felt them studying her. It was not her they were seeking, however, but a man in a crumpled black suit who cowered in a dark corner. Patrons stepped back, allowing the agents to pass through the crowded room, and no one challenged them when they grabbed the man and, despite his blubbering pleas for help, dragged him from the room. As the doors closed behind them, the gap in the crowd mended and boots trod over the trail of urine the prisoner had left on the floor.

The music started up again, but the jovial spirit was gone from the room. Voices remained muted and vodka was downed in bitter silence.

Dmitri's face quivered with anger. "This," he rasped, "is not what I fight for." He splayed his hands, palms up, helplessly. "This is not Russia!"

Alice's heart was only just beginning to slow to a normal rhythm, and though she wasn't sure Dmitri was right, especially when she thought of Feliks and Grusha and the people in the village of Bakhtin, she reached over and took the old fellow's hand. "This is not *all* Russia," she said gently. She leaned toward him and her voice dropped to a whisper. "But it is why I must leave, Dmitri. Why the three of us must leave ... if we can find a way across the border."

The old soldier's eyes watered as he met her gaze. "I will help you, Miss. I collect Denyan tomorrow and we will take you to the border. No one will question an ambulance."

Her hand stilled in his. "But you have to get back to the unit ... ."

"No, Miss. We are not going back. We are going home to our village." He smiled at her alarm for they had both seen the bodies of deserters hanging from posts as a warning to their fellow soldiers. "Don't worry, Miss. Denyan and I will have a tragic accident at a river crossing and nobody will spend much time hunting for two old soldiers." He leaned close to Tusya and Oleksi. "There is a backroad to a place on the Seym where you can hire a boat ... ."

ZGARDY
May – July 1919

Maryska was dying. At least, that's what she said when Natalya arrived early one May afternoon and found her shivering beneath a layer of soiled woollen blankets on the bunk above the mudbrick stove.

"The molfar's curse is killing me," she elaborated after her announcement. "I fall three, four, maybe five times a day. I am bruised and bloodied and my body is tired."

Natalya gathered wood and made a small fire, then brought some water to the old woman. Maryska sipped it thirstily, but when Natalya offered to make tea or fetch some *brynza*, she shook her head.

"It will only make me shit and if I shit there is a mess."

"My mama could help you," Natalya said, suddenly afraid the molfar's wife really was going to die.

Maryska cackled. "Ha!" she said. "The molfar's wife cured by a nurse? My husband would have to kill me so he did not die of shame. He would poison my food or push me off the cliff again."

Natalya stared at her. "The molfar *pushed* you off that cliff?"

"Why would he push me off the cliff?" Maryska shouted as if she hadn't just suggested that very thing. "I jumped and killed his child. That is why he saved me and made me live with his curse. To punish me."

Giving up on making sense of the conversation, Natalya brought out her blankets. "Mama says we need more corn. She was unhappy with the little bit I brought home last time."

"Humph." Maryska slowly shifted the pillow beneath her head. "Your mother does not believe in the molfar's magic. How does she expect him to produce what he doesn't have?"

Natalya glanced through to the storeroom where a large burlap sack leaned against the shelves.

Following her glance, Maryska shrugged.

"My husband says the war is over but his shepherds haven't

come back. He says maybe they're fighting a different war." She looked sideways at Natalya. "You'd think being a molfar, he'd know for sure, wouldn't you?"

"I think," Natalya said slowly, "he is not a very good molfar. Otherwise he would cure your sickness."

Maryska almost smiled. Then she glared at Natalya. "You cannot come here again. My husband has taken to checking on me. He wants to know when I'm dead so he can find a new wife."

Natalya felt like weeping but she knew better than to give in to her emotions in front of Maryska. Instead, she leaned down and kissed the woman's withered cheek and whispered, "I will miss you, Mother Maryska."

For a moment she was sure she saw tears in the old woman's eyes. Then Maryska turned to face the wall.

"Take what you want and go," she ordered. "And don't come back!"

Zhanna was not as upset as Natalya thought she would be to hear that Maryska would no longer be trading wool and food for blankets.

"Our gardens will soon be producing and after seeing what a fine job Catherine has been doing with her weaving, Boris Vitovskyi has offered to provide us with wool in exchange for blankets and a third of what he makes selling them at the market." She inspected the sack of dried apples Natalya had brought and nodded approvingly at an even larger sack of corn. "And now that the war is over, I could use some of that money to go to Kiev and see your sister and her baby."

Catherine broke a piece of honeycomb from a wedge that had been wrapped in a piece of oiled cloth and handed it to Pylyp. "You should write to Yuliya to send a ticket for you and Pylyp," she said casually. "Natalya and I can take care of the gardens while you're gone."

"With the wool Natalya has brought today, you could make a special blanket that I can take to them as a gift," Zhanna said, warming to the idea.

Natalya frowned at the two of them. "You could help Maryska, Mama. You know it isn't the molfar's spells that are making her sick."

Her mother shook her head. "The kind of sickness Maryska has, daughter, cannot be cured, even by proper medicine. But we will pray for her soul and I will ask Father Ishchak to do the same."

"I don't want her soul," Natalya said crossly. "I want Maryska!"

But her mother and Catherine weren't listening. They were too busy planning the trip to Kiev.

※

Two Sundays later, Father Ishchak announced that Maryska had died. Natalya was braced for the news, but she wasn't prepared for the deep sadness that engulfed her. She went through the motions of the mass without being aware of what she was doing or hearing the message the priest was delivering. All she could think about was the gnarled old woman who cackled like a grumpy hen and spoke her mind in a way no one else in Natalya's life had ever done. Now she was gone and once again Natalya was alone.

Everyone in the village attended the funeral held two days later. Not, Natalya knew, because they cared about Crazy Maryska, as they still called her among themselves, but because they didn't want to anger the molfar. Even Zhanna attended, though Natalya was sure she did so simply to maintain the good will they were now receiving from their neighbours. Father Ishchak led the procession to the church and was followed by the molfar, who was dressed in the finest, most colourful vest in the village and a snow-white shirt. Although he walked proudly, there was an air of despondency about him that caused Natalya to wonder if Maryska had been wrong. Perhaps he had not wanted her to die after all.

In the church, just as the mass was about to begin, there was a sudden stir near the door and a moment later the baron entered with Dominic Wojcik at his side. Natalya scarcely recognized the frail, white-haired baron who leaned heavily on a cane as he made his way to the front of the room. He was dressed in a light blue uniform similar to one he had worn when she visited him with her father, but this time his jacket bore the insignia of the Polish National Army.

"He's a broken man since his son's death at the Battle of Rarancza," Galyna Shevchenko whispered and was immediately shushed by the women around her.

Natalya shivered as she watched Dom Wojcik stride down the aisle. Then she shook herself angrily. This day was about Maryska.

The baron paused beside the coffin and crossed himself before hobbling to a special bench along the wall that was always reserved for members of the Potocki family, though they were seldom ever in attendance. When the nobleman was seated, Father Ishchak continued his mass.

Much later, after Maryska had been properly laid to rest in the church cemetery, the villagers gathered in the classroom where Zhanna and the other ladies of the church had prepared a small luncheon from food the molfar had brought from his farm. Natalya was given a tray of cheese to offer to the guests and she was halfway through the group when she came upon the molfar in earnest conversation with Galyna, who was nodding vigorously. "I know just the woman for you, Molfar!" the matchmaker said in a conspiratorial tone.

As his fist closed around a generous portion of *bryndza* from Natalya's tray, she remembered how Maryska used to sample the cheese then replace it in the crock. *She should have pissed in the crock*, she thought angrily, then smiled. Knowing Maryska, it was quite probable that she had done exactly that. Reminding herself not to eat any cheeses served that day, she moved on to Father Ishchak, who was talking with Boris Vitovskyi.

"I don't understand," Boris was saying, "how it is Zgardy has been placed under Polish control when the rest of Hutsulchyna is being ruled by the Czechs."

"It is complicated," Father Ishchak agreed. "From what I understand, the Romanians and the Poles are working together. Mostly because they don't want the Bolsheviks corrupting the Czechs or the Hungarians. And since Romanian troops have occupied Yeremeche and Kolomyia, no one is going to challenge them over a little village like Zgardy."

Boris shook his head. "But what do they even want with us, Father?"

The priest smiled. "Not us, brother. The baron. He has the capital to finance the rebuilding of his mill in Yeremeche but he'll only do so if his estate here is secure." He helped himself to some cheese from the tray. "Thank you, my dear," he said then added in a low voice, "It has been a while since you have been to confession, Natalya."

She felt her cheeks grow hot, and she ducked her head, unable to meet his gaze. "I will come soon, Father," she mumbled and hastily moved on, though she was certain he was fully aware of the guilt that consumed her and the secret she was keeping that she didn't dare to share with him or God.

⁂

For weeks after the funeral, Natalya continued to worry about Dom Wojcik's reappearance in the community, especially when rumours began circulating that the village was to have a new bailiff.

"The citizens of Zgardy will not tolerate another Wojcik as bailiff," her mother said when Natalya voiced her concerns, "and the baron knows it."

Every day, it seemed, there were more changes in the village. The bailiff's quarters were to be rebuilt, along with a proper school, and the logging operations that had been suspended after the outbreak of the war were to restart.

"Yevhen Hutopila will be the new chief forester," Boris Vitovskyi told her mother when he was delivering sacks of wool to the farm. A warm feeling spread through Natalya as she carried the sacks to the barn where they would be stored until Catherine was ready for them. *Papa would like it that Yevhen Hutopila has taken his place*, she thought, and for the first time since Maryska's death some of her sadness lifted. When they heard at church the following day that Dominic Wojcik had departed for Yeremeche where he was to be in charge of the baron's mill, Natalya almost cried out her relief. *Everything is going to be all right*, she told herself, and whispered a prayer of thanks to the Holy Mother.

Catherine did not join them after the service, and while Zhanna waited with Pylyp near the church steps, Natalya went in search of her sister. It was a warm day and the air was scented with the sweet perfume of woodland phlox. Hidden by the leafy branches of the beech trees growing close to the church, birds trilled their delight with the world and Natalya found herself sharing that feeling as she went around to a door at the back of the church.

"Catherine?" No one answered, but she was certain she heard voices coming from the far side of a shelter that was used to store extra firewood. "Catherine?"

She rounded the enclosure then drew up sharply and gaped at the man and woman embracing in the shadows. The man swung around and the light from a window in the hall illuminated the ragged scar down the right side of his face and the patch over his eye. Catherine pulled away from him.

"What are you doing here?" she demanded. Then, dismissing her own question, she said threateningly, "You'd better not tell Mama!"

"And why should she not?" Lech growled, putting his arm protectively about her shoulders. "Why should the whole world not know we love each other?"

"Because you are married!" Natalya said.

"Bah!" He waved his hand, as if brushing aside an insect. "In my heart I have only ever been married to Catherine."

"And I to you," she responded softly, taking his hand in hers.

Natalya's head whirled with conflicting images: Lech's father leading the soldiers to their house. Oleksi shouting at Catherine for dishonouring their family. Their mother kneeling before her icons. Over all of the images she heard Father Ishchak exhorting the sanctity of marriage and condemning those guilty of unrepentant adultery to spend eternity in the flaming pit of hell.

"Do whatever you have to do," Catherine said calmly. "But know this—I will not be parted from Lech ever again and remain living."

Natalya backed away from the shelter. "Mama is waiting for me. I will tell her you have returned home." And before either of them could say anything that would terrify and confuse her more than she already was, she ran back to the church.

※

Every year on the first Monday in July, the villagers celebrated the building of their church, an accomplishment that had enabled them to have their very own priest. This year the celebrations were to include an invocation for the reopening of the logging camp and a blessing of the first rafts of logs to be floated to the Prut River. Father Ishchak announced he would bless the rafts before his Sunday morning service, and with God's grace and donations from the whole village there would be a feast in the churchyard in the afternoon.

The villagers' excitement was infectious and even Catherine seemed to be caught up in it, singing as she went about her work and laughing easily. Natalya wanted to share her sister's enthusiasm, but she couldn't get past her growing dread that the affair between Catherine and Lech would be discovered. She felt like a mouse trapped between two cats, for no matter what she did—or didn't do—she was betraying someone she loved.

"I'm weaving that special blanket for you to take to Yuliya for the baby," Catherine said one afternoon when Zhanna suggested she accompany them to the village to help decorate the church. "You and Natalya go ahead."

Natalya knew her mother had written to Yuliya and Veniamin asking for the ticket, but she was hoping desperately that the letter would never reach them.

Later, as they walked home from the church, Natalya said, "Father Ishchak says the Red Army has taken over Kiev. He said it is not a safe place to go."

Zhanna smiled grimly. "Father Ishchak also believes Oleksi is dead. But he's wrong. I would know if my son were dead!" She paused for breath just below the gate to the farm. "God will hear my prayers in Kiev just as clearly as he does in Zgardy."

"I hope so," Natalya said, though she didn't believe God was listening to anybody's prayers these days. Certainly not to her own. She stared glumly past her mother to the meadow where the grass had grown tall and thick with fat seed heads ready to burst open. However, it wasn't the hay that made her stiffen, but something moving at the edge of the field—a dark figure that quickly disappeared into the forest.

Her mother lifted her head. "What is it?" She swung about to stare at the meadow herself. A glint of steel flashed closer to the barn, and Natalya saw Catherine swinging a long-handled scythe, swishing the sharp, curved blade through the weeds and grass. Zhanna clicked her tongue in disapproval. "She was supposed to be working on the blanket!" she said and hurried toward the gate. "We must go and help her."

Maybe she's already had help, Natalya thought as she trudged after her mother.

☙❧

For the rest of the day the three women took turns scything and raking and by the time they stopped for the evening meal, most of the grass was spread on the field to dry. Zhanna was so tired from the work and her walk to and from the village that she went to bed at the same time as Pylyp.

"I'll close up the chickens," Catherine said.

It was such a warm evening that as soon as she had cleaned up the dishes, Natalya went outside herself. There was no sign of her sister, but the barn door was open and from habit more than need, she hurried across the yard to close it. Once she reached the barn, however, she changed her mind and instead went inside and climbed up to the loft. Catherine was seated on the edge of the portal, staring out at the sliver of a moon perched just above the eastern mountains.

Natalya sat beside her on the ledge, her legs dangling high above the ground. Catherine did not acknowledge her presence, and after a moment Natalya said, "Galyna told Mama and me that Lech's wife has written from Canada. She wants him to join her there."

Catherine's hands fisted tightly in her lap but she remained silent.

"Will he go?" Natalya persisted.

"Why would he go back to *her?*"

"Galyna said the servants found Bolshevik papers among his things at the baron's mansion."

"They were his poems! But the servants can't read, so how could they know that?"

"Still, if he stays here, he will go to prison."

"He's going away," Catherine said, her voice as hard as her fist. "And I'm going with him."

The announcement wasn't a surprise, but it still caused Natalya's stomach to tighten. She stared at her sister with both pity and resentment. "The shame will kill Mama."

"I can't help that, Natalya! I love him."

"And yet you can't marry him."

Catherine lifted her chin, and staring out at the night sky, as if reading from the stars, recited,

> *What is this yoke that holds us to the ground*
> *Fettering soul to body with its weight?*
> *Chained by the false beliefs of men long dead,*
> *We plod the mire we've fashioned as our fate.*
>
> *Oh, dear heart, come aid me as I wrest*
> *Our freedom from these chains that bind us tight!*
> *Let us fly to lands where hearts are free to love*
> *And sins of yesteryear fade from our sight.*

"What does it mean?" Natalya asked, not liking the images the words provoked.

"Lech wrote it. He says the priests are lying about sin and

we're not being punished for things we did wrong, as Mama believes. He says we've let the church and people like Baron Potocki make all of our decisions for us and that is what is truly wrong."

Natalya fell silent, trying to make sense of what her sister was saying.

"Lech has a friend in Ternopil," Catherine said, her words coming faster. "He says in a socialist Ukraine everyone will live and work together and share what they have so no one goes without. The child growing in my belly will know a world of tolerance and plenty."

"A child?" The knot in Natalya's stomach tightened. She stared out at the dark mountains. There was nothing more she could do. Catherine had made her choice and now there was no turning back. "When will you leave?"

"In five days. The baron has arranged for Yevhen to take Lech on one of the rafts. I will go with him."

Natalya thought of the day so many years before when she and Catherine had watched Oleksi escaping on Yevhen Hutopila's raft. There would be no one to stand with her as she watched her sister do the same, and that thought brought her closer to tears than Catherine's announcement had done. Not trusting herself to speak, she scrambled to her feet and fled from the loft.

As the celebration of the rafts drew closer, the strain of keeping Catherine's secret made Natalya so tense that she quarrelled with everyone, even Pylyp. When she refused to take him with her to pick wild strawberries on the morning before the feast, he launched into a tantrum with all the anger a five-year-old could muster, screaming incoherently, stamping his feet and pounding his fists against her legs.

"Pylyp needs his breakfast," Natalya complained, blaming the incident on Zhanna, who had insisted the family needed to fast for the whole day.

"Take him with you," her mother ordered. "He loves to be in the woods." She had been cooking for the past two days, scrounging every morsel of last year's vegetables and whatever new greens she was able to harvest to bring to the feast, and the aroma of *kulesha* and *borscht* and *holubtsi* was torturing everyone in the house. Now she looked down at the bowl of flour she was about to mix with water to make *verenyky* pockets and suddenly pushed it away. "In fact, we should all go and pick the strawberries and I'll fill the *verenyky* with them instead of Crazy Maryska's musty apples."

Catherine was already putting on her scarf, but not to go picking berries. "I'm going to choir practice," she said. "Father Ishchak has asked me to sing a solo at the service." She avoided her mother's eyes as she made the excuse, and Natalya suspected that while her sister might indeed have a choir practice to attend, she was also meeting Lech.

"Then it is just us," Natalya said, grabbing her own scarf and some baskets for the berries.

With Pylyp in tow it took longer to reach the wild strawberry patch she had found one year while trapping, but the extra hands made the picking go faster, and by early afternoon all but one of the baskets was full of small red berries. Seated beneath a tree and sipping water from a jar they had brought, Natalya and her mother watched Pylyp investigate the woods around them. His mouth was red from the berries he had eaten, and with his hunger assuaged, he was in a much more agreeable frame of mind as he dug about the moss for beetles and salamanders and even spiders. He had developed a fascination for bugs and other small creatures and having captured one, he would often watch his prisoner for hours, sometimes nudging it this way or that to see what it would do before finally setting it free.

Maybe that's what God does, Natalya thought, watching as the beetle Pylyp had upended fought to regain its footing. *Maybe he knocks us over on purpose just to see what we will do and laughs, as Pylyp laughs, when our desperation makes us do something ridiculous. Like running off with a man who is already married!*

As if reading her thoughts, her mother said suddenly, "Your sister is angry with God."

Natalya froze, unwilling to venture into the quagmire of her sister's life, yet touched that for once her mother was addressing her as an equal. "She goes to church," she said cautiously, "and she's singing with Father Ishchak's choir."

Zhanna nodded. "Yes, but she does not pray. She bows her head but her lips do not move." She sighed. "She needs to pray. It is how we cleanse our souls."

Natalya said nothing.

Zhanna continued, "Catherine is like your father. She lives in dreams like his foolish love for that cursed rug." Her lips pursed with disapproval. "Dreams bring only sorrow, but your sister has not learned that."

"Yuliya does not believe in dreams," Natalya said. "She doesn't believe in love either."

"Yuliya will survive," Zhanna said with considerable satisfaction. "She is like me."

"And me, Mama? Am I like you as well?"

Her mother frowned. "No. You have a little of your father. A little of me. A little of something else. Your father said you were painted with a different brush than the rest of us." She shifted to a more comfortable position then waved a hand deprecatingly. "He was a dreamer."

The warm feeling that had flooded Natalya at her mother's revelations dissolved and was not restored even when her mother added, almost matter-of-factly, that Natalya was the daughter she trusted the most.

"I count on you to tell the truth, Natalya. I know you would never conceal anything from me that I should know."

Natalya thought of Catherine's secret and realized her mother wasn't sharing confidences because she felt close to her. She was seeking information.

"We need to get these berries home if you're going to make the *verenyky* in time for the feast tomorrow," Natalya said in a strange reversal of roles that lasted only as long as it took her mother to get to her own feet.

"We still have one basket to fill," Zhanna said firmly and, picking up the empty container, went back to the field.

※

Like many of the villagers, the Tcychowski family did not make the long trek to the landing where Father Ishchak was blessing the rafts, but came to the church for a late mass. They arrived just as the priest and the loggers and raftsmen returned.

The mass began with a prayer for the men of Zgardy whose lives had been lost in the war and for the first time Oleksi was included in the list of names. While many of the congregation responded with wails of anguish, Zhanna stood silent, her face set in a furious expression. She hadn't wanted his name to be read out today, but Father Ishchak had gone against her wishes. Natalya clamped her jaw tight. *Oleksi isn't dead!* she told herself and, following her mother's example, refused to show any grief.

When the mass was over, the priest announced that Catherine had written a hymn in honour of the celebration. Natalya watched as her sister took her place in front of the choir. She wore a white blouse intricately embroidered with her own designs of meadow flowers in an array of bright reds, greens and pale yellows and when she sang, her voice clear and rich, her gaze was locked on Zhanna's face.

> *Oh Mother Mary, wise and pure*
> *Who hath our sorrows to endure*
> *Forgive my sins, I beg of thee,*
> *Oh Mother Mary pray for me.*
>
> *Through long dark night, wracked low with pain*
> *My Lord's sweet voice called out my name*
> *When every hope I had was gone*
> *He lit the way to morrow's dawn.*
>
> *His love seeped deep into my core*
> *Brought laughter to my lips once more*
> *Now sweet flowers bloom and song birds trill*
> *My fears have gone, my sleep is still.*
>
> *Oh Mother Mary, pray for me.*
> *Oh Mother Mary, I love thee.*

Zhanna's cheeks grew wet with tears. "Vasyl must be so proud as he listens from heaven," she whispered when the song ended.

Unable to respond coherently, Natalya escaped outside and stood on the church steps for several minutes, taking deep breaths of fresh morning air. In the beech tree, leaves rustled softly and a blackbird trilled from the tallest branch, but she did not hear them. She heard only the song that she knew was not about God or the feast of the rafts. It was Catherine's farewell to their mother.

If only Oleksi would come! she thought desperately, staring down the road. *He would know what to do. He would stop this terrible thing from happening.*

But not even a dragonfly stirred along the dirt track.

※

Rough plank tables that had been erected in the churchyard for the occasion were covered with white cloths and, from baskets and wagons, women who had scraped their cellars and cupboards for ingredients brought out mouth-watering bowls of *holubtsi* and *banush*, platters of *brynza* and *kulesha*, and huge pots of *borscht*. Even the baron had contributed an assortment of delicacies Natalya had not seen since she was a very small child. She joined with the other women to carry food to the tables and, with a large jug of cold sour milk in her arms, was following her mother and sister when she saw Galyna Shevchenko bearing down on them.

"I have such wonderful news for you, Catherine Tcychowski!" the barrel maker's wife announced, her face beaming with success. "As you know, Crazy Maryska, may her soul rest in peace, passed away last month and our molfar has asked me to find him a new wife!"

Catherine set the platter of *verenyky* she was carrying onto the table and turned, unsmiling, to face Galyna. "And why should that be good news to me?"

"Because you are his first choice," Galyna gushed, almost bursting with excitement. "Is this not a miracle for someone such as yourself with no dowry and, let us face the truth, with age advancing fast upon you?"

"I'm twenty-one, Galyna Shevchenko. That's hardly aging," Catherine said coldly.

"Of course, he considered your younger sister as well," she nodded toward Natalya, who paled at the thought of the molfar even touching her. "She has a good, sturdy body ripe for bearing children, but I told him the eldest daughter must be married first. So it is you the molfar has chosen."

Zhanna, who had set her pot of *borscht* alongside the platter, swung about, hands on hips. "Marry the molfar? No daughter of mine will do any such thing!"

But Galyna gave no indication that she heard Zhanna's objections. "It is your blanket-making that has impressed the wizard of Zgardy!" she gushed. "He offers you his wonderful house and his fortune—which we all know he has hidden throughout the forests—in exchange for your hand."

Natalya stared at the barrel maker's wife. Had the molfar known all along that Catherine was making his blankets? Or had Maryska revealed their secret on her deathbed, perhaps to score one last victory over her husband?

Beside her, Catherine shrugged. "It is of no matter," she said firmly, "because I am not interested in marrying anyone. And especially not a man who bargains for a new wife when his old one is hardly in the grave!"

For a moment it seemed Catherine had wrought a miracle because the barrel maker's wife was rendered speechless, her mouth opening and closing like that of a fish out of water.

"You ... you ... refuse?" she gasped. Then, finally accepting this was exactly what Catherine was doing, her eyes narrowed and her lips twisted in a spiteful smile. "Well, perhaps like the whore of Babylon, you prefer to copulate with a Bolshevik pig who already has a wife, eh?"

In shocked silence Zhanna gaped at the matchmaker's smirking face and then at the panic in Catherine's eyes. Terrified of what might happen if either of them had a chance to speak, Natalya did the only thing that came to mind, and as the contents of her jug spewed over the matchmaker, coating her vest and skirt with sour milk, Galyna Shevchenko began to scream.

"I'm so sorry!" Natalya cried, whipping off her apron and dabbing at the woman's sodden garments. "I tripped ... I didn't mean to ...I'm sorry ... ."

Galyna twisted away from them as her two daughters rushed to her side. The eldest glared accusingly at Natalya and placed an arm around her mother's shoulders, "Come, Mama ..."

As they left the churchyard, Zhanna regained her composure. "Natalya, go and refill your jug," she said crisply then turned to Catherine. "What was she talking about?"

"She was just angry because I would not accept her proposal, and she will lose the fee the molfar would have paid if I agreed to marry him."

Natalya didn't hear her mother's response for other villagers had come between them, and by the time she had carried a fresh jug of sour milk to the table, Catherine was nowhere to be seen.

That night, after Zhanna and Pylyp were in bed, Catherine lit a candle and gathered her belongings, stuffing them into their father's old pack. Then she pulled the tapestry from beneath the mattress.

"I wanted to take it with me," she whispered, "but Lech says it will not be safe to have something with the tsar's crest in Ternopil ... " Her voice broke and she pressed the tapestry to her chest.

Seated on the bed, Natalya wanted to comfort her, but she

could think of nothing that would not sound like a condemnation. Finally she asked, "Are you not afraid of the molfar's anger?"

Catherine wiped her eyes. "If the molfar had any true power, little sister, he would have cured his wife and stopped the Germans from taking his herd. Anyway, according to Galyna, you were his first choice."

Natalya had wondered often of late what it would be like to be married, but not to the molfar. "I would rather die!" She crossed herself and felt a moment's gratitude to her mother for refusing the matchmaker's offer. Then she looked at her sister and felt more like crying. Catherine had been like a second mother to her, comforting her when she was hurt or sick, warming her bed on cold winter nights, sparing her from Yuliya's bullying. She never criticized, as Mama did, and was always there when things went wrong—when Oleksi left, when Papa was killed, when Savruk died. How could she now just disappear from her world? "I don't want you to go, Catherine," she whispered. "I'll be all alone."

Setting the carpet aside, Catherine wrapped her arms around her. "Shhhh," she soothed, smoothing Natalya's hair. "You'll be fine. You're strong like Mama and sensible like Papa. You always see what needs to be done, and you have the courage to do it. And one day soon you'll meet someone special. The two of you will have babies of your own and you'll help Mama and Pylyp take care of the farm."

Natalya shook her head. "Mama will hate me when she finds out you've left! She'll know that I knew and didn't tell her. And even God won't be able to comfort her if you turn your back on the church."

Catherine rocked her gently as if Natalya were still a small child and not a woman of sixteen. "Mama has a special blindness, Natalya. She will find a scripture to explain it all, and she will go on believing God has planned everything to teach her some great lesson."

She sounded so certain that Natalya began to wonder if she might be right, that their mother *would* find a way to keep her faith. After all, had she not done so all their lives?

"If I stay, Natalya, I will slowly die, so it will be the same for Mama either way. Besides, she still has you and Pylyp, and even Yuliya. Lech has no one but me, and I cannot reject him again."

Natalya met her eyes and slowly nodded. "I'm sorry I kept

his letter from you," she said in a small voice.

"I know, and I forgive you. Now go to bed. Tomorrow you will need your strength and your wits."

※

Natalya did not intend to sleep. She meant to savour the warmth and closeness of her sister for as long as she was allowed, but sometime during the night she drifted into a dream in which her family was together once more, gathered at the dinner table where Papa was eating his *borscht* with his usual gusto and Mama was nursing little Pylyp, while a young and carefree Oleksi teased Natalya as she and Yuliya competed for their mother's attention and Catherine and Leysa acted as peacemakers. Then, without warning, the blissful scene was shattered by soldiers clattering into the yard and her Papa running toward the burning barn. When she woke at dawn, she was bathed in sweat and Catherine was gone.

Relieved to see the door to her mother's bedroom was still closed, Natalya quietly ran down the stairs and out the door. A heavy dew drenched the grass and the air held a chill that matched the coldness in her stomach as she raced to the barn in the hope that her sister would be there. But it was dark and empty. Barely keeping her panic in check, she ran across the yard and through the gate.

I must watch the rafts, she told herself. *If I watch her go, she will be safe!*

But by the time she arrived at the lookout, the waters of the Imbyr River were already receding. The rafts and Catherine were gone.

KIEV, UKRAINE
November 1918

For the next five weeks after leaving Kursk, Alice, Oleksi and Tusya spent every waking hour either hiding from soldiers of whatever army was in control of the area or scrounging for food in a land where almost everyone without a uniform was starving. Then in Kiev after a Lutheran minister agreed to marry Alice and Oleksi if they brought him four loaves of bread, they wasted a full day searching for what they considered his outrageous fee, fighting an icy wind that cut through their clothes as if they were naked, then used the last of their pooled money to purchase the loaves he demanded. And when they returned to his church, they were annoyed because they were ushered not into the chapel but to an improvised dining room. There, on wobbly benches sandwiching a long row of tables, were at least two dozen gaunt-faced, raggedly dressed children, all staring with hollowed eyes at a steaming cauldron of soup that rested on the farthest table. Two women were ladling measured portions of soup into metal bowls that were silently passed down the line. When the last child had been served, the pastor beamed at his young charges.

"Today, children," he announced as if he was bestowing on them a great fortune, "we have a surprise!" He brandished the bread at them, but none of the children looked up from the meal they were already spooning up. His enthusiasm undeterred, the pastor gave the bread to the women, who carefully sliced two of the loaves and distributed one slice to each child.

Watching from a spot near the door, Alice glanced at Oleksi and Tusya and saw in their faces the same shame that she was feeling.

"Many of them live on the street," the pastor said later as they walked down a long corridor that led from the improvised soup kitchen to the main chapel where he would perform the marriage service. "They prefer that to the orphanages because of the typhus."

Tusya's voice was choked when he said, "It doesn't have to be like this. It *shouldn't* be like this!" Alice stared at him. Even in their most miserable hours of hiding, her brother had always managed to find something positive and usually amusing to say.

Oleksi said quietly, "One of those children reminded me of my little sister, Leysa."

⁓

The ceremony was simple, with only Tusya and the pastor's wife as witnesses. The couple were dressed in drab civilian clothes they had purchased from a street vendor—in Alice's case a black mourning dress. But the pastor's blessing satisfied Oleksi's need to have their union sanctioned by a higher power, and when they had both said their vows, Oleksi gently slipped the ring he had fashioned from a copper kopek over Alice's finger.

"I have no worldly goods to offer you, Alice Galipova. Only this ring and my promise that I will stand by you for as long as I live."

Alice almost wept at the intensity of the emotion she saw reflected in the eyes of this tall, gentle man who had come to mean so much to her. "One lifetime is not enough to hold the love I feel for you, Oleksi Tcychowski," she responded softly. "And I promise that I will stand by your side until the day I no longer exist."

As the pastor pronounced them man and wife, Oleksi took her in his arms and kissed her, and for just that moment the war and starving children and the challenge of getting back to Canada did not exist. Then Tusya cleared his throat and the reality of their situation washed over her. This might be their wedding day, but they were still far from Gdansk and a ship that would take them home.

⁓

In their civilian clothes it was easy for the trio to move about the city of Kiev without being noticed, but it was really not much safer for them than Kursk had been. Sprawled along both banks of the Dnieper River, it was currently held by the newly formed Directorate of the Ukrainian Socialists, which had recently wrested control from the White Army, but neither army was disciplined. Nonetheless, Alice decided to sell one of her three remaining diamonds here, although it meant exposing them to added danger from thieves or informants.

"The pastor gave me the name of a shop in the Jewish quarter," she shouted over the wind as they walked down the cobblestoned street toward the river. "He seemed to think the man could be trusted to give us a fair price with no questions asked." She tightened the shawl that covered her head and most of her face. The shop, near Alexander Square, was a good hour's walk away, and though there were streetcars running that way, they had no money left to pay the fare. By the time they reached their destination, they were cold, wet and in no mood to haggle, but that is exactly what they ended up doing.

The jeweller was a short, bearded man wearing a yarmulke on his balding head, a fringed shawl over his jacket and trousers. Between examining the diamond and negotiating with Alice and Tusya, he darted fearful glances toward the door where Oleksi was standing guard.

"It is a fine stone," he said finally, carefully placing it on a velvet pad on his side of the counter and prodding it with fingers extending out of fingerless gloves. "But of what good is it to me when everybody has diamonds to sell and no one has money to buy them?"

"Perhaps it is worth nothing now," Alice agreed, "but we both know that one day it will be worth much."

"And of what good will that do me if I am arrested?" he demanded, holding out both hands, palms up. "You have no papers proving you own the diamond. To accept it without them I would have to break the law."

Alice glared at him. "It isn't stolen. It was given to me by my cousin."

He shrugged. "Cousin. Mother. Grandmother. What does it matter? Without proof it might just as well have come from God. No one would believe that either."

Tusya picked up the diamond, enclosing it in his fist. "Then we will trouble you no more, my friend," he said firmly, and slipping his free hand beneath Alice's elbow, turned her away from the counter. "Come on, Ali. We have other shops to visit."

They made it almost to the door before the shopkeeper called them back.

"Let me look at the stone once more," he offered, fitting a jeweller's loupe to his eye. "Perhaps there is something that I missed."

In the end, although she was certain it was worth three

times as much, Alice agreed to accept the rough equivalent of two hundred Canadian dollars in a combination of Ukrainian, Polish and German banknotes.

"I have been robbed," the jeweller complained as he doled out the cash.

"I think not," Alice said tartly. "In six months this money will be worthless, but that diamond will be far more valuable than it is today." She divided the notes of each denomination into three piles, and after tucking one pile into an inside pocket of her cloak, gave the other piles to Tusya and Oleksi. Then, with a nod to the jeweller, who was still bemoaning his loss, she followed the men from the shop.

The wind had died and it was no longer raining, but Alice still had no intention of walking back to the hotel near the river where they had found a room. "We'll take the streetcar," she announced. "And after dinner we can go to the train station and find a schedule."

They were about to cross the street when two motorbikes careened around the corner, followed by a black roadster bearing the flag of the Ukrainian Galician Army. Just past the jewellery shop the roadster swung toward the sidewalk and screeched to a halt. They watched as the driver jumped out and opened the back door for a grey-haired officer dressed in a colonel's uniform. He alighted and came toward them smiling. "Tusya Galipova! I knew that was you!"

Tusya grinned back at him. "Mykola Shankovsky! I'll be damned!"

While Alice and Oleksi stared in amazement, the two men embraced and began talking at once. Then, remembering the others, Tusya introduced them.

"Mykola was one of my professors at the university," he said, "and one of Grandfather's students."

The colonel sobered and bowing slightly to Alice said, "I was sorry to hear about your grandfather's passing. He was a good friend." He turned back to Tusya. "What are you doing in Kiev? I thought you would have returned to Canada by now."

Tusya gave an abbreviated version of their escape from the Red Army. "Tomorrow we're taking the train to Gdansk and from there a ship home."

Shankovsky frowned and shook his head. "These days the railway lines are the most dangerous places to be. If the trains aren't stopped or blown up by revolutionaries, they're attacked by thugs and bandits who'll kill you just for the sheer pleasure of doing so. And that doesn't even touch what the real armies like ours are doing." Briefly he described the battles being waged across the country between the Ukrainian, Red and Polish armies, as well as with German communities whose inhabitants were refusing to be separated from their Fatherland. "Added to that, the Belarussians and Lithuanians in the north are fighting for their independence as are the Hungarians, the Czechs and the Romanians in the south."

Alice listened with growing dismay. "But how else can we get home?" she asked.

"We'll just have to chance it ..." Tusya began.

"I have an idea," Shankovsky said. "You can come with me."

They looked at him questioningly.

"I've just been assigned to a relief battalion that's heading for Baligród tomorrow morning. If you were willing to join our medical unit, I can guarantee you safe passage through the war zone."

"Baligród?" Oleksi's eyes brightened. "That's less than two hundred versts from Zgardy!"

"But we're going north," Alice protested.

"You can travel north much safer from Baligród than from here," the colonel said. He turned to Tusya. "I understand your sister's concern, but I believe you have a better chance of arriving at your destination if you come with us."

"I think you're right," Tusya said, ignoring Alice's glare.

Oleksi put a comforting hand on Alice's shoulder. "We will get to Gdansk, Alishka. But let us get there in a single piece by doing as this man suggests."

Alice shrugged off his hand and scowled at the officer. "And what guarantee do we have that your army will stay in one piece?" she demanded. "Or that you will let us go on our way once we reach Baligród?"

The colonel stiffened. "You have my word," he said coldly.

"And that's more than good enough for me," Tusya said jovially, slapping his friend's back. "We accept your offer, Mykola Shankovsky, and look forward to working with you."

"And I with you, my friend," the colonel said, relaxing. Then, after telling them where to report for duty, he saluted and returned to his car.

As the motorcade disappeared, Tusya turned to his sister. "We really don't have much choice, Ali."

"He does seem like a man who will honour his word," Oleksi added. "And this way I can say good-bye to my family."

Alice stared down at her ring, twirling it about her finger. Finally she let out a deep breath. "I *would* like to meet your mother and sisters, Oleksi."

He smiled and the gratitude in his eyes banished any further objections she might have had. She wished it also banished her growing fear that she was never going to see her father or Willow Bar Creek again.

For the next two months Alice had little time to think about whether they would get home or not. Every day she looked after wounded soldiers and the civilians who were unfortunate enough to get caught in the middle of the fighting. But unlike her experiences in Russia, the Ukrainian medical staff treated her with respect, and among them she found the same camaraderie she had experienced when she worked in the countess's field hospitals. The battalion's progress, however, was slow and involved endless detours as they dodged one battlefield in order to strengthen the Ukrainian Galician forces in another area that offered more strategic advantages, and then went back to collect the remnants of smaller companies. More than once Alice was separated from Oleksi and Tusya, who were left behind to search for survivors while the hospital moved on, and anxious days passed before they were reunited.

One day in late February while the medical unit was stationed in a small town roughly halfway between Kiev and Stanislav, they received word that soldiers in another unit had been presenting with the complaint of headache, fever and cough. Convinced that they had nothing more than a cold, the unit's harried doctors had sent them back to their quarters where they died within hours.

"The cause of their deaths," the medical director told Alice and her fellow nurses, "is a new form of influenza that spreads very quickly to the lungs."

Although none of the soldiers in Shankovsky's battalion had experienced any of the symptoms, Alice knew how fast such a virus could spread, and she was overjoyed when it was reported that the Supreme Council of Nations, who were assembled in Paris to negotiate the treaty to end the war, declared a temporary entente across Germany, Poland and the Ukrainian-held territories. What's more, they promised to enforce it. "Now we can go home!" she said later that night when Oleksi and Tusya returned to the tent they were sharing. But her joy was short-lived, for only a few hours later they were called to the command centre.

"We've just treated two soldiers with influenza," the chief

physician announced regretfully. "Our unit has been quarantined."

The fear in the small army encampment was almost tangible, and as one soldier after another fell victim to the virus, attempts to escape increased. After that, healthy soldiers were posted outside the compound with orders to shoot anyone leaving the area, and every night shots rang out, and more often than not would hit their mark. Fear shifted to panic when the medical staff also began to fall ill, and more and more bodies began piling up, waiting to be hauled away for burial.

Alice spent most of her days in the huge hospital tent, though there was little she could do besides applying cold compresses to foreheads burning with fever, providing heated bricks and blankets to bodies wracked with chills, and coaxing liquids down throats raw from coughing. Sometimes these measures worked and within a day or two the patient was well enough to leave, but more often the victim turned blue and began to cough so hard that bloody foam bubbled from their mouths.

During this time she saw Oleksi and Tusya only in passing, just long enough to ensure that, like her, they were resisting the disease, and after a week she began to believe they were somehow impervious to infection. One night, while her husband and brother were still working, she collapsed onto her cot and sank into an exhausted sleep so deep she didn't hear Tusya return until he moaned from his own cot.

"It is as if my head is in a vise and someone is squeezing it tighter and tighter," he groaned when Alice leaned over him. She placed her hand on his forehead and almost cried out at the heat she felt there. After removing his boots, she covered him with every blanket in the tent. Within moments he was throwing them off and she discovered his clothes were drenched with sweat. Oleksi arrived and helped to undress him, and by that time Tuysa was shivering. Alice hastily replaced the covers then ordered Oleksi to bed.

"You need sleep," she said when he objected, "or you will also become ill."

"And what of you?"

"I've already slept tonight. And when you've rested, I'll sleep again. Right now I need to be with my brother."

And since there was little either of them could do to help Tusya, Oleksi finally went to his cot. He slept restlessly and every time he moaned in his sleep, Alice held her breath, certain that he, too, was getting sick.

By morning Tusya was delirious, crying out for Alice, even

though she was by his side, and begging her to forgive him for not leaving Russia when they had a chance. No matter how many times she reassured him that it didn't matter, he continued to berate himself. Then he fell silent. All she could hear between his coughing spells was his raspy breathing, and she wished he was rambling again, for at least then she knew he was alive.

Oleksi woke and went to the mess tent for tea and bread, and when Alice had forced herself to eat enough to satisfy him, he insisted that she sleep, promising he would wake her if Tusya's condition deteriorated.

"Your brother will survive this," he said. "I have seen him fight many battles since we met. He is a man of strength."

"Not when he's sick," Alice said miserably. When they were children, it had always been Tusya who came down with whatever virus was being passed about the school, and he had taken twice as long to recover as anyone else. In contrast, Alice had rarely been sick, and when she did catch something, she recovered quickly.

"All the same, you must rest, Alishka, or you, too, will become sick." For the first time, she heard fear in his voice, and for that reason only she consented to go to her cot.

She did not expect to sleep, and she closed her eyes only to rest them, but the next thing she knew she was riding with Oleksi along a ridge above Willow Bar Creek. They were looking for something and then, suddenly realizing that something was Tusya, she began calling out his name, waking herself. For a moment she couldn't understand where she was, for the tent was silent and dark save for the flicker of a candle on a stand beside her brother's cot.

She erupted from her bed, screaming. "Tusya!"

"He's all right," Oleksi said softly, coming to her from the shadows. "He's sleeping."

Alice didn't believe him until she felt her brother's pulse and found that it was almost normal. She listened to his chest and heard the rasp as his lungs fought to suck oxygen through the film of mucous that was enveloping them. But his fever was gone and she knew if he could fight off the infection in his lungs, he would survive.

"Tusya," she said again, then looked at Oleksi and began to cry.

Mykola Shankovsky was among the victims of the plague that attacked his troops, and in June what remained of his decimated battalion was absorbed into other battalions. Alice, Tusya and Oleksi found themselves moving eastward as Polish forces, fortified by reinforcements from General Józef Haller's army, advanced from the west. The Supreme Council had given Haller permission to mobilize six full divisions of French-trained Polish soldiers to prevent the Red Army from moving further westward, but in fact, he had deployed several divisions to fight the Ukrainian Army instead and had occupied a number of strategic districts, including the city of Stanislav.

Determined not to join the retreat, Alice, Oleksi and Tusya managed to slip away with the help of friends they had made in their unit. By walking all night, they managed to reach Stanislav without being stopped, and by the following afternoon Alice and Oleksi were seated at an outside café near the Ivano-Frankvsk train station, waiting while Tusya purchased their tickets to Yeremeche. The lukewarm tea she was sipping and the hot afternoon made Alice sleepy, and leaning back in her chair, she nodded off, only to be jerked awake by a nearby commotion. As she straightened, she saw a thin, ragged boy racing toward them, weaving in and out of the stream of pedestrians exiting the station. A moment later a second runner appeared, this one an older man in a tailored grey suit who shouted in perfect English, "Stop him! Stop that thief! He has my bag!"

Although there had been a number of soldiers and police officers patrolling the sidewalk earlier, now there were none to be seen.

"Stop!" the man cried again, his voice growing more desperate.

As the boy ran past, Oleksi jumped from his chair, and at the same time Alice stuck out her foot. The boy sprawled at her feet while the bag he was clutching flew into the air, landing in a dry gutter. In an instant he was up again, but before he could take back the bag, Oleksi had grabbed it.

"You'd better disappear," he said sternly.

The boy, looking longingly at his prize, glanced warily at Oleksi then darted away just as the man chasing him arrived at their table.

"Thank God!" the man gasped as Oleksi handed him the bag. Setting it on the table, he conducted a quick inspection while he caught his breath. "My passport," he said, holding the document up, his face flushed with running and relief. He stuck out his hand to Oleksi. "You two just saved my hide!" After enthusiastically pumping both Oleksi's and Alice's hands, he settled into the chair they were saving for Tusya, and pulling a white handkerchief from his pocket, mopped his brow and introduced himself as Clyde Brandon. Then he added, "From Chicago," and looked from Alice to Oleksi, hoping they had understood him.

"And I'm Alice Tcychowski from Willow Bar Creek in British Columbia," Alice replied in English, then laughed at the shocked expression on his face. "Will you have some tea, Mr. Brandon?"

"Why, I don't mind if I do," he said, laughing. He removed his bag from the table and positioned it securely on his lap. "What on earth are you doing here?"

Alice signalled to the waiter to bring them more tea, but when a glass was set before him, Clyde Brandon did not stop talking long enough to drink it. He was, he told them, an inspector for an American relief agency run by a man named Herbert Hoover and he had been in the country for three months. "That man's been trying to bring food aid over here since before the United States entered the war, but the darned German command wouldn't guarantee the food would not be used for their troops. Honest to God!" He shook his head despairingly. "I can't tell you the horrors I've seen since I began touring this country. Whole families that are nothing but skin and bones, babies and children too weak to get out of bed, wearing nothing but little nighties because everything else has been sold or confiscated by the armies. I tell you, if we don't get these folks some food and get it to them awful darned fast, they aren't going to last out the year!"

Alice met Oleksi's gaze, but they both remained silent. There was little they could add to what the man had already witnessed. From the corner of her eye, she saw Tusya approaching the table. He looked warily at the stranger before collecting a fourth chair, deliberately placing it between Alice and the man.

"This is my brother, Tusya."

After the introductions were complete, Tusya held up three tickets. "The train leaves in an hour," he said meaningfully. It was obvious that he was still uneasy about the American, probably, Alice thought, because he never stopped talking, explaining all over again to Tusya about his job with the relief organization.

"Yep. Just have to make two more stops, then I'm heading back to Danzig ... or Gdansk ... or whatever the heck it's being called these days." He thumped his bag. "And thanks to you folks, I'll have no problem getting there."

Alice asked sharply, "You're going to Gdansk?"

"You betcha," Clyde said. "It's time I got back home to the States, where you can get a decent meal and folks know how to manage their affairs without shooting each other." He paused momentarily to gulp his tea, then flicked his index finger at the tickets protruding from Tusya's pocket. "Is that where you folks are headed?"

"We're thinking of it," Tusya said cautiously.

"Not *thinking*," Alice corrected. "We're going back to Canada as soon as we figure out the safest way to get to Gdansk and find a ship."

Clyde's brow furrowed slightly. "Things are pretty stable right now, what with the treaty being signed and all. But there's no guarantee that's going to last." He lifted his bag once more and started to rise from the table, then stopped. "I'm heading north tomorrow. If you want, we could travel together. Be safer that way, and I'm sure I can get you passage on my ship when we get to Gdansk."

Oleksi shook his head. "We can't leave tomorrow. We're going to say good-bye to my family near Yeremeche."

"He's right, Ali," Tusya said. "And I already have our tickets."

"But this is our chance to get home," Alice exclaimed, close to tears and refusing to look at Oleksi. "We've got to take it!"

Tusya looked at the American. "When does your ship leave?"

"July seventeenth," Clyde said. "That's ten days from now and it'll take me most of that time to make it back to Gdansk."

Oleksi's face brightened. "But you said you had to make two more stops."

Clyde nodded vigorously. "That I do! But they won't take more than a day each."

"Two days," Oleksi said. "That's all we need to go to Zgardy." He took Alice's hand, forcing her to look at him. "I must see them, Alishka! I have to know they are safe before I can leave them behind."

Clyde reached into his bag and pulled out a business card, which he handed to Alice. "It's up to you folks, but if you make it to Gdansk, I'll see to it that you get passage on my boat one way or another. In the meantime, there's some folks here who are expecting me to examine their relief plan." With that he rose, tipped his hat, and hurried down the street.

Alice studied the card, which read in dark embossed letters, *Clyde J. Brandon, Inspector, American Relief Administration*. Beneath the name was a telephone number and an address in Gdansk. Her fingers trembled. The name on the card made the city seem suddenly so close, and her dream of going home so near.

"Maybe," Tusya said gently, "Alice and I should go with this American, Oleksi. You could go and see your family and join up with us in Gdansk."

Oleksi looked longingly at Alice. "If that is what you wish, Alishka, that is what I will do."

She met his gaze and the tears she'd been holding back streamed down her cheeks. "I'm going nowhere without you, Oleksi Tcychowski," she said. "We will go to Zgardy today and the day after tomorrow we will take a train from Yeremeche to Gdansk."

Tusya slapped the table with the palm of his hand. "Well, that settles it, then!" he said, so cheerfully that Alice suspected it was his plan all along.

ZGARDY
July 1919

Never in her life had Natalya felt as afraid as she did standing in front of the farmhouse door, trying to summon the courage to enter. She could hear dishes clattering, which meant her mother was up and preparing breakfast, but still she could not move. Then suddenly the door was flung open and her mother stood framed in the entranceway.

"What are you doing standing there, Natalya? The water bucket is almost empty and there's scarcely enough wood for breakfast. And where on earth is your sister?"

Natalya took a step back. "I ... she ..." Her mouth was so dry it was difficult to form words. "She's gone, Mama."

"Gone?" Zhanna swept past her to the top of the steps. She clutched the support post and stared beyond the gate to the trail. "Gone?"

Pylyp, who had been standing behind her, came out onto the porch. He gazed at his mother and sister, his eyes wide with concern then asked with his hands where Catherine was. Natalya put her arm around his shoulders. "She went with Lech. On the rafts."

Zhanna stiffened then swung around. "You knew she was going to do this?"

"I tried to stop her, Mama, but I couldn't." Her heart was pounding so hard her chest ached. "I'm sorry," she whispered.

"How long?" Zhanna demanded. "How long has this ... this ... travesty been going on?"

Natalya swallowed hard. "Since before Yuliya's wedding."

She had never seen her mother so angry, but instead of lashing out with her tongue as she usually did, Zhanna grabbed Pylyp's hand. Jerking him away from Natalya, she pulled him into the kitchen then swung back to face her daughter. "Leave ... my ... house," she said, her voice cold and her eyes filled with hate.

Natalya began to shake so badly she was afraid her legs were going to give way. "But, Mama ... ."

Zhanna jabbed her index finger toward the gate then stepped back and slammed the door.

Natalya stared from the door to the window where Pylyp's face was now pressed against the glass, his eyes wide with confusion.

"I love you, Pylyp!" she mouthed just before Zhanna pulled him away from her view. And suddenly she was alone. For several minutes she stood in front of the door, willing it to open, and tried to think of what she should do. From what seemed to be a long distance away, she heard the rooster crowing.

Feed the chickens.

It was just a vague thought at first, but as the words repeated themselves in her head, they became a lifeline. Feeding the chickens was something to do. Something that was normal. Turning away from the door, she stumbled down the steps and made her way slowly to the barn.

❦

So long as she was working, Natalya was able to control her panic. When the chickens were fed and watered, she tackled the garden and by the time she had removed every weed in every row, she had convinced herself it wasn't hate she had seen in her mother's eyes but anger. She would forgive her daughters, as she always did, and then deliver a stern lecture on disobedience and disloyalty.

In the early afternoon, believing a fat trout might put her mother in a better frame of mind, Natalya took her fishing pole and walked to the creek. There everything was normal and as she sat on the bank of the creek, she heard a cuckoo calling from the branches of a nearby pine. She remembered hearing Galyna Shevchenko say, "If the first bird you hear in the morning is a cuckoo, a coin will find its way into your purse and your luck will be good all day." It was no longer morning, but perhaps the luck would still be granted, Natalya thought. In case it wasn't, she said a prayer, begging not only for mercy from God and her mother but also for her sister's soul.

Everything is going to be fine, she told herself as she headed home with not one, but two large trout, a sure sign that God, at least, had granted her absolution. *Mama will forgive me, too. After I've shown her how penitent I am and she's made me fast for a week and say a thousand prayers, she'll forgive me.*

But when Natalya returned from the creek, her mother and Pylyp were gone.

At a loss for what to do next, she set her fish in a basin on the table and stood uncertainly in the middle of the kitchen.

She's gone to see Father Ishchak, she told herself. *Surely he'll tell her she must forgive me. But what if she doesn't?*

Outside a horse snorted, startling her from her reverie. She went to the door and stepped warily onto the porch in time to see two riders coming through the gate. In the lead on a chestnut pony was a man with a dark wool cap perched jauntily over his curly black hair. His rumpled black suit and trousers were shabby, there were holes in his boots, and his axe was in a scabbard on his horse, rather than belted to his side, but the joy in his face when he saw Natalya made her forget everything except that her brother was home. As he leaped from his horse, she ran down the steps, screaming his name. "Oleksi!"

He engulfed her in a hug, then stepped back and inspected her. "You've grown into quite a beauty, little sister!"

With unladylike ease, his companion, a woman with blond hair cut almost as short as his, dismounted and came to stand beside him. He put his arm around her shoulders and drew her close. "Natalya, this is my wife, Alice Galipova Tcychowski!"

According to Oleksi, Natalya was the tough one of the family, but the red-haired beauty staring at Alice didn't seem very tough at all. She looked forlorn and ready to burst into tears at any moment. Extending her hand, Alice said gently, "I have heard much about you, Natalya. I am very glad to meet you at last."

Natalya didn't think Oleksi's bride showed any resemblance to the fine lady he had described in his letters. Her face was weathered and her black skirt and long-sleeved blouse were shabby and coated with dust. But there was a kindness about her that finally prompted Natalya to accept her hand. "Welcome to Zgardy, Alice Galipova," she said politely.

Oleksi swivelled his head from side to side, scanning the yard. "Where is Mama? And Catherine? And Yuliya?"

Brought abruptly back to her dilemma, Natalya let go of Alice's hand and sank down onto the bottom step. He didn't know that Leysa had died or that Pylyp was deaf and Yuliya was married and living in Kiev. And she knew that when she told him all this and told him of how she had helped Catherine elope, he would hate her as her mother hated her.

Alice exchanged a look of concern with Oleksi then sat beside her. "What's wrong?"

With her eyes fixed on the ground, because she could not bear to see the joy disappear from Oleksi's face, Natalya told them about the Russian soldiers and the typhus and Veniamin. Finally daring to look at him, she confessed to her part in Catherine and Lech's elopement. "Mama says I have to leave," she finished in a choked voice, "but I don't know where to go."

Beside her, Alice tried to make sense out of her mother-in-law's reaction. "I don't understand," she said. "Why would you have to leave? You've done nothing wrong."

"Because I didn't tell Mama that Catherine was seeing Lech. But it wouldn't have made any difference. Mama couldn't have stopped her. No one could." Finally she looked directly at her brother and said hesitantly, "Lech is a Bolshevik and he said they didn't have to get married. They're going to have a baby ... but I didn't tell Mama that either."

He nodded. "That was probably wise." He wasn't angry as she expected him to be, and he started to say something else, but a strangled cry caused them all to turn toward the gate where Zhanna was staring open-mouthed at her elder son. A moment later she was charging across the yard, skirting the horses and marching to the steps where she stood, hands on hips.

"As always, you are too late, Oleksi Tcychowski," she shouted, tears streaming down her cheeks. "Why do you come now when I have sold the farm!"

Oleksi's face reflected both astonishment and consternation as his mother waved a folded document at him.

"I've sold the farm to Yevhen Hutopila," she said accusingly. "Pylyp and I are going with him tomorrow to Yeremeche to catch the train to Kiev." She clutched the paper to her chest. "We are going to live with the only daughter I have left."

He placed his hands gently but firmly on her shoulders. "It's all right, Mama. I'm not staying in Zgardy."

Pylyp, who had followed Zhanna across the yard, grabbed onto the folds of her skirt as he studied Oleksi's face.

"Father Ishchak read out your name," Zhanna said accusingly. "He said you could not still be alive!"

"But, Mama," Natalya exclaimed, "you told Father Ishchak he was wrong!"

"And as you see, he was wrong," Oleksi agreed. "I'm not only alive, but I'm going to be a father!" Beaming proudly, he held out his hand to Alice, who reluctantly let go of Natalya and went to his side. "This is my Alishka."

The anger drained from Zhanna's face. She pulled away

from him and hobbled toward the step.

His brow furrowed in confusion. "Are you not pleased, Mama?"

Keeping as far from Natalya as was possible, she sat down heavily and, with both hands pressed to her temples, shook her head. "He said you were dead! I sold the farm because Father Ishchak said you were dead!" She lifted her hands skyward. "God forgive me, Vasyl! What have I done?"

"But I told you, Mama, I am not staying in Zgardy. Alice and I are going to live in Canada, and we want you and Natalya and Pylyp to come with us."

Natalya sucked in her breath. "Canada?" She tried to remember what Oleksi had said about Alice's homeland, but all she could think of was that it was far away from Zgardy. Farther away than any distance she could imagine.

Zhanna's shoulders slumped and she seemed suddenly to have shrivelled into an old woman half her size, a change so dramatic that even Pylyp was moved to sit beside her, patting her shoulder with his small hand.

"Canada?" Zhanna repeated the name as Natalya had done, as if in doing so she might make sense of what she was hearing. "Canada?"

Oleksi glanced at Alice then knelt before his mother and took her hands in his. "There are no wars in Canada," he said, his voice intense. "And we're going to have a ranch with a thousand times more land than Farmer Andronic! More land than even the baron. We will be rich, Mama!"

She met his gaze and for a moment his enthusiasm seemed to ignite something that was not quite dead within her. And then, as quickly as it had come, it disappeared. Slowly shaking her head, she withdrew her hands. "You go to Canada," she said wearily. "Pylyp and I are going to live in Kiev where he can go to a school for deaf children."

Natalya got to her feet. "And what of me, Mama?" she asked, her voice trembling. "Where am I to go?"

Zhanna heaved herself up from the step. "Come inside, Oleksi, and I shall make a meal. You and your bride must be hungry."

Alice stood irresolute, not wanting to leave Natalya.

"My sister will be fine, Alishka," Oleksi said, taking her arm. "I will talk to Mama."

For the moment it seemed the best thing to do, and so with a final, regretful glance at the girl, Alice followed her husband inside.

At dusk Natalya heard Oleksi and Alice's ponies whinnying in the paddock, and standing in the open barn doorway, she watched as Tusya rode into the farmyard. A warm feeling spread through her and she wanted to rush out and greet him, but when he glanced her way, she ducked out of sight, suddenly ashamed of her banishment. Through a crack in the barn wall she saw her brother greet him and as they both disappeared into the kitchen the aroma of fish soup and *kulesha* wafted across the yard.

She had made a fire in the pit they had used when the Russian soldiers took over the farm and, in a small pot she found in the tack room, had boiled some new potatoes and immature beets she dug from the garden. They tasted like sawdust in her mouth, but because she had eaten nothing else all day, she forced them down, then sat staring at the flames. The thought of being alone was terrifying, but even more frightening was the thought of going with Alice and Oleksi to a land so far from everything she knew. Far from the graves of Papa and Leysa. From the mountains and the streams she had roamed and fished and trapped since she was eleven. But most of all, so far from her mother.

Mama will forgive me, she told herself again and again. *Now that Oleksi has come, she will forget about Kiev. She will stay in Zgardy and we will go on as before.*

When the barn door creaked open, she felt a momentary surge of hope, but it was Alice who stepped into the firelight. "I brought you some dinner." She held out a bowl of fish soup then nodded at the remains of Natalya's meal. "But I see you've already eaten."

Natalya took the bowl and set it on the ground. "Mama won't like it that you're here."

Alice shrugged. "Your Mama doesn't like it that I'm anywhere. Not after Oleksi confessed we were married by a Lutheran priest."

A faint smile touched Natalya's lips. "Mama has very strong views."

"I'm discovering that" Alice said. "Well, I have some strong views of my own. But she'll come around—it will just take some time."

Natalya shook her head. "Not Mama." She felt her spirits spiral even lower as she realized the truth of what she'd just said.

There would be no forgiveness. Not ever.

Alice glanced around the dark barn. "Where will you sleep?"

"In the loft. There's hay up there." Natalya swallowed back a sob. Only a few days earlier she had helped Catherine pile the hay from the meadow onto a platform and winch it up to the loft. She tried unsuccessfully to wish herself back to that moment.

Alice said gently, "Canada is a beautiful place, Natalya, and my home is very much like Zgardy. I think you would like it there."

A silence fell between them and finally, not knowing what else to do, Alice got to her feet. "Things will look better in the morning," she said encouragingly. "They always do."

☙❧

But things were not better in the morning. They were worse.

It was barely light when Natalya woke to a shouting match. Scrambling down the ladder, she hurried outside to find her mother standing in the yard, a canvas valise in one hand and the other gripping Pylyp's arm. The boy was sobbing, his face skewed with confusion and fear. Oleksi stood in front of them, blocking their path.

"Don't be so stubborn, Mama," he shouted. "There's no reason for you to leave right now. We can travel to Yeremeche together."

"I will not stay a moment longer in a house of sin," she cried, crossing herself. "God forgive me, I have raised nothing but heathens!"

"But you don't understand what it was like."

"I understand the holy church, Oleksi. And when you turned your back on the church, you turned your back on me. I want nothing more to do with you and that ... that ..."

"Enough!" Oleksi roared, sounding so much like their father that Natalya gasped. Fists clenched at his side, he stepped away from his mother's path. "Go, if you must," he said furiously, "but do not ever refer to my wife as anything but worthy of respect!"

For a moment Zhanna seemed taken aback. Then her mouth twisted in a sneer. "Your head is full of nonsense! Like your father. He ruined all of you with his mawkish talk of love and chivalry and his ridiculous countess. And where did it get him, hmmm?" She waved her hand dismissively and, pulling Pylyp, still sobbing, along with her, she marched purposefully toward the gate. As the two disappeared down the path, Natalya came slowly from the barn to stand beside her brother.

"I should have told Mama, Oleksi. Maybe she *could* have stopped Catherine ... ." Her voice broke and she clamped her teeth, refusing to cry.

"It was not your fault, Natalya," he said. "Catherine did what she did because she loves Lech. You did what you did because you love her. And Mama ... ." He sighed and kicked a mound of dirt. "Mama does what she does because she loves the church."

ॐ

After a breakfast of lumpy *kulesha* the four young adults sat at the table not quite sure what to do next.

"We should leave for Yeremeche," Alice said. "Clearly there's nothing more we can do here."

Tusya turned to Natalya, who was seated beside him on the bench. "What will you do now?" he asked, but the way he was looking at her filled Natalya with confusion. He was much thinner than he had been the first time he came to the farm, but he was still handsome and there was something in his eyes that went beyond concern. She tried to gather her thoughts, to answer his question, but words would not come and in desperation she turned her head and surveyed the room. The floors and windows needed a good cleaning, as did the dusty, smoke-stained walls. She imagined Maria Hutopila and the other village women wagging their heads in disapproval. "What else would you expect of a fancy woman from Lviv?" they would ask each other smugly, pleased that they had been right all along about the former chief forester's wife.

Zhanna had taken most of the icons from the wall but had left the one of the virgin mother holding the baby Christ. Natalya's eyes burned as looked at it and saw, not the virgin, but her mother holding Pylyp, cradling him in her arms as if to protect him from all harm. As she had tried so hard to do for all of them.

"Mama will come back," Natalya said, finding her voice at last. "When she is no longer angry, she will come back. I must be here to welcome her home."

Oleksi shook his head. "She can't come back, Natalya. This is the Hutopila's home now."

She shrugged. "Then I'll stay in the barn and when she returns we will find a new place in the village."

"Your mother didn't sound as if she had any intention of coming back," Alice said, adding persuasively, "Why don't you come with us?"

Natalya frowned down at the table. How could she make this woman understand that it was impossible for her to leave? This woman who did not know their mother, who had never lived in Zgardy.

"I have to clean the house," she said, "or the villagers will speak badly of Mama and she will be ashamed when she comes back."

Oleksi said sternly, "Alice is right, Natalya. Mama is not going to change her mind, and there's no one here to look after you. It's better that you come with us."

"No!" Natalya was tired of arguing. "She *will* come back, Oleksi. She will miss Papa and Leysa and her babies, and she won't be able to stay away." Then, to keep from bursting into tears and to stop any further attempts to persuade her to go, she jumped to her feet and grabbed a scrub bucket from a corner near the stove. "I have walls to scrub," she said and hurried outside.

Alice stared after her, torn between wanting to leave at once and being unable to turn her back on this girl who was so young and so old at the same time. "We should help her," she said at last. "When the house is cleaned, she might agree to come with us."

☙❧

As she scrubbed the walls of her mother's bedroom, having removed every personal item Zhanna had left behind, Natalya remembered her mother saying there was no better remedy for grief than a bucket of soapy water, a stiff scrub brush and prayer. Since no one seemed to be listening to any of her prayers, she concentrated instead on the scrubbing and found the repetitive motion of the brush was soothing and helped her to think more clearly. The others were probably right in believing that her mother was never coming back, but if Natalya left now, she would never know for sure, or be able to forgive herself for betraying her trust. She would stay and let God decide how it was to be.

They made a burn pile in the yard of those things they were sure Zhanna, when she was thinking straight, would not want to fall into the hands of the Hutopilas or any of the other villagers.

"That's where this should go," Natalya said glumly as she pulled the tapestry from beneath the mattress on her bed.

Alice lowered the brush she was using to scrub one of the bedroom walls and inspected the rug. "Oleksi told me the story," she said. "It's very beautiful." She ran gentle fingers over the double-eagle crest above the Madonna. It was all gone, she thought. A whole empire lost because of one man's weakness. "I'm glad the countess never had to hear of the tsar's fate," she murmured. She hoped, as she had when she first heard the rumours of the horrible way in which the royal family had been murdered, that it was not really so and that somehow the children at least had escaped.

"Papa said the tapestry made him remember that everything a man does has the power to change the world in some way," Natalya said.

Alice glanced out the window at the pile they had readied for burning. "Your father was a wise man," she said. "But perhaps it's time to say goodbye to the past. Burning the tapestry would be like a funeral for the way things were and will never be again."

Through the open window crept a whisper of a breeze, scented with sweet clover from the meadow.

"It's certainly what Mama would want us to do with it," Natalya said.

But when the pile was lit and the flames were curling about the worn-out bedding and bits of broken furniture, she wavered. The tapestry was their history, their link to everything their father had stood for, and at the last moment she rushed forward and pulled it from the pile. As she began rolling it into a bundle, she glanced up to see the other three staring at her in astonishment. "Mama is wrong," she said defiantly.

By noon the house was spotless, and a crate filled with Zhanna's possessions and labelled with Yuliya and Veniamin's address in Kiev rested neatly on the porch. Still Natalya refused to leave.

"I'll stay in the barn," she reassured Alice.

Finally accepting that the girl's mind would not be changed, Alice wrote on a sheet of Zhanna's writing paper the address

Clyde Brandon had given them. She placed it and a bundle of Polish marks in Natalya's hand. "It's not much, but if you change your mind, this will pay for your train fare to Gdansk. We will arrange for money to be waiting for you at this address so you can pay for your passage to Canada. I've written my address on the paper as well, and I'll make sure that someone at this agency will help you get to Canada."

After that there was no further reason for them to linger.

Natalya stood on the porch watching as Oleksi and Tusya and Alice mounted their horses.

"She's only seventeen," Alice said quietly to Tusya. "How can we leave her here?"

"You were only a year older when you came to Russia, Ali," Tusya reminded her. "And you know that seventeen here isn't anything like seventeen back home."

"Besides," Oleksi chimed in, "Natalya is like my mother, Alishka. When she gets a notion in her head, even a lightning bolt from God himself won't dislodge it."

Sensing Alice's indecision, Natalya came down the steps. "I'll be fine, Sister," she said firmly. "The barn is safe and I have plenty of food. And if I have any problems, Father Ishchak will help me."

Their eyes met and Alice saw in Natalya a strength and determination that matched her own.

"Just remember, Natalya," she said in a strangled voice, "you have a niece or nephew on the way that's going to want you around." Then, lest she begin to cry, she turned her horse and followed her husband and brother through the gate.

As they disappeared from view, the tears Natalya had been trying to hold back flowed freely down her cheeks.

*E*PILOGUE

IMBYR RIVER, ZGARDY

September 1919

The postcard showed a picture of an ocean liner on the front, and on the back was Oleksi's note advising that he and Alice and Tusya had reached Gdansk in time to catch the boat to America. Natalya had tucked it safely into an inner pocket of the thick cloak she had made with Maria Hutopila's help, from wool Natalya had spun herself. It would keep her warm even in the coldest of winds. In another pocket was the address and money that Alice had given to her.

She stood, her feet braced against the logs, waiting for the raft to float. Within moments it was caught in the flood current and at once the two raftsmen in front of her began manipulating the huge oars, expertly steering their unruly craft through the rapids. As it bumped from rock to rock and was swept forward with ever-increasing speed, her heart thudded with fear and excitement. Down the canyon and around one bend after another, she fought to stay upright, but when they reached the spot where she and Catherine had seen Oleksi disappear so many years earlier, she dared to glance up at the lookout. As she had known there would not be, there was no one standing there watching her passage. No one holding their breath as she teetered on the logs. But somehow it didn't matter, and as the raft careened around the next bend, jerking her attention back to the river, she smiled. Oleksi had been right. Mama was not ever coming back. But that was all right, because Natalya was going forward to a new life and a new land, and she was ready for the challenge.

ACKNOWLEDGEMENTS

I am grateful to the many people who freely shared their stories, histories, pictures and maps that made the accuracy of places and events in *The Federov Legacy* possible. I am also indebted to those who captured in diaries, letters and memoirs the daily terrors, trials and triumphs they experienced as they lived through the wars and revolutions that plagued Eastern Europe in the first quarter of the twentieth century. These include, but are not limited to, Dorothy Cotton, Florence Farmborough, Malcolm C. Grow, James L. Houghteling Jr., David Paetkau, Maurice Paléologue, Bernard Pares, Arthur Ransome, William Thomas Stead, Albert Stopford, Violet Thurstan, and Laura de Gozdawa Turczynowicz. Their stories helped me to imagine the settings in my story more clearly.